LESLIE leaned away from Bernie's encircling arm to stare at them. They both looked radiant. Honor's hair the color of orange pekoe tea shone in the firelight. The inner curve of a breast came and went in the V-neck. Her long throat arched back and her mouth opened a little as she rolled the wine on her tongue. Bernie smiled in profile into the heart of the fire. The curve of his mouth was long and delicious. His curly hair caught the firelight. Leslie had a startling urge to make love to them both.

She sipped her wine nervously. The impulse was not real. No, she never wanted to make love to more than one person, and certainly not to both of them. It would be complicated and messy, like one of those construction projects, insert Flap B in Slot D.

They looked beautiful beside her and she did itch to touch them gently. But it was the wine and the dope together before supper. It was pure silliness. . . .

Fawcett Crest Books
by Marge Piercy:

THE HIGH COST OF LIVING

SMALL CHANGES

WOMAN ON THE EDGE OF TIME

THE HIGH COST OF LIVING

a novel by

Marge Piercy

FAWCETT CREST • NEW YORK

THE HIGH COST
OF LIVING

one

Leslie was balanced on the hard cushion of an antique chair designed for someone with a three-cornered behind. In front of her, too close, Hennessy straddled a chair backwards and loomed over her, telling loud anecdotes intended as far as she could guess as advertisements. "The minute Ted left the room, she walked over to me and stood there, just looking me up and down. Provocative. I could see she wasn't wearing a bra."

"Lots of women don't," Leslie said between stiffening lips. "It isn't mean to be provocative." She slumped forward. She too was not wearing a bra. Was that what had pinned him to her of all the women milling around this apartment? Some flaw, see you were asking for it.

"Listen, she knew. Then she leaned way over with her tits sticking in my face and she said"—he attempted to copy a languid expression, lifting one beefy shoulder—"she said, 'Mark, are you a good lay?' Just like that." He paused for reaction.

She stared at him, she hoped impassively. He had an almost handsome craggy face spoiled by a too square, too heavy jaw and an expression that was a perennial pout. His body, the upper part of his face seemed older than he was—a second-year graduate student like herself—while the lower half of his face seemed trapped in sulky early adolescence. If she said nothing, nothing at all, he might go away. But exactly like her, he seemed to know no one at the party. It was Cam's fault they were here, because Cam was acting in the damned play she had also gone to tonight. *The Importance of Being Earnest*. Support dead fags. She was itchy with discomfort in this fancy room with its mixture of wonderful-to-look-at, impossible-to-use antiques and modern couches like velvet-covered marshmallows. The walls of the livingroom were decorated with drawings of naked women, and she did not like that; she did not like the way men used bodies like hers to pin up on their walls and sell toothpaste and decorate glassware and magazines.

"So I said, 'Well, nobody's complained yet.' 'No?' she said. 'Let's see.' And she put her hand on me, right you know where. . . . You're awful quiet, Leslie. Don't you believe me?"

She tried waiting him out, but he waited too. Could he really think not wearing a bra was an automatic general come-on? She had on a denim shirt, and her concession to the party was a fancy leather vest covered with an intaglio flowery design, two years old but still beautiful, that Val had given her for their second anniversary. "Sure I believe you, Hennessy." Politeness got the best of her.

"What's this Hennessy bit? Call me Mark. Jesus, we see each other every day."

Almost. They had the same boss. She refused to call him Mark. Formality was a poor defensive weapon but a comfort. He was inching his chair forward again until he had walked it well into the space she counted as her own, forcing her against the misshapen back of the chair. She imagined lashing out with her foot, a quick chop to topple him. Her mouth twitched in a quarter smile.

Taking that for encouragement, he reached for her hand. Big hot grasp. She could not kick him, because they worked together for George: Professor Sanderson. George was her bread and butter, her thesis adviser, almost her fate. George had brought her along to Detroit and the University when he had changed jobs, carried her along with an appointment as his research assistant with his files and his map collection. Therefore, she could not kick the

8

chair out from under Hennessy, but she could pull her hand away. "Sorry. I have to pee."

Through the crowded party she nudged her way, past the couples dancing, the thud and growl of the speakers. She got stuck next to a long glass table. On it besides glossy art books was an ashtray in the shape of a woman. It wasn't the kind of cheap thing her brothers might have had, like a hula girl on a highball glass. It was artful, sort of African, and therefore all the more shocking, as it was supposed to be. The butts ground out on the woman's hollowed belly jarred Leslie. She gritted her teeth, suddenly hating the whole room of strangers. There didn't seem to be another woman alone who wasn't trying to pick up one of the available men. What was she doing here, among women who looked through her? She wanted to break the ashtray, but there were too many people around. She did something else, fingering her vest. She had seen an extension in the hall. She scooped up the phone as she walked past and took it on its long cord into the bathroom, shutting the door.

She dialed Valerie's number in Grand Rapids. Let the owner of the ashtray finance her call, Paul What's-his-name. Creighton. The director of the play. Her heart was pounding in her throat, her wrists. It rang and rang. Why did she think Val would be home on a Friday night? Because she did not want Val to be with anyone else. The phone was answered. She shut her eyes, shut them tight, to hear Val's high voice.

"I'm sorry, the number you have dialed is not a working number. This is a recording. Please check your number and try again."

She dialed Grand Rapids Information. "Do you have a new listing for Valerie Mendoza?"

They had no listing. Broke? Phone shut off? But Val had not vanished; she had moved in with somebody and that was the truth. She knew it. Let it not be Lena. But she was sure it was.

Enough. Time to get out. She wriggled along, awkward, diffident, to the bedroom at the end of the hall. Even the bedroom was full of people drinking and talking. There she saw Cam Rogers sitting against the bedroom wall, beside the bed heaped with coats. Cam worked for George too, as his secretary. She'd sit beside Cam and pay her a few compliments about the play before rescuing her pea jacket from the bed and going home where she belonged. "You were wonderful," Leslie began, squatting down. But Cam wasn't listening. Her head tilted against the blue wall, she brooded. "Is something wrong, Cam?"

Slowly Cam turned, focusing on her. Drunk? "Hi there, old Leslie. You liked it, huh?"

She had begun to be casually friendly with Cam, a big amiable scattered woman who when she wasn't working for George studied dramatics and acted with the local theater group. Cam did not attract her; she was too obviously heterosexual, even victimized, a big soft woman not quite able to carry off her own act. Her hair was bleached and she made jokes about dark roots; her eyes were elaborately made up in two shades of eye shadow and her long lashes seemed to molt. Her daring purple jumpsuit was creased in the wrong places where she had been slouching against the wall. Leslie could take one look at Cam and draw in with the scent of her musky perfume that Cam would always be falling in love with someone who wouldn't love her back, and now Leslie searched where Cam was bleakly staring and tried to decide who might be making her unhappy tonight.

A girl wearing a long bottle green velvet dress was sitting on a hassock, her back toward them, kicking off her uncomfortable shoes. She balanced a wineglass on the palm of one hand, running the other through fine wavy light brown hair that shimmered over her shoulders and halfway down her back, smooth and controlled as satin. "All right, it can be amusing! But to pretend you're fulfilling some grand role in society, that's silly!"

The voice was familiar: low pitched, husky, but knife-edge precise in its diction. Yes, it had been Cecily's voice in the play. Honor Rogers. "Is that your sister?" she asked Cam.

Cam nodded heavily, as if her neck were too weak to

support her head. "My baby sister." She nodded again. "Paul's letching for my very own little sister."

"Paul?"

"Our director. *Him.*"

The owner of the ashtray, the apartment, the party. He was in his middle or late forties and chunkily built with a face carved in broad lines and dark angles, crumbling only a little. Leslie asked Cam, "Are you worried? Or do you just think you ought to be?" She had never had a sister; the idea intrigued her. Younger sister, vulnerable, looking up to you.

"It's all my fault. I brought her down to try out. I never thought she'd get the part, I just wanted her to get a kick out of it. . . . I had to do some fast talking to persuade Mama too."

Paul squatted, saying something into Honor's ear. When he stopped she flung back her long swan throat and laughed till her body shook. Paul grinned, with his teeth showing, his forehead wrinkled. Her dad's age. That annoyed her. Her boyish father would look at his wife and three sons and a daughter and two dogs and seem to wonder who the hell they were. How had he come to wake up with these noisy carping strangers on his back? The way he would look at them coldly, blankly, especially when he'd been drinking. This man was more self-important, more aggressive. She found his lust ugly, butt grinding out on the ceramic belly. Now he was taking Honor's arm, leaning close again, and the girl swung around to face them, freeing herself with a shrug.

"Did you have fun playing Cecily?" Leslie asked.

Somehow it was the right question. "Yes, but not as much as I'd expected. It's work, actually. Stupid rote work."

"Our Cecily doesn't approve of work. She wants to swallow a part like a birth control pill," Paul said wryly.

"The costumes are fun, anyhow." Honor ignored him, looking at them out of enormous eyes that seemed above the bottle green velvet such a pale brown as almost to be golden, like a cat's eyes. Her forehead and cheekbones were high, her nose long, her skin pale and rosily translucent. Her mouth and chin were delicate. "I wanted to come to the party tonight in mine—all frills and ribbons and a dear ridiculous parasol. But Paul wouldn't let me. He was petrified I might spill something. They rent their costumes, you know." Her eyes shone gold with mischief.

Leslie sat up straighter against the wall. Nineteen? Even though Honor was, odds on, talking to her to annoy Paul, turning her back on him as part of the same game as flirting outrageously five minutes earlier, she enjoyed the moment. "I'm Leslie McGivers. I work with your sister."

"Oh, Cam's talked about you." Honor raised her thin arrogant eyebrows. "She says you're brilliant. That George"—Honor drawled the name, looking under her lashes to see if Leslie noticed she used his first name. Ah, she was young—"brought you with him from Grand Rapids. That you have a black belt in kung fu and George treats you like his daughter and you eat rapists for breakfast."

"A brown belt in karate." But look at me with your golden eyes. Nobody has looked at me anything like that way for months. Christmas. Val with the snow in her shining black hair.

"Cam admires you, so I think you must be special. She hardly ever admires another woman." Honor beamed at her sister.

What else had Cam said? That she was a dyke? Paul glanced at her quickly then through her. She did not register on him. He had risen to his feet and he stood now at Honor's shoulder peering down into her green dress, at her breasts. But Leslie did not think Cam had guessed. No, Honor flirted with everyone; probably she flirted with the mirror when she brushed her teeth.

Another woman who had just come in slipped her arm through Paul's. "Come and dance. It's time for our ingenue to go home to her mama. . . . You know, Cam, I have a little sister too, but I keep her where she belongs. At home in the closet."

Honor rose. She was tall, perhaps five eight and a good two inches taller than Leslie, who instinctively stood with her. "It *is* time for me to be in bed, even if I don't sleep in a closet like Cinderella."

Groggily Cam stumbled to her feet and began pawing at the coats on the bed. Leslie took hers as it heaved up. As they went past the crowded livingroom she saw that Hennessy had pinned another woman against the wall, hunched over her with his extended arm blocking her escape. ". . . and when I opened my eyes, there she was climbing into bed with me . . ." Together they picked their way out and went down the broad stairs. Cam tripped on her big clumsy shoes and Leslie caught her under the elbow, set her back on her feet.

"You'd better drive," Leslie said to Honor.

"But I hate machines. I don't know how!"

"I'll drive, I'll drive," Cam muttered, fumbling for her keys.

It was an old dust-colored VW with one fender bright blue. "Why not take a taxi?" Leslie suggested. "I'll go up and call one for you."

"Mama would be upset."

"Yes, we do not upset Mama!" Cam declaimed. "It costs too much."

"How would she know? Get the car in the morning."

"She'd know." Cam giggled. "She's sitting up waiting. She always waits. She has to check us in and check us over."

"Camille!" Honor sounded icy. "She worries. We don't live in a neighborhood where you stroll around at night." She put her hand on Leslie's sleeve. "Could you drive us? Please."

"I'm not drunk." Cam leaned on the fender, still going through her purse. "The keys're here somewhere. I can drive perfectly."

She saw Paul at the second-floor window looking out at them, probably trying to decide if it was worth his while to come down. He turned then, as if deciding. "All right," Leslie heard herself say. "But I hardly know the city." Now how the hell would she get back home from wherever?

Thus she found herself patiently driving the battered

13

VW whose gears slipped, whose brakes were mushy, whose choke did not appear to be connected with anything, while Honor gave her directions. "You turn at those lights, or maybe it's the street after, I'm not sure. Let me see. Not that one. Oh, that was it! We've gone past it!"

"The virginity of a younger sister," Cam was saying from the back seat in a loud flat voice about three inches from Leslie's ear. Cam's chin came to rest on the back of the driver's seat. "It's confusing. The virginity of most people is like they haven't got around to it. Except most people aren't virgins. But Honor—it's a positive thing. Like a Samoan princess."

"Be quiet, Cam. Or help me give directions!"

Finally Leslie parked in a bus stop and looked at a city map from the glove compartment. Honor and Cam lived on the near northwest side about six blocks off Grand River, and she plotted a reasonable route via the John C. Lodge Freeway and then south on Wyoming. "You're delightfully practical, Leslie," Honor said. "I'm always so tangled up in my own fantasies that I never notice the obvious, such as where I'm being driven. Also, it's so dull—signs that tell you not to do things. The only street names I ever remember are the pretty ones, the old French names like Beaubien and Saint Antoine, even if everybody pronounces them wrong. But they're all slums or factories. Or rubble fields. I can't imagine why you'd choose to move here."

"This is a metropolis compared to Grand Rapids, and Grand Rapids was wildly cosmopolitan after Ludington."

"Is that where you come from? Ludington? That's where the ferries cross, isn't it?"

"The Chesapeake and Ohio Car and Auto Ferry. Have you taken it?"

"Never," Honor said tragically. "We only noticed it on the map, Mama and I. One of those things you imagine doing. I dare say it'd be disillusioning—a second rate imitation of a real voyage on a real sea."

"With a bit of wind you wouldn't think so."

"Really? Does it get stormy?"

"A tanker broke up out on Lake Michigan the year I left home. Broke in half in a storm. Nobody got off." Defending her home now, as if she'd ever go back. But Honor had annoyed her. Really, she might be beautiful but she was ridiculously affected. Probably gone to some fancy private schools where they all tried to sound British.

"I've never been anyplace. Except in my head. But being a tourist sounds tacky. I'd like to travel, but for some compelling, some inherent reason."

Leslie laughed. "Like being a fugitive?"

"Don't laugh at me, Leslie. I hate to be laughed at. I always find a way to punish Paul when he does that."

"When Daddy was going to take us all to Niagara Falls, you wouldn't go," Cam said suddenly, chin on the seat back.

"Well, imagine going to Niagara Falls with Daddy and you and Mignon!"

Mignon must be another sister, whom she imagined as older than Honor, just as beautiful and already interested in women. And throw in a legacy from a rich aunt. "Does she live at home too?" Please not.

"No, she's in Columbus with her family," Cam said. "Poor Mignon."

"Why do you say that?"

"I don't know." Cam yawned warmly in her ear. "We always say that. Why do we always say that?"

"Because she has three children at twenty-four, she's sweet and darling, her husband only married her for her looks, and she's losing them already." Honor shook her head and her long hair slithered back and forth. "Stop, Leslie, right now!"

"We're nowhere near your house yet."

"That dismal-looking diner. We need to make Cam presentable."

"Come on, Honor. Cam's an adult. Surely she can come in a little soused."

"Not wih *her*," Cam said. "But I'll keep my mouth shut."

"Camille! You can't walk without shuffling!" Honor screwed around in her seat.

"Yes I can. Right past Mother dear. Nighty-night."

"Besides, she'll be brimming with questions. You know."

"Why didn't she come to the play if she wanted to keep an eye on you?" Leslie parked and they walked back half a block. The all-night diner stood across from the gates of a Kelvinator plant and served the night shift. There were eight or nine men in the place, including two cops at the counter. Walking past them all to the booth, Leslie felt peppered with stares. She always felt conspicuous, but here were Cam in her purple satin jumpsuit and Honor in a long velvet gown.

"Been out on the town, girls?"

"Partying," Cam started to say when Leslie nudged her into a booth at the end. Edgily she pulled off her gloves and her left hand rubbed the callused edge of her right palm. She noticed she was sweating. But she was not really *with* Cam or Honor; neither of them, that is, was her lover, with whom she walked always warily, always in fear of being attacked. Her jaw gave a twinge and she discovered she was gritting her teeth. Neither Cam nor Honor seemed nervous. Cam was drunk past caring and Honor seemed flattered by the comments, the stir. She had taken several minutes shrugging off her coat before sitting in the booth.

"Leslie, you look quite grumpy. Are we keeping you from something? Or someone?" Honor raised her little eyebrows, undecided whether to flirt or be annoyed.

"Only a room with the heat turned off. Don't worry." If only she could stop herself from worrying. It was a sickness to be balanced always on the blade of anxiety, twanging alertness. Yet the first time she had been attacked, she had been purely thoughtlessly happy, overflowing with a clear liquid ample joy as she walked with Val out of a Howard Johnson's and across the parking lot. Two men blocked their way. At first she had not understood. Val and she had been walking intertwined, that was all. She could still see that man's face bloated with righteous anger then a fist coming. She had not known how to fight. She had never hit anyone except for pad-

16

dling her dog Satan when he had been naughty on the floor, or once in a while whacking her youngest brother. All she had done was scratch the man's cheek before he had left her in the parking lot with a broken jaw.

She had played that scene fifty thousand times. "A male atmosphere like this one makes me edgy."

"It's pretty . . . greasy." Honor giggled. "Our entrance was the event of the night. Here comes our waitress."

Leslie relaxed. She was ridiculous sometimes. Maybe it was the four months of working on the rape hot line right after she had come to Detroit. Black women, white women, old ladies, kids, all bleeding. Never again, she could not take it. She could not live with that knowledge of pain. Just to mind her own business and survive, somehow intact. "Three black coffees—"

"I don't wish coffee, and I don't take it black," Honor interrupted, bridling. "I would like tea."

"Not for you. For Cam. And a glass of milk for me." It was the only thing she could find to consume. She was too wired to drink coffee and she would not eat bad food.

"Oh, that's a good idea. I'll have milk too, instead. And pie— What kind of pie do you have? Blueberry with strawberry ice cream." When the waitress had left, Honor leaned forward. "I'm sorry I jumped at you. I thought you were being officious. You're so practical!"

"So practical. I spend my days sorting hundred-year-old rent receipts. Or I feed a balky computer information on capital formation trends and capital accumulation in selected northern industrial centers during the post-bellum period. At least with the Simpson papers I dig up ancient scandals, like finding fossil condoms in a bed of sandstone." She wasn't doing anything wrong, just showing off a little.

"Simpson papers? What are they?"

"The Simpsons are local money. They left the University their family archives and a tidy sum. We've got grant proposals out for the capital development project, but the Simpson papers are what's supporting me."

"Were there really old scandals? Incest and mad wives in the tower like Mr. Rochester?" Honor asked.

17

"Business chicanery mostly. But there's syphilis and even a bastard daughter who perished in a fire.

"Arson?"

"They had lots of fires. All the flimsy wooden buildings. Open fires, candles, oil lamps, straw. It was a raw place in the 1870s, which is when the daughter bought it."

"It's a raw place now." Honor shrugged. "I think you're hired to make that up. I know, in grade school we studied all that: Founded by Antoine de la Mothe Cadillac in seventeen-whatever. But you know it's a lie. Henry Ford founded Detroit in the twenties, and everything before that is invented. It was put together like a freight train made up of odd boxcars marked Chevrolet and Great Lakes Steel and Wyandotte Chemical. It was all put up at once and now it's all rotting at once. That's what you can see. Antoine Mothball is just a story they make up to teach in school."

The coffees arrived and Cam began drinking the first, shuddering. "Mama's so fussy about you. What does she expect anyhow? The princess can't even pee."

"I don't think I'll ever permit myself to get drunk! Ever!"

"Listen, I'm the one in the pot. If anything happens to you, it's my fault. If you quit, it's my fault. Paul will fire me. Don't quit on us, Honor, listen to me."

"It's so dull. It looks lovely from the audience, but it's just sweat and bother. The illusion's gone and a play is not any more exciting to be in than studying for a chemistry quiz."

"You like the curtain calls well enough," Cam mumbled, shaking her head and doggedly drinking the coffee Leslie nudged at her.

"I like the costumes too. It's not fun to be female any more. I'd love to flirt endlessly with a parasol. All right, you're safe. I won't quit unless Paul drives me mad. He's wicked." She smiled broadly. "Besides, what else is interesting in my life? Nothing even as exciting as memorizing lines ever happens at General Custer."

"General Custer?" Leslie asked.

"Her high school," Cam said.

"You're in high school?" Leslie sat up even straighter than she usually did. I didn't touch her and I never meant to.

"Oh, Leslie, did you think I'm older? I think I look older, especially when I'm dressed up like tonight. Do say I look older."

"Older than what?"

"I do love to be told I look at least nineteen. I don't think I'm anything like a typical high school girl. Really, in many ways I'm more mature."

"And in many ways you're not," Cam snarled. "You don't even go out with boys, but you walk in and start carrying on with Paul. He's forty-seven and he goes through women by the six-pack. Don't think you'd mean anything more to him than a quick fuck."

"Cam, you can't really imagine I'm about to let him . . . go *through* me? I just find him more interesting to flirt with than a sixteen-year-old with bleached hair and pimples."

"I don't know. I look over the local talent when I'm passing the school, and I see a few I wouldn't kick from my double bed." Cam winked at Leslie.

"They're stoned all the time, they play music so loud you can't talk. I don't know what to say to them—they never read a book from one year to the next. And they have a one-word all-purpose vocabulary: fuck."

Cam ran her hand roughly through her blonded hair, trying to focus. She started on the third cup. "Besides, what happened to that boyfriend you had? He wasn't half bad-looking."

"What 'boyfriend'? I don't have 'boyfriends.' "

"Bernie something?"

"He is not, *not* my boyfriend. He is my friend. Period." Cam yawned hugely. "He's queer, huh?"

"We're all rather peculiar," Honor said icily. "Bernar' "—she pronounced it as if it was French: bearnarr—"is my very best friend, even though we met only two months ago. He's the only person in the whole world who actually talks with me."

Leslie remembered something. "Listen, if your mother's so possessive and concerned, how come she didn't go to the play tonight? Then she could keep an eye on you in person."

"Oh, she would've, believe me, if she could get off work. The telephone company's sickening. She works afternoons and evenings—the two to ten shift—as a floor supervisor. That means she stands behind the operators. But by ten-thirty she's home. Waiting." Honor looked directly into her eyes. "I like you, Leslie. You talk with me too. Hardly anyone does. Come and visit me. I have morning classes and I'm home from General Custer by one-thirty, except Tuesdays and Thursdays, when I'm on library patrol till four." Honor's last words that evening were "I'll be very hurt if you don't come."

two

Hennessy was coming on to Cam, hanging like a slab of plaid-shirted beef over her desk. Leslie saw George notice. George viewed everything that happened in his fiefdom as his business. She had seen him offended when he discovered a minor liaison between his students, not offended for the affair but because he had not known. Ignorance was possible weakness. Now from his inner office he observed Hennessy and Cam.

Summoning Leslie with a wave of his hand, George shut the door. He had an orderly mind and a disorderly office full of coffee-ringed papers and books propped open at some dusty page. A beautiful old map of Detroit hung over his desk, the neat wheel-spoke patterns of the original city radiating. He liked maps and she had pleased him at Christmas by giving him an ordinary soil map of Michigan.

He asked, "How're you doing?"

"Okay."

"So uncertain? Big city still hard on you?"

"Not in the long run, I think."

He had not asked her to sit and she waited. He gave her that small square grin of his. "Sit. Always on protocol. Take nothing for granted." George was loose limbed and professorial-looking—patched-elbow jackets over corduroy jeans, medium brown hair just to his shoulders with a gentle wave, gold-rimmed glasses and mild brown eyes, a bushy dark brown mustache more definite, more aggressive than his hair, the vain little ways of a man used to being admired. Last September he had come to the city university in a position of strength with an associate professorship and the Simpson papers. What he really wanted to work on was not those family archives but his quantitative history project, the capital development grant he was angling for with half a dozen foundations. That would really set him up. He was still feeling his way in Detroit, systematically checking out alliances and enmities in the history department and incidentally economics because of his econometric interests. He was putting together a model of how everything worked that would be tight enough to run on the computer, while he seemed still to be blinking at it all and just in a friendly laid-back way trying to find his footing in a new situation, a new city.

"I've begun to get into the Simpson papers," she was saying. "The bank archives are richer for us than the family documents. It could be interesting after all."

"Red." He tapped her arm very lightly for emphasis, not contact. "Don't talk about the fun parts."

"Don't talk about the papers?"

"Right. Set it all down but pass nothing out of our cozy group. Chortle only with me. There are powerful Simpsons."

"The representative."

"He's the stupid cousin from the wrong line. They only send the failures into electoral politics. No. Chrysler and Goodyear and salt. The salt money is the oldest. I don't want them getting the wind up."

"I won't," she said, remembering then that she already had, in the diner.

He was watching her face closely. He grinned again. "But you won't do it anymore."

"Only once I did."

" 'That was in another country and besides the wench is dead.' . . . Hey, has Mark Hennessy made my secretary yet?"

"Not yet, I believe."

"Why? I shouldn't think it would be hard."

22

"For him, it would be hard." She did smile then. "He even tried me."

"Well, Red, you don't wear a sign. And in this department you better not."

Her face caught and she waited. "A lot of warnings today."

"I don't have to warn you about that. We both know the world is sick and wants to die. In a year or two—"

"You'll own this place." She could not be above a little flattery, when she was sweating fear.

"I wouldn't take it, Red. It's not financially sound." He leaned back on his spine, sticking his feet up on a pulled-out writing surface of his oak desk. "We're coming in here strong. They need us more than we need them. We brought income. . . . Let's start the regular Thursday nights this week."

"Starting this Thursday?" She went to the dojo Thursday nights.

"Sure. I'll announce it in the seminar this afternoon."

"You want me to come early and help Sue set up?"

"Give her a call and ask. She's got a woman who comes in three days a week, but I don't know if that suffices. Okay, scoot."

At her desk in the outer office she shuffled papers, brooding, reviewing. Well, he gave his warnings and made it plain enough. Her relationship with George was naked: the power, the obligations, the rewards. If the power were less blatantly unbalanced, she might even like him, but it did not do to dawdle on that aspect: like criticizing the color of the sky.

Mostly she was grateful because George did not force her to lie to him and because he accepted her as useful, as intelligent, as a good student. He had selected her and her alone to carry with him to his new position and a better fellowship than she could have gotten any other way. He used her and let her work for him without there being any sexual overtones. None. He was neither attracted to her nor repulsed nor excited nor agitated by her being a lesbian; it was merely a piece of data he filed. It meant she could do certain things and not others. For that tolerance

23

she was grateful enough to try to do well the extra tasks that fell on her such as house hunting for him through June and July before he moved his wife and children, such as going early on Thursday to that house finally selected and following Sue's orders in laying out the goodies for the weekly informal, supposedly noncompulsory meetings of the Simpson papers staff and his own graduate students he liked to hold in his house, on his own territory.

She felt lonely. She almost missed the time on the rape hot line. It amused her in retrospect how she had selected that her second week in Detroit, thinking she would meet women. Oh, she met women; bleeding, lacerated, vomiting, catatonic. Even the women who worked the hot line seemed to shrink from each other, as if each held too much pain to care to deal with any woman similarly brimming over. She had made only one friend on that job, Tasha, and she felt guilty before her now for quitting. Tasha felt she had let them all down. Now Leslie tried to wear out her loneliness in work, and usually she succeeded.

She lay on the mattress in her apartment, one cold room. She looked forward to spring when it might be more pleasant, for it faced the flat roof of a grocery next door, with a fire escape just outside where she ought to be able to sit in good weather (the previous tenant had left a metal chair rusting there). She had just installed a new lock, scraped old linoleum off the floor, and scrubbed the boards.

She lay on her side, facing the wall that had on it a poster for a women's poetry evening that Val had silk-screened two years before. Because she was afraid she might be getting a cold, she was drinking rose hip tea. The hot sour tea, the poster kept Val floating just beneath the fragile web of the Simpson archives, her classes, her need for a thesis subject that she spun constantly to keep herself walking over the deep pool of depression always waiting there. That Val should be with her and wasn't, that somehow she had botched it, that she was here and

24

Val was a hundred and fifty miles away and every day, every single night, that was so. Tears gathered behind her eyes. She did not cry but drank the hot tea and tried to persuade herself to read for a paper she was writing on the railroads and tried to persuade herself she could take the evening off and go to the movies; only she could not imagine that there could be on the screens anyplace images that would speak to her pain, her need, her loneliness, images that would make her feel good. Then the phone rang.

It was not Val. That fact alone kept her numb for a few moments. It was Honor. "Leslie, when you were being so kind and driving us home Friday night, you dropped your scarf in the car."

She had realized it right afterward, before she got to the corner. She had paused in the street, shrugged, and gone on. Cam could easily return it. If Honor really wanted to see her, her scarf would be held for ransom.

She sat in the bumpy lurching back of a filthy DSR bus making its endless way across Detroit. First she was regretting not having enough money to own a car. That was a sin. To be car-poor. Second she mistrusted herself. She did not want Honor, she did not want to make love to the girl. What did she want? To soften the outer edges of the loneliness that occupied her, frozen hard like a ball of ice impacted with soot and grime. To have someone in the city who wanted her to come, who served as an afternoon's target, was maybe enough. Snow was beginning thickly, softly. The bus went slower. She could visit Tasha of course, but not without experiencing pressure. Why had she withdrawn? Was she doing anything for women? Damn Tasha. She had left school, she had time for that sort of thing.

When she got off, Honor was standing in the doorway of a laundromat, and Leslie was moved that anyone would come out in the snow for her.

"I thought you might not remember the house. Besides, the snow looked inviting and I thought I'd like to get out at least briefly."

"Weren't you out earlier? To school?"

"I couldn't go today. My nerves were ringing this morning like a thousand alarm clocks. I felt so down."

Leslie smiled at her exaggeration. "There's a performance tonight?"

"I'm neither stage-struck nor stage-shy. I'm only sorry it palled so quickly." A cold wind burned Honor's face above a bright blue scarf. She spoke of tedium buoyantly. "Mind the broken front step."

The house was a small frame bungalow that stood side by side with mostly two- and four-family frame houses with just room between to squeeze in a driveway. They had little front yards and little back yards. The stumps of dead elms thrust up along the street, with a few young saplings perishing by the curb. All the yards backed on a row of small factories, tool and die shops, a box manufacturer. On Honor's house the old white paint had blistered and begun to peel. From the porch ceiling on rusty chains a settee swing hung that no one had bothered to take down for the winter. Honor was struggling with her key in the lock. "Stupid door! It won't lock from the inside or open from the outside. It drives me crazy!" Finally she kicked it open.

Leslie followed her into the small stuffy overstuffed livingroom. At once loud howls and fierce barking came from beneath their feet. "Bottom! Samson! Shut up! Oh, shut up, you noisy rotten beasts!" Honor stamped her boots on the floor. The howling sank into growls, lower but persistent and accompanied by the clanking of metal on metal.

"You have dogs?" They sounded more like a wolf pack.

Honor shook off her coat, yanking at the door of the hall closet.

"This doesn't open either," she said through gritted teeth. "Oh, the dogs. German shepherds somebody gave Daddy to settle a debt. He's always being taken. He was supposed to breed German shepherds and make a million. That was between the edible ice cream carton and the burglar alarm that did something like bark. They stay in

26

the basement howling. Sometimes we put them in the yard to eat small children. Daddy takes them for walks. At least no one will dare attack him. We've never been robbed or broken into, but maybe that's because all the neighborhood junkies know there isn't ten cents in the house at a time."

The bottle green velvet gown of the party, the careful accent in the mellow voice were born out of twenty-five-year-old flowered slipcovers washed gray and old linoleum imitating old brick on the floor of the kitchen, the room to which they immediately gravitated. Honor said, "Please, would you do me a favor and call me Honorée? I know it's affected, but so am I—that's how I survive high school—and I'm in a French period. Honor is so drab, like Faith and Prudence or Chastity. While Honorée sounds like a king's mistress."

"I find king's mistresses even duller than Puritans, but sure, I'll call you Honorée." The girl was affected, but placed in the house she became more interesting, like an orchid growing out of a rack in the sidewalk. No fancy school, no set of mannered friends, no nouveau riche milieu produced her. Honor had made herself eccentric, old fashioned, flamboyant, as another girl would diet herself bone thin as a model. Leslie felt equally bothered and intrigued.

"What can I offer you? Orange-spice tea? Hot Vernors?" Honor was balancing on one toe in front of the refrigerator.

"Hot what?" Vernors was the local spicy ginger ale. Something in Honor's pose made Leslie ask, "Do you dance?"

The girl swung back to stare. "How did you know? I've always longed to be a ballet dancer—that's the source of all my frustrations! But it's too late. It's been too late ever since I can remember. How perceptive of you, Leslie! Did you want to be a dancer too?"

"I don't think I want anything but permission to be myself."

"You mean a gulf between what you want to be and what you are?"

"Nope. I'm working on what I want to be, but nobody can stand it." Oh, come one. Just walk in and start: Hi! I'm a dyke! Image of a stupidly grinning face and outstretched hand. "Tea, please. What were you upset about this morning? That made you not go to school?"

"Oh, I had a fight with Cam about flirting with Paul. Then I told Bernie—he's my best friend—and he wasn't sympathetic. In fact, he was even more disgusting than my know-it-all sister."

While Honor fussed at the stove, Leslie looked around. Linoleum with a pattern of bricks worn through to backing in front of the stove and the sink where a faucet dripped, all the appliances a generation old. Nothing was entirely clean or thoroughly dirty. Obviously they soldiered along, but the absent Mama Rogers was not first a housewife. Honor, who never seemed to wear pants, had on a long pink dress that brought out the bloom of her skin. It was the only new thing in the room. The little edging of lace at the cuffs and throat had not begun to fray.

Honor brought the steaming brew in small teacups. "Aren't they luxurious? We found them at a yard sale. There's only two, and one's mended, but I pretend not to notice the crack."

The cups were paper thin. She felt elephantine handling hers. No, she didn't think they were luxurious; she thought they were bothersome.

"Leslie!" Honor shook her head, smiling. "That's Rosenthal bone china. It's quite strong. It won't crumble in your hands."

"I'm not convinced. How do you know whatever it is?"

"Mama knows everything like that."

"Did she use to have money?"

"Mama? As a matter of fact, her father ran away when she was eleven and her mother began going in and out of mental institutions. She lived in foster homes till she was old enough to work. Mama's brave, a real fighter. I'm not that way at all. I don't have to be—she does everything for me. But isn't that a romantic and terribly sor'id background?"

28

Honor pronounced the word oddly and Leslie puzzled a moment. "Isn't there a 'd'? Sordid?"

"No." Honor frowned slightly. "There is but you don't pronounce it."

"I think you have 'forehead' in mind or 'toward.' "

"No, it's 'sorid.' I never mispronounce—it's sloppy."

She hesitated, then let it go. They had both learned most of their vocabulary from reading, only Honor was bolder using the more literary words out loud. Leslie heard herself giving a presentation in her first seminar back in Grand Rapids and making awkward circumlocutions to avoid saying "hegemony" because she discovered when she opened her mouth that she had no idea how to say it. She experienced a shiver of identification with the girl. "My family lives in a house not so different from this. It's on an eroding hill of sand. A not quite stabilized dune."

"Is it on the lake?"

Leslie snorted. "No ordinary people like my parents can afford that! Only summer people and people with money. No, they live ten blocks in. It's a house that wasn't meant to be year-round, then somebody stuck a half basement under, jacked it up and put in a furnace. The wind howls through the cracks. There's sand in everything—in the beds, in the rugs, in the corners." Vividly she remembered a typical gesture—running her hand through her hair with the nails digging hard into her scalp when she was nervous and worrying, and bringing out her hand with sand hard packed under the nails. Sand at the roots of her carroty hair. "In season—the summer—my mother waits tables. The rest of the year she doesn't work. I mean outside. There were four of us kids and in fact she always worked hard. My father was a fisherman, but you know the fishing has pretty much run out, the lake's dying. He used to work seasonal in a canning factory, apple picking, house painting. They should have left years ago, but they grew up there."

"My father's an X-ray technician at Mount Carmel. He fought in Korea, and after he came home he studied on the GI bill. He and Mama met while he was still in uniform." Honor insisted she come to the little livingroom to look at a photograph, which showed a skinny young anyface with crew cut squinting into the sun in an Army uniform, in front of a picket fence lined with hollyhocks. The uniform looked too big and he held his cap in his hands as if asking for something. His neck was very long, the only feature she could identify with Honor, and he did look tall.

Honor picked a bolt of material and a pincushion off the sagging davenport. "Mama is making a delicious dress for me—a thick soft corduroy with a paisley pattern. I can even wear it to school, though anything I wear is wasted." Honor looked down, biting her lower lip. "I sit in class and part of me waves my hand and answers questions. But most of me is living elaborate novels in my head. They go on for months. When somebody speaks to me—some jerky boy, even Mama—I feel as if they're invading my real life and what they want is unreal. I sound schizophrenic, don't I? I'll regret confessing this to you."

"Why? You'll leave home soon and things will start to happen. Then books won't be more interesting than the people you meet, people you have something in common with."

Honor stood before her clasping her hands. "You don't think I'm weird?"

She shook her head, realizing that Honor had the same big full body as Cam. With the long neck and Botticelli face, she had automatically equipped Honor with a slender sylph's body; but Honor was wide hipped and moderately busty, pear shaped. I don't desire her, it's the truth, she isn't even my type. I like her, she moves me, stifling in a narrow existence, full of energy and dreams. But what strange claptrap romantic dreams. "What do you usually read?" she started to ask, when Honor interrupted her.

"Look!" Honor pulled back the cuff of her left sleeve, showing a long raw cut on her arm. "I did it with the potato peeler."

"For shit sake, why?" It couldn't be a suicide attempt,

for the cut was only skin deep, but there was no way it could be an accident.

"To punish Bernar'. For saying nasty things because I like to flirt with Paul. I wanted to show him how much he was hurting me. I wanted to make the pain visible so he'd stop."

"And did he?"

"Of course! He kept saying I'd get tetanus. It cowed him completely. You'd think he'd be tougher than that, with the life he's led."

"But why did you cut yourself up? Does Paul mean that much?"

"Paul? Of course not. I did it for me. To prove I could. And to show Bernar' he can't turn his sarcasm on me. . . . I felt proud of myself. I thought he'd fall off his chair!"

"Exactly who is this guy?"

"My sort of adopted brother. Where to start?" Honor cast herself down in a swirl of skirt.

"Is he in his French phase too?"

"He calls himself Bernie, but he truly is French. French-Canadian, anyhow. You must meet him—"

"Why must I?"

"He's between us in age— How old are you Leslie, exactly?"

"I'm twenty-three, inexactly. What do you mean exactly?"

"It sounded nice balanced on the end of the question. I suppose you could have been awful and answered me, 'Four-thirty in the afternoon with Scorpio in Uranus.' Bernar's twenty-one, but a sophomore. He only just decided to go to college. He's quite mature. And terribly bright and fascinating." Honor paused to make sure she had Leslie's attention.

"Are you in love with him?"

"No, I like older men. Bernar'—he's the brother I didn't have, instead of my competitive sisters. I adore him, but he isn't romantic at all. I can't imagine him making a pass. Not even like the crude proles do at school: 'Hi, how ya doing, foxy, ya wanna fuck?' " Honor burst into

31

giggles. "You think I'm exaggerating! Last week I was standing in line in the lunchroom— Oh never mind. Everything those animals do is too boring to repeat. They swagger around, but Bernar' was genuinely tough. He was a real street kid. He knifed a boy when he was fifteen and got sent to a reformatory. He had to take exams to get into college, because he never finished high school."

"I see," Leslie said, conjuring different known jerks. "For a while in high school I rode with a gang of bikers, but I don't think that entitles me to special consideration. After all, it was fun." In a way. The riding was great, the sense of community had warmed her, the speed, the energy; but the sex had been mean. Finally she had fallen in love with another biker's old lady. At first she had not been able to figure out what had come down on her like a landslide of soft warm sand. Like a paralyzing case of flu she could not shake, she had endured the love as if it had been the disease it felt like.

"But, Leslie, he's had a hard life. His family was dreadfully poor. His mother died when he was thirteen. He's been knocked around and he's had several ugly homosexual experiences. That's one more thing he must struggle to overcome."

"Why? Maybe he likes men."

"But it's against his religion. He's a devout Catholic."

"In case of contradiction, something goes. Goodbye the church, I'd think."

"Don't be so cynical, Leslie!"

"Believe me, that's not what I'm being. . . . Maybe I'm not pure enough in heart to meet him."

"Don't be silly. No, you must. I have to arrange it!"

"Honor, Honorée I mean, people you like will not always like each other."

"Leslie, you haven't even *seen* Bernar' and already you're explaining to me that you won't get along. You're really prejudiced!"

three

Sunday morning Leslie rose early to work out. Her room was over a shoestore, forcing her to practice falls when they were closed. Tonight at the dojo she must do better; this last week she had been embarrassed by her clumsiness. Muddied in spirit. Doing her warm-up, she found her gaze seemed to catch on the poster, catch and stick.

Crosslegged she sat down to think. Sometimes her whole life seemed a votive candle burning slowly its scent and light smoke of loneliness, of desire, of missing. Finally she got up and tore the poster from the wall, folded it neatly, and threw it in the garbage. *That's my last duchess hanging on the wall,* said a voice from high school English, Miss Greening, who had saved her from slow death in Ludington. Now the walls were bare. She had never liked the poster, for the winged woman bothered her. Should a woman lust to fly? Fly away? Part pigeon, part mammal. No, it was stuck to her wall because Valerie made it. History formed you. But history is what you carry inside. Relics do not increase clarity. Valerie lay sleeping in a room nothing like this. A spasm of pain left her doubled over, although she did not really move from her crosslegged straight-backed sitting.

Eight-thirty. Valerie would still be in bed. She knew what the room looked like where Valerie slept. Or did she? Relics do not increase clarity. No, she knew what the room had looked like before Valerie came to it. Many times she had entered the bedroom of Lena Kornhauser to throw her coat on the bed whose headboard was covered with wild female cupids and doves in papier-mâché painted yellow and green and violet. The bed's furry coverlet would be almost hidden under heaped wraps. Lena gave excellent parties for local lesbian society. Valerie and Leslie were invited only to the larger bashes, being of the poorer more uppity element, the feminists not in with Lena. From an old Dutch family (anything that had arrived before 1880 was old), Lena had income from real estate and a department store, but she made money in her own right. She owned two good women's clothing shops in the best malls—no one went downtown in Grand Rapids. Her reputation was as a sculptor in plastic—big sensuous pieces in amberlike resins all soft lumps and female curves.

Lena did a piece or two a year. Leslie, for whom work was a passion, slightly despised her. She was taller than Leslie, blond and blue-eyed and usually tanned. She had to be forty-five but looked ten years younger, most of the time. Lena cultivated an air of luxurious decadence: a Victorian house whose upper floor had been cut into expensive apartments but whose more than ample parlor floor was art nouveau and Grand Rapids Gothic, cocaine and cognac (both brought in from Chicago), velvet draperies and spun glass Venetian knickknacks, the most extreme clothes from her boutiques.

Leslie sat straight-backed and crosslegged and identified the flame in her solar plexus. Yes, she hated Lena. She could not exactly make it come out that Lena had taken Valerie from her, because it had never been clear that Val would follow her to Detroit. Val did not like to say yes or no bluntly. Or perhaps it had been clear, but not to her.

Money.

It was easier by far to think about Lena than to think about Val. Had she destroyed the poster in anger? She did not like to think that. Would Val ask what had happened to the poster, the day Val finally came back with her?

She had a sudden picture of herself sitting on the floor of the almost empty room surrounded by the bleak gray February city in her white baggy costume with her shoulder-length carroty hair pulled back in a rubber band and her face blank with concentration, balanced against the room two hundred miles away with purple draperies and oriental rug, the scent of perfume and incense, music blaring from the speakers. Of course at nine on Sunday morning music would not be filling the house; she was thinking of parties. Valerie's black hair would be fanned over the pillow and she would perhaps just be waking groaning with vexation and wriggling into the covers. She did not think Lena would be bringing Val breakfast in bed, as she had. She had the habit of getting up hours earlier than Val on the weekends. On weekdays they got up together at seven-thirty, she for her classes and Val for work. Breakfast in bed had been her homage to Val's different temperament, to the poverty they had to share, to all the places they could not go together. Finally, what was Lena's fanciful lush interior but a place where women in couples could be together at their ease without pretense or self-consciousness or danger? The rich contentment of being able to take for granted the simplest of connections.

"You're never at ease anyplace!" That was Val's voice, high, woodwind. Truthfully, she had never been at ease at Lena's. Whatever she touched she felt might smear on her hands like butter cream frosting: the flocked wallpaper, the plush of the loveseat, the velvet of the draperies, the vases of glass flowers, the spotlights discreetly commenting on the rounded amber sculptures. She drank too much out of discomfort. Once she had nervously during a political confrontation disguised as chit-chat eaten a whole plate of little cakes—petits fours, Lena called them—out of that nervousness. She had immediately gone and vomited neatly in the toilet, flushed it away, washed her face and come back. Still she had felt guilty. At the least it was wasteful, although she could not think of any purpose to which the small pink and green cakes should

35

have been put, except perhaps fed to her older brother's children, her nephews and nieces, to make them, too, sick.

Abruptly she rose and began exercising—her blows, her kicks, her forms—until she was drenched with sweat under the loose costume. At eleven she lay on her mattress hot and relaxed and aching, happy. Now she would eat breakfast. Yogurt with a little honey, apple juice with two heaping tablespoons of nutritional yeast, Red Zinger tea. As she rolled to her feet she took off the Brunhilde bra with its hard protective cones she wore only for karate—because she was a little too full not to bounce around and could easily be injured—and stuffed it in the laundry bag, entirely wet. Right after breakfast if there was hot water she would bathe; if there was none she would shower. Then she would look at her notes and computer correlations on the bank archives from the Simpson papers and type up a preliminary report for George. Finally, in the early evening, she would go to karate.

"You're crazy, I mean it. You work as if you loved it!" Val's voice again, high and timbred like a clarinet.

It was true, she did love her work. She felt privileged to be allowed into the stacks of the library, she loved her desk in George's anteroom, her books and papers. It was orderly. It went somewhere. It built and made sense. It was different from blood on the floor and diapers in the pail and the smell of spoiled fish. She had always had to pretend she hated doing homework so that her brothers, her friends, later her roommates would not despise her. Books retained a special power: tickets to elsewhere. She had grown up in a house without books, without magazines except for an occasional Sunday paper or comic book, and they had proved to be doors to a different life, to respect and dignity. Social mobility, sure, but more.

Late Monday afternoon found her in the back of the shabby jouncing bus headed to Honor. As she walked past the laundromat, the liquor store, to turn at Honor's street, the late sun flashed out between spongy mountains of cloud. When the sun has been gone for days, it comes like an annunciation, she thought, wanting suddenly to be on skates. She could feel herself gliding, the cold air sawing at her face, the blades skimming, digging in as she swirled in a rush of ice particles. For a while in high school she had been serious about speed skating. But there was no one to coach a girl, no one really to skate with or against. She could beat everyone who would race her at the local pond, but it wasn't popular, tearing down the ice as if she was crazed, running long-legged and loping on skates. Speed skating had helped build her thighs, and that was useful in karate. For a thin woman she·had strong thighs.

Already she could see the little white house crouched behind its rickety porch. The walk had not been shoveled, just a rut gouged through the snowbanks not quite to cement but down to ice. Gingerly she picked her way up the slippery walk and the salted steps to ring the bell. Then guessing it too might not work, she banged on the door for good measure. The dogs heard her and barked furiously, clanking their chains.

Honor came gliding in a long dress of the blue paisley corduroy her mother had been sewing. Her face was flushed and she was playing with a cameo at her throat and still calling something over her shoulder Leslie could not hear for the dogs. "You're here! Wonderful! Come in, hurry. Isn't it nasty out? Bernar' has come already—he met me at school—and we're waiting for the fudge to cool. Why are you walking like that?"

"I pulled a muscle last night. It'll be all right in a day or two."

"It must be dreadfully painful! Would you like my heating pad? I always use it when I have the curse."

"It's not a curse. If you take a calcium-magnesium supplement, it prevents cramps. Also, masturbating helps."

"Shhh! Bernar' will hear you. It may not be a curse for you, but it certainly is for me! Let's not be sor'id. . . . Come, tell me how much you like my new dress and I'll introduce you to Bernar'."

"If I don't, you won't?" Wan hope. "All your dresses are fine, if you like dresses."

"No, no, you're supposed to tell me how pretty I am in the dress! To compliment me, not the dress. Come, smell the fudge."

"What I said about periods is true," Leslie said stubbornly and was towed into the kitchen.

He was standing at the window with one hand raised against the cracked sash. Posing, she thought. There's nothing to see except the house six feet away, the aluminum siding and the grade door. After a count of ten he turned, tall, skinny, at least as tall as George and even skinnier. His face was thin too. His hair was a lighter brown than Honor's and kinky; his nose was long and straight, as was his mouth, and he would be called good-looking.

Honor was introducing them and neither was listening. He caught her gaze and then she was damned if she would be stared down. His eyes were gray. Cold, very cold. Then abruptly he dropped his eyelids in disdain and his hand inscribed a gesture of Take it. If you care for such petty victories.

"And you have such a lot in common," Honor was finishing hopefully.

They could not help quickly glancing at each other, almost in complicity. It was like introducing Bonnie and Pierpont Morgan and saying, You've got loads in common to chat about, you both take such an interest in banking matters. Still she was delighted that he wanted to meet her as little as she wanted to meet him. That was a good start because it implied no further development. She never felt much in common with gay men; it was like telling her she ought to feel empathy with child molesters because they were both defined by the law as sexual deviants. She was only at ease with gay women, really, and she was less ill at ease with straight women than with the gayest of men. After all, they were still men. What was he doing hanging around Honor anyhow?

Leslie unfortunately had to cross the kitchen to a chair, and she could not suppress her limp. She hated limping. It was a loss of control. She was paying for having pushed too hard, fighting a little outclassed. "I'm not usually a cripple," she said sourly.

"Leslie hurt herself doing judo."

"Karate."

"Isn't that a lot of hassle?" Bernard came slowly to the table and sat on the other side of Honor. "I don't see the point. I mean someone with a knife could cut down a karate expert as easily as your helpless grandma."

Attack disguised as defense. She was supposed to say something indicating she remembered he had knifed a boy, thus making Honor feel protective. "Of course. And if someone threw a hand grenade at me or lobbed a mortar. One armed warhead and the whole city would go up. But people hardly ever attack you with a machine gun or even a straight razor compared to the number of times you might have to show simply you do mean to defend yourself. Every woman has the experience of attempted rape—attempted, if she's lucky."

"Do you think you could actually fight off a man?" Honor asked.

"Sure. It was a man I was fighting last night, in kumite. I'm in a mixed class. It's harder"—she grimaced at her sore leg—"but more useful. I've never been attacked by a woman." Actually that wasn't true. She got in a fight in a bar her very first month in Detroit when a woman had swung on her with a bottle. But that had been over in two minutes and nobody hurt. She would not admit that here. Honor would think she went arount like a comic book bull dyke picking fights in bars. She did not like bars. They were smoky and hurt her sinuses and gave her headaches, and there was nothing to do in them but drink and get into trouble.

Honor was making a monkey face. "I just can't imagine you actually . . . fighting with a man. I can't picture it!"

"It's not wrestling," she said dryly. "The only body contact is blows. You fight the same way whether you're fighting a woman or a man. . . . You wouldn't think it weird if I went to Rouge Park and played tennis with a man."

"Would you enjoy that the same way?" Bernard asked innocently. His voice was deep and silky. Everything about him reeked of practice.

"I'm no good at tennis. What are you good at?"

"Want to challenge me? Not much. What am I good at? Loving and lying, I suppose."

"Well, the second might get you into the government. The first, onto the streets."

"I have been on the streets."

A moment of pure malice passed between them bright as a beam of light. Honor blinked, her eyes darting from one to the other. Then she stood with a toss of her hair and a flip of her gown. Both their gazes followed her. She stood a moment in dramatic silence and then laughed that heavy sensual laugh that had caught Leslie's attention at the party. "Let's see if the fudge has cooled enough to eat."

She did not think Honor had understood what he had just said and for a moment she was tempted to explain. His eyes waited on her like hungry pikes. Perhaps Honor would romanticize hustling. She was naive enough. Leslie said nothing. Outside it was getting dark. She had not asked if she was being invited to supper and she was beginning to feel empty. She hoped that Honor did not intend the fudge in place of a meal. It was a little after five. Briefly she felt like an ancient among adolescents.

"Leslie, take some. Don't sit there wishing!" Honor and Bernard were eating as fast as they could.

Reluctantly she broke off half a square. "Sugar is a drug."

"Absolutely," Bernard said. "That's why it's such fun."

Slowly she chewed the fudge, chocolately and full of walnuts. It felt like heroin charging her blood. She was too hungry not to finish her half square but she could not eat more. Their capacity amazed her. Already each had eaten three large squares. At last Bernard sat back with a sigh, licked his fingers in a catlike gesture, and then lit a joint he extracted from his woven belt.

"We're both candy freaks," Honor said. "I can see you

aren't. Or is there a secret candy freak in you struggling to come out?"

"Yes, Leslie, do come out," he said musically.

She tensed. Well, they each knew where the other stood. Or was it a blind shot? She had to bring the matter up with Honor, she intended to, but not with him there. "No, I'm a hot freak. I eat Mexican peppers while steam issues from my ears, and my sinuses miraculously clear."

"What kind of hot food? I've hardly had any." Honor leaned forward, still nibbling fudge.

"Indian curries. Szechwan Chinese. Mexican. There's a lot of Mexican food in Grand Rapids in the ghetto. I heard there's a new Szechwan restaurant here—"

"I liked it," Bernard said. "A friend took me. We could all go if we could figure out a time Honor wouldn't be caught."

"Caught eating Chinese food?"

"I couldn't go in the evening because Mama manages to get in a phone call. . . . We could go in your car. Bernar' has a car, just as tacky as Cam's."

"It's an old Mustang but it still moves, kind of." He offered her the joint suddenly. She had not thought he would.

"Go ahead, Leslie, don't let me bother you," Honor said. "I'm sure Mama would smell it on me somehow. It's not that it's mysterious to me. I tried it first in the sixth grade."

If she did not share his toke as well as not eating the fudge, she was rejecting too much. It was not that she didn't smoke but that she didn't want to smoke with him. She took it. Was she imagining all kinds of subtle hostility between them? She could have sworn that he was amused at her hesitation and at her acquiescence. She could be making it all up. No, not all. His gray gaze measured her and there was amusement in it.

Her belly growled. She was very empty. "I wonder if there's anything to eat? Like cheese?"

"Poor Leslie," he crooned. "You aren't used to the house rules. Never mind, you can share my hero. We

41

never eat from the refrigerator because Mama would notice. I'm not supposed to be here very much."

"She's so . . . anxious about me, she'd want to know exactly who was here and what we talked about, and she'd want to meet you at once."

The phone rang. Honor hurried to answer it in the livingroom. Rather than speaking to each other, both looked after her and shut up the better to listen. "Yes, Mama. . . . No, not yet. I was just about to pop the casserole in the oven. . . . Low heat, yes. Do you imagine I plan to burn it? . . . No, Cam has a date, she won't be home till late. . . . Yes, Mama, it's on again this weekend. It isn't a long run after all! . . . Just doing my school work, my French. . . . I was in the kitchen. I told you, I was just about to heat my dinner. . . . Yes, I put the dress on as soon as I got home from school. You'll see how ravishing it is when you come home, Mama darling. . . . Yes, I'll show you what Mr. Haggerty wrote on my theme, and all I'll tell you is that it's quite flattering. . . . I am not! I'm perfectly healthy. . . . Really, Mama, I'm not as sickly as you like to imagine! . . . Oh, that was a touch of the sniffles. . . . Well, sometimes I don't want to go to school. It's boring! . . . Well, if it wasn't then, it is now. . . . Yes, Mama, I did already. . . . Yes, love and kisses. See you at ten!"

Bernard met her gaze and a strange hostile complicity jelled between them. He shrugged one shoulder. "The voice of the dragon in her ear."

"Have you met Mama?"

He nodded. "You'll have to, if you stick around. It isn't . . . infinitely avoidable."

"I suppose then I'll meet her. You survived."

"Survived what?" Honor glided in.

Leslie fumbled for an explanation but Bernard said smoothly, "High school. But I didn't go through. So I didn't exactly survive it."

"I'd forgotten, excuse me," Leslie said dryly. Yes, he was a good liar. He had scored a point on that exchange.

When Honor brought her tuna and noodle dish to the table, Bernie pulled a hero sandwich from his coat, where it hung on the doorknob. As he went by the sink he picked a knife from a drawer and carefully cut the sandwich in two. Half he put in front of Leslie. "Take, eat, it is my body," he said lightly.

Once again their gazes snagged while the retorts she could not *yet* make flew barbed through her mind. Honor said, "Really, Bernar', isn't that blasphemous?"

"Only the religious ever blaspheme. Nobody else knows how."

"How nice to have extra sins," Leslie said. "However, eating your hero won't be mine. I have to work tonight, so I'd better be on my way."

"If you wait, Bernar' can give you a ride home. He has his car," Honor wheedled, playing with the ends of her hair. "You don't have to go yet."

"Tonight I do."

"The bus runs so seldom."

"I still have to work. I'll call."

Taking his half a hero back, Bernard did not bother to hide his pleasure. The field to himself. She would make sure to see Honor alone next time.

four

Leslie came early to help prepare and lay out the buffet with Sue, who used the time to pump her about people at school. George was upstairs in the family room building a wooden skyscraper with Davey and Louise, and Sue also wanted to tell Leslie about Brenda arriving without warning the weekend before to make a dreadful scene, and how cruel and unfeeling George had been. Sue had had to clear it all up as usual, and send Brenda back to Grand Rapids on the bus after a good cry.

"Really, I don't hardly know *what* she thought she was going to stir up." Sue paused. She was a big-boned attractive woman with short straight hair of a wonderful color. It was half natural straw blond and half prematurely gray. The result was a beautiful ash color that reminded Leslie of the furniture in her parents' bedroom. Her mother had got it when the hotel closed, where she used to wait tables in the summers, and she called it Hollywood Oak. The veneer was that same ash blond. There were a double bed, a vanity, and a chest of drawers; one of the treats of Leslie's childhood had been to help her mother empty the drawers and line them with shelf paper. Then Leslie was allowed to play with her mother's things, and they were together, the two of them, all afternoon in the room where she was not usually allowed.

"What was she expecting?" Sue paused again. She had a seductive voice, basically Texas overlaid with good

Eastern schools. Her drawl expanded and contracted according to mood, how social, how flirtatious or how serious she was feeling. "Shouldn't it have dawned on Brenda if George wanted to see her he'd have shown some sign? Our George is no slowpoke about chasing down pussy."

"Maybe Brenda wanted the scene so she'd know it was over." Leslie was slicing a salami.

"Why do they always think it won't be over? Should I make a dip for the chips? I'm bored silly with dips."

"Don't. They all taste like sour cream with something odd in it."

"Brenda cried all the way to the bus. Imagine coming to the house that way! . . . Why do they carry on like scalded cats?"

Leslie raised her brows. "Is that a serious question?"

Sue pouted, sleeking her hair. She had put on a long blue and green Mexican hostess dress. "Do they figure he's about to leave me? That's what makes me spitting mad!"

"You never seem spitting mad."

"All right, mildly bothered. I don't like it slopping over anywhere near the kids." She smiled absently, stooping to rummage the lower cupboards for more crackers to put out.

"I suppose you only see the ones who make a fuss."

"Oh, he's honest. Honest George. He does tell me about all of them. Otherwise I'd poison him, right? Give me a hand up. I've got to lose weight this spring. You're always so neat and trim. How come you never gain an ounce?"

Leslie set Sue on her feet. Sue held on to her arms for a moment. "Maybe I should study karate?" Sue peered into her face. "But I wouldn't, would I, honey? I'd never keep soldiering at it. I'd just go in there twice and pull a muscle I never did hear of before and give up."

The truth was Sue was lazy and never studied anything past a couple of lessons, whether it was trancendental meditation or conversational Russian. She read an enormous amount, far more than George, who stuck to journals and books in his own field. She read serious novels and books about genetics, books about education and art and the Etruscans and medieval icons, biographies of Freud and Helen Traubel. As compulsively as some women ate, she read. Sue had enjoyed a good education in the English department at Bryn Mawr, but she never seemed to have sheltered any ambitions Leslie could discover. Leslie could not understand such a large amorphous curiosity, a morass into which all that information and literature sank. Yet it was characteristic of Sue that no matter what book anyone might mention, she would have read it or would have acquired it and be about to. Reading seemed to be Sue's profession. If she could be inveigled into real conversation, frequently her ideas were interesting. But nothing led to anything else. Maybe it was because she had never had to work, Leslie thought, puzzling over Sue.

Once the students arrived, Leslie detached herself from Sue. The livingroom of George's house reminded her of a failed church, high and gloomy with shadows clustering like bats in spite of the Design Research furniture. The livingroom stretched a full two stories, facing the cold gray north for a supposed view, a weak slope to the trees still standing in a thin band between this house and the next, and it looked like a room the sun never entered. Sue collected art. The livingroom was arranged to show off the prints, the hard-edge paintings, the welded metal sculpture, rather than to facilitate sitting or talking. As a result, George's students ended up in two huddles. The first was centered on George, who usually sat by the fireplace in a leather sling chair, while at his feet the nervous masses huddled yearning to be noticed. Those were the students who kept their minds buzzing on number one goal, impressing George. The lazier, more confident, the hungrier, hornier students clustered in the kitchen near the food and the drink.

Leslie wandered back and forth, a little bit the maid emptying ashtrays, collecting empty beer cans and glasses abandoned where they could be broken, putting out more chips or ice—a little bit the ersatz daughter of the house, called over by Sue or George to hear some point or tell some anecdote: the only female Sue trusted. His newer students tended to resent her ambiguous role, not comprehending it was all just part of her job.

Who would George take up with? He always had something going, carefully casual and limited affairs with young women. They were pretty, uncommonly so, and quite young. Sometimes they were students, sometimes secretaries, and sometimes somebody's girlfriend or sister. Valerie and she had once invented a murder starring George as corpse in which ever so many characters had motives for offing him. They had such fun they listed twenty-seven suspects, including Sue of course, his students, his colleagues, his ex-affairs, young men whose girlfriends or sisters he had briefly enjoyed. He never had an affair with a married woman or anyone belonging to a peer. He had been murdered by having the stem of his pipe coated with strychnine: he chewed his pipe more than he smoked it.

She smiled at the memory and then saw Hennessy trying to catch her eye. Cam was not here; the play had two more weeks to run. In one of those loud buffalo plaid shirts he liked to wear, he looked like a hunter and she felt like a hunted deer. Pivoting, she dived into the pool of listeners at George's feet. Actually it typified these gatherings that nobody ever listened to anyone except George and the voice of their own anxiety. They never heard what anyone said, even the person just beside them. But Hennessy wedged himself in next to her, his thigh heavy against hers. Hugging her knees, she ordered herself to be elsewhere; she would review her sensei's admonitions for the last two weeks and think how best to apply them.

Her new sensei, Parker, was the only man she could remember that she considered beautiful, as beautiful as a woman, although she did not desire him. She had never had a male sensei before, but Parker was good at instructing women. He was of medium height, his skin was copper-black, he was graceful and very, very strong. He looked sarcasm oftener than he spoke it. He had ways of glancing at her when she was clumsy that made her shrivel. She liked him immensely but could not tell from his vast fairness whether he liked her. Perhaps he perceived his students only in terms of their karate accomplishments and problems; she would like that.

She jumped, realizing George had addressed her and probably repeated whatever he had said, because everyone was staring. She felt herself blush as if she had been dipped in boiling water. Hennessy said, "Hey, now I know why George calls you Red. Not just from your hair." He patted her head as if she were a spaniel, grinning down at her.

"What were you dreaming about?" George stroked his mustache peevishly.

"Why the papers, master, only the papers."

"Then you must've found something more interesting than I have, to blush like that."

"It's a reflex. . . . Can you figure what possible survival value it could ever have had for my ancestors to suddenly turn beet red? Fitting into a predominantly red landscape?"

"Bright as a baboon's behind. But evolution works by sexual selection as well as natural selection." George would pronounce on anything. He had a weakness for biological theories, Ardrey and Wilson. She was off the hook, but he wouldn't forgive a second lapse, for her attention was part of what he was buying. That quality of attention first made him notice her as a student, he had told her. "You'll have to do everything not twice as well but five times as well." He did not bother to tell her she'd have to be a decent politician to survive. She knew that, but she was not convinced she had the capacity. Maybe she could be seven times as good and they'd accept her.

Honor was wearing a lacy nightdress with a lavender housecoat over it, trailing down to her narrow high-arched bare feet. "I'm afraid I'm catching cold. I feel frayed around the edges. That's why I got into my nightgown when I came home." She glided off to the room she obviously shared with Cam, one twin bed made up with an old-fashioned prim-faced doll sitting on the pillow—a doll that must have belonged to her mother—the other a

48

tangle of covers and run pantyhose, rumpled bikini under-pants. "Do have some of this cough medicine. It's delicious and habit-forming."

Leslie glowered. "It has codeine in it. Why not just shoot up? A, you don't have a cough yet. B, if you did, the last thing you should do is suppress it! Coughing clears your lungs."

"Leslie, you're so righteous! What's the difference between drinking wine and drinking this, except it has a lovely cherry flavor?"

"I don't mean to be . . . righteous. I try to avoid the lesser temptations."

"I can't even resist a second slice of lemon meringue pie, which isn't my favorite, so I'm sure I could never resist a big juicy temptation, if I had a crack at one. . . . Paul's the closest to a temptation I've met, and his ugly little dirty jokes turn me off." She sat on the bench in front of a skirted vanity and motioned Leslie to sit beside her. The frilly dressing table was piled with a dusty havoc of glamour—half-used lipsticks, hand creams, throat creams, cakes of eye shadow, an electric curling set, powders and rouges that Leslie presumed were really Cam's. "Look at this wicked new lipstick. It's mauve."

She took Honor's wrist, gently. "Please don't put that crap on. You're naturally . . ." She could not say "beautiful" again. Sometimes it seemed to her every time she looked at Honor she told her how beautiful she was. ". . . lovely."

Honor grimaced into the mirror, making a face with one eye strained wide and the other squinted. "If I'm . . . lovely . . . as you say . . . why does everyone hate me?"

"Who hates you? What are you talking about?"

"Nobody in the play likes me. I can tell. I don't know how to talk to people. . . . And at school, they hate me."

"Listen, the kids who enjoy high school, they're all assholes, Honorée. Believe me, everybody you'll be friendly with when you go to college, when you ask them about high school they were all miserable."

Honor put her elbows down hard on the vanity, shoving aside the cosmetics. "Such an ugly thing happened. In

49

the cafeteria. Buck Rogers—his name is Bill but he calls himself Buck, and every time we're in the same class, we have to sit by each other when they do it by alphabet. He plays basketball and he thinks he's sexy. . . . Ugh, he's so gross!"

"What happened?" This was the cold, she was sure, what was really ailing Honor.

"He said to me in front of the whole line, 'Hey, Dictionary—' "

"What?"

"Oh, that's what some of them call me. Miss Dictionary. They're such cretins. . . . Anyhow, he said—very loud—'Hey, Dictionary, I can't decide what's bigger, your tits or your ass or the words you use, but I'll tell you what. I'll fuck you anyhow, if you'll wear a gag. How about it?' " Honor gave a yank to her own hair. "I felt so stupid, I couldn't think of a come-back. All the conversations that go through my mind all the time, and I always give myself such witty dialogue, and I couldn't think of anything to say. I almost cried! I felt so humiliated. . . . I'm never going back!"

"He probably really is attracted to you, and he doesn't know how to approach you, so he punished you for it."

"Sometimes I feel like such an anachronism. I want to be a Great Lady, and whatever will I do with my life?"

"Finish high school and get away from home for a start. It will get better then, believe me."

"How can I leave Mama? I think she's bred me so I can't. I'll turn into an old maid and age behind drawn blinds playing with cosmetics and dresses."

"Are you aging at— What age are you?"

"Seventeen."

"You're not getting social security yet," Leslie said mockingly, but she shivered. Was never leaving a possibility? Was that why Cam had brought her sister to the theater? Nervously she picked up a small metal box from the dresser and fiddled with it. Suddenly it began to tinkle out music. "What?"

"Mama and I found that at a garage sale. We search them out sometimes on weekends. Dad never goes. He doesn't like to do anything Mama does. He likes to hang out with what Mama calls his cronies—two friends he plays penny-a-point pinochle with every Friday night. They must be the last pinochle players in the world." Honor took the music box from her. "I bet you didn't notice what's inside?"

"Some earrings."

"Those are real garnets. They belonged to my father's mother. But I can't wear them, they're for pierced ears. Mama won't let me get my ears pierced. She talks about infection. It makes me furious! I'm trying to get Bernar' to go with me to have it done. I'd have the nerve then. Once it's done, what can she do? I don't suppose your ears are pierced?"

"Wrong. I had it done when I was fourteen. I used to wear big gold hoops."

"I should think silver would look better with your hair?"

"I used to be partial to a shade of red-gold I thought matched it. Now gold's so expensive it's ludicrous that when I was fourteen and a biker's old lady I used to wear gold in my ears."

"I've never seen you wear any jewelry but your man's watch." Honor lifted the loop of Leslie's hair that covered her ear, on its way to the rubber band that confined it. "You do have a little stud—but just on one side. Did you lose the other?"

"Val—Valerie and I—used to buy a pair of post earrings together. We'd split the pair and each would wear one. Val has the mate to this turquoise stud."

"Valerie. I thought you didn't have a sister."

"No, we lived together for three years."

"I don't know if I'd like to live with another woman. I've had it with sisters."

I've got to do better than this, she thought. "We were lovers, Honor, Honorée."

"And when you were fourteen you really slept with a boy? Is that what you mean by the phrase you were a biker's old lady?"

Leslie laughed with relief. Honor wasn't going to faint

51

or scream. "I don't think I was ever a virgin. I probably had sex some time up in the sand dunes when I was nine. I suppose before fourteen it doesn't count. Yeah, I was involved with first one guy, Billy, and then Cliff. I was involved with Cliff from, let's see, around Christmas just before I turned fifteen until halfway through my sixteenth year. It was practically like a two-year marriage. Cliff was my first marriage and Val my second."

"It's amazing to imagine having sex for years by the time you were my age. Just think, you'd already broken up with Cliff! Oh, there must be something wrong with me!"

She blinked. Honor had taken it like a sugar pill. Or had she? Had she just somehow not listened? She could hardly say, Hey, never mind the early heterosexual stuff, you have to focus on what matters to me. "It was my first try at breaking out of the house. Not a smart way. It's lucky I didn't get pregnant and stuck for good. But the gang seemed high on energy, style, speed. That's what drew me. Except I liked books. They were escape too. I always liked to read from the time I discovered that. They were someplace else, like the gang."

"How did you happen to go to college?"

"I had a high school teacher who decided I was a diamond in the rough. Miss Greening." She had loved to talk to Miss Greening, Miss Greening loved to talk to her. Both of them were perishing of loneliness. Because she had already been in love with a woman, although nothing passed between them, she felt more sophisticated and more corrupt than Miss Greening, who did not know what the attraction between them was. She knew. She was grateful, but knowing made her fierce and bumbling, awkward and lumpy. Miss Greening helped her, gave to her, shared with her, and she was deeply, passionately grateful. Even though she was not physically attracted to the dumpy gray-haired woman, she wanted to make love to her out of love itself. But they remained Miss G. and Leslie, and all that was ever given to the affection was a peck on the cheek at final parting.

"Every time I turn on the stupid TV, I see some man I

could have a passionate affair with," Honor mourned, holding her hair on top of her head and turning to and fro to eye herself. "Why don't I meet any in real life? Maybe they all left Detroit. . . . I had a fantastic dream about Paul. I do have the best dreams! If I could film them, I'd make a fortune! They're like ten-course dinners. I dreamed I was married to him. He was, how shall I say? playful -but affectionate."

Leslie laughed. "Sounds like a Saint Bernard puppy."

"Sunday I told him I'd dreamed about him, and he forgave me for our tiff Saturday and got all enchanted up again."

"Are you really interested in him?"

"He's fun to practice on. I can't help it if I'm feeling fine. I'm not going to act dull and dreary on his account," Honor said loftily.

"You don't even like him, do you?"

"What has liking to do with it?"

"I wouldn't want to . . . touch someone I didn't like a lot."

"Pooh. I don't think sexual magnetism has much to do with liking. I like Bernar' more than anyone—except possibly yourself, Leslie, and I've known him longer—but there's no electricity. I can't imagine him sweeping me up in his arms and throwing me on the bed."

"Gay men seldom do that sort of thing," Leslie muttered. "But why do you want to be raped?"

"I don't want to be raped! I don't even like having my hair pulled when Mama's trimming it. But I want a masterly sort of man. If I were tremendously experienced and sophisticated, like yourself, Leslie," she added wickedly, "I'd know just what to do, and then I wouldn't need to imagine the man taking charge. All I know is how to flirt, and I'm still learning that. How else will anything ever manage to happen?"

Tuesday she was coming home just after ten in good spirits. She had made a breakthrough, she had done very well in karate class. Her instructor had given her a nod and said, "Like that, watch," to another student. Afterward she had showered at the dojo and rubbed out her bruises and changed and even hung around socializing in the glow of the thing well done. As she passed the dark shoestore with its heavy metal grates pulled over the windows and approached the street door that opened on her stairway, she saw someone in the doorway lounging, and at once she crouched into a ready position, letting her gear drop.

"Really, do I look like a ravening menace? You're much more dangerous than I am on a dark street."

She recognized Bernard's voice before she picked up her gear and moved close enough to see him slouched outside the locked door.

"Are you waiting for me, or do you just like to piss in hallways?" Leslie unlocked the door and started up the straight steep flight. "That bell downstairs doesn't work by the way." Her adrenaline slowly subsided and she felt annoyed.

"Yes, someone's been using it for a pissoir. But as you guessed, I'm waiting for you. Don't look quite so gloomy about it, it's time we tried to talk instead of throwing darts over Honor's head."

"I don't know. I thought we could manage to avoid each other." She stood aside for him.

As she flicked on the overhead light and followed him in, he prowled about looking and then he whistled. "I have never seen a barer, more ascetic pad. I mean, the solitary cells at Saint Boniface were fancy by comparison. Saint Boniface was my alma mater, a home for uncurably delinquent boys. At least we had graffiti. What do you do here? Do you eat, do you sleep like an ordinary mortal, or do you go into hibernation? Maybe you walk in and turn yourself off like a robot?"

"I don't care for a distracting environment," she said with a little amusement, hanging her pea jacket on a nail. She put her gear on its shelf and sat down crosslegged on the floor. "Do have a seat."

"I could go sit on the toilet. I assume you haven't removed it? Or I could sit on your bed—your mattress. If you wouldn't mind? I have a feeling you would."

54

"No more than I mind your sitting anywhere else. Do make yourself . . . less uncomfortable."

Sprawling then, arranging himself gracefully on her mattress covered with the only spot of color, an old but satisfying Indian blanket, he dug in his pocket and pulled out a flask of Old Goat Blended Whiskey. "What a relief, your mattress is foam rubber. I was worried it might be nails. . . . I thought this might make things go easier."

"Do you usually drink that?"

"No. But I was weighing how much alcohol power I could buy for my money. We could drink that." He pointed to a bottle of Benedictine she had been drinking a little at a time before bed.

"I'm not going to get drunk with you. And I don't like whiskey." She got up and took an opened bottle of California chablis from the refrigerator, left over from George's Thursday night. Sue tended to load her with whatever was left.

"You're not offering me the Benedictine?"

"Want me to sit here counting every drop? It's my bribe to myself."

"All right, I'll drink your wine. I'll save this for a seduction. Or use it for paint remover when I refinish my desk."

There they sat, he in a graceful sprawl on her mattress, she crosslegged on the floor with one hand on her knee and the other holding the tumbler of wine cold against her palm, while a silence fell from the air between them palpable and awkward. She had a feeling she was better at silence, better at waiting.

She was right, because Bernard began to shift and then rose on his elbow and fixed her with gray eyes narrowed with irritation. "The thing is, it's dangerous for us to act hostile over her head. You almost couldn't resist saying something cute when I dropped that cue about hustling. I hope you didn't bring it up later?"

"You must know from Honor I didn't."

"And you must know she's too fine to carry tales."

"Aren't you scared that's too sticky for me too?"

"Then you're a fraud. You put up a front of being

55

tough. So I treat you differently, expecting a different response."

"What?"

"How you bristle. What are you afraid of?"

"Afraid?" She was losing the advantage. "Don't confuse distaste with fear."

"Are you so scared of me that you'd rather go on fencing than try to communicate?"

"Why do you want to communicate with me?"

"Got nothing to say worth hearing?"

"Why should you listen?"

"Why should I listen to Honor?" He held out his glass till she refilled it.

"We can get to that in a minute. Why did you come here?" For the first time she drank some of the wine. It wasn't good but it was cold. Then the cold wine hit her belly, which doubled up in protest. She winced.

He was watching carefully. "What's wrong?"

"I'm hungry is all. I haven't eaten since lunch."

He got up to inspect her refrigerator. "Almost as bad as the room. Well, I see sprouts and eggs. Got soy sauce? If I cook a nice Chinesey sort of omelette, will you talk to me?"

"Soy sauce on the shelves to your left. Yes." Because in a moment of weakness, she was tired of doing for herself. She wanted to be cooked for, coddled, yes.

He lit a joint and went to work humming softly at the hotplate. She was weary and her back ached. What she really wanted was to lie down or, second best, to lean against the wall. Would she let herself? Suddenly she was tired of her continual discipline, like a spring she had to keep winding every five minutes. She could feel the one big swallow of wine she had taken. She inched backward until she was resting against the wall. Ah, better. Actually she wanted to collapse. With him gone. But she could not quite wish that with the smells coming from the hotplate. She was enormously hungry.

He brought over the plates of eggs. "See you look almost human now."

"Meaning I look for the moment worn out and defense-

56

less." She took a plate and ate. The eggs were good, which she said between mouthfuls. When they had finished he took the plates to the sink. She was not sure whether he meant to wash them, but she called, "Leave them."

"So you're ready to talk to me?" He strolled back and sank on the edge of her mattress.

"All right." She laughed uncertainly. "I have the feeling we should shake hands. But suppose we just talk more to the point. Square one is that I'm as queer as you are, if not a little queerer."

"Yeah?" He batted his lashes. "What else is news?"

"It's not supposed to be news. I've been out since I was eighteen. I was married to a woman for three years—we considered it marriage. I've told Honor. Not that it sinks in, and I can't exactly sit around Mama's house waving copies of *The Lavender Woman*."

"You're not real out. Not flagrant, as we say."

"I was outer in Grand Rapids. I don't think I'd hit it off in my department. But I'm farther out than you are."

"I'm not closeted or out. I'm confusing and confused, dear heart." He rolled over on the mattress, staring at the ceiling. Then he sat up and glared around. "What a monastic cell. Nothing to fiddle with. No bric-a-brac, no casual clutter. I bet there isn't a book over there that isn't for school." He actually got up and peered at the board and brick shelves, the books piled in cartons. She waited through his fit of restlessness till at last he came back to the mattress again, facing her. "Are you interested in Honor?"

"We both are, obviously. What else brings us together?" She sipped her wine. This time, with the food for cushioning, it did not hurt.

"Now you see it, now you don't; watch the moving shells and not the moving hand. You know what I'm asking."

"I'm a little in love with her. I don't mean to have an affair. She's too young."

"Oh, yes," he sighed. "On the other hand innocence is lovely, isn't it? It's so different."

"From you and me?"

"From me. Oh, Leslie, I'm not sure about you. I think maybe you're more innocent than you think you are." He grinned. "If I were you, I'd make love to her."

"And her mother too?"

"Mmmm. Your objections are practical." He waited while she shrugged. "What do you want then?"

"To be her friend, I suppose."

"You supposes and who disposes? Will you wait for her?"

"Come on! I admit I fantasize that in a year, after she leaves home, when she knows who she is, then I might be good for her. But I'm not stuck there crouching like a cat outside a mousehole. Did you think that?"

"That you might seduce her? Why shouldn't I think that?"

"I never in my life seduced anybody to anything. I can't. I'm not so stupid as when I was younger, when I could never even ask for what I wanted, but always had to wait suffering and in silence for it to offer itself to me. Now I can ask. But I can't try to . . . push on others, to make them want what I want. . . . I can't." Maybe that was what had gone wrong at Christmas with Val, why she had not been able to get her to leave Grand Rapids and come to Detroit.

"You're less calculating then I am. And more bourgeois. You'd really like to carry her off to a house in the suburbs and raise begonias."

"How do I know?" She shook her head impatiently while her hair caught at the nape slapped the wall. "With Val I couldn't even walk down the street with my arm around her without some ape wanting to cream us. What in hell do you want with her? Hey?"

"I'm a little in love with her too." He drank off the rest of his glass and poured more. "But you at least know you could make love to her. . . . Actually I don't want to. She doesn't move me that way. . . . I adore her, but truly as a sister. Don't raise your eyebrows. Why can't I desperately want a sister again? I'd like to keep house with

58

her too. I'd love to get rid of Mama and move in and have a little warm house to hold me. Why not?"

"And a moment ago you were calling me bourgeois."

"It's a state we both aspire to, in our various pitiful ways." He smiled. "I want her to save me. From myself. My rotten life. My desperation. I want her to believe in me. Violins please."

"We're both crazy, and she'll go to bed with that lecherous creep Paul."

Bernard rubbed his chin. "I think that can be stopped. I'd be furious, I'd howl for months! But Paul's a busy man and Cam's usually on the spot."

"Ber— I don't know what I call you. I can't bring myself to call you Bernar'.'"

"Oh, Honor's French phase. Call me Bernie—half the world does. I'll call you Red."

Perhaps she jumped, for he raised an eyebrow. "Please don't," she said, "it has too many smells attached."

"Did your lover call you that?"

"Val? Never. It was my high school name. Red—or Ready."

"What were you like then?"

"Very chicky. Then bummed out and quiet. I was going to ask you something: Was Cam ever involved with Paul?"

"Cam? Why did you think so?"

Leslie shrugged. "The *way* she was upset over him coming on to Honor."

"Will find out. I hang around there with Honor. Paul's gone so far as to ask me if I want to try out for a part."

"You don't want to?"

"Not all gay men want to be actors, didn't you know?"

"No, but most vain men have fantasies about it." She smiled, her head lolling against one shoulder.

"I try not to be vain."

"Do you try very hard?"

"I have no vanity, no respect for myself, nothing to stand on. You don't know me yet."

"How could I, even if you were transparent as a clean

59

window? Instead of kinky and weird and sideways. I'm tired. Very tired. Go home, Bernie, we'll talk again."

"Will we?" He stood over her.

"Sure." She laughed weakly, her eyelids at half mast. "We have so much in common. . . . Truthfully I enjoyed it."

He kissed one finger and touched her nose with it. "Good night, Leslie. Don't be too sleepy to lock the door behind me. I found it real unpleasant waiting in your doorway."

five

Grumpily she sat on the arm of an overstuffed couch next to Honor, who was next to Paul. Paul had his arm around Honor and was cracking innuendo jokes in a steady stream she tried to shut out. The evening before, Bernie had come by to ask Leslie to fill in for him as he had to work and could not cover Honor the last night of the play, "when Paul may be especially clever or especially desperate, so you go and play St. Bernard in my place." Therefore here she was perched uneasily on the arm of the couch smoking a joint Bernie had laid on her as recompense.

It felt funny to smoke a whole joint alone, but nobody was paying any attention to her, which suited her, and Honor never smoked. Indeed, did she love Honor? No. That she was sure of. She had fallen in love only twice, once with Penny, when she was sixteen, and once with Val, when she was nineteen. Well, she should watch out, if such natural disasters came in three-year cycles. Of course they didn't. Instead it was reasonable to assume that if recovering from the first—unconsummated, unacted—had cost her three years, then recovering from the fully realized second might take six.

She did not think of herself as volatile dry straw catching at the first spark. No, slowly, painfully she succumbed, like a waterlogged green bough that took hours and piles of kindling to set smoldering. What worried her was that every time she had fallen thoroughly in love she was engulfed entirely before she allowed herself to realize what was happening.

It's true, she thought, I don't make love. I fall in love, I make it happen like lightning striking. Therefore she stared sideways at Honor tossing her hair with a hand dramatically aloft and wondered. Penny had been big and blond, ample bodied as Honor was, but languid, easy, like a pool of sun-warmed water, her eyes big and brown and slowly blinking. She would never be attracted to Penny now. The last time Leslie had been in Ludington—the dramatic throw-it-all-on-the-table Thanksgiving—she had run into Penny coming out of Meijers Thrifty Acres. Penny had looked flabby, spent, one snowsuited kid tugging at her and the baby stuck in a shopping cart with the groceries she was pushing toward a station wagon.

Valerie. Her mind balked. Valerie's poignant face. Moon round yet hollow cheeked. Skin like dark buckwheat honey. In the summer Leslie never tanned as dark as the skin of Val's winter belly. She freckled too much. Val's skin was clear, so clear it seemed to have lighted depths. Valerie Mendoza. Everything about her was special and strange. Half of her was Scotch-Irish like Leslie but the other half was Filipino, which was itself part Japanese and part Spanish and part Tagalog. Her hair was black and slippery smooth, cut straight across her wide forehead in bangs and then straight again at her small shoulders. Her eyes were slanted and dark, but her nose turned up like Leslie's own. In repose Val's face seemed faintly amused. Her body was lithe, compact, perfect except for an appendicitis scar that proved she was mortal, that and her left breast being slightly larger than her right. Suddenly Leslie found herself squinting to keep back tears in the middle of the alien straight noisy party that happened around her like a swarm of insects. Honor could survive her absence long enough for her to scout something cold and unalcoholic, like water to drink. She found the small stool-and-counter kitchen.

Cam came over to lean on her arm. "Well, so much for that play. What're you drinking?"

"Ginger ale. I have to get up early tomorrow."

"Listen, you've been wonderful for Honor. I appreciate it. I really do."

"What do you mean?" Leslie asked warily. Was Cam being sarcastic? Yet she seemed as blowsily open as a big cabbage rose.

"I know she's bright—she's always been a bookworm and teacher's pet—but I worry a lot about my kid sister. Mama keeps her on such a tight leash, I wonder if she'll ever get loose. It isn't natural for her to see so few people. She's not ugly or anything, she ought to find a boyfriend. She doesn't even have girlfriends the way I always did, someone to giggle with and go shopping. She just knocks around alone playing games with the mirror and trying on my clothes when she thinks I don't know it and using my make-up and eating too many sweets and pretending she's in a movie. But I can't get through to her. She thinks I'm trying to boss her around. It's hard to be an older sister, you better believe it."

"But that'll all change when she goes away to school."

"*If* she goes away. There's not much money. Who wouldn't like to go to a school in some place like Colorado or New York City? Mama's not real keen on it. It's a race between her wanting to hold on and wanting to push Honor. Besides, Honor's lazy. I'm scared she'll never leave home. You know, she doesn't even wash out her own underwear? She gets away with murder."

Leslie grunted, shifting from foot to foot. She wanted to hear everything about Honor, but she did not want to be guilty of disloyalty. With Cam she drifted back into the livingroom. Honor was standing tapping her foot to the music in the blue paisley corduroy dress. Paul was wearing a suede suit and he looked hot, red in the face, fiery rather than sweated. He kept touching Honor on her arms and shoulders, her waist, her back. Once as his hand slid out of sight low on her back she pointedly moved away. But not far.

"That's why I'm glad you've been spending time with her. Because she listens to you. It's miraculous!" Cam laughed, throwing back her head so that for a moment in gesture she resembled her sister. "She worships you. All day long it's 'Leslie likes my new sweater. She says it's becoming.' Or 'Don't bother me, I'm reading a book about Emmeline Pankhurst Leslie gave me.' 'I have to have the kitchen. Leslie's coming and I must bake a cake.' "

"That's not for me. Don't believe the propaganda. Your sister's the one with the sweet tooth." And Bernie.

"She's going to ruin her complexion." Absently Cam touched an old scar of acne near her temple. But Honor's skin was flawless. How could Cam help being jealous if only because of their mother's preference? She found Cam's view disquieting. It was like looking at op art, lines that kept changing focus. She tended to think of herself as dancing attendance upon Honor. More than likely Honor was using her as a blanket excuse. Her name was sui generis or gender safer than Bernie's and probably stood for both of them.

"I like her, genuinely," Leslie said brusquely. "She's not quite like anyone else."

Cam gave her an amused sideways glance. "You can say that again. Lord, why couldn't I have a nice giggling gum-chewing teenybopper sister like everybody else? I'd put up with it, I'd be so tolerant! Instead I have a kid sister who offers to write my paper on Ibsen so I won't flunk out, but only if I'll pay her five dollars a page."

"Why does she want the money?"

"Mama keeps her on a short allowance. Presents, yes. Money, no. I'm not nuts about George. Between the two of us, he's such a damn perfectionist. But I do need the money!"

"Why don't you leave home, Cam?"

"Love to. I can't afford it yet. I don't do well enough in school for one of those effing scholarships and I can't pay rent. . . . Actually, I'm paying off a debt." Her gaze fixed on Paul with hostility tightening the mouth. "Once I get that paid off, I'm going to take an apartment with Mona— You know, she played Lady Bracknell."

She wished she could ask Cam if Paul was the father or

if he had done something else. "Is it Paul you owe the money?"

Cam looked startled. "No, Mona. She's my best friend, and she doesn't have it to spare. So I really want to pay her back."

Well, Leslie thought, that answers that. But has Honor never guessed? Well, why would she? I wasn't so smart figuring out other people's problems when I was seventeen. Oddly then she thought of Bernie: that this was the sort of question she could set him. She tucked the matter away to wait until they talked privately the next time.

Because of seeing Honor home from the late party, she was short on sleep when she woke. She worked out for a while and was just about to eat breakfast when she became aware of a woman yelling at her from the street. Only Tasha could make that much noise—she had a carrying voice.

Leslie ran down to let her in. The day was mild, if wet, and Tasha's jacket was unzipped. Leslie felt a surge of warmth at seeing Tasha, her light brown hair in two long braids, her overalls two sizes too large—aimed at concealing her hips and breasts—her big eyes and big nose and big mouth and bushy brows crowding the small triangular face. Tasha was short for Natasha, which Tasha had named herself, after her own grandmother. Her mother had named her Michele. "Who ever heard of Michele as a Jewish name? If we don't come from anywhere, how can we go anywhere? All women, we need to understand history!" Tasha was always vehement, even when she was ordering a corned beef sandwich to eat on the hot line.

"Tasha! It's wonderful to see you!" Leslie tugged her in, almost embraced her, didn't quite. Something held her back.

"So how come you waited so long? Never mind. Listen, I came over this morning because we need help. You got to work the hot line tonight. Half the staff's out with the flu. It's ridiculous. Listen, Leslie, I'll say please if I got to, I'll get down on my knees. We can't train a new person before tonight. I'm on tomorrow, I was on last night. I tried to reach you last night. I called until almost midnight. You sleeping someplace else?"

"I was out." She could hardly say she'd been keeping an eye on a young woman to make sure she didn't get laid. "Working," she lied lamely. "I'm awfully busy with George and the papers and my classes. Haven't even written my thesis proposal yet."

"George should drown in a puddle," Tasha said. "Are you working tonight? There's nobody else. And the weather's mild."

"Tasha, tonight I have karate. I can't work the hot line."

"For once you couldn't skip it? Okay, what time do you get off?"

"I could get off by nine."

"Okay. There's nobody else. Start when you get there."

"Only this once, Tasha. Only tonight. I can't do it anymore. I don't want to!" She felt as if Tasha had left her no choice and she burned with resentment.

"I thought maybe you'd come out and have brunch with me?"

"I can't. I'm busy. I have to work now if I can't work tonight." Of course she could study on the hot line, she knew it. Tasha left, her head lowered. Leslie was immediately sorry she had not gone with her. But to see a friend for the first time in a month, and all she did was draft you; on the other hand, it was her fault she had not seen Tasha.

She had known Tasha was interested in her. It was a matter of tiny hints, little flashes of warmth. About personal things Tasha was shy. But Leslie had still been thinking about Val day and night, sure she would bring her back at Christmas. And Tasha was not pretty. Leslie always seemed to fall for women who were—oh, better looking than herself. She had simply pretended not to see those little gestures of affection, and Tasha had understood. Nothing had been said, and nothing ever would be. They would have gone on being friends if Leslie had not quit the hot line and then withdrawn from Tasha.

Now she was sorry she had turned her away. Maybe Tasha would come by tonight while she was on the hot line. But Sunday night while she sat at the phone nothing happened. For once there were no assaults and Tasha never came by.

Bernie could get away earlier Mondays than she could, so he would already be there when she rode over on the sad broken-springed bus. An expressway view of Detroit: a cement ravine full of cars lined with a fringe of worn wooden houses. Yet when she hopped down, it was all she could do to hold herself to a sedate trot. She wanted to run, to leap in the air.

The sky was pale gray and high. Nothing had color. All was the hue of dirty cement: the air, the streets, the sidewalks, the sky. It had rained and it would rain. Tomorrow it would rain some more. The next day they would have some rain too. All the trash, the dogshit, the beer cans of the winter were exposed by the glacial retreat, and where the sidewalks ended the mud began. Yet, yet it was spring. Dogs ran in a pack across the small spongy waterlogged lawns, and she too wanted to run. At a jog she bounded down Honor's street.

Suddenly she slowed. Stung, smitten, ravished by longing. She stood still under a half-dead blasted sapling, the end of a branch dripping steadily on her head. Her thighs tightened and she sighed; she sighed heavily and aloud. Her hands clasped and unclasped. She could feel the longing through her whole body. Spring, spring, and she wanted a bike.

Sweet Jesus, she hadn't been on a motorcycle since she was sixteen. Yet she could feel the sensations as if it had been the week before. Always her passions came on her and struck her with a thunderbolt: Paul of Tarsus on the highway. She wanted a bike.

It needn't be a big hog, not the Harley Davidsons or the oversize Hondas of her wanton youth. No, a middle-sized sensible tidy bike. As if that quibbling mattered. She could not afford such a creature, not in any sense. It was not a strategy for survival; it was a strategy for getting wiped out fast. She could not pay for it; she could not feed it and keep it. The sight of a woman zooming along astride a cycle brought out the killer lust in drivers of automobiles and they would leap barricades to run her down. Large semis would be driven back and forth across her. She was mad.

She had come to a halt under the sapling that dripped like a leaky faucet right on her bonehead. Oh me, oh me. Did she want to die young and leave a pancake-flat corpse that could be used as a doormat at George's? She did not want to ride that creepy bus and she could not afford any car, whereas she could do without this and that, what? What could she do without? She could feel the wind tearing at her face and the pavement beating up through the machine into her muscles and the clean feeling of speed, of control, of skill rightly used. The brisk no-nonsense pleasure of scooting through stalled traffic.

She made herself walk on toward Honor's broken stair and tilting porch, but each step was a step not relished, disgustingly slow, pokey and uninteresting in the method of ground travel. Perhaps the desire would lessen, perhaps it would release her, this longing that had seized her like a hawk taking a mouse in its talons and borne her aloft.

Honor let her in as if on the run and swept back to the kitchen. The house smelled of baking, the chocolate chip cookies with which Bernie and Honor were already stuffing themselves at the kitchen table. The conversation her coming had not succeeded in interrupting was about Love. Oh shit, she thought.

"I think of love as a fencing match. Taste my absolutely habit-forming cookies! You try yourself against the other being. One word of submission too much, one gesture of stiffness, one hint of mockery, and it's clumsily broken. It's, as Leslie might agree, a martial art."

"You confuse love and power, because you've never experienced either of them." Bernie propped his chin on a hand, leaning his elbow on the table.

"Every child has experienced a lack of power, Bernar'. And when *you* talk about love, I think of Mama. That's not the kind of love I had in mind."

"How can love not be loving? Love is acceptance—the

68

stronger the love, the more absolute the acceptance."
Casually he scooped up another cookie.

Leslie drank her tea, bored on the outskirts of the conversation. She considered Bernie's definition self-serving: that was, indeed, the love he craved from Honor. Adolescents talk about Love. Later you find out there is only loving, only being loved, each individual by individual. She felt weary and dense with experience before them. "Have you ever loved or been loved, I don't mean by the wayside," she asked Bernie.

He frowned. "I loved one person who loved me—not at all by the wayside. And one person loved me I wish I could have loved."

She admired the skillful, apparently casual avoidance of the pronoun. She often had to do the same herself.

"Who was the one you mentioned first? The girl who loved you and you loved her?" Honor reached absently for a cookie.

"Ann-Marie, the sister who was less than a year older than me."

"Oh!" Honor tossed her head scornfully. "We aren't talking about sisters. You're cheating. That's not passionate."

"How do you know?" He raised his head from his cupped chin to give Honor a level stare.

"Oh, if we're talking about incest. But we aren't, are we? Nothing so interesting," Honor said.

"Again, how do you know? How can I talk to you if you think you know what I mean before I speak, and then you don't hear what I'm really saying?"

Leslie simply did not believe him. "We're dealing with a point of fact. Did you sleep with your sister?" She was still bored. The kitchen felt close, she had to blink hard to keep her eyes open. The radiator burbled and clanked; the oven still sent out waves of dry heat, although the last cookies were on a sheet cooling. How could she afford to study karate if she bought even a small used lightweight bike?

"For years. There were four of us and only two bedrooms."

"You're playing word games." Honor tossed her head.

Bernie leaned toward her. "You use your hair like one of those large exotic fantastically silky Persians use their tails. You punctuate with it. A swish of your hair, a lashing to and fro." His voice was silky too.

"Heavens, a tail!" Honor tossed her hair again, as if trying to see herself. "Meow! I had a cat once." She sighed. "A Persian kitten like you mean. But a chow caught it out in front and ripped it open. Mama brought it in. It was dying and it crawled toward me, up to my feet. I wanted to stroke it, to comfort it. It was crying so piteously! All I could feel was disgust. Its fur all matted and oozing blood. I couldn't make myself touch it. . . . I felt so guilty!"

Bernie as usual had committed himself neither one way nor the other but laid down a complicated trail. However, he had changed the subject. Better dead cats than Love. She said, "I don't understand how any woman can be genuinely revolted by blood. Menstruation makes us used to blood. Our own. I'm serious, Honorée. Don't make faces at me. To be repelled by blood is to reject your own body."

Bernie looked at her from under his lashes, his hand stroking the sides of the delicate china cup. "Can't you understand rejecting your own body?"

"No. I am my body."

"You don't believe in a soul?"

"No, and I can't ever forget my body—this society won't let me. Then in affirming it, I affirm being animal, mammal, functioning woman—"

"That's too abstract for me," Honor said scornfully. "Leslie, you're forever making up rules and then following them. Like kids who force themselves to walk only on the cracks or never on the cracks. If something's disgusting, it's disgusting. There's no use arguing."

"The trouble with that is, it presumes everything that goes through your mind is honest." Bernie put his cup down. "Suppose you have a toothache and hate the whole world."

"If I had a toothache, I'd have sense enough to know

70

it." Honor carried off the empty plate to refill from the cookies cooling. Looking after her, Leslie noticed that Honor was wearing pants—gray wool slacks and a dark gold wool sweater. She looked fine in pants, although another pound or two and she would not. She was just within the border where voluptuous passes over to plump.

"But in a relationship, truth doesn't lie on either side," Bernie said carefully. "You can't be honest by yourself."

A tactual quality in the talk puzzled her. Serious, yes, they talked as if talking mattered enormously. In a way it was very young and yet that summed up nothing, because youth culture did not encourage intense, rather intellectual verbalizing. To her they seemed to be talking at times about something undefined, closed and half secret, which they brought out before her in tentative display. "I've just figured something out. What we have in common. We all believe in words. We get satisfaction from discussing. As if it changed anything. We're nuts to put everything into words and feel the pressure of another mind turning over."

Honor smiled almost sadly. "I'm sure if I had to pick only one thing to do through eternity, I'd pick talking. . . . Please don't patronize me by saying I haven't tried everything yet."

Bernie looked at his hands on the table. "Nothing in my life has felt like I'd want it to go on. . . . Maybe a moment or two when I felt accepted. . . . Once or twice at mass when I felt something touch me."

"How about you, Leslie?" Honor asked.

"I can think of times with Valerie. . . . I can think of times too when I've felt an intense serenity. A white space—"

"You sound like the TM folks," Bernie said.

"Not meditation, though obviously there's stillness in being still. But there's also a stillness at the center of motion—"

"We are being mystical today," Honor said crossly. "Just as there's a chocolate chip at the center of this cookie?"

"When I'm doing something well and not thinking

about *how* I'm doing. When I don't cloud it with worries or motives—like last night at the dojo, when everything flowed through me just right—"

"You mean to say when you're leaping around in baggy pajamas hitting each other and making noises like a cat whose tail has just been trodden on, that you feel serene?" Honor turned up her gaze theatrically.

Bernie leaned way back in his chair. "Leslie, you're a jock."

"I guess." She felt suddenly depressed: she saw herself as strange, outcast, twisted, peculiar, one of a kind and that kind not worth making twice. That sense since early adolescence. "Maybe I am crazy." A rare pang of the confessional urge pricked her. "Maybe something's bizarre in me. That wants to be John Wayne. I have this insane desire to have a bike—a motorcycle. I really do."

Honor stared and then went into a fit of giggles. Bernie shrugged. "From a practical point of view, it's hard to live in this city without wheels. And it costs less to operate a bike than my greedy baby buggy."

"Sure," Leslie said glumly.

"But that isn't the point of the passion, is it?"

"It bothers me, it bothers me. I say, Come on, do you want to be a man? But I don't. I don't even like men, present company excluded and maybe my boss George."

"Who's he?" Bernie asked suspiciously, sitting up.

"Cam's boss too. I haven't met him yet." Honor nibbled a cookie. "I'm dreadfully curious. But he's married."

"On the other hand, why buy that? It isn't because it's macho I want a bike, it's because it's fun—a hell of a lot more fun than putting your hair up in rollers and knitting argyle socks. I like to go fast. I like the control, the sense of being on the road, out in the air, in the wind, the weather. It feels alive. That's joy! Not a machine that shuts you off the way a car does, a metal box around you. No, it's a metal horse!"

"A metal horse! My, my. Leslie, you're finally romantic about something. A greasy machine that makes as much noise as it can. It's like developing a passion for a riding mower." Honor grimaced. "I can see myself explaining to Mama, No Mama, I haven't taken up with Hells Angels, really. It's only Leslie, the one-woman motorcycle gang. Resist! Buy an electric can opener instead and sublimate!"

"You haven't seen her room yet," Bernie said. "She'll buy an electric hair shirt first."

"When did you see it, hmmmm?" Honor arched her neck in mock jealousy.

"Why should everything beautiful be defined as masculine? How come freedom and skill should only belong to men?"

"How can you call a smelly noisy puttering motorcycle beautiful? I think that's perverse." Honor rose. "I must put on my supper. I'm so stuffed with cookies I don't want it, but if I don't eat, Mama will be convinced I'm perishing and frail, her consumptive darling."

"I can see it as beautiful inside that Kenneth Anger leather S-M death's-head cult," Bernie said. "But where do you fit in?"

"Look, if I was nuts about horses, you wouldn't think I was craving to join the cavalry and shoot Indians, so why assume I can't honestly want to be on top of a bike? It feels good, damn it. Sometimes I feel like I'm shriveling up in school. The rest of me. What isn't required by classes and seminars and George."

"What does George require?" Bernie asked. He had seized on that name. He broke out his hero sandwich as Honor ate spaghetti warmed over and Leslie brought out her container of yogurt.

"Only complete fidelity." She laughed. "Only my life."

"Leslie, Cam is going out with a creep who also works for mysterious George. Mark, I think he's called."

"Hennessy. He's a disaster."

Then Bernie had to know just who Mark Hennessy was and why she called him a disaster. He finished his hero and lit his after-supper joint. Things seemed to become quickly ritualized among the three of them, and it was already understood that Bernie would smoke dope all the time they were together but that Leslie would join him

73

only right after they ate and sometimes just before they left, on the nights she stayed as late as Bernie did.

"My birthday is coming," Honor said as she stacked her dishes in the sink.

"Like the millennium." Bernie stretched out his long legs, passing the joint to Leslie.

"A lot sooner. April fifth. I want each of you to buy me earrings for pierced ears."

Bernie sat up groaning. "That again. Your mother will make holes in me. Don't you think, Leslie, her desire to be immolated is a little suspicious?"

"You don't also want your feet bound and your ribs broken for an hourglass figure?"

Honor stood. "Do not, do not, do not ever patronize me!"

"But Honorée," Bernie groaned, "it is murky."

"It's not! I want to wear the garnet earrings that belonged to my father's mother. If you're truly my friends, you'll support me."

"Your mother is going to murder us," Bernie grumbled.

"It's my birthday. And I choose to celebrate it by wearing my heirloom earrings. I'll take care of her. That's what I want for my birthday and nothing else. From you, that is. I'm asking her for a watch."

"You want us to go with you to have your ears pierced," Leslie said, finally understanding.

"Right. A simple request. Mama says it's unsanitary. She says only peasants and hippies have pierced ears. I have pointed out that my grandmother, who was beautiful according to every photograph I've seen and who was married three times and buried all three husbands, ran a dairy farm with pierced ears. I want her earrings as much as you want your motorcycle. But I have them. It's more frustrating that way, to have them and not be able to wear them. . . . And if having holes punched through my ears appears to you to resemble the sex act, I'd say that's your problem." She looked from one to the other while an upturn appeared at the corner of her mouth. Then with exaggerated dignity she sat. Only to jump up again when she saw the clock.

"Mama'll be here any moment. Out with you. Empty that ashtray. Bernie, take it out back to empty. Grab the flashlight. Leslie, clear the table. I'll wash up." She flung open both kitchen windows so the cool wet air flowed in. Quickly, madly she sprayed with an air deodorizer and washed the few dishes they had dirtied and put them away.

When Bernie returned with the ashtray she washed it too and wiped the table frantically. Then she stood flapping a dish towel as if to change every breath of air in the small kitchen.

"Does she go through this every time?"

Bernie nodded. "We're the secret callers. The worm in the heart of the quiet afternoon."

"If you'd rather wait for Mama and chat with her, that'd be lovely," Honor said coldly. "Do have a couple of seats. You can offer her a toke and discuss my ear-lobes."

six

Perhaps other people, strangers, were still unreal to Honor. Perhaps Leslie and Bernie were both more riddled with outcast resentments and a sense of being forced into role playing than she had realized. But whenever the three of them left the shelter of Honor's untidy shabby kitchen, in fact they acted on stage. They fell into games. They assumed parts. Honor and Bernie did so at once, without speaking a word of conspiracy or even of consultation. She was sucked in reluctantly but could not resist, could not cast herself as a double outsider beyond their game too. Thus when Honor had to be fortified with a hot fudge sundae to face her immolation, in the ice cream parlor Bernie became Willie the Idiot Boy and they were his keepers.

When they entered the jewelry shop in the mall— selected after they had squandered half the time they had on previous jewelry shops Honor pronounced too "sor'id" for her to endure—in the big shopping plaza with its glassed-in malls and piped music, occasional pieces of sculpture big and metallic, shrubbery in pots, they had not allotted parts. But by the time they were in the shop five minutes the roles emerged. If this game had a name it would be Governess, because Bernie and Honor became at once snotty and confined. Obviously they were in tow to her. Yes, her purse, her authority ruled them. They called her Madame.

She was Madame: herself, not herself. She was cold and rational and judgmental. She sneered at their enthusiasms. When they asked, she refused or condescended. The names too magically appeared. Honor was Violet, Bernie was Tate. Part of the insulation the games conferred was that it didn't matter if anyone else believed them; they were more play than disguise.

Honor was covering nervousness with extreme hauteur mixed with bursts of giddy flirtatiousness toward the stout glib young man who was selling earrings. The piercing came free with the jewelry. Honor had gone through half the earrings in the place before settling on little gold-filled studs with filigree balls, one of the cheaper pairs they had looked at, of course. Madame's role was to say no to most of them, which Honor hadn't the money for anyhow: arbitrary, scornful, rotund noes.

"Those aren't bad. They'll do. Hurry, please. I must have you back by six." That was true, because Honor's mother always called her on her supper break. If Mama did get a moment to call earlier, Honor could claim to have run an errand. "Yes, Mama, I just stepped out momentarily. I was only outside for two minutes peeing in the yard." Honor imitated herself making excuses to her mother.

Bernie nodded approval. She had seen him pocket one of the pairs, flattened irregular silver loops that looked hammered. Although she was sure the clerk had not noticed, it sharpened her haste. But Honor had not seen and would not be hurried. She very clearly did not want the clerk to touch her, and she was fighting a delaying action by pretending to contemplate pendants.

At any moment the clerk might notice the pair had vanished. She would have liked to boost a pair too, because she did not want to pay for earrings. She did not approve of jewelry, which seemed all built on slave bracelets and wedding rings, signs of bondage, decorative brands of ownership. Yet she herself had pierced ears and wore that remaining turquoise stud. Did Valerie still wear its mate? Lena would make fun of such a lopsided arrangement. Indeed she could remember Lena's voice, a

77

voice with a dry sexual authority. "Did you know, my dear, that men started that fad of one earring? S-M, I assure you. For indication, you see: sadists on the right and masochists on the left. Yes, you're on the masochistic side today, Valerie. I must say, I don't know that it pays to advertise." That was Lena at a long mahogany table with a centerpiece of those glass flowers she collected, as they ate a cold pale green avocado blender soup. . . .

Honor's fingers were digging into her arm; her gold-flecked light brown eyes were pleading. " . . . right now!"

So they all went to the back of the shop, where Honor sat on a folding chair that looked as if it belonged at a bridge table. Then the clerk daubed her ears with alcohol and neatly with a shiny punch perforated first the left and then the right lobe, all the while keeping up a banter as she saw him wink at Bernie, lounging against the counter looking ostentatiously bored but with his gaze always on Honor. From time to time the clerk managed to brush against Honor's stiffened body as if that too were part of a game, his game, the contact casually forced that could not be objected to. "Remember to drop the earrings in alcohol at night for the first month to sterilize them, honey. Now press this cotton ball, that's a good girl, just press it hard till I tell you to let go. That's right, honey, just that way, you're a fast learner. . . ."

As they straggled out, Leslie was musing why the tension had not annoyed her, the fear of Bernie being caught. It was almost pleasant, the tension, and it reminded her of something half familiar. Almost sexual. Honor let out her breath in a harsh snort. "That's over!" She was glaring. For a moment Leslie thought Honor was angry because of Bernie's shoplifting. "Ugh! It did hurt. But not even much. And it feel so . . . messy." She discarded the wads of cotton batting into a wastebasket and washed her hands together in recoil. "I suppose it'll be worth it to put on Grandmother's earrings. But the thought I allowed that oaf to touch me, to rub against me, to call me honey, makes me feel like spending a week in the bathtub. The two of you were no help at all!"

Honor suffered herself to be led to Bernie's old Mustang, of a metallic faded purple color. It seemed put together of sardine tins and clattered and clanged on the smallest bumps, and Leslie fancied she smelled fish in the air. It had a moldering salty odor. Bernie's theory was that some large animal had died there in the midst of its winter hibernation on the used car lot and had not been removed until spring. What was left of the upholstery was spotted and stained, and some of the large discolorations in the back seat did suggest blood. It slumped toward the rear wheels as if sitting a little on its heels. It squealed turning corners at the sedatest pace, it squealed backing up, it laid down a palpable fog of exhaust like a black plumy tail, and it was a drunkard.

"But it's like riding in your great grandfather. The miracle is that it moves." They were always in danger of running out of gas because Bernie refused to put more than two dollars' worth in at a time, claiming the car might break down any minute.

Normally Honor sat in the front as her due, leaving the back seat to Leslie, but now she crawled back after Leslie and curled up, her head hanging. "I feel like the chauffeur," Bernie complained. "Do I smell bad?"

"Shush," Leslie said, and put her arm tentatively around Honor. Honor did want comforting and cuddled nearer, letting her head fall against Leslie's shoulder. "Someday I'll do something Mama forbids and it'll be exciting and glorious instead of crummy. Someday!"

"Does it hurt?" Gently she stroked Honor's hair.

"A little. I just feel icky." Honor's head was pleasantly heavy on Leslie's shoulder. The girl pressed against her like a tired child, looking as if she could not quite decide if she wanted to cry.

Sue had taken the kids to visit her parents in Houston, leaving George a temporary bachelor. Not that he would act the way she had observed other married faculty behaving, like horny little boys let out to play. Because of George's famous arrangement, he could always play. Instead they worked early and they worked late. Normally, George was controlled by a desire to spend time with his children. Whatever tenderness lurked in George poured out over his son, Davey, and his daughter, Louise, and his own widower father who lived upstate. Leslie thought of it as vertical tenderness: no competition, no envy. At night George rushed home to his children; when they were out of town nothing restrained his zest for work.

He sent her out for Chinese food in cartons. They did not let up until ten, when he drove her home. He parked, so she invited him up. She was not surprised, because although he hadn't visited her since they'd moved to Detroit, he had used to have a cup of coffee with Val and her in Grand Rapids. Occasionally Val would cook a supper, not for him and Sue but for him and his current youthful girlfriend. She imagined he was curious about where she was living and whether she was living with anyone yet.

Chuckling, he looked around. "Is the university paying you too little?"

"Sure. But there's an aesthetic of emptiness."

"Yes, but don't you think that blanket's a little gaudy?" Easily George sat on the floor, arranging his long legs. "That was mediocre Chinese. We'll have to locate a decent take-out place for worknights. Next time try one of those Black chicken-and-ribs joints." George was a gourmet. He counted every bad meal a missed opportunity.

"There's a Syrian place we could try if I borrow your car."

"Just don't get it in an accident. I'm supposed to fly down Thursday and come back with them Sunday," George said plaintively. "What a ridiculous potlatch of money. I don't want to hear Sue's mother carry on about how she'd torture the kids, which she calls raising them. Arguing politics with her old man. He tries in his crude way to patronize me as an ivory tower academic as opposed to his two-fisted businessman. Whereas the only reason he never succeeded in losing Sue's nest egg is because her grandfather was smart enough to tie it up in trusts that petty crook can't undo. He's a barbaric old hard-drinking failure. Why should I spend half a grand to

80

fly there for two days of watching him drink himself stupid and trying to abuse Sue?"

"You're well on the way to persuading yourself not to go."

"The bitch is I can't figure out if Sue will be mad if I don't show. That is, how mad?"

"George, whatever I guess is likely wrong."

"You think I'll blame you for bad advice?"

"Sure."

"But think how much more annoyed I'll be if you advise me to do my duty and fly down, when I'm itching to be told not to."

"What you need is a good excuse."

"I'll have to come clean with Sue. I can't fool her."

They were supposed to be truthful, which amounted as near as she could see to George advising Sue of his infidelities. Sue had none. She was busy with the kids and the house, and she never met men who weren't George's colleagues or his students, none of whom were apt to take the risk of getting involved with her. Their arrangement seemed to Leslie to come down to a rationalization of the fact that George had more freedom, more power, more choice than Sue did. But she kept her mouth shut.

"She'll probably think it's some girl. I'm getting too old for all that anyhow." George patted his belly, not believing it for an instant.

"No doubt you've been busy getting settled."

"The only stunning women around are Blacks, and that's just too complicated. This town is so charged, we couldn't even go to a bar together."

"You could spend a day doing something she asked you to fix in the house. That'd cost you a day, but three less than flying down."

He chewed that over, rubbing his mustache. "I could arrange it so that . . . Hmmmm. If I actually got a plumber to fix the hot water system . . . I could send you or Cam out there to wait. . . . We'll call plumbers tomorrow morning." He looked around her room as he talked as if taking an inventory.

Finally she teased him. "My life is not only an open book, but practically an empty box."

He tapped his mustache, smiling with his best father-confessor air. "Surely you don't need to be lonely here. There must be lots of places you can meet women. There seem to be plenty of women's activities on campus."

"Sure. I can go volunteer for the rape hot line. . . . I don't especially want to meet anyone. Not yet."

"Have you heard from Valerie?"

"Not since I saw her at Christmas. She never writes. I know she moved because the phone's disconnected."

"Is she living with somebody else?"

As if she had been caught unbraced by a blow. "I suppose. I guess I'll find out when I go see her. Maybe I'll do that spring vacation." She sounded ridiculously vacillating, but it hurt so much to talk about.

"I don't mean to pry." But he did. He was always curious. She felt George was genuinely sorry she did not have something going here, in part because he wanted things to go well for her as he wanted what was under the hood of his car to work well. She hoped she wouldn't have to spend Friday sitting in his house waiting for the plumber.

"I'd better be going." George meant it, for he got up dusting his pants. She saw him to the door and down the straight steep flight. The street door clicked shut behind him. Then she locked her door and stood in the center of the room. She wished he had not mentioned Valerie. She took off her boots, stood with her hands laced on the top of her head, and waited to see what she felt like doing with the short end of her evening.

A fumbling at the window. She froze. Wind? No. She found herself crouching, then, thinking better of it, she reached into the rack over the hotplate and pulled out the stoutest knife. She walked toward the window. She was frightened, her body sang with tension and she felt over-wound as if an arm might suddenly fly off. Lightly she crossed the room on the balls of her feet, almost bouncily, and then, hefting the knife, drew back the blind. A man crouched there pawing at the window. "Hail!" she screamed and feinted with the knife, the glass between them.

"Hi yourself, Les. Let me in." Bernie's silky voice came unmistakably through the window.

As the adrenaline receded, she felt weak. "Bernie? What the hell are you doing on my fire escape?"

"Let me in. It's cold."

She unlocked the catches. He was dressed just as he had been earlier in the day, with his old leather jacket on and a plaid cashmere muffler around his neck. As he climbed in she shook him roughly by the shoulder, then slammed the window and locked it again. "I do have a door."

"Yes, but no buzzer. Am I supposed to stand in the street bawling *Les-Lee, Les-lee,* like an eight-year-old? Leslie, come out and play-ay! It's cold and crappy standing on your street. I keep expecting to get mugged, and rough trade keeps trying to pick me up. I have as much trouble standing on a street corner as you would, my dear, and you shouldn't forget it."

"The hell you do. And you don't fear rape. And you don't have to come crawling up my fire escape like a cat burglar."

"But I am a cat burglar."

"I think not," she said coldly. "Maybe a shoplifter. Well, take off your jacket and enjoy my amply furnished, sensuously outfitted digs. Everyone complains but everyone comes visiting. . . . How long were you out there?"

"Oh, since ten-thirty. Thursdays through Sundays I work as a waiter at a restaurant near here—À Votre Plaisir. Supposed to be French. The menu's sort of French. A couple of Cubans own it and everybody in the kitchen is Puerto Rican."

"Since before I got here with George?"

"Just a couple of minutes before."

"Why didn't you rap on the window sooner? Were you listening?"

"Of course." He sat on her mattress. "I was so intrigued to see you arrive with a man, how could I possibly butt in? I was ravished by curiosity."

"You and George. You have a lot in common. You're both uncommonly nosy."

"But I'm smarter than he is, because I know about him and he doesn't know about me. . . . He's younger than I expected and much better looking, with that wicked little mustache. Is he after you?"

"My god no. George knows I'm gay. And he's compartmentalized. He'd never lay a hand on Cam either, because she's his secretary."

"Are you so sure? He has a way of looking at you."

"He looks at everybody that way, it's habit," she said shortly. "Naturally I'm so devastatingly attractive no one can entirely resist me, but George manages."

"When did you tell him you're gay?"

"Shortly after I became his assistant. I figured he'd find out anyhow. . . . He's good about it."

"I don't believe it. I don't believe in liberalism."

"Well, it's points in a way. Better than having a Black secretary even. Sue is never jealous of me. In some funny way he does get on better with women. Man are competition. I'm his loyal dependent, and as he says, I won't get pregnant or married in whatever order."

He lay back thinking. Then he sat up and leaned forward. "So you saw my light fingers at work in the jewelry store. What did you see?"

"I saw you take the earrings."

"Which?"

"I did see you, Bernie. I think they were hoops."

He thrust his hand into his jacket and brought out the hammered silver hoops on his palm. "These? Come and look."

Gingerly she tucked herself onto the far end of her mattress. "They're pretty. For Honor's birthday?"

"The same. How about these?" Again he reached into his jacket and this time he brought out crescent moons in filigree. "You can give her either pair. I know you don't have much cash."

"That wouldn't be right."

"Dog-do. What am I supposed to do with them? Go

back and get my ears pierced? I have enough troubles. Come on, tell me which you want to give her."

"Either pair. See, I didn't take much persuading. I'm saving what bread I can to go to Grand Rapids over spring vacation."

"You get to give her the hoops, since you caught me in the act. Frankly, I'm surprised. I thought my hand was quicker than anyone's eye. Now guess what?" Again he stuck his hand inside and this time he brought out two stud earrings. "Last act. For Madame."

She kept her hands in her lap. "No."

"I know you like this kind, because I've seen you wear one. Look, these are little scarabs. It isn't turquoise like yours. It's some Mediterranean blue stone, I don't know what they call it. Scarabs are fancy beetles." He dropped the tiny studs on her thigh and they rolled off. She would not pick them up.

"No, really. I don't . . . care for presents."

"Then take them as mortification for your spirit. Or your flesh. You like to be ascetic and mortified."

"No. I like to be serene. That's different."

"Letting me bribe you into liking me better would ruffle your serenity?"

"I don't like being given things."

"I don't believe you. At least look at them. They won't explode."

She dug them from under her thigh and dropped them on the blanket between them, rolling them out like tiny blue dice. "It was nice of you to think of it."

"We both think it was sly. But not sly enough. You don't want to be treated like Honor."

"You'd think that the fewer things I have the simpler it would be. But it's like adding objects to this room. Everything takes on significance. If you came tonight and there was suddenly an armchair, you'd stare at it and ask about it—"

"I'd for sure sit in it. Although I don't mind sitting on your bed, it makes you so nicely nervous."

She felt her cheeks heat. She wanted to go sit against the wall away from him, but that would be obviously a retreat. He was right, it was absurd that she should object to his occupying the mattress when she provided no other place to sit. It was also absurd that she should allow him to embarrass her; he was no prick-waving straight shooter like Hennessy about to harass her.

"You have such a ravishing blush. You light up like a red neon sign. You also have such a fetching air of intact chastity—you really act much more virginal than our certified Honor—that I think you underestimate the ordinary male's reaction. Why are you sure George isn't interested? I had the opposite impression."

"Stop it, Bernie! Don't tease me that particular way. I work with him. Make me paranoid and I won't be able to. George's sex life is very regulated and gratifying: he has babies with his wife and he has a string of young girlfriends his wife knows about."

"I don't think you like George after all."

"Why would I possibly like the sex life of any straight male? It's so easy for him, it's as if he has a license to hunt his pleasure and come home to Mommy. . . . But he's bright, he's effective politically in the department, he looks out for me. In fact I admire him, workwise."

"Un sot trouve toujours un plus sot qui l'admire. That's Boileau. To the effect that the biggest fool can always find a woman to look up to him."

"I understand French and it didn't say anything about women."

"Maybe I'm just pursuing my favorite pastime, feeling sorry for myself. Maybe I'm jealous."

She laughed sharply. "So hire me as your research assistant and give me my Ph.D."

"Even little brothers get jealous. My ego blisters. I don't like the way he makes himself at home. You won't even take my little bugs for your ears, which I stole at risk of jail, literally risking my precious ass to win your heart and mind. Your heart and mind being all of you I can reasonably use, but c'est la guerre. . . . The afternoon bummed me out. I'm sure Honor will blame us because she didn't enjoy it—which I told her beforehand, and that's worse and makes me more in the wrong. Now

86

she'll get an infection, watch, and it'll be as if we'd given her the clap."

"You're more comfortable with sexual analogies than I am. And they annoy Honor."

"Annoy and titillate—my function in life. I'm feeling blatantly sorry for myself tonight."

"Not just because of this afternoon?"

"No, my smart friend. See, when you pay attention to me, you become smart. You're only stupid when you squander first class attention on academic hit men."

"Or an expert interpretation of number seven position of not answering a question."

"Yes. 'Why I Am Depressed,' by Bernard Guizot. Okay, as I was being my simpering waiterly best tonight in À Votre Plaisir, in comes my former lover Burt, not alone. He has another young man, not so good-looking as myself, I might add, but then I'm not being wined and dined. I'm serving them. Humiliating, no? A turn or two of the screw. . . . Now you might expect I'd not be all that unhappy to see Burt with somebody else, since I left him and since it was Burt who loved and I who was loved—"

"He's the *person* you mentioned so delicately by that tong-shaped word, who loved you and you wished you'd loved."

"That doesn't mean I wasn't fond of him and capable of being jealous. I'm naturally jealous, I'm always being jealous of someone or something. It does not add to my . . . serenity. It's a vicious habit, like eating small children."

Her vivid brooding on Lena and Val. "We were in the restaurant," she prompted him.

"Where I was serving overdone duck with a too sweet sauce made from frozen orange juice. The food is lousy there, by the way. . . . I was hurt he'd come in. And the injustice, bringing that smirking young thing."

"Why did you leave him?" She could not imagine leaving anyone who loved her if she was going to go on in the same place. It seemed spoiled arrogance to relinquish anyone who would actually claim to love you. How would you know you would ever again encounter someone crazy enough to approach, to give, to accept?

"We were fighting. Burt's more together than I am. I say that admiringly. He's involved in the whole gay political scene, the committees to protest this firing or that lack of hiring, to petition the city council, to picket a bar or a movie." Bernie lay back on one elbow, his eyes fixed on her, not unseeing as he got into the flow of his story but carefully watching. "He can't be shut up in the usual way of being fired from schoolteaching or advertising, because he inherited real estate. Up around Petoskey they're building a resort complex, a ski run on an artificial mountain put up out of industrial garbage. . . . Burt's solidly built, athletic. He plays tennis and squash, he skis, he's a good swimmer. He hangs around bars only to socialize, to keep his eye on the community, or when he's between what he'd consider real things. He's thirty-four. He makes enough to live what he calls comfortable—which seemed to me like baronial splendor. Burt really is good. He doesn't go around picking bums out of the gutter and handing them five-dollar bills. But he has clear principles, clear politics, and he lives that way. He's responsible for getting me into college. He paid for my first year. It was his idea."

"I still don't understand why you left him. The more you say, the less it makes sense."

"Maybe it doesn't make sense to me." He frowned, the corners of his long mouth turning under. Unconsciously he picked up the earrings and started to play with them, then dropped them when he grew aware. "He put pressure on me."

"To love him back?"

"I was fond of him. But you can't make yourself be passionately attracted to somebody just because you ought to be. . . . In fact that makes it worse, that you ought to be. It's like eating wheat germ. I know it's good for me, but I can't make myself lust after wheat germ the way I do for a double chocolate cake with chocolate frosting. . . . But he put political pressure on me. He wanted me to be proud of being gay."

"He was right," Leslie said. "Do you want a drink?"

"Enormously. I thought you'd never ask."

"I'm not sure I have anything, which is why I didn't. I usually get the leavings from George's Thursday night, but there wasn't one this week." She poked in the small refrigerator. "I don't. We'll drink the Benedictine."

"Pour me some. Then you'll have to accept the earrings, it's only fair."

"We might as well kill the bottle. I think your friend Burt was right. All those sad old types who thought they were sick or evil, isn't it pathetic? How can you let this society make you feel ashamed that you don't get your pleasure from raping women in hallways or buying them on streetcorners or marrying one and keeping her in a box and going pump, pump, pump on top of her the correct two point four times a week?"

"The point four must be premature ejaculation." He laughed. "You make it sound wondrously appealing. Have you ever made love with a man?"

"I don't know that I'd call it love. I made a baby with one once."

"Really? Did you have a child?"

"I lost it. Before I realized I was pregnant. I was fifteen and on the pill and I just went on taking it, not up on the situation. It was a bloody mess." She was standing in the girls' lavatory at school with blood running down her legs, running down as if from the faucet left wide open, and she was in terror and mortified at the same time because she was getting blood on the floor and she kept mopping at herself with little pieces of toilet paper that would only come out one at a time, little harsh sandpapery squares in the room that always smelled of tobacco and dope from the girls coming in to smoke there. "But as a matter of record, I've slept with two men. Not since I was sixteen and knew myself have I known a man," she finished with a self-mocking smile. "How many men have you slept with?"

"You're kidding. How the hell would I know? I suppose several hundred. I'd have to sit down and do an annual average."

"One, two, three, many? As a quantitative historian, I'd have to disallow your evidence. If you can't count, you don't count."

"Do you count hiccups? When I was with Burt, only him."

"You were faithful!"

"Don't bitch. It's not your style, not becoming. You have to look with big serious brown eyes and count my sins."

"Which even you can't count. You were hustling?"

He nodded. "I didn't have any other useful skill. I was kicked out of high school, and I didn't have the class to get off the streets into a regular sugar daddy. I was a mean young punk. But not half as mean as what was about to happen to me."

"Which you'll drop hints about forever to Honor, but make damned sure you never describe."

"I'll describe it to you, my bus station johns, my chicken hawks. Tell me what you want to know in how much detail."

She grimaced. "Why am I so lucky?"

"Aren't you going to ask me how many women I've been with, for your quantitative history?"

"I didn't think you had. I suppose I'd rather you haven't."

"I'm not sure whether I actually have or not." He laughed at himself, shortly. "I wasn't lying about Ann-Marie. We did sleep in the same room and we were very, very close. We were born in the same year. She was only eleven months older. My mother thought she couldn't get pregnant again when she was nursing. We were almost twins. Ann-Marie was another me. She was as big as me, as tall, as tough, as fast. She could run, she could fight, she could throw rocks and snowballs straight as any boy. If I got in a fight, she'd pitch in. She was skinny and hard as wood."

"When we were eleven they, the old folks, decided we couldn't share a room. I was given Mike to share my room with, a squalling baby, while Ann-Marie was stuck in with the little girls. We were pissed. We knew it had

90

something to do with sex. Also, in confession the priest was starting to ask questions about sex. He was Irish, we didn't trust him. It made us more curious. I don't know exactly what we did. I know we fooled around a lot, but how can I tell whether we committed literal incest or stopped short. . . . It sounds funny, but I'd give a lot to know. I have the feeling I could remember if I let myself. . . . Because after Ann-Marie was killed—"

"Killed? How?"

"We used to hang on with our sleds to the back of cars to get a free ride. She was just thirteen and I wasn't thirteen yet. She was hanging on a laundry truck and she went under the wheels. Her head cracked . . . like an egg. A bloody egg."

"You were there?"

He nodded. "I was sick the rest of the winter. I was sure what we'd done killed her. That the Church was right and she'd died of our sins and gone to hell."

Her palms sweated around the earrings she found herself clutching. She had to say something. She couldn't just sit there. But she could not think of anything to say that was not ridiculous in the face of his story.

"It happened so fast that I kept screaming at her. Then I started punching the driver. He was cursing. He hit me back and knocked me down. I didn't feel a thing. I think for a year it was like I was asleep. I wouldn't talk about her. I wouldn't even go to the cemetery with my folks. I've never seen her grave."

Her eyes burned and two fat drops ran down her face. Embarrassed, she scrubbed her cheek with the back of her knuckles.

"But of course it's useful too, isn't it, to have such a neat childhood trauma to blame everything on. Sometimes I don't know how I'd get through life without good old Ann-Marie's death to haul out as a convenient excuse for why I'm such a pervert-monster-callous-cold bloodedthieving whatever it is I've done lately."

"Bernie, you're never satisfied. You want me to pity you. When I do, you mock both of us."

"All true and many more." He settled back with her

91

pillow between his head and the wall. "To finish up my fabulous sexual history, I've been to bed with two women since and not been able. Including the woman I traveled all over Europe with for half a summer. Except once when we were phenomenally stoned on very good hash and opium at once in Amsterdam when something happened. It's so unreal—I remember caves and waterfalls and rainbows more than anything concrete—but she was sure I'd balled her not once but half the night. I'll never know. I never had trouble performing with men. Except once when some john held a knife to me. And once or twice when Burt was really putting the pressure on. But ninety-nine times out of ninety-nine point four—that's where the point four belongs—I'm weatherproof."

"It's exotic. I've always wondered why men make such a fuss. Afer all, if you're impotent with a woman, you could please her anyhow and maybe better."

"But it's not under voluntary control. That's the rub."

"Your . . . prick may not be. But your hands are. Your mouth is. Your elbows and your feet for that matter. You couldn't come, but you could give pleasure perfectly well."

"It's strange to think that way. Of course, rationally you're right—"

"In what way am I wrong? Only in some weird male point-counting."

"No." He shook his head. "Not only. Because it's weird for one to give pleasure and one to get it. A lot of gay sex has been set up that way. One of the things that's good is the growing tendency for things to be more mutual."

"I've never known women who didn't make love . . . mutually."

"I've known many men who don't."

Leslie sighed. "Sometimes I think we'd all be better with more jogging and less sex."

"Do you find all the working out you do reduces your desire for sex?" Bernie leaned on one elbow.

"We've finished the Benedictine. Maybe I'll make up some frozen juice. I'm feeling dry."

"You didn't answer my question."

She stood at the sink running the water. "I thought it was impertinent. But I almost never experience general sexual desire."

"Truly? I sometimes think that's all I ever do experience."

She turned with the pitcher, smiling. "I guess we do belong to different sexes."

"Don't you ever feel just plain horny?"

"Even that term is male. A horn."

"Don't you have anything like wet dreams? Dreams about sex with strangers, people you wouldn't touch awake?"

"Bernie, we've been talking about sex for *two hours*."

"Ann-Marie isn't exactly sex. But in ten years we'll talk this way about money, right? But we won't trust each other enough to do it frankly."

"How much do we trust each other now?" She brought the juice. They could use the same glasses.

"Les, take the earrings. I won't ask you again. If you say no, I'll throw them down the toilet."

She frowned. "All right, I'll take them. I'll keep them for a while. If I feel good about it, I'll wear them. But you mustn't badger me."

Bernie sank back, his head on her pillow, and shut his eyes. "I badger not. Who, me? Lord, I'm tired."

She finished her glass and poured more grapefruit juice. "Don't fall asleep. It's very late. It's after one."

He did not open his eyes. "I'm exhausted."

"Then you'd better go now."

He lay still and answered after minutes in a voice thick with sleep, "Oh, let me stay. I'm half dead."

She shook him. "Bernie, no. Get up and go home."

He made himself limp as a rag doll. "Cruel Leslie. Why? So dark, so late, so cold, so far to go. Blood on the sidewalk."

"Blood on the bed if you don't move." She hauled him up and propped him against the wall. "Where are your shoes?"

"Let me stay. Why not? I don't mean anything by it

but the coziness and I'm tired. I not only wouldn't try anything, but I can't."

"It amuses you to push on my limits. Well, you hit a wall. Not pushable."

"You're more pushable than you think." He put on the shoes she had been trying to cram on his feet. "But I go. To my death by mugging."

"Good night, Bernie." She took hold of him and hauled him up just as he was starting to slide toward the mattress again. They were both laughing silently. "No, out the door this time!"

"You're so conventional. Let George come in by the door. I like the other route." He let himself be shoved out.

When she went to bed, of course the earrings were there, hard little blue eyes she rolled in her palm. And beside them, the earrings for Honor. She did not want to give Honor jewelry, but she felt obliged to. What she imagined giving Honor was a beautiful antique dagger in a silver sheath to wear at her waist. Tasha had told her about a culture in the Caucasus where women had carried such knives until recently and worn the Amazon cap. But she had no money for antique daggers and Honor could scarcely wear one to school or on the streets of Detroit, no matter how practical that might in truth be.

She tossed both pairs of earrings in her drawer among her woolly socks. A book about freedom? A compass? A rucksack? *Ideas of the Women's Suffrage Movement?* Martha Shelley's poems or Judy Grahn's? For Mama to read. Well, why not? Because she would be thrown out of the house. Undressing in under a minute, she crawled into bed with her head simmering.

Why can't I open her life up a bit? If I can't make love to her, I can help make her into someone worth loving. But the glib recipe bored her. Honor would be eighteen in a couple of days, and eighteen was not a child. At eighteen she had been going to college, supporting herself, having her first real affair with a woman, Sandra, for whom the relationship was equally new and experimental. Sandra and she had been intense, explosive and quickly burnt out, but quite real. The affair had changed her. It had transformed her from a girl who suspected she was perverted, that she had nameless or too easily named dykey longings, who fell shamefully and silently in love with unattainable women who belonged to men, to a woman who could and did love another woman and who would love others. It was a sunny transfiguration, a beautiful simplification. She had been only eighteen. Eighteen was no longer a child. Bernie was not a rival, for as he said he couldn't make love to Honor.

Lying on her mattress in the dark, she could feel the weight of Honor's head on her shoulder and she could feel the caress of silky hair on her cheek, could feel then Honor leaning against her to be comforted. Tenderness held back at the time flooded her now till she began to sense that hot tension gathering low in her abdomen. For the first time she wanted Honor. Her fingers caressed the silky hair, the head, the nape, the face, the arm as they had in the car, but then she let her palm slide down Honor's back, then she was kissing her mouth. Her tongue pushed against her own teeth and a vein throbbed in her labia. Unlike Valerie or Sandra, Honor was bigger than she was. The awkward car with Bernie in the front seat dissolved around them and she was holding Honor standing body to body, their arms taut around each other, their breasts exquisitely swaying together, belly to belly softly and the pressure of mons against mons. The vein throbbed like a swollen heart.

She opened her eyes to stare at the ceiling, deciding not to make herself come. Another twenty-four hours, including the presentation of her paper on railroads to her seminar (only one other woman in it), and it would be Saturday, Honor's birthday. Honor was summoning them into the problematic presence of her mother to celebrate it. Leslie was nervous but determined. How could she ever pass for that fabulous creature of Mama's imaginings, a proper ordinary young woman friend?

seven

Mrs. Rogers was a big woman, as tall as Honor and Cam and stout rather than fat. Stocky, big bosomed, and wide hipped, she had the armored care that a woman who goes out to work maintains over the equally overweight woman who stays home. Her own mother had never been able to maintain that surface; always something straggled, as with Cam. Mrs. Rogers' hair was dyed blond, kept short and curly in a simple hairdo probably reinforced with a permanent. Her glasses had light blue rims. Her eyes behind them, magnified, were light too. Leslie could not tell if they were pale brown like Honor's or light blue like Cam's. Finally she saw that Mama's eyes were blue. Her make-up was pink as was the dress, a little tight, a little worn, with an odd-looking flounce at the waist as if she, the clever seamstress, had made it over for some ulterior motive: to disguise weight, to cover a stain. On the whole Cam looked more like her mother than Honor did, but her mother did not seem to favor her for that.

But Honor did not resemble her father either. He was of a piece: gray sweater, gray pants, gray hair, gray skin. He did not look well. He was skinny and always coughing or smoking or both. His cough was incessant but quiet, smothered, and no one but she seemed to notice it. Even with a pronounced stoop to his shoulders he stood as tall as Bernie, but he did not seem tall, because he took up so little space and did it unobtrusively. He emitted a steady litter of ashes—he never seemed to look for an ashtray until he was ready to stub out a butt, and once she saw him squash one underfoot in the kitchen as if he were on the street—and parts of the daily paper, clippings he tore out and dropped on the arms of chairs, tools he carried around and forgot on the telephone table or the back of the toilet, half-used white handkerchiefs and books of matches with their covers ripped off, leaving the matches exposed like fangs. Mostly he ignored the rest of them, including Honor and certainly including Bernie and her.

Mama did not ignore them, however, but watched carefully. "It's so nice Honor has made some friends." She pronounced her daughter's name "Honor." Leslie could not decide if it would annoy Mama more if she stuck to the pronunciation she had carefully schooled herself in, "Hon-or-ay," or if it would annoy Honor more if she dropped that affectation. She avoided using Honor's name and mumbled when she could not avoid it. Bernie caught on and looked amused. As she waited to hear what he was doing, she did not notice him using the name at all. "So nice Honor has made friends. I've been upset that she hasn't made friends at school. . . . Of course, Honor is intellectually precocious, so she'd rather have older friends. But I'd have thought she could have gotten to know some of the nicer girls at school. Others in the Service Society perhaps."

"The SS. Oh, Mama, they're all such . . . flips. They do nothing but giggle about boys."

"They must do something or they wouldn't be in the Service Society. It's nice for your college friends to take an interest in you, but it's important to have friends your own age. You have more in common."

"Mama, I don't have a thing in common with *anyone* at General Custer! And they don't like me either. I'm not common enough." Honor laughed nervously.

"There's no reason to be defensive." Mama pursued the point like a glacier moving down a river valley scraping everything before her to the last pebble. Leslie found her palms sweating. "I'm sure you could be very popular with the other girls in the Service Society if you spent a

97

little effort listening to them instead of drowning them out with what you think."

Yet Mama obviously doted on Honor. Her gaze was always brooding on the girl like a big cooing dove when she wasn't giving one of them a quick inspection. It wasn't that Mama lacked pride in Honor but that she believed in upping the ante constantly. Mama was so unlike Leslie's parents. Her own mother complained constantly but rarely criticized her and never with such will. Her mother had worried Leslie would get into trouble, which meant pregnant but also in jail, kicked out of school, caught at something. Caught, that was it. Caught with your pants down, caught in the till, caught shoplifting, caught smoking dope in the john, caught with a belly. When Leslie began to do very well in classes halfway through high school, her mother had been pleased but surprised. It would never have occurred to the small harried woman to suggest how Leslie act in school. The idea of Leslie going to college had simply astonished her mother, who never got to finish the tenth grade. Mrs. Rogers told them exactly how many colleges Honor had applied to and what was wrong with each.

"We'll open the presents now," Mama said. "Then let's have the cake."

They sat in the livingroom, barely fitting in. "Do get started," Cam said with her eyes on her watch. "Mark will be here soon."

"I don't know why you invited him on your sister's birthday, if he doesn't want to take part with the family," Mama said.

"Why should he want to watch my kid sister open presents? It's me he's interested in. I'm glad somebody is."

Bernie smiled at her with his eyes only, sideways glance on the sly, and she thought, as if they had spoken aloud, that yes, in a funny way this afternoon was like a childhood birthday party with the presents in piles and the cake and ice cream waiting while the party girl's mother directed the show and behind the door two kids were punching each other in the snoot. Yes, and she had never had the money for a real present. Oftentimes her mother tried to cover with something around the house (oh, they can't tell it isn't new) or at least better than that, some twenty-five-cent nothing from the dime store. This afternoon too cooked up the sense of being observed: whether you measured up, if you had manners, if you ate too much, not to mention whether your gift was ample.

"I'll open your present first, Cam." There were quite a lot of presents—from Mignon, the married sister, and individually from nephew and niece, from other relatives, from a Mrs. Gordon who worked with Mama. Cam had given her a pair of ice skates, which Honor exclaimed over without conviction. Cam wants to get her out of the house too, we're secret allies, Leslie thought. When Honor came to their presents, Honor opened first hers and then Bernie's, an order that made Leslie jealous. The earrings, the book of excerpts from the journals of women she had finally selected as at least carrying some quiet freight of content with it, the unlocking of a door or two in the imagination. When Honor opened Leslie's present, Mama seemed about to speak but did not until Honor had opened Bernie's. "Oh, I'll put one on each side! I'll have to use that antiseptic gunk. Just wait!"

Honor ran to her bedroom. Mrs. Rogers eyed them both. "Apparently you knew Honor had her ears pierced, against my wishes. I hope you didn't pick out those earrings before she had it done?"

"Oh, no," Leslie started to stammer as Bernie said in his best humble smooth tones, "I think Honor asked each of us for exactly the same thing on her birthday. That's what she wanted."

"But we can't always give Honor everything she wants, can we?" Mrs. Rogers picked up her card. Leslie felt prickly, although she had written nothing more compromising than "Happy Birthday to Honorée on her 18th Birthday! Love, Leslie." Mrs. Rogers' eyebrows rose. "But Honor isn't eighteen. Heavens! They grow up fast enough as it is!"

"But . . . how old is she?" Bernie said.

"She's seventeen today. Whatever made you imagine she was a year older?"

"I . . . thought she said she was seventeen last month," Leslie said.

Honor came running back in turning to and fro to show them one earring of each pair. "How can I be bothered saying sixteen and eleven months? I rounded it off."

"I've told you a thousand times, you shouldn't exaggerate. It gives people a misimpression." Mama turned back. "Perhaps you didn't realize I was against Honor having her ears pierced. It's unfortunate. Rewarding her for disobeying me—it does give that impression. Or perhaps since you thought she was eighteen, you didn't think my objection mattered?"

Right on the first guess, Leslie thought. Bernie had drifted over to sit beside her on the sagging couch, and they huddled side by side. She had the feeling that if they dared they would be holding hands for comfort, although they did not even exchange glances but sat eyes forward. Honor, very slightly smiling, was unwrapping her next present.

"Really, Mama." Cam stood up. "If Honor asked them for earrings, what were they supposed to do? How the . . . heck do they know if her ears are pierced? What difference could it make to anybody except you and her in the whole wide world? Honestly, do you think the neighbors are gossiping because Honey has holes in her ears?"

"Don't call me that old nickname, I hate it," Honor said. "What a gorgeous dress. I have to try it on at once!"

I'm in love with the wrong sister, Leslie thought. Cam fidgeted with an eye on her watch. Honor returned in the new dress, filmy and pale blue. Rosy with pleasure, she swirled. It was not particularly flattering because it billowed out below the high empire waist and made her look pregnant, but it was cut low front and back. Honor was ravished by it because her breasts showed. What were all those dresses for? Honor hardly went out. She wore them around the house, parading in front of mirrors; she showed them off to Bernie and her. Where was Honor supposed to go in them and with whom? They were the trappings of Mama's fantasies that none of them belonged in.

Of course Honor Rogers must be a girl with an ambitious mother. Honor was Mama Rogers' creation. Every cent that could be leached from the house, from the food bills, from taxes and mortgage went into or onto her. The third daughter, the last chance, the beautiful youngest princess. Maybe the elaborate dresses had no more function than the clothes made for dolls, to be put on and taken off at affairs of the mind? It frightened her. It frightened her for Honor. What did Mrs. Rogers want? What did she imagine? Leslie saw mother and daughter living in a private Victorian serial, waiting for the rest of the cast to arrive, the wicked tempter, the virtuous suitor, the lord of the manor.

Then she had to glance at Bernie, who was sitting very still and straight with his hands on his knees and his mouth crimped into a polite smile; but the line of his jaw was unusually sharp. He was clenching his teeth. As if we could carry Honor off between us. I couldn't keep a cat. I couldn't keep Valerie. It comes down to money. She clenched her own teeth. I will, I will stick it out. I'll stick out anything George hands me, I will! I'll go on my knees crawling through that obstacle course of a department. I'll earn the damned degree. I'll be so good they have to let me in, they have to accept me, because I'll be so much better than anyone else, yes, they have to. I'll do it!

Honor, perched with the blue gauze draped around her chair, was opening her last package. It held an old fashioned gold locket on a fine chain. "Mama, it's beautiful!"

"Thank your father too," Mrs. Rogers said with cool justice.

Honor looked around. He had wandered into the kitchen, where he was doing something with a screwdriver to the toaster. "Dad, thank you for the locket."

"The what?"

"Cal, what are you doing to the toaster?" Mama asked.

"The pop-up mechanism is jammed."

"But we just turn it sideways, Daddy, and the toast falls out," Honor said.

"I'll have it working in no time."

Mrs. Rogers grimaced. Honor came to her and bowed her long swan neck to have the locket attached. "But, Mama . . . I did tremendously want a watch. You know? I told you."

"And I told you you'll get one when you're eighteen. You'd only break it. You're not very good at taking care of your possessions. Cheap watches look cheap. You want a good watch."

"But I'm always late."

"That's no one's fault but your own. You have an alarm clock. There's a clock in the kitchen. Taking responsibility is part of growing up. . . . Don't you care for the locket, my darling? It's an antique."

"It's lovely, Mama. Of course I adore it. . . . What shall I put inside?"

"Whatever you like, dear heart." Mama beamed. "It's such a sweet fragile old thing. Makes me think of pressed violets and locks of hair of lovers long dead. I think photos are . . . a little cheap. You don't have to put anything in it until you have a memento you cherish."

Bernie got up restlessly, apparently determined to actively charm rather than passively suffer. He headed for the locket to admire it, starting out, "It's really a lovely piece of antique jewelry." Then he realized that admiring the locket close up would bring him nearer to Honor's half-bare breasts than seemed wise in front of Mama and he came to a sudden halt, tilting a little back. She had the sensation that invisible strands of nerve fiber ran from Bernie to herself, along with bolts of amusement and dismay as one or the other committed their little faux pas and bobbled uneasily under that pale blue maternal gloat. "You could have a kind of religious souvenir—"

"Oh, we're Presbyterians. We don't go in for that sort of thing," Mama said reprovingly.

Bernie sank down again. But they were all gently herded toward the kitchen for cake and ice cream. When they arrived, pieces of the toaster were spread over the kitchen table. "Cal! I had the plates laid out." They were stacked in the sink. "It's time for cake. For Honor's birthday."

That look. Like her father. Where did all you strangers come from as I'm getting off here in my own free space? Leslie turned away in that mixture of anger and complicity her own father aroused in her, because they were in some ways too much alike. She looked like her old man—red-haired, short and stocky, neatly built, turned-up nose and brown eyes and freckles. Her old man wasn't old, her boyish, frolicking, whining daddy. She focused with difficulty on the entirely other man who did not drink and space out, but spaced out diddling with a toaster. He was immovable. Words did not penetrate. He said, "Eat whatever you want in the front room. I'm working on the toaster here. Broken appliances are dangerous."

Close to her ear Cam giggled breathily. "Isn't he great? Nothing bugs him. He just coasts along. She can jump up and down and yell and he just says, Mmmm. Oh!" she said louder as she realized Mark was peering in the window from the porch, rapping on the glass. "Forgot to tell him about the doorbell!"

It must be raining much harder than when she had arrived, because Mark came in dripping from his mackinaw and his boots and his plastered-down hair. Even his ears dripped. Everyone—except Mr. Rogers—lined up at the window to stare at the force of the rain. Biting her lip with annoyance, Mama moved the cake and ice cream into the livingroom. Cam took Mark's arm, beefy in red and black plaid. "I'm all ready. Don't want to keep you waiting."

But Mama invited him to dessert. "After all, it's your sister's birthday. Why leave before we've had our celebration?"

Mark showed no signs of impatience to re-enter the gale. "Ice cream and cake, sure. Happy birthday." He looked around trying to figure out whose it was, then he saw Honor in the long blue dress. His gaze fixed on her breasts. "Wow. So this is your little sister. She's not so little, huh?"

Bernie, who was carrying plates along his arm at his

103

waiterly best, put down his load and narrowed his eyes at Mark. Facing away from Mama, drawing himself up stiffly, he stood taller than Mark. "Bernard Guizot."

"Huh? I'm Mark—friend of Cam's. Hi, Leslie." He smirked at her. Something wrong. It was not the old ogling or the more recent sullenness. She felt a prickling of unease. "Funny place to see you," he went on. "What are you doing here?"

"Attending Honorée's birthday party." Leslie tried not to read more into his question than she should. "How are you?" Perhaps dying of leukemia or advanced congenital syphilis?

"In the pink. You still taking that karate stuff and throwing men around?"

"What's that you're talking about?" Mama's eyebrows rose.

She had to explain. It was dull as usual. Mark was wolfing down chocolate cake and Neapolitan ice cream, but she knew it was too much to hope that he would suddenly choke to death. Mrs. Rogers was daintily shocked. "It's hard for me to imagine any"—her tongue hesitated before finding a noncommittal enough noun—"a woman hopping around that way. It looks peculiar enough when young men do it. I think it's the effect of all the violence on television and in the movies, although I haven't gone to the movies in years. Don't you think it's a passing fad?"

"Mrs. Rogers, you know what the streets are like. Rape is the commonest violent crime. Don't you think it's a good idea for a woman to be able to defend herself?" Speech number two in a taped loop. Why couldn't she just say she liked to have muscles as well as fat, and she liked being healthy.

" . . . and I'm always telling Honor the same thing, it's not safe to go out. If Cam wasn't running around every night of the week, I wouldn't have to worry so. I don't even care for Honor being here alone in the evenings."

"It's turned into a popular sport." Bernie was trying to take the heat off her. "It does make more sense for a woman living in the city than swinging a racquet or running around dribbling a basketball."

104

"Gee, I thought you would've gone in for . . . *basketball*." Mark spoke with heavy emphasis, giving Bernie the same smirk. Oh, he'd been doing his homework.

"I'm not a good sport," Bernie said. "When I'm forced to fight, I fight dirty and I fight to win. . . . Would anyone like some more delicious cake? Can I cut anyone another piece?"

As Mark finished his plate, Cam grabbed it. "Now that we've eaten, I guess we should run along." She pried him out still looking back at the cake and at Honor.

"Really!" Honor said when the door had opened to the wind and the water and shut again with a slam. "Where does she find them?"

Mrs. Rogers only smiled.

Soon afterwards Bernie and Leslie escaped. His left rear tire had gone flat and he had to pump it up while they both got soaked. Then they huddled in the car cold and wet and furious, with the rain drumming on the metal roof like a personal attack. "Like to get him to take a poke at me, that asshole," Bernie groused. "I could lay him out."

Leslie looked doubtful. "He's solidly built. Why bother?"

"Because that's the only kind of strength he'd understand. You judge too much by broad shoulders. I know how to fight at least as well as you do and a lot dirtier, I bet."

"You're taking over his macho code. You think knocking him down proves you're a better man."

"It's an impossible bind. The old story of the images in other people's heads. But don't you ever intend to use all that training in mayhem?"

"It's the relationship it gives me to my body I value, not fantasies about breaking somebody's head because they're nasty to me. . . . I think he's heard something."

Bernie finally got the car engine to turn over. "I have to go to work at five. Let's get a drink. There's a gay bar where nobody'll pester us. Come on. Have a drink with me and I'll drop you home before I turn myself in to À Votre Plaisir."

"For once I feel like a gay bar. That woman!"

"When will Honorée go through a normal adolescent rebellion? When will she tell Mama to soak her head in a bucket of piss?"

"I suppose we're her rebellion."

"Poor Honorée!" Bernie chuckled. He started rolling a joint with one hand while driving through the flooded streets till nervously she took the makings from him and rolled it herself. Handed it back lit. "Ah, service. Know what's better than service with a smile? Service with a whimper. . . . I don't mean to imply you deal from less than a position of strength, I'm chattering. If the dope doesn't cool me out a little my head will fly off."

From the car they ran from the neon-rimmed door, pelted by the hammering surf of the rain coming horizontally, lashing their faces. They staggered into the dim reddish interior, almost empty, not even smoky yet. The bartender gave them a look of vacant hostility, then recognized Bernie. "You're crazy to come out today. If I didn't have to work, I'd stay in bed in this crazy weather."

"That's where I should have stayed, in bed, but I'm too wet to care. An Irish coffee."

"The coffee sounds good." Leslie shivered. "Black and a shot of that Remy Martin there on the side."

Bernie's teeth were actually chattering. They hung their sopping jackets over a couple of chairs and sat in a booth. The pulsating wail from the jukebox did not bother her. She warmed her hands against the mug. "Instead of coming here, you should have gone home and changed before work. You really are cold."

"Frozen." His teeth were chattering wildly, but as he sipped the Irish coffee gradually the shaking stopped. She took his hand between hers artificially warmed from the mug, and began chafing it. He said, "Yes, take care of me a little. I'm feeling ever so sorry for myself."

"You want to know what the worst thing for me was?"

"That dude's entry all smirking with knowledge of exactly what labels to apply."

"That'll make trouble," she said slowly. "But, no, actually. When I found out Honor is only seventeen *now*."

"Oh!" He laughed. "She's such a baggage. She said fifty times she was seventeen already. She makes complete fools of us both. But Mama's not only a nuisance but evil."

"She's our opponent at tug-of-war. Honor means everything to her, which is a bad idea all the way around, but what else has she got? She's bound to lose. Honor is seventeen anyhow, not seven. She'll leave home."

"I hope so. Sweet Mother of Mary. But I wonder. Does Rapunzel get away from the witch? It's a fight to the death." His hand between hers turned and firmly squeezed the topmost of hers. Immediately she took her hands away and put them around her empty mug. "Why won't you let me be affectionate sometimes, Les? When I feel affection. If I was a woman friend, you wouldn't be offended. Is it a kind of strong physical repulsion?"

"I'm sorry. Maybe it's habit. I'm not used to being touched."

"I wonder how you manage in matches?"

She smiled. "But that's the point: not to be touched."

"You're quibbling."

"I'll tell you something funny. There's a whole school of karate where you work entirely without contact. You never actually land a blow. In any kind of karate you're always supposed to be able to pull your punches. To do that." Abruptly she launched a straight-knuckled punch at Bernie's glass, stopping short just before she grazed it. He jumped and she smiled again. "But they fight without touching. . . . For me a lot of the benefit was ceasing to be afraid of pain. The sky won't fall if I make a fist, and I can survive blows hard enough to knock me off my feet. . . . When I've been matched in tournaments between schools with people trained in no-contact—and of course with them you have to fight no-contact—I always lose. Because when I *feel* a blow isn't really going to land, instinctively I don't really try to block. Nothing lands, but they get the point."

"Is there a parable in all that?"

"I'll try to think about not bearing to be touched. I am sorry. In the gay women's community back home everyone was always kissing hello and hugging. I've got out of the habit here."

"But I'm not talking about that in-group 'Oh Hello Dahling' pecking. I mean the simple expression of affection."

"I think it has to do with Val. Rejecting not being with her. I don't believe it yet. I pretend I do, but I don't. I know she's mine, really, if I can just get to her. And except for George I haven't been close to a man for years. Get us another round. We'll just have time before you have to go to work."

The place was beginning to fill up, men in couples, men alone mostly. He waited at the bar, chatting, while she counted on her hands the days till spring vacation. She had given up hoping for a reply to her letter, but she was most of the way to convincing herself to go anyhow. Bring Val back. She saw herself as marking time with Honor and Bernie, friendship, company. If she really got involved with another woman, something in her believed that she would therefore lose Val. As long as she was still faithful to Val, Val would somehow belong to her. Could be gotten back. She sighed, banging her fist on the table.

When he brought the drinks back, she leaned against the booth wall flexing her fingers behind her nape, elbows poked out. "You deny you feel comfortable with a gay identity, Bernie, yet when you feel upset, look where you go. Your own turf."

"That's like saying a poor kid wants to be poor because he knows the streets of his own home slum. How comfortable for him to be poor then on the crummy ratty murderous streets he's familiar with."

"All right. It may not be fun to be Black, but now at least often Blacks can pull some strength from that identity. We've all seen people call themselves Black and talk about Black is beautiful whose skin is no darker than ours. Why should they pass when their identity can encompass self-love now?"

"Les, you won't see, will you? Except for Burt, with

nine tenths of my gay experiences I had as much choice as a public urinal. I'm not sure how much choice I had with Burt. It was a better turn of luck. If he'd been a captain of the Mafia instead of gay liberation, I'd have followed him anyhow, I was broke and in trouble, in real trouble. I never had it easy, one of those callboys who lie at home in comfort and handle a few choice clients who lavish favors and gifts on them. I could imagine getting into that. Maybe I'd be good at it. I'd sure feel different about myself. . . . But when I was fifteen I had fucking bloody hemorrhoids. Can you imagine that at fifteen, from doing too many johns and not knowing how to protect myself? How can you expect me to salvage a lively pride out of that?"

"Living with Burt was a real relationship, right?"

He raked at his hair. "Sometimes I think I'm basically destructive. All the way through. . . . It's funny being in this area again. Since I left home—since my mother died, since my home broke up, I mean—I hadn't ever come back. I met Burt in Chicago and he brought me here. I grew up downriver on Lake Erie, Les, I have this totally mad idea for spring vacation. It's only a week away. I want to drive downriver some afternoon with Honor and you and see where I grew up. I really want to do it."

"Maybe right at the beginning or the end. . . . I'm going to see Val. I have to talk to her. I'm going to bring her back here with me."

"Do you really believe she'll come?"

Leslie bowed her head. "I don't want to think. To create strategies and try to be clever. I'll go, I'll see her, and I'll know. As you say, it's only a week away."

Tentatively she put out her hand and he took it. Two cold hands touched gently among empty cups and glasses. She heard a loud voice then arguing with the bartender and turned her head.

Tasha, dripping from a waterlogged poncho, was hauling a poster for a women's dance out of a plastic bag. She got the bartender to let her put it up, and a Black woman with her was sticking in thumbtacks. Tasha turned then and realized someone was staring at her, looked puzzled and then recognized Leslie. "Hi!" she bellowed. "Leslie!" Then she saw Leslie holding hands with Bernie and she did not come over. Jesus, Leslie thought, and it was all she could do not to jerk her hand away. I'll have to explain it to her. Why? It's none of her business. But Leslie remained embarrassed.

eight

Although the temperature was in the forties, the day felt balmy because of the first sunshine in two weeks. Leslie wanted to rise into the air, to flutter up like a dirty pigeon and beat to and fro. She walked instead into an overheated house. Honor met her in a dressing gown. "I just got home. I was at a stupid meeting of Service Society students from all over the city. I do those dreary extracurricular tasks that are just unpaid slave labor—library staff, hall guard, lunchroom monitor—because it looks good on college applications. . . . I was just trying to decide what I should put on?"

The dressing gown was flimsy and peach colored. As Honor stood against the light, Leslie could see right through the material. She was galvanized by an urge to grab Honor, to kiss her finally, to hold her and swing her in the air, big as she was, to hug her. To draw her down on the dingy slipcovered couch and unbutton the wispy silly dressing gown and make love to her, starting with her long neck, the full breasts, the swell of belly. She took a step toward Honor and gently held her hand.

"What should I put on? It's unfair we have our vacations at different times! Such a waste. Bernar' and you and I could do a thousand exciting things. The school is under Mama's secret direction, don't you think so?" Honor chattered, oblivious to her touch.

Leslie sighed and let go. Even the sharp access of

111

desire had nothing to do with Honor, but was instead a great thaw occasioned less by the sun and the peach flimsiness than by Val having finally called her last night. "Put on slacks and a sweater and come out with me. The day's beautiful. We have an hour of sunshine left—let's use it."

"Walking bores me. I mean, we have to have a goal. I know what, I need some creme rinse for my hair and we can look at nail polish. I'm trying to decide if I want to get into polish." Honor allowed herself to be bullied into dressing and putting on a jacket. "It *is* lovely today—robin's egg blue. . . . I was so annoyed at the hypocrisy. . . . I'm sure prime ministers and secretaries of state don't take themselves nearly as seriously as officers of high school honor societies."

As they walked to Grand River, Leslie allowed the fascinating conversation to play in her head a mere five or six times. She kept a tight rein on herself and was careful that she seemed to listen to some of what Honor was saying. The phone had rung at eleven. She had gone to bed, although she was not sleeping. Rather she was reading a long paper, dense in words and bad mathematics but thin in content, from the *Journal of American History*. She could see her arm reaching for her phone as it glowered on the floor beside her mattress like a white toad. Again and again her arm moved in a jerky arc of irritation. Who the hell is calling me now, this late? And heard that high sweet voice.

She had been so excited she could not remember the exact words of the first exchanges. Through the phone she could hear music in the background and voices. Valerie spoke softly, cupping the receiver.

"Yes, I'm glad you're coming," Val said, quite as if they had discussed her vacation at length and agreed. She could remember those precise words and the lift of her heart.

"So am I glad, oh, Val, very glad. Should I come Saturday? I can take a morning bus."

"Not unless you have other friends to see. Monday we'll manage it. Where will you be staying?"

Val was therefore not inviting her to come and stay. And could not see her Sunday. "Are you . . . actually living with Lena?"

"Yes, of course. Where will you be on Monday?"

"I'll stay with Mary and Liz. I'll ask them, but I'm sure it's okay."

"Better check. They're a hotel for runaway wives these days. But it's a good choice, Mary and Liz. I'll call you out there Monday." Valerie hung up.

Monday we'll manage it. Now what did that mean? That Lena was possessive and jealous? That Lena had forbidden Valerie to see her? A good choice, Mary and Liz. What did that mean? Mary and Liz were more her friends than they were Lena's. Liz and Lena had had a fight a couple of years before on whether to form a coalition with a male-dominated Black group on issues of minority and women's hiring, and neither woman had trusted the other since. Liz called Lena a racist, and Lena called Liz a fool. Didn't Valerie's being willing to make the phone call, to create the chance, didn't that prove Val was still wanting Leslie? Hope tormented her in a cloud of biting flies and she twisted her head as she walked. Constantly Honor reproved her for walking too quickly. "We aren't racing to Grand River. Nobody here will give you a gold medal for a fast mile!" Imagine her wanting to throw Honor down on the couch. She had an impulse to confess to Bernie at the first opportunity, but that gave a moment's urge too much weight.

"Why don't you ever come and visit me?" she asked Honor. The words were out before she considered them. "I always come to you. You must get bored with the house."

"But Mama. You know she calls."

"How can she mind your visiting me?"

"She'd find something. She'd object to my coming home after dark alone."

"I'll bring you back. I'll escort you door to door." She saw herself endlessly trundling across Detroit on the buses and she winced. Why had she offered that, why?

"I am curious. Bernar' insisted your apartment is a

113

nun's cell. I've never seen Bernar's lodgings either. Have you?"

She shook her head no.

"Why don't you? You don't have problems with mamas. Go and give me a report. I love to have each of you talk to me about the other. It's endlessly fascinating to shift perspective."

"When you say that, you make me feel vulnerable. To think of you together talking about me."

"Of course we talk about you. Don't you and Bernar' talk about me all the time?"

"Actually, no."

"Well, then, what on earth do you and Bernie talk about when I'm not there, if it isn't about me?"

"We don't spend that much time together. At first we were sniffing suspiciously. Testing each other. Now we argue a lot about how we experience being gay."

"Gay—Bernie uses that word too. I hate 'in' words."

"The other choice is saying homosexual to cover both. I'm not homosexual. I don't like homos, which sound like men to me. What a long awkward word. 'Come to me, my homosexual baby,'" Leslie crooned while Honor laughed, looking around.

"What do you find to argue about?" Honor was frowning slightly, peering at her. "That you should like men and he should like women?"

"How we each feel about being gay."

"Sounds dull. I'm glad you do it together instead of attempting to include me, since I haven't even had a chance to be heterosexual yet. Like the angels, I have no sex life at all. . . . I do envy you, able to run around and have assignations. You can visit Bernie. He can visit you. You can race around the city to shops and museums and restaurants, while I'm doing my homework."

Looking sideways at Honor, who was slowly twirling and untwirling a curl, Leslie realized with a chill that Honor was in fact jealous.

At the Cunningham's, Honor brooded on the nail polishes. "I'm trying to decide whether painting my nails is a vice I want to take on."

"Why bother? It can't be good for your nails. Cam is always daubing at herself, yet I can't see she looks any better for it."

Honor frowned at her extended right hand. "I don't enjoy my hands. How peasantish they are. I covet Bernie's hands. He has the hands I ought to have. No, you're right, Leslie, I'll pass it by. I don't want to call that much attention to my hands. Now if women polished the tips of their breasts, that'd be another matter."

As they walked back along Grand River, past the wig shop, two bars, one closed by the police and boarded up, an empty store with a broken window, a dry cleaner's, a liquor store, knots of men stood in front of the bar and again in front of the liquor store. Leslie moved over to pass in between the men and the girl. Past the muttered, the loud comments, the leering, the obscenities, Honor kept quiet. Then when they turned onto her street that went straight for half a mile to her house (and straight for miles after that in both directions in a grid pattern with numbers that rose into the 20,000s), Honor said, "I really do like my breasts. I'm proud of them, I like to look at them and touch them. But when I walk past a group of . . . louts like that, it's ugly. Maybe I don't want to be touched at all by anyone. To be . . . used. To be torn open and used."

"You could make love with women for years and still be untorn."

"I've read about women raping other women. In prison."

"I've known hundreds of lesbians, and I have never once known a woman to force another woman. Ever."

"What I'm trying to say is, maybe I'm narcissistic. Will I ever fall in love? Perhaps Mama has trained me to be so self-involved I'll never, never care for anyone else except as a friend. Every day I imagine making love. I imagine the scene, the mood, how I'm dressed, what we say. But when it comes to what they call the nitty-gritty, I fade out."

"Could that be lack of experience? Or maybe you're not attracted sexually to men."

115

"I like the way Bernar' looks at me. He flatters me. It feels sexual, but there's no threat in it. He won't ever . . . attack or make a pass. Not that I'd want him to. I adore being friends with him."

"I also . . . admire you," Leslie said quietly.

"I love to be admired. The both of you make me feel wonderful, ever so much better than those street louts or the goon squad at school. Maybe what I need is a civilized lout. I don't know. Sometimes I see myself in Faulkner. You know, our house as decaying manse. Mama and I ending our days together, tremendously old women. Her still sewing perfect lovely gowns for me and insisting I can't wear them to the corner for fear of being ravished. She's ninety-five and I'm almost seventy and we're living in a maze of bric-a-brac." Honor screwed her face up, holding out a palsied hand and speaking in a cracked voice. "Now, my baby, how are you feeling this morning? You look frail. Fine, Mama, shall I wear the pink marquisette or the blue voile? The blue voile, my darling, but do put on your shawl. And take a parasol to protect your tender complexion from the sun. Nowadays people are all courting skin cancer, the way they expose themselves. You have a lovely bloom and you must protect it. Now don't walk too far and tire yourself. Perhaps to the garbage can in the yard and back." Her shoulders were hunched, she held her hands as claws. "And don't speak to the neighbors, they're not what I'd call nice."

Leslie laughed, a little scandalized that Honor could satirize her dependency. "Your mother didn't care much for Bernie and me, did she?"

"Whatever made you imagine that?" Honor snapped back to defend her mother. "She wants to meet both of you again soon."

"She was angry about the earrings."

"Really, Leslie, she had wonderful things to say about you. She said you could be terribly attractive if you tried. With natural red hair and a creamy complexion, there are dozens of colors you can wear that make me look sallow—if you didn't run around in jeans all the time. Right after you've washed it, your hair gleams. Of course it's

116

not thick like mine, but if you wore it curly the effect would be stunning. She says you have perfect posture—the way I ought to, she says, although I do think I have a devastating walk—and a good figure, if you dressed so it could be seen sometimes!"

"I have good musculature too." They were passing a coal yard. Leslie stripped off her pea jacket, thrust it at Honor, rolled up the sleeve of her workshirt and made her biceps hard. "See?"

"Leslie!"

"I worked for my muscles. I was born with my hair, and my hips just grew. But every muscle represents years of effort."

"You say you don't want to be like a man. Why are you ashamed to look like a woman?"

"I dress for comfort, durability, cheapness. I'm not entirely indifferent. In addition to my everyday gi—gi, that's what I wear for karate—I have a special gi that's bleached, for ceremonial occasions. Honorée, the way I look, that's how I look when I wake up, when I get out of the shower, when I make love. It's just me, all the way through."

"I see that you want to be loved in despite. You want to say, Take me or leave me. Bang. Just as I am."

Leslie was unable to turn her head. She could not tell if Honor was speaking personally, saying, You want me to love you in despite. Or generally. She could not tell. She could not turn her head and look at Honor. "Maybe." Finally she turned, but now Honor was waving languidly to a girl who shouted from a passing Rambler. Loved in despite: was that true? Every time she had Honor neatly classified in age group and virginity, Honor startled her. "You mean to say that I . . . I ask too much?"

Honor was staring after the car, shaking her head. "She was my best friend. Barbara. In the seventh grade till the ninth. In our sophomore year she fell in love with a creep named Zack. She had sex with him in cars, in drive-ins, at the beach, on the playground, in the bleachers, every place I suppose he could manage to ram it into her. Really. I don't know what she got out of it. She told me once she never had an orgasm. But if he frowned, she cried. She cried, she took Quaaludes, she cried and drank, she cried and got pregnant and had an abortion, she cried and he left her anyhow. Now she's involved with another jerk I can't tell from the first except he has pimples and plays ice hockey and is even stupider. Mama wants to know why I don't have girlfriends. Barbara was my best friend. We had secrets I wouldn't even tell Mama. We were going to live together when we grew up, and after we got married we were going to name our daughters for each other. Maybe that's the one she had out at the hospital."

"It hurts a lot when women let men come between them. Are you afraid to be close to another woman because of losing Barbara?"

"Barbara lost Barbara. I'm not afraid—I'm close to you. Not to mention Mama. I'm sorry I went on about Barbara—my man, my man, anything for my man. You tell me I'm too traditionally feminine, but I'm not that traditional. I find her a mess. There's no . . . style, what Bernie calls grace."

"I don't think any woman sets out to make a fool of herself. What she imagines happening is romantic love. What she gets is a bloody mess where pulling out feels as if she'll lose everything she put in. See, I remember all that. I was Barbara in high school. Except I was too stupid to know when I got pregnant, and I lost it, like you'd lose your dinner if you ate something that upset your stomach."

"I'm glad you told me about being pregnant. Bernar' told me, but I wanted you to feel free to talk about it yourself."

"That's years ago. It doesn't press on my mind." Yet she was upset to think of Bernie telling Honor behind her back.

Mary picked her up at the bus station in Grand Rapids to drive her out to the farm. Like herself, Mary came from a small city in Michigan, Holland in Mary's case, where the tourists flocked for the tulip festival and carried home plastic replicas of wooden shoes and windmills.
118

Mary was plump and flaxen blond. She taught chemistry in night school and commuted from their farm, filled in Saturdays in a medical lab.

It was dark when they arrived. The house stood at the head of a circular drive; anyhow a sand track ran in a circle in front of it past the rusting skeleton of a car. A front door, hardly ever used, led into the old parlor. They went around to the back, entering a long porch where potatoes and onions, garlic and apples were stored in bushel baskets. The kitchen was steamy and thick with good food smells. "We killed a chicken for you," Liz said, kissing her. "It may be tough, but it'll taste good. I made soup from it."

Liz came from the UP—the Upper Peninsula. She had grown up on skis and she was sturdy. Her light brown hair was cropped, she was a little shorter than Mary and Leslie herself, and she had a loud abrupt infectious laugh that had been the first thing Leslie had noticed about her in the old days when they had met in a local lesbian rap group. Liz had a four-year-old from a marriage still legally in force, although her husband had disappeared right after the birth of Rosellen. When Leslie first met her, Liz had been on AID, but the farm was in both women's names now and they farmed seriously. They raised all their own vegetables, most of their own fruit, and they sold lettuce, beans, corn, tomatoes, cucumbers, peppers, and pumpkins from the tailgate of their truck in the farmers market in Grand Rapids.

The kitchen was hot from the wood stove they cooked on. All the kids were there—Rosellen and Mary's fraternal twins, Bob and Yevette, who were six. Mary was divorced and once in a while she got forty a month child support. Still it was Mary who had saved the money for the down payment on the farm and it was on her feeble credit they had finally procured a mortgage. The house was seventy years old and needed work; in fact work sank into it almost without a trace. An army of women could have swarmed over it for a year with saws and hammers and left it only habitable. Mary and Liz and the kids seemed mostly to camp in it, using the livingroom and

119

kitchen heavily while they put their effort into the land. The land fed them. The house would come later.

"Did you get the furnace fixed?" Leslie asked, sitting at the long rough table.

"Not yet. It's so old. I don't know that it's really worth it." Liz shook the short brown hair out of her eyes, giving a last stir to the pot. "Oil's so high. There's all the wood we can burn in our woods, and we have to thin the trees anyhow. Part's natural woods, but part was planted in Christmas trees, Scotch pines, and they're too close. They never got harvested and it's a mess." She brought the soup to the table.

Every plate was different, from rummage sales, and "Everything comes from the land, everything!" except the cheap red wine in gallon jugs. "But we don't see why we can't make our own wine eventually. We have grapes started. Bobbie! Quit picking out the pieces of chicken. Just take it as it comes, Bobbie! Or I'll have to serve you instead of letting you take for yourself like a big person."

"What's this about runaway wives?" Leslie asked.

"Oh!" Mary laughed. "We're part of the underground railway of abused women. There's houses in Chicago and Minneapolis. I hear maybe one's getting organized in Detroit. Is it true?"

"I hadn't heard," Leslie said guiltily.

"Well, if a woman or her kids are in danger and the man discovers where she is at one of the regular houses, we're one of the hidey holes she can come to with her kids till she can get help or figure out what to do. We just get the cases in real trouble—I mean they're all in real trouble—mortal danger."

"What do you do with them?"

"We play with them!" Yevette said loudly. "Sometimes they got real babies."

Over more of the wine, wrapped in an old quilt and cuddled on a straight chair near the potbelly stove in the livingroom, she listened as they caught her up on the world she had left to pursue her degree with George: matings, partings, firings, hirings, parties, and quarrels. "We

120

didn't ask anybody over tonight because of what you said about Val. Are you officially here or not?"

"Not yet." Leslie sounded grim even to herself and she tried to smile into Liz's square face and Mary's round one. Her own was baked dry on the cheek toward the stove and frozen on the far cheek. She felt awkward. She was happy to see her friends again, yet clearly she had not come to be with them. Everything in her was in abeyance. Her whole body held its breath and she was rigid all the way through with waiting.

nine

"Mary can give me a ride into the city. Or I can hitch a ride easy. I can walk to Route Forty-five—it's only a mile—and hitch in."

"What for?" Valerie sounded miffed. "Where can we go in town? I'll drive out there. I'll arrive, oh, about one. I have a class I can cut."

"Class? You're going to school?"

"Tell you all about it. One o'clock, see you."

"Drive? You have a car? You're borrowing Lena's?" But Val had hung up.

At one the house was empty. The twins were at school, Mary was teaching, Rosellen was following Liz through the muddy furrows. They had a share in a tiller, and Leslie had spent the morning plowing in cover crops on the upper fields, which were dry enough to work. She took a shower—hot water was one luxury they had—combed her hair back, put on the vest her lover had given her and began to pace.

She vibrated nervousness checking the house. She was sleeping in the room that had been the parlor of the old farmhouse, next to the room they used now as a livingroom. It had been fixed up to accommodate the abused women Mary and Liz occasionally sheltered. She tossed her sleeping bag on the central bed, a sturdily built platform with a mattress on which she had in conscious hope put clean sheets. The rest of the room was filled with

122

bunk beds, shelves holding an assortment of toys and clean linen, a rag rug, bright red and white curtains. She opened the door between the old parlor and the present livingroom so the potbelly she had stoked well with wood might send some heat in. In case, in case.

The livingroom was a big square room with windows on two sides hung with curtains in a blue print. An old couch, V-shaped with hard use, faced a couch constructed of a plywood platform with pillows on it. Liz must have built the bunks and the couch. Otherwise there were straight chairs and a bookcase running to children's books, *The Encyclopedia of Organic Gardening*, Department of Agriculture pamphlets on bramble fruits and potato storage, old and new herbals, *Patience and Sarah*, and Mary's chemistry texts. It was already one-forty. If only she could turn off her mind, turn off her nerves. Be frozen until Val's arrival thawed her to life. Where was she?

At two-fourteen Val arrived. She was driving a rakish red Toyota she brought smartly around the loop screeching to a halt beside the porch. Holding aside the blue curtain, Leslie watched Valerie, dark hair swinging at her shoulders, give that little quick shake of annoyance as she hopped from the car and skipped toward the door. Val seemed slender and shining, she seemed to move twice as fast as anyone else. Yet forever Leslie stood with one hand outstretched and fingers planted against the pane, staring, and watched Valerie approach. Leslie found herself shaking. The door opened. Was shut. She turned from the window, moving as if through turbulent murky water, but she could not walk into the kitchen beyond.

Finally she stumbled forward. Just inside the kitchen door Valerie paused, looking around with an expression of dismay. "Here I am, hello!" Leslie bellowed, to wipe off that look of disappointment or whatever it was. "How are you!" She wanted to bolt forward and embrace Valerie, but she did not dare. She did not know how things stood; if they were only to debate, discuss, remember, be polite and distant.

Valeria shrugged off her coat—suede with cuffs and

123

hem of fur and new to Leslie—and sat with a half-checked gesture, stopping to remove a child's crumpled sock by one corner and put it after a moment's hesitation on the table. "So sorry I'm late. I couldn't get away sooner. I have to leave here at four at the very, very latest. We're invited out tonight."

We. Coupledom, excluding her. Lena and Val. Setting sharp time limits like the blade of a guillotine descending. All right, ask something, get her to talk. "You're back in school?"

"Part time. I don't think I could stomach it in bigger doses. It's harder when you've been out—been a real adult."

"Are you in art school?"

"Lena says the art school here sucks. All hard-edge male stuff. I'm taking a women's theater course. We're into creating new rituals, and I'm doing the set designs. . . . And parapsychology. We've done the *I Ching* and palmistry and now we're doing the tarot. That's the course I was going to cut, but I realized Beta, who's teaching it, will be at Grace's tonight. If she asked me where I was, it'd be awkward. I felt I did have to put in an appearance."

In other words, Valerie was studying nothing whatsoever. "What made you go back to school?"

"It's silly not having a degree. It won't take that long. And the theater course is exciting. I like doing art work that's part of something else. School's amusing."

"Are you working? You must have quit your job at Bolt's." I.e., is Lena keeping you?

"I can't go to school and work full time. I work Fridays and Saturdays in Lena's shop in the Grandville Mall."

"Do you like that job?"

"Leslie! How could anyone *like* working at some boring job? Do you like brushing your teeth? Would you like to do it for eight hours?"

Boring: it was Val's universal condemnation. It was boring to be poor; it was boring to have to take rotten jobs to survive, it was boring to be out of the closet and

124

hassled all the time. "Boredom isn't the worst fate. If you want to learn any real-world skills from plumbing to chemistry, you have to be willing to be bored for a while."

"Real-world skills! You mean the male world."

She was on the verge of starting an argument, as she had at Christmas. Their words seemed to come out in flat plastic trays covered with transparent wrap, boxes in which each word was displayed like a bright red waxed apple or a dyed orange. She had lost Valerie, lost her entirely, lost her to new suede coats with fur hems and a jaunty red Toyota and classes in palmistry and doily making. She tried to form a question: something not dangerous. Something that wouldn't explode. "Would you like some coffee? Or tea? Herb tea?" Valerie drank them all according to mood. She always wanted one absolutely and the other would not do. Since Val still hesitated, saying only, "Mmmmm," Leslie went on: "Or wine? There's red wine."

"Red wine at noon?" Valerie laughed, a sharp expulsion of breath in a single "huh," dainty as a cat's sneeze. "Why not?"

She would buy more wine to replace what they drank. The gallon jugs were stored on the porch with the fruit and potatoes, wine brought in by the case from a dealer in Grand Haven. Mary and Liz claimed it was better and cheaper than anything closer. It was certainly cheaper. She poured them each a tumblerful. What did asking for wine mean? Valerie was not a drinker. Had she become one? Lena drank scotch, she drank fancy aperitifs. Or was it a sign that Valerie too was nervous? Her own heart was hammering, the pulse working in her wrists, her throat, her temples as she carried the tumblers to the table and then the jug. Then she dragged her chair nearer to Valerie's and held out her full tumbler. "To *you*."

Valerie laughed the short hissing laugh and her small chin dipped. "To me? Should I drink to me?" She held out her tumbler and they clunked dully, heavy practical glass against glass. Val's face was round, her features delicate. She had an upturned nose like Leslie herself. Her

125

eyes were a much darker brown, her skin was dark honey. Her eyebrows were high and thin, stylized like the painted brows of courtesans in Hokusai, whose prints Valerie had put up on the wall of their bedroom. Her hands were small, her feet small, her body compact and tightly made. Her lower lip was bigger than her upper, giving her face in repose the impression of being always about to smile. "Red wine at noon. Anyhow in the afternoon," Valerie said, watching.

Suddenly she recognized: a phrase from a song, from an album they had played a lot. Joy of Cooking's first record. The album had come out a couple of years before they met, but they had bought all Joy of Cooking's records. She waited for the song to move in her head, rhythmically sad and slow. Piano. Two women's voices intertwined:

> The life that I chose
> is nothing at all
> without white wine in the morning sun
> red wine at noon
> and I'll be here when the evening comes
> and where have you been so long?

Valerie put down her tumbler half empty. "I don't enjoy sitting in this kitchen. A drag. It kind of leans on you saying, Clean me, do something!"

"We could sit in the livingroom."

Valerie walked before her, shorter and slenderer. Leslie walked after, carrying her glass. The wine was already flushing her face. She had not eaten since seven-thirty. I could put on a record, she thought, like that one if they have it. We could dance. Drink more wine. Then slowdance. I'll put my arms around her neck, hold her close. The hell with it; she hasn't given me enough time for a seduction. It's now or never.

Stooping, she put her glass on the floor and threw her arms around Valerie from the back. Arms over arms, clutching, embracing, she pulled Valerie off balance against her. She burrowed into Valerie's shoulder-length

126

glossy black hair to kiss her nape, to move her lips into the curved niche between shoulder and ear. Her mouth grazed in the hollow of the delicate ridge of collarbone. Her hand moved under Valerie's crossed arm and gently circled the nearest breast, five fingers radiating to stroke toward the center where the nipple under the light jersey was already hardening.

Valerie twisted then, turned around all at once in a swift dancing catlike swirl, and they were embracing mouth to mouth. She felt feverish. She wanted to touch every place, to caress entirely, to take all of Valerie on her tongue, to kiss every mound and flatland of her world of skin. Under the graceful curve of half-shut lid, Valerie's eyes glinted. Ha-ha, they said, amused, delighted. They gleamed under the sensuous lids until she kissed the eyes shut, and then they gleamed again as her mouth sank back to Valerie's.

They were turning about, half wrestling, half walking. Before them the mattress lay like a plain of snow. They were thrashing from their clothes, sweaters and socks flying. How skin dived into skin. How they fitted, silky, furry, sleek. This is what she should have done at Christmas instead of being rational and arguing and sulking. Yes. The right way, the right place to be. It was flower into flower, breasts making love rubbing against breasts. Diana of Ephesus. The secret meaning of that image besides the mother of wild things was a woman making love with a woman, a mound of living breasts nudging each other swift and squirming and hot and passionate as little piglets, little piglets at the tits. But the tits were hungry piglets themselves, both question and answer. Mouth on mouth. Eyes becoming one round huge eye staring into the other.

Gently Val drew back from her to unloop the rubber band that bound Leslie's club at the nape and her hair fanned out to mingle with Val's, red-amber and black-cat black. First one cheek and then the other joined, silken peonies. They rubbed noses, they had almost the same nose. "The same, the same," Val crooned. Upturned, delicate, a little flattened. Their mouths joined again. Sucking the juices from a peach. Honey and peach and peony, mound of belly heaped upon mound. Mons on mons gently rubbing, half ticklish, half torturous, all desire. Your flanks, Valerie, are petals of a yellow rose. Buttocks slung lower and softer than mine.

When she slid her hand between Valerie's thighs, first twitching the labia together, gathering, then slowly, gently parting, Valerie was already creamy and hot. But Valerie immediately slid away from her hand and went down on her. They hardly ever made love to each other at the same time. Usually Valerie made love to her first—because invariably she came more quickly—and then she made love to Val, taking as long as might be needed. Today she had expected to make love to Valerie first because she was the suitor, the beggar, the pilgrim.

When Valerie touched her, a bolt almost of pain went high into her. She could not bear for Valerie to tease or excite her long, touching gently with her fingers and then with her lips. "Please," she said. "Now." Valerie's tongue lapped at her, enfolded her, grew large and molten and seemed to penetrate her as her three crossed fingers actually did, plunging in. She could not move, she lay absolutely still while the wave rose, stood, crested and broke into pleasure. She came within a couple of minutes, her thighs squeezing Val's head.

They lay still a while resting, relaxing. She noticed that in their haste they had forgotten to shut the door. She hoped no one would come into the house. After she made love to Valerie, she would close it before they began again. She did not think Liz would come back to the house if she could avoid it, for Valerie's car was plainly visible from the hill where they were planting parsnips in the recently turned soil.

Then she rolled over and began to nuzzle Val's breasts, small and firm with large nipples like dark purple tulips. The tongue tip went back and forth, back and forth, round and round, while her fingers stroked toward the center. Then she paid court to the wide honeyed belly, kissing in wide circles, fingers trailing after, now barely touching, now the nails just scraping, now seizing fistfuls

128

of flesh. Then she parted Val's thighs to blow on her while Val giggled. Then she began again with the toes, making love individually to each brown pillow. When she came slowly back along the thighs, Val began to move her hips in slow circles, and she went straight to the small rosy nub of clit with her tongue and then, as Val rocked harder, entered with her hand. Her head was pillowed on the supple thigh. Val tasted of soap and perfume, of salt and cream, ammonia and marshland. Val moaned and thrashed and Leslie went on, now slower, now faster. She felt calm, patient, her hand steady and love pushing on her from inside like a roaring flood of sweet juicy wine.

Kitten Val. Stray kitten, sleek and pampered now. Val who had cried and cried. Who stared into the mirror with hungry eyes and turned away pouting, sulking. Beautiful Val who mistrusted her beauty and her self. Val came in from the cold kitchens of a divorced and remarried and married again mother, this child wrong name, wrong color, wrong sex, wrong father, wrong face. This child on speed at seventeen, straight again by nineteen. This baby born again crying at Leslie's breasts. Val the kitten, Val the tough-talking sour skeptic disbelieving in love. Who cried and cried against her until the pillow was soaked, until the tears ran down over her breasts like sweat, like salty broth, who shuddered with tears and clutched her hard enough to leave bruises and slowly, slowly, slowly uncoiled. Val who said, I'm frigid, so what, sex is a scam. Who believed in pain and cold and loneliness and relief that came in pillboxes.

The first time she had taken Val in her arms a look like a sneer had come over Val's face and Val had leaned back looking at her as if to say, What a fool you are. Then, eyes shut, mouth closed on a grimace, Val had permitted herself to be kissed. Who said, Go ahead, what do I care. But whose eyes had filled with the first tears between them when Leslie drew away immediately and stepped back, rebuffed. Who Leslie knew managed to run into her at carefully contrived accidental meetings for weeks. Leslie had known Val loved her long before Val had realized that, and that knowledge had given her patience. Patience flooded her now like gentle warm milk as she labored on with her mouth and hand to give pleasure, to open the knot that locked in her lover.

At last she felt the vein start to throb, the beat inside as Val contracted, and she moved faster, till Val came moaning. Slowly she ebbed, waited, stopped at last, her face resting against Val's wide-spread thigh.

Finally she got up and shut the door, realizing they would pay for privacy in cold air. Well, they could keep each other warm. Val reached out a languid arm and read her watch (new, fancy, on a plaited leather band) where she had placed it beside the mattress. If I could love the thought of time from her head.

They lay with mouths joined and bodies intertwined, legs and feet, playing between each other's thighs in hot stickiness, sometimes teasing, withdrawing, teasing with fingertip and pushing with joined fingers or fist, while occasional waves of orgasm swept over one or the other, never quite beginning and never quite leaving off, a strangely peaceful state on the edge of too much where she felt as if she were an extension of Val, could feel every motion, every sigh and shudder. By now there was no difference in responsiveness between them. Val was roused to full openness now, and she was satisfied and wearied to half relaxation. She imagined dying. What would ever end this? They could remain locked into each other until they peacefully, happily melted together. She was willing. She would fuse into Val. They would fade into each other. They would melt and dissolve smeary as nebulae. They would steam away to make a pattern on the ceiling like a double flower. She was willing.

But Val wriggled free suddenly and reached for her watch. "Oh, goddess, I'm late! Shit!" With a quick thrust she kicked out of bed and went scrambling for her clothes. "Brrr. It's freezing in here. Really, why do they have to live like pioneers? Do they think it's noble or something?" Five minutes later Val was dressed, through the door and gone.

Leslie lay on the bed prone, as if she had fallen from several feet up. The breath seemed to have pushed out of

130

her. She felt as if she were bleeding, bleeding from her breasts. She shivered suddenly with cold and covered herself with her unzipped sleeping bag. She lay in the chilling room until she heard loud voices, the voices of several children arguing, and saw it was dark outside. Then she went to wash herself. Wash the stickiness, the scent, the perfume of Valerie from her.

Supper was a big brown stew of root vegetables—carrots, parsnips, onions, potatoes, nutlike Jerusalem artichokes—with an oatmeal bread and wax beans from the freezer dressed with soy sauce and ginger.

"Mary, Yevette took my glass. My Evel Knievel glass!"

"Liz, I don't want that stuff, I don't!"

"So I've been going to the small farmers association, but it's hard to get through. Mary preps me on the pesticide stuff, but they don't want to listen yet."

"I have sixty tests to grade by Thursday. Yevette, I'll smack you. Give Rosellen back her Evil Knievel glass. Rosellen, quit carrying on. She's giving it back," Mary said.

"At my friend Tasha's house they just let the kids struggle."

"That ends up with the strongest running the show, the bully," Mary said. "So I referee."

"Would Bobbie really push the girls around?" Leslie asked.

"Leslie!" Liz giggled. "What assumptions. Yevette is the house bully. Bobbie, eat it! You do too like it."

"All the students care about now is grades and curves. Boy, is it depressing. Are they straight and conservative!" Mary wailed.

Afterward Leslie did the dishes in the deep old sink for what felt like a couple of hours. When the children had been routed into bed, the adults gathered again at the long rough kitchen table. Leslie said, "I'll chop some wood in the morning to make up for all I burned keeping the house warm today."

"That's super." Mary squinted curiously, her honest round face wavering between wanting to ask and wanting

131

to wait to be told. Finally she had to ask, "How did it go? Will she come back to you?"

"I don't know." She swilled the harsh red wine. She had found out nothing. They had hardly spoken. She was furious at herself.

"But what did she say?"

She said, Oh, oh, oh! "Nothing concrete."

"I'm sure Lena knows you're in town." Mary shook her head. "She'll pretend she doesn't. She likes to cool things out, always. Then she wins. You wear yourself out and she's still there waiting."

Mary was talking about political controversy, but Leslie winced. At least they were lovers again. The connection still held, strong. "You don't trust Lena."

"Never. It'd be a lot better to have a house for battered women in town. She could use one of her buildings. But she won't. She worries about property values like any other landlord. . . . I hate to say it, but we're expecting a guest tomorrow. For a couple of days. Husband fired at her and the kid with a shotgun—somehow managed to miss them but killed their dog. Don't bring it up unless she starts talking about it, okay?"

Another couple dropped in, Vicki and Meg. Like Liz and Mary they had children, they rented an old farmhouse although they raised only a few vegetables, they lived on marginal jobs and little money. Joints traveled around the table, they drank the coarse wine and gossiped. She tried to stir herself and ask about everyone she should be interested in. It had begun to rain again. The wind went around trying the doors and the windows, rattling the sills, while the rain drove against the western side of the house. She felt cut off from the women in the room. If she were living here alone, having lost her lover, they would be wary of her. She had seen it ten times. Couples. She would be lonely here without Valerie, she would be forced to find another lover just to be welcomed back into the community again. This was the only place she had ever found acceptance as a lesbian, yet the narrowness of the world they created here grated upon her for the first time. She preferred these women—Vicki and

Meg, Mary and Liz—to Lena's affluent professional propertied lesbians with their satin shirts and their stylishness and their sour wit. But she had lost her cohesion with them.

"Oh, Kathy. She's having an affair with a man," Mary said contemptuously.

"With a man?" Leslie repeated.

"Some big slob she met iceboat racing," Liz added.

"You win some, you lose some," Meg said.

"But I thought she had her head straightened out!" Mary's round face was pink with feeling. "Then to go back to it all. It's depressing! Then she keeps dragging him around with her. She wanted to bring him to Beta's party, imagine that!"

"But Beta's had men sometimes. That Ronny. That black guy Rich," Leslie said mildly. Suppose I told them my best friends in Detroit are a straight woman and a man.

"But they're gay. And Lynn will be there. Lynn was in love with Kathy," Liz said.

Meg said, "Kathy was just experimenting. Now she's done playing with us. Too bad if you happened to get hurt."

"Do you think she's really straight? I think she's fooling herself," Mary said. "She got scared. You watch. She'll keep switching. Getting involved with a woman and then running back to reassure herself with a man."

"She's a dangerous fool," Meg said shortly. "I don't want to deal with her any more. I can't stand women who hurt women and then go and cozy up to men. If she falls through a hole in the ice in her precious boat, it's no loss to us or any other woman."

How could she have spent two hours with Valerie and asked her nothing? How could Valerie have granted her only two hours? In the morning she would call. It was ridiculous to have to meet her clandestinely. They had lived together for three years; why did she have to sneak around and make assignations? I had her in my arms and I let her walk out the door. I took the quick comfort and let the important matter go. I've lost her. No, this afternoon, mine. Hold her. I feel so cold.

Phone conversations like five-minute vacuum aspirator abortions. "I can't."

"Why not?"

"Don't be difficult."

"But you're impossible! We have only a little time!"

She would hang up with her heart thudding and could not accept that the conversation was over. Too short, too violent, too mean. It was not what she meant to say. She paced and sometimes she called back and sometimes that worked and sometimes it was worse.

They sat in a coffee shop selected by Val on the sole criterion that nobody they knew would see them there, a greasy spoon in the factory district near the river, brick streets that trucks rumbled through. They sat in a booth and argued in voices pitched barely loud enough to hear each other.

"She's found out you're in town," Val said, hands laced over her coffee. "She plans to invite you to supper."

"I won't go."

"Why not? She'll be suspicious."

"She ought to be. I want you to come back with me."

"Leslie! Stop it. You know I can't!"

"Why can't you? You aren't doing anything in particular. You're going to school part time taking silly courses and you're working part time in Lena's store. What's wonderful about all that?"

"I like my classes. Really, Leslie, you're male dominated in your values. You believe all that nonsense, you think if you work hard and jump all those academic hurdles, they'll reward you just as if you were a man and give you a job and let you in their club?"

"But what are you learning? Just nonsense."

"Things *you* call nonsense. . . . You're so sure you're right, you don't even look at our work before you pronounce one of your judgments from on high! I don't think doing water colors by myself is higher or superior to de-

134

signing sets for our group. Maybe I work better with the content given. . . ."

Leslie had a moment of doubt. But no, it would just be the bunch of them running around like little girls in their mother's old white curtains declaiming poetry. Valerie just didn't want to buckle down to working alone.

" . . . I wish she didn't make me work in the boutique. It's boring and my feet hurt. But it's better than working at Bolt's thirty-seven and a half hours a week!"

"It wouldn't be better if you had to live on what she pays you. Val, come with me. We don't need much to live on. You can work part time in some store in Detroit."

"Detroit has terrible unemployment, and how can I leave in the middle of the quarter?"

"Val, I love you. I still love you."

"I love you too. That's why I don't feel guilty being with you. We were together before I ever met Lena, so it isn't like being unfaithful."

"It's not Lena you're unfaithful to, it's me. You can't love her."

"But I *do*."

"No! Come back with me. I'll do anything. I'll rent a car to move your stuff."

"Leslie, don't push me around again. I'm in school, I do love Lena. You went off to Detroit because you wanted to. Damn it, Leslie, you always want to turn me into a wife!"

That old accusation, from their last year together. After all, if Valerie would really buckle down to something, she would respect that. "I have to get a degree!"

"Now I'm getting a degree too. Even if you call it silly. At least Lena thinks about what's good for me as well as what she wants."

"A car, a suede coat, classes, a Navajo bracelet with real silver and real turquoise." She pointed to Val's wrist.

"Why shouldn't she give me things? You would if you could. Or would you? Maybe you'd insist we live on beans and rice forever?"

"I'm getting my degree. It'll only take two years more.

I swear it, two years. Then we'll have some money. Two years isn't forever, Val."

"Nothing is, I suppose. Why do you want to waste the time we have together arguing?"

"Because we needn't have only a couple of days. You can come with me. I don't want to leave you here."

"But there's no reason for me to be in Detroit. I don't like Detroit. I don't know anyone. The only reason I'd go is to be with you, and you'd be studying and working and at the dojo all the time, just the way it was here. What would I do with myself? My friends are here, I have a life here. I can't just walk out on Lena after all she's done for me."

"That's called a price tag. They know about that in boutiques."

They sat in the kitchen of Liz and Mary's farmhouse, keeping their voices down. "It is depressing here, it is! It's cold and it's cluttered and it's ugly. Everything lying around. It's a mess! They must like it that way, but I don't," Val said scornfully.

"But you used to be comfortable here. They have kids and kids make a mess. They farm, that's dirty. Food grows in dirt, you know."

"Don't take on that high superior moral tone with me! You don't like mess any better than I do. I remember you going on about dishes in the sink!"

"You're in the crowd now around Lena and Beta, the ones with money and snob appeal. We're all supposed to be sisters, but they have more money and more control and more options, and they decide things to suit themselves."

"You like to be uncomfortable! You think that's superior. But it isn't. It's just uncomfortable!"

They could not use the old parlor because Pattie (the woman from Chicago who had a black eye and a bandaged-up hand) was in there with her little boy Dick working jigsaw puzzles. Pattie was nervous of being around lesbians anyhow, and had thawed only a little toward them. Val and Leslie had to creep upstairs, where

136

the stove was lit only at morning and night and the air was heavy with cold.

This time she made love to Val first, in Mary and Liz's bed. After Val had come and began to make love to her she could not respond. When Val touched her she was dry; it almost hurt to be touched. Gently Val's mouth wet her, but instead of becoming excited she began to cry in hard racking sobs. She stopped and took control of herself. Sitting up on the high pine bed, she seized Val by the shoulders. "I can't, I can't! I don't want to feel it if we can't be together."

Val put her hands on either side of Leslie's face, giving her an exasperated smile. "Leslie, why make things difficult? It was so lovely Monday and yesterday, so lovely. You're the most wonderful lover, it's just beautiful to be with you. Why can't it be like that? We can see each other when you have a vacation. It doesn't have to be over. Why do you want to be so demanding and absolute?"

"Because it hurts."

"You make it hurt, silly. Go back to school and you'll be super busy with classes and your work and your Great God George and your karate and your discipline, and you won't think of me once a week. Come on, we could easily go on seeing each other when we can, and things could work out fine for us! You say it'll only be two years."

"I can't wait." She felt as if she were choking, as if her vocal cords were swelling in her throat and choking her, swelling with tears and the words she could not find to say.

ten

"Even if you didn't have a good time in Grand Rapids, I'm glad you're back early. Besides, whoever heard of anyone having a good time in Grand Rapids? It's a contradiction." Honor paused in front of the high fireplace. "Can we have a fire?"

"We don't need one, for a change." Then seeing Honor's drooping neck, arc of disappointment, she added, "Oh, why not? I think I remember how to open the flue. I've seen George do it twenty times." Making a fire was one of the few tasks at which she had no practice in George's house, because he fancied himself a great fire layer. It was a ritual with him and the kids. Exactly so much paper, so much kindling, three logs in a geometric arrangement carried out with earnestness and frowns of concentration. Davey dragging a log by its end across the Danish shag rug.

She and Honor made a messy fire but it burned. The fire was unnecessary because for a change the weather was good. Her last day in Grand Rapids rain had fallen, and rain had shrouded the bus on her return. But today, Friday, it was high spring. Spring came to Michigan suddenly, violent and languorous at once. The air was so soft she melted into it.

George had not joined Sue at her parents', making Sue resentful. The plumbers had come but they had not finished. Now George was off with Sue and children on a four-day Puerto Rican jaunt supposed to restore harmony, and Leslie was house sitting and plumber watching. That gave her George's car, after she took them to Metropolitan Airport. When the plumbers finished in late afternoon she drove to Honor's and brought the girl back to keep her company while she cleaned up after the plumbers and tested the hot water.

Now she poured Honor a little Tío Pepe in a wineglass as they sat contemplating their fire. Honor wore an apple green dress down to the floor with a high stand-up collar and a V-neck, and she looked particularly rosy. But then she was particularly happy. Even visiting this house was a treat. Bernie had traded the early part of the week with another waiter who was also a student and wanted to go home to Port Huron for spring vacation. Bernie worked lunches all week and suppers too in exchange for Friday and Saturday off.

First they would all eat at the Szechwan restaurant Bernie had found. Then Bernie and Honor were going to a ballet; the American Ballet Theater was in town, and they had tickets. They had not got a ticket for Leslie because she had not imagined returning early. Tomorrow Bernie wanted to visit his old home.

"Something odd happened while you were gone," Honor said, looking less happy. "Monday night I went to rehearsals with Cam. They're doing Pinter's *The Caretaker*. I suppose I wanted to flirt with Paul a bit. I miss that. Cam doesn't have a part—she's very disappointed—so we just stood around. Bernie came over too. Then Paul did something ugly. I was walking past him and he reached out and pinched my buttock, very hard. It wasn't even sensual. It hurt and I cried out. Then he laughed and asked me if anything was wrong. I asked Cam to leave. We had her car. Bernie didn't know what had happened and I didn't want to explain with Paul standing there gloating because he'd humiliated me. So we left and Bernie hung around."

"His pinching you isn't odd, just nasty. What do you want from him, Honorée?"

"Nothing. I hate him. He's a pig. But Bernie told me

139

Wednesday that Paul had . . . propositioned him that night after rehearsal."

"I don't suppose Bernie was interested."

"Do you believe it? I mean, why would Paul do that? He's ridiculously heterosexual. Staring at my breasts, pinching my behind, always leering. Cam warned me he's a womanizer. . . . Why would he suddenly switch?"

"Sex is sex to lots of people. He wanted someone and thought Bernie was available. Doesn't even mean he's interested in Bernie. Because a person doesn't act out same-sex attractions doesn't mean they don't exist. Everyone of us had a mother, for instance—"

"But Bernar' is always seeing homosexuality every place, you know how he is! He could have . . . misinterpreted Paul."

"People don't make those kinds of mistakes. I've been stupid and not seen when people were after me. They were too subtle or I was preoccupied. But I never thought somebody was coming on when they weren't, whatever they might say afterward."

"I can't believe Paul would be interested in another man. He's just too much of a letch about women." Honor fidgeted with her hair ends.

"Why does his wanting to fuck Bernie mean he wouldn't like to get his paws on you? What does it matter anyhow? Nothing happened, right?"

"Bernar' could be wrong about Paul."

"Why does it matter so much? Does this turn you off? Or make Paul's interest in you less exciting?"

"Here comes Bernie, that's his car." The high anguished shriek it made whenever asked to negotiate a corner, however slowly. "But you ask Cam if she's ever heard of Paul being interested in men before. . . . I can't ask her myself because I'd have to explain. But you can easily ask her."

The purple Mustang rattled up the drive, something loose dragging beneath it, perhaps the muffler; and as it clanked along it laid down a gray wake of fumes that slowly rolled through the hedge bordering the drive onto the neighbor's lawn.

Bernie sat down between them on the long couch that had recently appeared in the livingroom—very low and long and excessively soft so that Leslie sank in it as if into a feather bath—covered with a Chinesey print of chrysanthemums in gold and green. He poured himself a generous glass of sherry and began imitating the unseen neighbors behind the hedge.

"Do you smell that, Ralph? What is that?"

Ralph, coughing. "What is it, Ida? Is something on fire?"

"Do you suppose they're having a barbecue?"

"On their front lawn? I hope they're not that type."

"Ralph, do you suppose their house could be on fire?"

"If it is, I suppose we'll hear about it soon enough." Coughing. "Perhaps we'd better go inside."

"Honorée," he added in his own voice immediately, "you look absolutely beautiful."

"So do you, actually." Honor laughed. "You're competing unfairly."

"Do you like this? I stole it especially for the occasion." The shirt was a dark silky-looking blue. He brought out his makings and started to roll a joint until Leslie stopped him.

"Don't waste your own. I know where it is here." She got George's downstairs stash from the kitchen, where it was hidden in a large jar whose label claimed it held oregano, the pizza spice, from Kroger's.

"This is lovely." Bernie kicked off his sneakers and settled far down on his spine. "The fire is silly but pretty, the sherry nice, the company extraordinary, the setting is bourgeois cozy. I'll take it all, wrapped up."

"George's sherry, George's dope, George's sofa, George's fireplace, George's car, George's house. Hmmm. . . ." Honor rubbed her nose. "I'm curiouser and curiouser and curiouser about George. Cam is always alluding to him as if to some act of God. Does he really have an existence in the flesh, or is he a fictional person like a corporation?"

"A bit of both." Leslie surprised herself with a cough of embarrassment, half giggle, half disclaimer. She felt

141

guilty sitting on George's brand new couch discussing him. She also had a moment's uneasy fantasy that a tape recorder hidden in the down would record every word of her disloyalty. She shared the joint with Bernie.

"Puerto Rico, adiós. Then the plane describes a graceful parabola and falls gently into the sea. Blub blub. Adiós a George y mujer y niños. Under the waves all. And we just quietly move in. Think how exceedingly comfy we could be here together, we three," Bernie crooned.

"Until the first mortgage payment is due."

"Les, be good. Right now, this moment, we live here," Bernie coaxed.

"Yes, Leslie, you're suffering pangs of reality. We have quite enough of that every day. This is vacation. They've left us this playpen. Bernar', pour us both some more delicious sherry."

"Be careful, Honorée. Don't drink it too fast."

"Leslie! I told you to relax. I'd think it was gross to get sloppy! But I think I could drink you under the table."

Bernie obediently poured more sherry into both their glasses and his own, standing empty. Then he put out the roach's tail in the ashtray, commenting, "They don't go in for the quality imported stuff. This is good old Toledo Green, a little moldy from efforts to jack up the kick." He put an arm around each of them and his feet up on the coffee table beside the Tío Pepe. "Ah, satisfaction. A jug of wine, a stash of dope, and the two of you beside me in civilization! I could think of a lot more to ask for, actually, but this does fine for a basic set-up. We'd have to redo the place, of course. The taste is a little wobbly. This couch, for instance. You couldn't do much but cuddle on it. If you tried to make love, you'd suffocate in the stuffing, you'd lose your partner and end up making it with a dead goose."

"Yes, let's throw all this failed art out in the back yard and do something interesting with the space." Honor stared up into the gloomy rafters. "A trapeze, perhaps. Myself, I actually like this couch. I'll lie on it and eat

142

chocolates when I've grown weary of the trapeze—Is there anything to nibble on?"

"Don't spoil your appetite for supper. We want to try lots and lots of dishes," Leslie said.

"I have one Mama, Leslie. When I run away from home to join the circus of the two of you, I don't want to be mothered at all. I'll wear spangles and décolleté as low as I want and eat chocolates by the pound and hang from my heels and have a pet monkey that pees on the furniture!"

"Leslie will be the strongwoman and also the knife thrower."

"Well, she can't throw them at me!" Honor said.

"She can throw them at me. I know she wouldn't miss, and if she did, she'd feel so very bad it would be quite worth it losing a finger or an ear. . . . I of course am the sword swallower. The magician. The famous disappearing man. We must all take several parts in a small traveling circus. We'll ride bareback on the circus ponies round and round. We'll do trapeze tricks and catch each other death defyingly as with no nets at all we fling ourselves through giddy space. And Leslie will tame the lions—which will consist of me in a mangy fur suit growling and snarling. She may lay her head in the lion's mouth. Thus giving head I stand, the perfect circus lion. Then Honorée is shot from a cannon and I am the ringmaster and I saw Honorée in two—"

"Oh, no! I'm not to be had so cheaply, at half price! I'm going to dance on a horse's back in ballet slippers and orchid tutu."

"I like those Chinese acrobats who make human pyramids," Leslie said. "We coud paint me with spots and I'll be the leopard lady. I can growl too." She produced a sample.

"But can you purr?" Bernie asked.

"I can. Listen." Honor did, from deep in her chest.

She leaned away from Bernie's encircling arm to stare at them. They both looked radiant. Honor's hair the color of orange pekoe tea shone in the firelight. The inner curve of a breast came and went in the V-neck. Her arms

143

looked plump and rosy, even the elbows gracefully rounded, dimpled. Her long throat arched back and her mouth opened a little as she rolled the wine on her tongue. Bernie smiled in profile into the heart of the fire. The curve of his mouth was long and delicious. His curly hair caught the firelight. He looked lean and wound as a balanced spring. She had a startling urge to make love to both of them.

She sipped her wine nervously. The impulse was not real. No, she never wanted to make love to more than one person, and certainly not to both of them. In reality it would be complicated and messy. It would be like one of those construction projects her brothers used to hate to get for Christmas. A flat box with a brightly colored space platform or rocket launcher depicted on the cover, with no resemblance to anything inside. A bunch of pieces and directions. Insert Flap B in Slot D. Glue inside edges. Do not glue Flap A–2 to Flap A–3. Then draw inner tabs through outer ratchets along side F. No, she could never desire Bernie, not for an instant. It was preposterous.

They looked beautiful beside her and she did itch to touch them gently. It was the wine and the dope together before supper. It was sexual overflow from what had and had not happened with Valerie. It was the result of not having done karate all week. She had been drinking too much. It was pure silliness.

"I suppose there are five or six bathrooms in this mansion. What I need is only one, but that one rather soon." Honor rose and swept her gown over her arm. "Where would I find it?"

"There's a lavatory off the kitchen, just to the left."

With his free hand Bernie sipped his wine. Then his arm tightened on her shoulder. He gave a little tug drawing her nearer. "What happened?" he asked, turning to look hard at her.

"It's over. I've lost her."

His hand dug into her upper arm and he stared into her face. "Are you sure? You did see her?"

She nodded. "Yes on both counts."

"If she's hostile, that doesn't mean she'll stay so."

144

"She wasn't. Except when I tried to push her. She was ready to fit me into her schedule. Ready to make love. At times that wouldn't annoy her keeper. Who's keeping her in Toyotas and school and new clothes."

"That's stinking." He took her face in both hands. "I can't tell how bad it is. You say it . . . numbly."

"I cried for two days. I am numb. I can't tell what I feel."

The way he held her was odd. It was not gentle. It was not the way he always touched them, very airily. She realized he wanted to take hold of her, the energy was something held back. She was not frightened, blinking at him. She felt a little smile tugging at her lips. "I'll let you know tomorrow how I am after I find it out tonight. It's good for me to be alone."

"Are you sure?"

She was not frightened because she wanted to explain to him that it was silliness. It came from drinking sherry on an empty stomach and smoking dope and sitting in front of the fire on a too soft sofa on the first evening of balmy warm spring. The air was soft. The wine melted them to taffy. "I'll survive."

Honor called from the kitchen. "I found some cookies. Either we go eat now, or I'm going to have some. I'm starving!"

They used Bernie's car. "But tomorrow we'll take George's," Leslie promised.

"Tomorrow!" Bernie sang out. "I'm edgy about it. Really, you must promise not to be disappointed. There's nothing to see but scummy water and ugly houses and for thrills an occasional junkyard. You have to promise not to expect anything."

"Oh, but I'll be tickled to be traveling in George's brand new Cordoba with an FM radio. We can pretend we're on a real trip." Honor was bubbling again.

In the back seat Leslie felt guilty. They did not try hard enough to take Honor out of her house. They did not insist enough. The girl was overwhelmingly excited by a trip to a house in a subrub with a real fireplace, a visit to what would doubtless be an ordinary Chinese restaurant, the prospect of a Saturday morning drive in a new car out to a rural slum thirty miles south. They did not try hard enough. Honor was hungry for experience, yet they came to see her out of their lives without attempting to let her into theirs, without trying to free her. Leslie promised she would do better. She would begin immediately and seriously to free Honor from her mother's excessive protection. She would not take advantage of the situation for any gain to herself. She would not think of herself as the world that Honor needed to explore. She would not confuse her attraction to Honor with anything necessarily liberating. If after Honor was freer in her choices she chose Leslie, that might happen, it might well happen. She would be a good friend to another woman, and that woman would grow stronger.

Sometimes she thought Honor enjoyed lying to Mama, that it became an end in itself. She drove George's Cordoba to the Rogers' house first thing Saturday morning because Honor was supposed to be spending the day with her only, rather than with her and Bernie, because as Honor explained, Mama knew she had gone to the ballet with Bernie the night before and had insisted upon reacting to the event as if it were practically a date. Therefore on Saturday morning Honor decided it would be necessary to de-emphasize Bernie. Although it made more sense geographically to pick up Bernie first, she drove to Honor's without him.

When she rapped on the door, however, Mrs. Rogers let her in and Honor was nowhere visible. "Do have a cup of coffee," Mama said, smiling faintly.

"Er . . . Honor isn't ready yet?"

"Honor forgot I had made a doctor's appointment for her this morning for a check-up. Her father has taken her."

"Oh. Will she be back soon?"

"I don't know how she happened to forget. Wishful thinking, no doubt. Are you sure you won't have some coffee?"

"Perhaps I should come back later." Bernie was going

to be crushed with disappointment. Why hadn't Honor called?

"I did want to speak to you for a moment. If you have the time?" A gentle irony tinged Mama's voice. She had a fine speaking voice actually, low, musical, but as capable as Honor's of taking on a cutting edge. Baby blue eyes fixed on her, waiting.

Leslie sat on the edge of a chair. She accepted coffee and waited, wondering where Cam was. Beyond an occasional rattle and clank of chains from the basement and a low mutter of growling, she heard no other sounds of living beings in the house. Dead, all dead. Mama had poisoned them all with her coffee. They lay each in their bedrooms in the awkward postures of strychnine seizure. Within seconds she too would be lying on the carpet turning blue and lashing her spine like a rattlesnake until she gave a final spasm and lay still. Mama would plant them all in the back yard in the sorry bulb bed that ran against the western side of the slot between neighboring slots, back to the tool and die shop. She would die with Valerie's name on her lips and be buried between Honor and Cam.

"I expect you think I'm a bit overprotective with my daughter?" Mama did not go on but waited and finally outwaited her.

"Well, you know, er . . ."

"That I'm overprotective?" Again she waited, smiling faintly. Her blonded hair was less curly this morning and her scalp shone pink where the morning sun turned her hair to insubstantial fluff. She sat well on the sagging couch, braced against the sag. Her shoulders did not give at all. She was a well-built woman still, wearing one of those cotton housedresses of the sort her mother used to wear. Middle-aged swaddling clothes. This one still had some crispness, pleasant blue and white flowers that reminded her a little of the chrysanthemums on George's new couch.

"Well, er, I suppose it's a question of what you're protecting her from, in a way, you know. Er, ah, I mean, some things we all want . . . her to be protected from . . . but, then, again . . ."

"What kind of things?"

"Lightning and grizzly bears, rapists, that kind of . . . But she has to meet people and learn to act independently too and take her place . . ." She could not quite croak out "in society" or "in the world"; the clichés simply dissolved in her mouth to a solid wad of glue and she was stuck.

"Yes, I know you do think I'm overprotective. But what you don't understand is that Honor is more delicate than she appears." Mama's eyes grew large and watery with sadness. Her lips parted slightly and she looked earnestly into Leslie's eyes. Her head was tilted to one side, her plump hands caught each other in her lap.

Would she be surprised if I kissed her? Actually the problem was that she was responding to Mama as a woman rather than as the prop, Honor's mother. That was inappropriate both from Honor's point of view and Mama's. But she could not fend off a pang of empathy for the woman there, married to a preoccupied gray ghost, with one daughter off in Ohio being privately and distantly unhappy, Cam about to leave home as soon as she could finance it, and the swan's-neck daughter stealthily preparing to snip the threads of coercion. Mama was still attractive, although she put no effort into it. All the effort, the energy, the fantasy were sucked from her own life into Honor. What did Mama think of what she had settled for? Was it fun to be a floor supervisor for the phone company? Did she worry about being laid off? What would she do after Honor too fled the house? Did Mama look forward to a pension? Did she ever lie in bed and want to die rather than to get out of bed one more day?

"Honor had rheumatic fever when she was eight, you see, and it left her with a weak heart. She may appear robust, she may appear normal, but she's not. She has to avoid violent exercise and too violent emotional upheavals. You know she doesn't take part in the more demanding parts of physical education at school? She's excused for medical reasons. Because of her heart. I imagine in fact you didn't know. Honor doesn't like to talk about it. I think she's secretly ashamed of not being normal, of having to take care of herself in a way that few children her age must. But it requires a certain amount of restraint on the part of everyone around her. Not to allow her to overdo. Not to overstimulate her. I think yesterday was very exciting for Honor, and no one is happier than I when I see stars in her eyes. But when she wanted to skip her doctor's appointment this morning to go running around some more, I had to put my foot down. You must agree to help me protect her also, to be a true friend to Honor. Because her heart could give way. She's not able to do all those things a normal teenager could."

"I don't believe a word she said," she told Bernie. "I'm going to ask Honor."

"But if it's true, she might be furious."

"If it's true, I want to know. And I want to know what doctors she's seen and what their opinions are and what can be done about it. I can't believe she has to go through life with a label invalid around her neck."

"It is a bit pat. Mama reveals all. Fucks up my day as if incidentally."

She was driving and Bernie was navigating. An early overcast had moved off east and the day was warm, suddenly, by eleven. "It must be seventy!"

"Why couldn't she come? But thank you anyhow for carrying me on my sentimental journey."

They were driving down West Jefferson, the old bricks showing through the asphalt. The river was always beyond the factories, beyond the rotting empty green grounds of deserted Fort Wayne, beyond the mills of Great Lakes Steel. On their right ran a row of old bars, unbroken fringe to the decaying ethnic neighborhoods beyond. They were headed downriver. "Why am I always thinking that we're playing at being adults? I just had the feeling vividly. That here we are in George's car, playing. Is it because we waited so long to grow up that we don't feel grown ever?" she asked him.

"To be grown up in America, it's to buy a car like this

one. The poor never grow up. George is Daddy. Besides, you and I will never be Daddy or Mommy, so how can we grow up anyhow? What do you want to be when you grow up, my son? I want to be an old fag, Daddy."

"Is that why I always think that I'm playing whenever I find myself feeling good? Because the way I feel good I'm not supposed to be feeling? Right now we look like we're supposed to. A couple out on a Saturday drive," Leslie said.

"But we aren't doing it right. We ought to be on I-Seventy-five in this car, not clumping along between the mills and the bars. It makes me think of my old man, that's why I dig it. We're sneaking south."

"Besides, we won't be poor. We're both wiggling upward, Bernie, we've shed our class. We've flayed ourselves bare and plastered over our bleeding flesh with accents and books and classes and everything we weren't and wanted to be."

"Do you like yourself?" He had a southeastern Michigan map open on the lap of his jeans. He had shrugged off his jacket and rolled up the sleeves of his shirt. One arm rode on the rolled-down window, the other on the back of the seat.

"I guess not. Not yet. I'm an unfinished project and I show too many signs of haste and wretched planning." She laughed shortly, more of a cough.

"How come you didn't go home this vacation? It can't be more than an hour or two further on the bus from Grand Rapids to Ludington."

"I'm disowned." She laughed, again with no mirth. "Sounds melodramatic, like disinherited. You'll never see a dime from my purse again, that is if I ever have one."

"Ah. They wouldn't join the supportive parents of gays associated."

She snorted. "Yeah, that did it."

"Why did you tell them?"

"Don't you have to finally? I mean, sometime? It made me feel so . . . weird when I came home. All the questions about boyfriends and when are you going to get married and don't you want to meet a nice boy. I wanted my mother to understand."

"So one Christmas morning you said, Guess what?" He made a gesture of opening a raincoat to expose himself.

"Actually I brought Val home with me for Thanksgiving. After all, I was twenty-one. We'd been together for two years. Yeah, I had a fantasy. I wanted something from my mother, some sign, some approval." She took her hand off the wheel to scratch her head roughly. "I can't go home now. For real. They won't have me. You wouldn't think it would bother me, but it kind of does. People murder and their family sticks by them. It makes me mad, really."

"It makes you feel rotten, really, you goose."

"Should I pretend it doesn't?"

"To me, no. Orphans together."

"I wanted to tell my mother. I wanted her blessing. I wanted to say to her, Look, here's Valerie. I love her and I live with her, see?" She made a face so fierce it stretched her cheek muscles. "To hell with all that. It stinks. I'm a theoretical lesbian nowadays. The rest of my life is just as unreal to them—grad school, George, quantitative history."

"My home fell apart. It started when Ann-Marie died. Then my mother. She was still young, she never got fat like other mothers. She was thin as a girl. People would think she was our sister. She had TB on and off but she died from breast cancer. She didn't even know she had anything wrong. She had so much trouble with her lungs, the other thing came out of the blue. The doctor who found the lump wasn't even that kind of doctor, he hit it by accident when she came in for the TB test. They said she had cancer, she went in the hospital and they cut her breast off. She came home and she cried a lot, she was so embarrassed, and then they took her back in. They said it was all through her body. She died in the hospital."

"But your father, wasn't he still alive? Had he left you?"

"No. He was the quiet kind of alcoholic who goes along for years and once in a while he has a stupid acci-

151

dent and gets fired, but mostly he manages. He wasn't a noisy drunk, he didn't beat anybody up. He was just quietly drunk almost all the time. He liked to be oblivious, that was how he coped. But he couldn't cope with four kids. The school started complaining because we were missing a lot and the social workers descended like flies. We were managing. I mean, we were used to managing. We made our own meals. We used to put a lot of jam in the oatmeal and cook it up that way for breakfast—two cups water, one cup oatmeal and one cup jam. We had hot dogs and TV dinners and fish sticks. Gourmet cooks we weren't, Les." He put his hand on her knee, demanding her attention. "We'd wash the silverware and put it all in a pile on the table in the middle and everybody'd take what they wanted. We each got one sheet to roll up in. Things like that bothered the social worker pests. That we didn't make the beds. Everybody got a sheet and a blanket and we slept in our rolls. We were into cowboys. We called it our bedroll. Even the little kids could manage to roll up their bedroll and unroll it at night."

They were pursuing Jefferson along the river in Wyandotte, past the North Works of old Wyandotte Chemical (now BASF), past the trim rows of the turn of the century houses, dark-stained brick-red, past the new condominiums on the river, past the South Works, where the air began to be painted with stench, where the old houses were wooden and run down and closer together, downriver. They rolled up the windows. Politely she pried his hand off her knee. "That's the foot that works the accelerator, Bernie."

"See, we took care of the old man, instead of him taking care of us. We were dirty and shabby but we got ourselves fed and dressed and pretty much we managed to attend school. When we got colds or flu, we took care of each other. Every night we made some kind of supper and in the morning breakfast, and we ate everything on the floor by the TV set. Every few days when we ran out of plates we did the dishes. Once a week we'd put all the garbage out. The neighbors were bugged by us too. . . . I think basically all the adults around were freaked out that we were obviously managing. I think they really hated that we didn't need them. It made us outlaws."

They had passed Grosse Isle, where the comfortable houses stared back at the industrial shore, and he was getting more and more excited. He ran the window down again and leaned out. A flat landscape. Between the road and the river a maze of small waterways ran, some called brooks, some, rivers, some called simply drains. Nothing was elegant here. The houses were plain, the marinas places where working-class families kept a small motorboat. Occasional farms appeared, but the factories and mills dominated the landscape still, the twin stacks of the Enrico Fermi Nuclear Power Plant sticking up over the marshes to the south like blind spires of a warped cathedral. She realized that the river had given way to the other lake, Erie. Occasionally, crossing one of the railroads that carved up the flatlands, she caught a glimpse of it looking soft and blue under the balmy sky, although she knew it was dead as a beaker of sulphuric acid. It had been killed before she was born, when her own lake, Michigan, had only been beginning to die.

"Okay! Yes. Turn here!" He sat forward, his hands spread white-knuckled on the dashboard. "I left here a ratty desperate punk. Raw, stupid, illiterate. Right again. There."

Past wooden houses, a stream where men were fishing with poles and square nets. "For catching suckers. Trashy fish that feed along the bottom." He smiled at her and she smiled back. "Why am I so happy?" he asked her.

"Happiness is basically irrational."

"Is unhappiness irrational too?"

"No!" She laughed.

"I do think you believe that. That misery is natural."

"They separated you? Your family?"

"Into foster homes. At first I was with my little brother Mike. After I got into trouble, we were never together again. I wasn't allowed to see him."

"Do you know where they are? Do you ever see them?" They were bouncing along a dirt washboard road now.

"I have a fantasy of tracking them all down. Finding

them. Collecting them. I was never back here till now. Somehow I want to be more . . . accomplished, successful. I want to show up in a car like this one, money in my pocket. Then I'll collect them all and we'll live together. Sure, it's pure bullshit fantasy. Probably we'd have nothing to say to each other. But, Les, the fantasy is strong." He leaned forward, grabbing her arm. "Park! Park here. Come on. We have to get out. We have to go on foot."

Obediently she found a fairly dry clay patch where she could get off the road without getting into the wetter-looking clay slough beyond. She locked the car and tied her workshirt around her waist. The sun was warm on her body through the Gertrude Stein tee shirt. The air felt thick and damp. It was obviously chemical, but after the city it had an odor of something natural—green and growing things, waters in which something lived. Sniffing, looking sharply ahead, Bernie strode back and forth impatiently. Then he darted ahead down a path along a stream edge that seemed raised a little between the marsh and the stream itself. It ran too straight to be natural. At some point the drain had been dredged and straightened and the banks heaped up. The only obstacles they came to were smaller creeks feeding in, which they had to leap across, unless there was a board for a bridge someone had left there. Sometimes she followed Bernie's thin impatient back across a half-rotted plank. Sometimes he jumped the creek and plunged on without looking to see if she followed.

As they came out on a gravel road, Bernie turned right, trotting. She caught up and they jogged side by side. They crossed a small bridge and he struck off again through a woody field. How green it was. In spite of the rusty garbage, the aluminum beer cans, the broken glass that underlay the weeds, how green it was. Everything was leafed out already. She was trotting behind him in a delirium at running outside, movement in the free air, at being among green and wet and growing creatures. A debased landscape but still a living one. Once or twice she leapt high in the air behind him.

It was flat country. Winding waterways, small houses,

little flat bridges, train tracks, junkyards and dusty stores, aging gas stations where they worked on aging trucks, reeds and cattails, marshy mazes, scum and bubbles, oaks and poplars. Along the road's edge viburnum was blooming in flat white sprays. Not like her own lakeshore, near Ludington. That was all hill and dune, scrub pine and blueberry. There no factories stood, but the busy tourists came in the summer and left the boarded-up motels and restaurants and miniature golf and petting farms by the side of the road empty and stark the rest of the year. Yet something was familiar. Rivers flowing to a lake you could not see across, whose storms were a fact of life. The sense of being marginal places, the margin of an inland sea, the margin of the economy where unemployment was normal.

He stopped so suddenly as they came out of the weeds on a broken stretch of sidewalk bordering a narrow asphalt road that she would have run full tilt into him if her reflexes had been duller. "It's gone," he said.

Ahead of them was a burned-out bowling alley. KEEP OUT, the signs said. The fire had gutted it some time ago, a year, two years. The scorched wood was weathering.

"I can't believe it. That was my house. I lived there."

"In the bowling alley?"

"There wasn't any bowling alley! There was a house. A gray house all stuck together. It looked like a farmhouse even if it wasn't, all those sheds added on. A lean-to on one side, a room stuck on the back. Then came the Framing's house, then us, then Stosenko's. They're all gone."

"Riverview Family Bowling," she read off what remained of the facade. "Well, they sure had a real fire."

"Was it real? Probably they went broke in this godforsaken shithole and set it on fire for the insurance." He clutched himself across his chest, standing first on one foot and then on the other.

"You wanted terribly to see the house?"

"But it's not here. Maybe it never was." He turned and grasped her by the upper arms. "Maybe I made it all up. I've lied so much. You know how much I lie. How can I tell any more? Maybe I come from San Diego and I don't remember. Maybe my mother didn't die and I don't

155

remember. Maybe she's alive in New Jersey. Maybe I'm the one who's dead."

She let him shake her for a moment. Then she unpeeled his hands and held them together steadily, meeting his gaze and trying to calm him. "It was torn down. The bowling alley is probably a few years old. You haven't been here for six, seven years, right?"

He leaned on her. "But it never occurred to me it wouldn't be here. There's nothing, not even a foundation. Even the alder tree, the poplar. There aren't even the trees. Not the bushes, the ground, nothing."

"Let's go. Other things will be here. Other things you remember. Come on, show me around. Keep walking." She pried him along, dragging him away from the wreck of RIVERVIEW FAMILY BOWLING.

He did not speak till they had passed several small ramshackle houses, one with a boat a man was caulking on a Saturday late morning. "You're right, there's got to be something." He stopped in front of a vacant lot. In the yard to the right a big brown dog barked at them, straining at a chain pegged in the ground. To the left stood a grocery whose windows were clogged with old soft drink advertisements and the posters from last year's church bazaars and rummage sales. Each building was surrounded by a little wooden and cement block dike. Flooding? "Yes, this way." Again he was off, bolting like a rabbit for cover into the thickets, on a path that led kitty-corner between the house and the store and disappeared into scrubby growth.

They came out of the bushes on a rickety dock. Just off it a rowboat had sunk. One still floating was padlocked by a rusty chain to a corner of the dock. "Look! This is still here. Wait."

He knelt and with his pocketknife started working on the padlock. Nervously she looked around but saw no one. The dog had stopped barking, out of sight back on the road. She could hear the distant whine of traffic on the highway and the mew of gulls going over.

"I'm sure you can find a can to bail with," he said without looking up.

156

She had plenty of choice on the shore. When she brought a paint can back, he had the locks off and he was already in the rowboat fitting the oars into the oarlocks. "Take off your shoes and bring mine with you as you climb in."

His sneakers were on the dock. Giving him the paint can, she sat down on the edge of the wobbly dock and took off her own boots, handed them over too, and then stepped with a great lurch down into the boat. "Isn't this technically piracy?"

"When they catch us, they can hang us. It'll take them a while to float the sister ship to this one." He pointed over the bow to the sunken boat. "We don't have to bring it back here. It belongs to the guy who owns the grocery store. I'm sure it's the same jerk. What other loser would buy a sink like that? I hate him. He wouldn't give us credit. He was a shit. He called us drunken Canucks behind our backs and charged ten cents more on everything. I'm glad to swipe his boat. . . . He used to shoot birds in the marsh. Ducks, I guess. We used to always be scared he would shoot us too. When we were out on the water and we saw him, we used to hide. Mostly it was a game. I don't remember him ever actually taking a shot at us. But he was the enemy."

"See, now it's real to you." She would never steal a rowboat, but she could not help enjoying enormously that he did, involving her without choice. She worked so hard to be respectable, to get the scholarship, to get the assistantship, to get the fellowship, to get and keep the job, it was a relief to be loosed into chaos and mischief.

"Ah, Les, I could make him up too. But, yeah, I'm happy again. Out here things have to be the way they were. Nothing that couldn't thrive in pure pollution was alive when I was a kid, so it's not like I would come back and posture and say, Jesus, look at them bottles and cans, wow, what ecological destruction. This place has been a big garbage can for sixty years."

She sat in the bow being ferried, and that felt odd. "Don't you want me to row? Come on, let me. Then you can look around better."

"I want to row first. I'll let you, don't worry. You have to keep up the bailing, this thing leaks like crazy and it wouldn't be fun to sink. The bottom here is muck. I mean you really sink in it. We had sicknesses all the time, probably from hanging around on the water so much. It's like swimming in shit. So bail! I'll let you have your turn, never fear, because I'll get tired. I'm not in such wonderful shape as you are and I'm bound to feel this unusually healthy exercise and start groaning and complaining. Then you can take over, soon enough, soon enough, my dear, and then you can row until you give out, probably never, but now bail away. . . . Didn't I let you drive this morning? Just because it was your boss's car. Old George. I wonder about him. Are you sure he never tried to ball you? . . . I don't believe in the altruistic motives of men, none of us have any. . . . We're almost into the maze. I love this area, a watery jungle. I love it later in the year when the reeds grow up and hide you. All mazy and lost, streams and backwaters of the Huron. We'll probably get lost. Why not? Why shouldn't we lose ourselves? . . . I stole a book once called *The Floating World* from the pad of a university type who picked me up for sex. It was about Japanese society in the eighteenth century, and I was terribly disappointed. All painters and prostitutes and nothing at all to do with water and boats. . . . This is my floating world. Can you imagine how weird it is out here when the wind blows hard and the sky and water are iron gray and everything shooshes and moans? . . . Or when the fog comes in thick and yellow, warm almost, muffling everything, magnifying sounds. . . . It's hot out here. I think I'll take off my shirt."

She reclined in the bow, bailing, sometimes trailing her arm in the water. The cold water slid to and fro in the boat, lapping at her bare feet. She would have liked to take off her shirt also, but she was not wearing anything under it. She was annoyed that she could not do so in front of him, but she could not. She rolled up her jeans, and the sun lay on her skin warm and palpable. She felt as if she could lick it off, she could drink it slowly like orange-pineapple juice. Everything in her was slowing.

158

Yes, she had been running for days, for weeks, for years. She had been running all the way from her sandy windswept house in Ludington. She had been running since the day at sixteen when she had fallen in lust for Penny. She had been running since Miss Greening had saved her from her class fate by involving her in school and then in college plans. She wanted to lie down under the sun among the reeds in a floating world and be baked and lolled and lulled and lullabyed into oblivion.

"When we're happy, I boil over, I bubble. You sprawl. You get still like a cat in the sun."

She nodded, smiling.

"Do me one favor. Take off that wretched rubber band and let your red, red hair loose. It would be so splendid in the sun."

"If you and Honor don't stop picking on me about my hair, I'll cut it all off. I'll shave my head."

"Ah, that would be exciting," he crooned. "Ascetic and sensual at once. People would always be wanting to finger your scalp."

"I can't win." After a few minutes she took off the rubber band. He rowed slowly, and sometimes the current carried them onward almost without rowing. Other times they were held in a backwater, and if he stopped and rested the oars they drifted so gradually they appeared to remain still. Once or twice he backed them into a dead end where the boat could not penetrate the reeds. She lost all sense of orientation. The sun felt hot and she was drowsy and calm. The sun licked her arms and legs, hot and a little caustic. She could not even regret Honor was not with them. She felt a pang of guilt at how thoroughly she had forgotten how the day had begun; but she could not imagine Honor sitting happily in the rowboat with water sloshing to and fro, she could not quite imagine it. No, she was freed from everyone here, from ceaseless lonely wanting, from Val, from George, from her department, from Honor. She was free as a dirty gull circling over the reeds. Her eyes half closed. They closed completely. Warm and lapping. Water world.

eleven

They hit with a crunch and she woke. For a moment consciousness hurt. She was startled, her head full of bees. Her eyes itched.

"You were sleeping." He raised her by the armpits. "Wake up. We've arrived!"

She stumbled from the rowboat onto a low clay shore where he had grounded the boat. To moor it he wound the rusty chain around a sapling. "Where are we? Where have we arrived?" She looked around for houses.

"I found my island. I'd about given it up."

"Island?" It was brushy and low, only a couple of feet higher than the water.

"Gaudalcanal. Come on." He led off through the alders.

"Where are you going?"

"Follow me. And the path."

"What path?" But she followed his thin back. He had his jacket slung over his shoulders and hers as well. "Wait. My feet have turned tender. Let me put my shoes on." She went back to the boat for them. "What did you call it? Guadalcanal? Name of a battle in World War Two, Pacific theater. Yes. Solomon Islands. Coconuts and gold. . . . See, how lucky to have a historian along."

"My old man fought there. The family story was that he got malaria fighting in the jungle on Guadalcanal and that's how come he started drinking. It was romantic-sounding, the place where Papa started to drink. So that's what we named this island."

"How big an island is it?"

"Maybe a couple of hundred yards long. Look. Here's the duck blind!"

It was a low open shed of weathered boards slapped together and much patched. Inside the air was damp and musty, while wasps buzzed ominously around their heads. Bernie could not stand upright. He stooped to crane out the slit of window. "Well, this has lost some of its magic."

She snorted. "Maybe it's lost *all* its magic."

"Never mind. I know where we'll go. Are you hungry?"

"Now that you mentioned it, yes. Why did you have to mention it?"

"Then we'll eat. Come on." He led the way among low scrubby trees, slightly uphill. Then over a faint ridge and down again. They had risen perhaps a total of twelve feet above the marsh.

"We come out of the bushes and there's a Howard Johnson?"

He slapped the pocket of the jacket he had slung over his shoulder. "Foresight. I swiped chicken and goodies from the restaurant. You don't appreciate me, Les. And I'm so good to you!"

"If those wasps would leave us alone, we could eat in the duck blind. Or the boat. Why can't we eat in the boat?"

"Because we're going to eat. . . . if it's still here. And it is!" He led her out on an old concrete apron. Square holes stained with rust marched down the edges, where girders must have stood to support a vanished building. All that was left was a square of crumbling concrete with bushes growing through the cracks. It began on the gentle slope and ended about ten feet out into the water.

"What was it?"

"We never could find out. It was old when we were kids. We used to camp here. Ann-Marie and I even spent the night a few times. Very spooky. Damp but magical."

The sun had baked the concrete so it felt warm as she sat on it facing into the marsh. A mile away a factory belched red smoke through five high stacks. Out beyond the maze of rivulets and open waters and marsh and islands, the main channel of the river meandered toward Lake Erie. Gulls hung over something in that channel toward the invisible lake, but she could not see what gathered them in screaming numbers. A dump or a sewer mouth? A great blue heron was stalking in the reeds a hundred feet away, but when she pointed it flapped heavily away.

"I'm glad we came out here," she said. "Now gimme."

Out of his pockets he took the chicken, six somewhat flattened sandwiches in plastic bags, pickles in another, a peeled but whole cucumber rolled in salt, three hard boiled eggs, a half bottle of red wine and a corkscrew. "This is none of your rotgut special. Look here. Saint-Estèphe. That's a town in Bordeaux. This got all shook up, but it's not a fancy wine and it's young. I learned to sound knowledgeable about wines in that gyp joint. Monsieur would like the Rothschild Mouton-Cadet. It's not very good but the name is fancy and famous and monsieur will like that snob appeal and it will set him back fifteen small ones, so he can suitably impress whoever he hopes to fuck, across the table. . . . My ancestors could have come from Saint-Estèphe. Actually I don't know where they came from. My old man had trouble remembering where he was supposed to be born. We'll have to drink it from the bottle because I forgot to bring the wineglasses, hanging from my ears no doubt. I'm sure an old trooper like yourself won't object."

"I thought we were supposed to have white wine with chicken."

"Pas avec un poulet rôti, madame! Besides, I have no means of chilling a white. If you don't want it, of course I will be obliged to drink it all myself."

"Don't bet on it. Um, the chicken's good."

"Best thing on the menu. It's actually sautéed and then steamed, but they call it roast." He got the cork out and passed the bottle to her after taking a swig.

They ate quickly, their feet hanging off the end of the cement apron at whose base the water murmured, faintly rippling. They ate their intended food and then they split what had been brought for Honor. "It's good, it's good," she said, eating quickly and then reaching for the bottle.

"We still have rotten manners, my friend. We eat as if somebody"s going to take it away if we don't finish before they grab it."

Within twenty minutes they had eaten every crumb. "Did you bring dessert?" she asked.

"Aw, come on. It's impossible to boost éclairs under my shirt. The same for chocolate mousse."

It was a little cool facing into the breeze over the water. She backed away from the edge and spread herself out flat on the hot concrete. Out in the main channel she could hear motorboats, but only a cabin cruiser rode high enough to be visible. She yawned, yawned again. "I don't know why I'm so sleepy. Maybe all the running this week."

After a moment he stretched out beside her, spreading his jacket under his body. "What I forgot is a blanket." He took a joint from his shirt and lit it, sucking smoke and passing it. She shook her head no. "I'm too relaxed already."

"Never too relaxed. That's like too happy. Neither of us is the relaxed type. It's a rare pleasure."

"I feel like a snake sunning. . . . I don't mind snakes. I never was afraid of them, even the massasauga rattlers we'd find in the gravel pits."

"Only people make me afraid. No animal has ever attacked me. Except for bacteria and viruses, if they're animals? . . . We were sick a lot as kids. We had the reputation of being dirty and tough. There weren't hardly any French-Canadians in our neighborhood. My parents' friends lived in Detroit Beach, near Brest, fifteen miles, something like that, south of here? The people were Polish, Irish, and the ones who called themselves just plain Americans—the Wasps—and then the kids up from Appalachia that everybody called hillbillies. . . . At school they were always hauling us out to the nurse's office. They were terrified we were going to turn out to have TB and spread it around. We were the first to catch anything and give it to everybody else. . . . We weren't stupid, any of us, except maybe Denise. I think Ann-Marie was the smartest. But they made us feel they didn't want us in school, and we didn't want to be there. We hated to be split into different classrooms because of our ages and having to sit way at the back. When Mother was sick or away in a sanatorium, we just wore whatever wasn't too filthy. And then always trying to get money out of you for this and that, and of course we never had any unless we took it off some other kid."

She yawned again. Her eyelids drooped. "You were a lot closer to your sisters than I was to my brothers."

"Especially Ann-Marie. But yeah, we played together. Sometimes my mother was home and sometimes she wasn't. Sometimes she had to work and sometimes she had to go in the state sanatorium. We were a tribe, we stuck together. We kept each other warm. I miss that, yes, I miss it still. I've been cold all along my side ever since." He took hold of her by the shoulder and hip and turned her, half pushing, over on her side to face him. "Please don't go to sleep. Please, Les. Don't go to sleep and leave me here alone with my ghosts. I need not to be alone here."

"Sorry." Her eyes fluttered and drooped. She felt thick. "You should have brought coffee instead of wine. I'm trying to wake up. We could get up and run."

"On a full stomach? No, I'll pinch you whenever you start to drift off." One hand lay on her hip to prevent her from rolling onto her back again. She wriggled uncomfortably. The cement cut into her bottom hip. "Here, lie on my jacket. Put yours down too. Like that."

She lay stiffly on the jacket facing him. The distance was too short for her to be quite at ease. Soon she would get up. She must wake herself. The wine, the food, the sun made her fat and heavy. The blood buzzed and simmered in her head, a huge overripe melon full of flies. Her arms and legs were distant and floating like logs in a tepid pool.

"Ann-Marie and I were nuts about naming. We named everything, every channel of the river, every hump and tussock that could be labeled island, every pimple that might be called a hill, every slag heap we could think of as a mountain."

"Nobody comes here except to shoot ducks?"

"This island? Nobody except us. We used to catch bullheads. Ugly bastards as slimy as nightmares. They lie in the mud of the bottom and wiggle antennae. They can give you a nasty cut on the hand. Slime monsters. You don't scale them. You nail them to a board and skin them alive."

"Ugh. Why do people always describe as nasty the creatures they're going to torture?"

"Touché. People used to say they tasted like chicken, but I thought they were better. . . . Ann-Marie did make a map of our world. We had it on the wall. She made lines for latitude and longitude, just like the maps in the textbooks, although we didn't know what the lines were for. We just knew they made maps real." His quicksilver eyes were burning with excitement, he spoke rapidly, his voice rising and falling. The gaze of his eyes was bright and intense, a hook she kept slipping off, drifting down. "My youngest uncle, Jean, got killed in Vietnam and they brought his body home. We went up to Sherbrooke for the funeral. It made a big impression on us kids. When our dog got struck by a car, we carried off a flag from the drugstore—under Ann-Marie's skirt, bless her pure gall—to bury him in. We called him Al Capone. We shot off a cap pistol at his funeral and Ann-Marie made a speech. We always had mutts, we had the rowboat, we had each other. Our junk-heap wilderness."

"In a way you had a happy childhood," she mumbled through closed eyes, wanting to prove she was listening.

"Hold me, Les, be affectionate. I need you to stay awake and be with me. I feel extremely close to you. For years I never remembered my childhood. I never talked about it except to make up lies." He held her against him loosely.

She felt uneasy against him on the spread jacket. She could imagine them seen from above, embraced like lovers on the cement apron. She felt like explaining to the

165

blank air it was not so. But she was sleepy and relaxed still. She had promised to try to be more affectionate. She put her hand tentatively on his shoulder, bony, sharp, hot in the sun. The bare skin startled her and she blinked her eyes open for a moment before she remembered that he had taken his shirt off ages ago. "Lies?" she repeated. "Like pretending to come from a middle-class background? I've done that. Sometimes it's just keeping your mouth shut when people make assumptions. Or talk about *them*."

"There are other ways of lying. Telling it like it was, except that it didn't feel that way. I've never told anyone but you that I had a happy childhood, Les. A father who drank, a mother with TB, a dirty drafty house where the power company cut off the electricity every six months and we'd stumble around in the dark. Who else but you could believe I was happy? You aren't supposed to love your older sister the way I loved Ann-Marie. Not just because it was sexual, and it was, but because you aren't supposed to love a sister that much. If we hadn't been so mean and tough, they would have called me a sissie. Hanging around with girls. Tired to your sister's apron strings. You know how cruel boys are to boys? Almost as mean as they are to girls. How kids hate each other, it's wonderful we don't all break each other's necks in the seventh grade. We would if we could. We'd bash each other's heads in if they'd let us. We'd eat each other's brains with a spoon like a vanilla ice cream sundae."

"Ugh, that's a bit graphic. I hated grade school. For years I had dreams of being tortured there. It was a prison. No wonder Honor hates school."

"I can't stand lying in this beautiful hot sun—the first good sun of the year—with my clothes on. I look splendid with a tan, and my hair bleaches some. I hate white marks on my body. If I had another sugar daddy, I wouldn't have to work in that crummy gyp joint. . . . Not that I want one. I don't want to take any more lovers because I need money." He sat up and stripped rapidly, kicking his pants off. He had nothing underneath them.

166

She edged away, carefully not looking. "Don't you want to sunbathe?"

"I wouldn't be comfortable."

"Oh, Leslie, are you modest? I can't believe it. I have no modesty whatsoever. I could walk naked up the street if I felt like it."

"It's not modesty!"

"What is it then?" He chuckled. "Are you afraid I'll ravish you?"

"Don't be absurd."

"Well, at least take off your shirt and enjoy the sun."

She remembered wanting to. She did feel a little formal lying completely dressed beside him completely nude. "Nobody comes here? What about the duck blind?"

"In the fall they shoot ducks. Nobody comes here to smoke or drink or fuck. It's too far. There's hundreds of nearer places you can find. The neighborhood's full of little dead ends, clumps of trees and bush, old junkyards where you can crawl into a wrecked car."

Stiffly she took off her tee shirt, but she could not keep herself from crooking her elbow across her breasts.

"What a day!" he said. "I feel as if the sun is licking me. Isn't that erotic? Burt had a dog named Lucky Pierre. A poodle. But not one of your yappy little dogs. A big dog-sized hairy intelligent poodle. I really loved that dog. I miss him. Burt used to accuse me of loving the dog better than him. But it was easy to love Pierre, he was such a passionate sunny spirit. I've never been able to have a dog since I was a kid. One other thing I can't afford. I don't get meat myself when I'm not eating at the restaurant."

"What kind of dog was Al Capone?"

"A yellow mutt. But with wonderful speaking eyes. He could beg the life out of you, he could coax your supper off your plate when you were hungrier than he was. . . . I've tried for years to perfect that look. If I had my old yellow dog's look just right, the world would be my salted peanut."

"I think you're perfecting it," she said sourly but relaxed again in the curve of his arm.

"Ann-Marie was the hero and I was the villain. Or else

167

we'd be something like *Star Trek*. I got to be Spock, which is the best part, naturally, secretly lusting after the captain forever. Or explorers or pirates, guerrillas, bank robbers. I was always willing to be the villain when we had villains. I'd kidnap Denise or baby Mike, and Babette would be my sidekick. I didn't mind dying at the end, because I got to be dramatic and evil before. Ann-Marie was the hero type—like you. A striver and strainer, as the Blacks say. They all live across the river, downwind from those belching stacks. We looked down on them, I can't for the life of me imagine why. We all lived in the same dumps and grew up to work in the same mills or collect the same unemployment, and they had more fun. We were convinced of that, deeply convinced, and we hated them for it. Anyhow they looked like they were having more fun." He cuddled up to her, his cheek against her shoulder. "I still miss Al Capone, I miss my mother, I miss Ann-Marie. I miss her more lately because I let myself remember. You and Honor make me remember. I shut myself up, cold. Sometimes I think all you have to do to be desired, to be an ultimate sex object in this society, is to be cold all the way through. The world will cream a path to your door to impale itself on you if you're only an icicle."

"You don't seem cold to me."

"I'm not with you. Or with Honor. Because I'm coming back to life. And I feel safe with both of you. You're all I have of . . . real connection. I still have the needs of a child. I'm not a child, you know—that makes it harder. There are few kinds of hell I haven't seen from the inside. I could tell you stories that would make Honor grow pale and your eyes melt with that serious glow."

"Bernie, you haven't a pose that annoys me more than your world-weariness!"

"Dear heart, when you've been rolling in shit you must have something to say for yourself. You have to make the best of it, and the best is to boast that at least you did roll in shit."

She sighed. "You make sure we never know how literally to take the shit."

"Listen, once I saw a punk movie in New York playing in a rerun house where I was sleeping. It was about an Italian street urchin who witnesses a crime and blackmails a respectable family to take him in. He's hungry, he's tired of stealing his bread. Well, one thing and another, their influence melts his grubby proletarian heart. And when he can no longer blackmail them and they can hand him over to the cops, they reach out with loving arms to clasp him to their familial bosom. You follow?"

"Follow where? Every poor kid dreams at times that she's really the lost foundling of some rich pig." She looked away from the intensity of his demanding gaze. His hand, fallen on her rib cage, dug into her flesh for emphasis.

"At the end of this sentimental tearjerker, our filthy street beast stands silhouetted against the waves of an ocean beach. His foster father holds out his arms to him. A moment of stillness. Our beast can't believe they really want him, the crumb-bum, him, the proletarian turd. Then he tears down the beach into his new father's arms to a thousand violins and the crashing of the surf. Here I cried." He grinned mirthlessly, his hand hard on her rib cage as if to prevent her from rising in revulsion and moving away. "I cried like an old maid at a wedding. And when I recovered from my embarrassment at my own secret taste and maudlin tears, I knew precisely what I wanted. Simple. I want a home. Will you laugh?"

"No. I'm in exile. From where I don't want to be and ran away from at the first opportunity. An old maid is a woman who hasn't sold herself in marriage to a man, by the way, Bernie."

"For most people home is the taken-for-granted. I'm sorry, I won't use the phrase again. It's the place you fight to leave. Afterward you speak of making yourself at home in other houses. But I still wander outside the first shelter. . . . My life is just a messy interminable game of parchesi. Where the whole object is to get the little wooden idols home and you almost make it and then somebody knocks you all the way back. . . . You know the whole concept is phony. It's just an empty square where nobody's waiting. But sometimes I think I'm stuck in that kid's game. It's déclassé. Other people get to play adult games like backgammon and twenty-one, poker and chess. Here I am living my life out in a crappy children's game that relies entirely on chance!"

"I had a home once—with Val. And I muffed it. I couldn't have her and a meaningful job, her and a decent income. But I couldn't hold on to her in the long run without job and income."

"You came back from her shining. Something turned on in you that you haven't managed to smother yet. I keep wanting to touch you. Maybe I think it will rub off . . . or I don't want you to squash it again."

"I have to." For a moment her eyes burned. She was caught by surprise. How close her emotions seemed to the surface today. In a sense she was still on vacation—beyond discipline, away from control, from all the armor that sustained and protected her against the hundred casual and calculated onslaughts and insults of every day.

"No. You don't. We don't have to go on being caught in our own traps always. I don't even have to spend my life caught in an old parchesi game." His hand slid up very gently over her breast, exploring it with fingertips only.

She tensed under the hand. "Don't."

"What's the difference between your rib cage and your breast? Because society draws funny lines on the body?"

"I was born in this society. My breasts are personal. . . . I suppose the touchy-feely scenes make me uncomfortable because where do you draw the line? But there's a real difference between taking my hand and touching my breast."

Yet he continued his soft tentative caress. "It feels different to me too. If I touch you on the rib cage, on the back, it's like touching myself. Bones, lean meat. If I touch your arm, it's like being with a man who's more athletic than I am. So it's as if *I* had breasts. . . . The couple of other women I ever touched were all soft and strange, spongy. Except for Ann-Marie. She felt lean and

170

sinewy like you, except for her small breasts that were just starting."

She gathered herself together, tensed to move. "Don't though. I'm not comfortable. Stop."

"Am I not being gentle enough?"

"Bernie, to me it is erotic." She was embarrassed, but she could feel her nipple harden and her breast grow warmer with blood.

"To me too. Isn't that a surprise? I think it's fabulous."

She started to roll away from him but he anticipated her. The other hand that was behind her pulled her to him. He rubbed his lips against hers as if curiously back and forth. Then he was kissing her mouth not gently but hard.

She was shaken totally awake now and she thought, Oh shit, and cursed herself for stupidity, yet she was scalded with surprise. She could not quite believe what was happening. It was like suddenly arriving in a puddle of hot oil. Why hadn't Honor come? This would never have happened. She lay passive in his arms hoping he would just as suddenly stop. He was kissing her so that she could not speak, and she tensed with astonishment. Almost she expected him to stop momentarily.

But he was not stopping. She bucked quickly for space and tried to wriggle from his grasp. He let her fall onto her back away from him and then he moved over her. She felt a kind of hot shock at the weight of his body on her. He was naked, his body heated by the sun, and she felt his erection against her thigh. She turned her head away from his mouth and spoke into his sharp collarbone. "Bernie, don't! You must stop."

"I want to, Les, I have to. Hold me, please. It can work this time, I know it. It can work."

"I don't want it to work. Get off me. If I have to stop you, I'll hurt you, Bernie!"

"We could be together, I know it. Hold me. Don't fight. Let it happen. Please, Les, I'll make it all come out. It'll work." He tried to cover her mouth with his again. His hand was fumbling now with her pants. He got the zipper open and his hand moved down her belly that felt

171

cool against the heat of his touch. She felt at once an aching twinge of desire as his hand covered her mons, and a stronger bolt of anger, the confident cock shoving like a club against her thigh, him and his hand trying to breach her. She fought free with her left elbow till she had enough space to drive her right fist into his solar plexus. He groaned and went limp and she thrust free of his weight, rolling off to the side and coming up on her feet.

Grabbing her shirt, she ran from him over the broken concrete to the trees, zipping her pants. When she turned at the wood's edge, looking for the path and staring back over her shoulder to see if she was pursued, he lay curled up on the pavement where she had left him. She paused to pull her shirt over her head. Then she ran up the slight rise and down the other side. She followed the dim path past the duck blind humming with wasps and then back through the bushes and willows to the sedge where the boat was moored. There she stopped.

How could she get in the boat, row off and leave him on the island? How would he get back? Even if he had gone out of his mind and attacked her, he was still Bernie. She simply could not go off without consideration of how he was going to get home. Reluctantly, making faces at herself, she trudged slowly back.

When she emerged on the apron again, he was still lying where she had left him; for a moment she was afraid she had killed him. But in that constricted space she could not have hit him hard. He lay with his eyes closed, clutching his stomach with both hands. As she watched him on the ground, he was too familiar for her to stay back. Tentatively she took a few steps. "Bernie?" He opened his eyes and looked at her without expression she could discern. "Are you all right?"

"Not noticeably."

She came closer until she stood over him. "Are you hurt?"

"Entirely! Les, I'm sorry." He sat up. "I kind of wish I was dead."

She reached down then to help him up.

172

"You don't mind touching me?" He raised an eyebrow. "You're not afraid?"

"I'm not afraid of you. How could I be?" She clutched her arms around herself as if she was cold. "How do things get so messy?"

"Yes, you can handle me. Alas. I wasn't cut out for a rapist."

"Bernie, don't misuse words. It wasn't rape."

"Well, attempted." Moving gingerly, he stepped into his pants.

"You knew I could stop you."

"But you're not angry with me now. I can tell." He looked at her closely and shrewdly.

"I'm confused." She did not move off from him.

"You couldn't pretend it never happened?"

She shook her head. "No. In a hundred small ways. Like now when you put on your pants, I'm aware there's nothing under them."

"Except me." He laughed thinly. "Am I nothing?"

She shook her hair roughly, pulling it into the familiar club on her nape. "I'm aware now you aren't. I mean . . . that it's all sticky, as if we and every word and everything for miles has been covered with a film of hot taffy. I'm aware of you physically now. I'm confused, I mean it. Do you think that just sort of happened by accident?"

"I wish it had. No. I think somewhere in my spine—I must think with my spine like an extinct dinosaur because I certainly don't seem to use what brain I have upstairs—I knew I was bringing you here to try to . . . be with you. To try. I was so caught up in the fact that I could, I overlooked whether you could or would."

"You startled me."

"Maybe deep down I'm convinced you're really Ann-Marie. Now she could never refuse me, she could never say no to me when it came to the crunch. Maybe I was convinced I could have you too because I think you're really Ann-Marie and therefore you're really mine anyhow. So I have some ancient right, you see."

"The only brother I feel related to lives in Seattle and I

173

never get to see him any more. But a peck on the cheek is a big display." She picked up their jackets and handed him his shirt.

"Well, I'm perverted in all sorts of ways, we know that," he said sourly. "Actually I didn't think you'd leave me here. I had a cold moment and then I felt sure you would, responsibly, trot back to fetch me. You'll have to row us home."

"My pleasure." She lèd the way over the ridge. "Don't limp so. I didn't do a thing to your leg."

"The idiotic things you get pleasure from. A rowboat rather than me." He stopped limping. He kept quiet until they had pushed the boat off. Then he sat facing her as she rowed, giving her directions through the maze of reeds. "Are you sorry you hit me?"

"No. You made me angry. You shouldn't jump on people."

"I did begin very gently, as I recall, then I got too enthusiastic." He stared at her. "You aren't going to run away from me like you did right afterward. Or are you?"

She shook her head no. "I'm confused by what happened."

"Euphemisms. What I did."

"*Besides* what you did, things happened. We have to talk. I feel a little . . . unraveled. I have to sense my way back toward you again. I want to feel open, I want to feel like your friend. I don't want to withdraw. It'd be easy to. It's terribly hard not to. But I'm trying. You have to try too."

"In spite of such emphatic rejection. What am I to do?"

"Just talk to me, Bernie. Till we understand each other again."

"Oh, talk!" He threw up his hands. "I'm wonderful at that. I should have stuck to talking this afternoon."

twelve

Leslie brought George's Cordoba home to its attached garage. She had promised to feed the tropical fish in Davey's room, the hamster in its cage in Louise's, and to water the houseplants. But basically Bernie and she came back to the house because it was other space, less constricted than trying to talk in her room or presumably his, less awkward than talking in a bar or coffee shop. A gay bar on a Saturday night did not seem the right ambience.

"I could make supper," Bernie said. "I'm a good cook. One of my survival skills: How can you throw me out on the cruel hard streets when I can bring you a prefect omelette for breakfast? I bet there's goodies in their freezer. This strikes me as a well-stocked house."

"They didn't exactly invite me to move in while they're in Puerto Rico."

"Any chance they'll come back early? Suddenly appear?"

"No. George has to call, so I can pick them up at the airport."

"So you really think they counted every last steak in the freezer?"

"I'm sure not. Sue never knows what she has on hand. Every Thursday night we have to run out for things she's forgotten. He has little parties for staff and students on Thursday nights."

175

"How cozy." Bernie looked in the freezer. "Roast beef. Pork loin roast. All those take too long. Wait, what about Cornish game hen? I could defrost it in kind of a hurry under running water in its little plastic bag. What do you say?"

"Why not? Do I have to help?"

"You have to clean up."

"Fair enough." She did her George chores and then sat in his chrome and leather swivel armchair and took his copy of *Time on the Cross* which he was using for the methodology seminar and started reading where she had left off in her own copy. She took particular pleasure in observing and in some cases copying George's notes. Bernie was busy in the kitchen for a long time and then she heard him running the water for a bath.

In another half hour he emerged flushed and almost steaming, wrapped in a dark blue velour bathrobe she supposed was George's. "I figure we can wash the towels in that busy laundry apparatus downstairs before we clear out. Cover all traces." He leaned against the walnut desk combing back his hair with his fingers. It was flattened to his scalp in ringlets. "So much lovely hot wtaer. The heart of luxury. I live in a dreadful roominghouse. My landlady's okay. She's a fat middle-aged Black who grew up in Detroit and she's lived in that house for twenty years. But there's never enough hot water, nothing works right, it's noisy and drafty. When the furnace is turned on, the hot air blows right up into my room through a register in the floor like a desert wind. When the furnace is off, a cold wind blows through the cracks around the windows. I almost never get a bath because there's not enough hot water. And most of the guys are pigs. They never clean the tub. So I have to take lukewarm showers."

She put down George's book, realizing the truce, the recovery time, was past. "Is it too late for me to take a bath before we eat?" That would put off confrontation. As she ran the bathwater she thought, There is a real connection. We both live in ratty cheap lodgings without enough heat or hot water, and a bath like a good meal is a real treat. Lush towels. Sharing small pleasures like

176

booty stolen from the comfort we're both struggling toward: that's the real part and the confusion this afternoon only passing static.

Still, her naked body wavering in the baby blue tub discomforted her. She had only a shower, like Bernie, and no full-length mirror; she hardly ever saw herself naked. Image: Valerie and herself standing nude side by side with arm around shoulders, leaning together in front of a big mirror with a carved mohogany frame. Somewhere they had spent the night. Unmade bed behind them, a big fourposter rumpled with their lovemaking. It was the house Lena had before she bought the Victorian mansion in town, a farmhouse near Lake Michigan she had filled with antiques and semi-antiques bought at the auctions she attended weekly, although she always implied that the finest pieces had been handed down in her family. Yes, Lena had given a party for the summer solstice with a live women's band brought in from Chicago. Not only had she and Valerie been invited, which wasn't unusual for an enormous party, but invited also to stay over for the night and share a special outdoor breakfast Sunday. That was odd because they were not in Lena's crowd of lesbian couples with university and professional jobs. She sighed, realizing Lena had already been interested in Val, but Leslie had been too lost in herself to notice—her assistantship, George, her degree, stacking plans on plans.

Skeptically, she squinted at her body looking vast and pink underwater. Why had he wanted to do that, to try to have sex with her? Yet she had partially responded. If it had not happened so quickly, what would she have done? He had made it easy for her to grow angry and reject him violently. She was relieved but confused, and she felt open to him still.

She did not want to lose him. He was the only person she talked to openly and honestly about her life. Honor had to have more independence, more sense of options and choices before they could communicate fully. With Tasha she had often hung back, sheltering herself from judgment. Not really wanting to describe the work she did with George, the Simpson papers, the history of capital

177

development, sure that Tasha would be critical. Would find political objections. Would manage to threaten her position, her security.

She tried to imagine Bernie as a woman, but she failed. He only came out in drag. She could hang the paraphernalia of conversational womanhood on him, but that made him more gay. She was glad he was not a transvestite, because they made her uncomfortable; she disliked men taking on the attributes of the enslaved woman as an aesthetic ego trip. She felt awkward enough around Honor sometimes. Bernie was not a woman but not a straight man either. In no way did he remind her of the boys she had been involved with so many years before.

Somehow it would sort itself out. She grimaced at her body and rose dripping to wrap it in a thick towel twice the size of the much laundered three towels she had at home. Carefully she cleaned the bathroom after herself. Then she discovered why Bernie had put on George's bathrobe. She was hot and damp from bathing and she seemed to have swollen. She could not fit into her pants.

Stubbornly she went and sat on the floor with her legs crossed until she had cooled enough to force her clothes on. She had washed her hair and now she toweled it part dry, leaving it loose to dry itself while she ate. She hoped supper would be ready.

Bernie too had his pants and shirt back on. She felt relieved. It was going to be easy after all. They would talk and everything would simplify. He was dashing around the kitchen from stove to chopping board to refrigerator. "Good. You can set the table."

She did. "Do we have wine?"

"The best I could find is a Paul Masson chablis. I've got it in a pan with ice water. Tell George to purchase a proper ice bucket."

He had used orange juice on the skin and filled the hen with pine nuts and kumquats. It was succulent. It was delicious. They sat at right angles eating fervently with their fingers. He had also made a rice pilaf and broccoli with lemon butter. "It's all wonderful," she said, but not until twenty minutes later when she had eaten all she could.

178

"It is awfully good, isn't it? Did Valerie cook for you?"

"When we bothered. A lot of times we just ate on the run, a can of tuna fish. Or we'd make a big spaghetti or rice and beans and eat it for days."

"I just have a hotplate. Doesn't make for gourmet splendor. I try to eat enough at the restaurant to carry me the rest of the week on eggs. . . . I do love to cook. It's a way of flattering someone. Are you flattered?"

"I'm satisfied."

"Now make me a fire. It's turned cool."

When she had lit the fire, they sat on the soft couch facing it with their feet on the coffee table, where he had set out coffee and Metaxa he had found in the liquor cabinet. He said, "How quickly we get used to being George. You have a surprising taste for luxury."

"But I couldn't be George. Even for a good meal and all the comforts of this house."

"How come? I thought that's what you were working for. I thought you simply admired him to the stars above."

"I couldn't take the kind of . . . arrangement he has—the roles, the distance, the maneuverings. I mean, there are things I like about him and things I don't. In some ways he is ruthless. Not to me. But toward others It's not my business."

"Burt lived this well. Not a big house. He had an apartment. But superior in the line of the food and the drink and the tailoring. Do you appreciate what I gave up in the name of some obscure principle of honesty or free choice or whatever you want to call it—if you want to call it anything. Fido, perhaps?"

"Are you sorry you left him?"

"You bet. When I wake up too early because the room's icy cold and I have to drag my clothes six blocks to the laundromat and get in a fight wih some junkie who tries ineptly to pick my pocket. When my boots wear out and I can't buy another pair and it's cold and slushy. When I have a paper overdue and I have to work till midnight at À Votre Plaisir and some drunk gives me a hard time and I owe my landlady rent so I try to sneak in and

179

out . . . I have trouble writing papers. That's the worst thing about being a student, aside from the sense of pretending. Of acting out 'student' when I'm really a hustler, an adventurer. . . . I'm glib enough, I can talk my way in or out of almost anything. But not on paper. In French it's just as awkward. I speak French, by the way, quite as artificially as I speak English; I relearned them both and in no way do I sound like what I am. My old man wouldn't believe it if he heard me speak French. He'd puke. It'd be exactly as if I spoke with a fake Oxbridge drawl. My French is more affected than my English even. . . . *You* still have a Midwestern accent."

"Academically, what's wrong with that? My specialty is American history, nineteenth century."

"Your voice amuses me: that it's high pitched and so Midwestern. Like a little girl's voice. Do you know that tension raises your voice?"

"Are you annoyed with me?"

He slumped further. "Edgy. I'm feeling rejected."

"So now you're telling me I'm not so nice after all."

"*Nice?* Like me you're much too offensive and defensive to be nice. Burt was nice. If I survive till I'm forty, what fun it'll be to be nice. Until then I'll be awful. Years of lying and manipulating and scheming and pretending and politicking. . . . The Supreme Court of the land has officially ruled we aren't people. It's okay to outlaw us, forbid us jobs and housing and education. Bust us. Perhaps it's okay to refuse to sell us food and okay to hunt us down in the streets again. Perhaps we could be burned alive at state occasions."

"Well if you'd managed to penetrate me this afternoon, do you think that would have made you more of a person? In the eyes of the Supreme Court, no doubt."

"Les, you can't honestly believe I was trying to prove something on you? Like trying to hit a bull's-eye!"

"Do you honestly believe you weren't?"

Turning, he seized her by the shoulders. "You may reject me, you have, but I do not deserve contempt!"

"Bernie, I was trying to be truthful."

"You aren't going to slug me for touching your shoul-

180

ders? The shoulders are acceptable? Be careful. The armpit is potentially erogenous. And I'm within a hand's breadth of what has been officially established as forbidden erotic territory."

She grimaced. "You fight dirty."

"I fight to win. I told you that. I can't afford to fight any other way. Sportsmanship belongs to the leisure class."

"What's the *it* you'll win?"

He let go of her shoulders and turned back to the fire, burying his head in his hands. "I wanted it so simply this afternoon, it seemed very clear."

"Nothing with us could be simple. It isn't simple for us to be friends."

"That wouldn't have happened either if I hadn't been pushy."

"Why were you?" She willed him to drop his hands from his face so she could see him.

He spoke through his fingers. "I don't know. You were getting all involved with Honor, and in self-defense I had to psyche you out. Honor means a lot to me. I had to protect myself. . . . Beyond that it's nothing rational. Don't you believe we don't always have clear reasons? Especially people like you and me, who always do have reasons. That some things grab you? Sneak up on you?"

"Yes, but . . . not usually friendship, you know."

"Everything gets mixed up with me. I must be crazy!" He took his hands away then and she saw that he looked on the verge of tears. She felt an immediate surge of sympathy. She wanted to put her arms around him, but she could not. "It goes back to my childhood. Maybe the rest of my life the only women who'll ever turn me on are women like my sister, like Ann-Marie. And they'll never want anything to do with me. Maybe she was the only person who ever loved me. Me as I am. The only one who could!"

"I do feel close to you, Bernie. But I don't know if I can want you. Physically. I don't know if I can."

"I keep having the conviction that I could seduce you. But I don't know how to seduce a woman, I don't know

181

quite how to begin. The women I tried to be with, it was their idea. You don't know if you can? Ha! I'm the one who most likely can't. I'm the one who should be protecting myself." He held out his hands, palms up.

She had the sense that if they did not at least try, they would withdraw from each other. It seemed so complicated, she felt exhausted in advance. Yet she wanted to comfort him. He knew how to wring her of pity and compassion. It could not work out well. She regretted it all, the whole day, everything that had provoked the snarl. She put her hands on top of his. "Your hands are cold. Should I build the fire up?"

"You know that's not the problem! Only a little friendly loving would warm me tonight." Tentatively he took her hands in his, waiting to see if she would pull back.

She did not, but gently squeezed his hands. She did not speak, because she could think of absolutely nothing to say. She felt as excited as she might in a dentist's waiting room.

He smiled for the first time since he had tasted the game hen. "I don't know, Les, there are a lot of things I could do with a hand or two. Do you feel quite safe like this?"

"No." She smiled too, stiffly.

"Oh, Les, I wish I could wake up beside you, and we'd been lovers for five years. We wouldn't even be hot about it. We'd roll into bed automatically and say, You wanna tonight? We'd take each other for granted, and I'd tell you the pretty boys I noticed on the street and you'd tell me about the new woman you have a crush on, and we'd be comfortable as dirty old shoes. God, to have someone to take for granted. . . . Oh, Les, you've terrorized me to the point where I don't dare move. I can't read your mind. I don't dare risk experimenting, because if I guess wrong you might break my jaw."

"Bernie, I don't know. I'm willing to try to be close. But it does feel awkward. I don't know where or how to begin either. I'm scared of freezing up."

"If you do, we'll stop. It's soothing to think you might

182

not be able to manage it either. Suppose all we can do is hold each other? That might be comforting. We could be like old Puritan lovers, we'd get in bed with a bundling board and hug each other. Come, lie on the couch beside me."

"Take off your sneakers first. The couch is new." She lay against the back of the couch and Bernie lay on the outside. She felt sunken in down, and lying with one arm around each other's backs and the other crushed between them in the soft concavity of the couch was not stimulating. They held each other in a serious and unimpassioned grip. His chin dug into her collarbone. After a while her fingers crushed between them began to tingle from bad circulation.

He moaned. "This is ridiculous. I'm smothering in goose down. My backside is being roasted. Let's put a screen on your fire and go borrow a bed. We'll tumble in and if we fall asleep what does it matter? We'll have a good sleep in George's fine motel, and in the morning I can make you a delicious breakfast before we have to vacate all this splendor."

It was a relief to get up. Surreptitiously she rubbed her numb hand. In some way by agreeing she had defused the whole thing, and probably they would sleep here and nothing more would happen and he would feel neither rejected nor curious. Cheerfully she led the way upstairs. They would wash the sheets with the towels, and everything would be in fine shape for George and Sue.

"Oh, we'll have to take Mommy and Daddy's bed. King-sized. It's big enough to dance on." He scampered across it, twirling and hoofing like Fred Astaire, and then sprang down. "Why couldn't we borrow somebody's house every weekend? Think of all the people who travel. We could break in. We wouldn't steal a thing. Just borrow the facilities, drink a little of the booze, eat a little of the food, sleep a little in the bed. Goldilocks all over." He kicked off his pants, flicking them with his shirt on a chair, slung back the covers dramatically and hopped into bed. "How can you take all night to get undressed? It's all those frills and furbelows you wear."

She stood flatfooted, unable to move. She felt as if her joints should creak like old wood. Finally she shut off the light, undressed and got into bed. It was so big that she felt quite alone in the dark until his hand encountered her.

"You feel better in the dark?"

"Yes," she said thickly. Her voice did sound high and girlish. Almost scared. "If you don't mind."

"I would rather see you. To be reminded it is you. In the dark we feel even stranger." Slowly his fingers explored her arm. Cautiously she turned and began to caress his shoulder along the angular collarbone, down the shoulder blade to the sleek skin. They did not kiss, they did not lie against each other, but from a little distance they explored each other slowly and carefully with fingertips and palms. A visit to another country, over the border.

After a while in the dark she smiled because sometimes his touch tickled her till she clenched her teeth and sometimes it felt exquisite. His chest was odd, flat, hard. Nipples without hills. He was too skinny to have even slight breasts. His belly was oddly flat too with a puckered scar. She could not bring her hand lower than the middle of his abdomen. It was as if she hit a barrier. She fled to his back, where nothing disturbed her, not even the high firm buttocks. Near the cleft he had a thick growth of wiry hair, thicker than on his chest, where the hair grew only down the middle, a river of hair with a little lake on the upper belly.

Gradually they moved closer, still stroking each other. It would be much easier just to talk. "Do you wish you were in love?" she asked him. "Are you really sorry you didn't love Burt?"

"Sorry because of how it worked out. Like I failed him. Didn't meet his needs. No, being in love is a disaster. It's the same game people pull on me, wanting the unattainable because it's withheld. When I've fallen in love, it's been some tepid beautiful stud. Even blonder, more beautiful and middle class at least and lucky besides. I'm thinking now of the worst time, in Chicago before I met Burt. . . . Les, I can't get it up. Nothing's happening."

She worked to keep relief out of her voice. "Should I touch you?"

"It won't help. Just hold me."

Facing, they embraced, less awkwardly. He chuckled. "Instead of a love that dare not speak its name, we have here a love that doesn't know what to call itself. It *looks* straight but it's even kinkier."

She relaxed against him, smiling in the dark, her body cuddling into the angular planes of his. His penis was limp and small against her belly, unthreatening, undemanding, gentle and soft as a breast. For the first time, very tentatively, she brushed her palm against it. "Maybe you're right. Maybe it is kind of relaxing to come together this way and hold each other. It feels good to me. . . . It was so open and relaxed out on the water. In the sun. Now I feel almost as loose. As if we're floating."

"Suppose we did live together. And Honor. The three of us could make a home for each other."

She snorted, "Honor has a home. I don't think domesticity has the same exotic pull for her."

"But it wouldn't seem domestic to her. It would be freedom to her and domesticity to us. . . . I'd try to be less sloppy. To please your austere compulsive neatness. We could have a real apartment. Could you give up your cell?"

She curled into him, her cheek against him, the skin sleek but the minute prickles standing out like lopped-off wires where the razor had passed over. "I don't know. . . . Yes. I could. I haven't always lived like that. It's been a paring-down time. A way of making visible what's been happening in my life, in losing Val." Suddenly she heard herself and it became real. That this week it had finished, irrevocably, and Val was lost. She remembered Val against her, the right feeling of the right body, and tears gushed out as if bursting from her. Tears ran from her eyes over his face and she said in a choked voice, "Losing." Then the tears stopped as suddenly as they had begun.

"Lost, yes, all lost," he said half ironically, with lips and tongue following the tracks of her tears to her eyes, moving his mouth and tongue over her closed lids. Then they kissed for the first time, the first time she was kissing him back. Tongue kissing always excited her, it felt so interconnected and wet and intertwined. He seemed to like to kiss almost as much as women did. She had always thought of men kissing as something they did to get you excited and then they started what was the real stuff to them. Kissing was close to an end in itself for her, and for a long time they kissed each other. Her body began to feel larger, as if the blood were pushing out against the skin, arching her buttocks, thrusting the tips of her breasts out, billowing through her thighs. Without thinking, she moved against him, that half-circular rocking action of her hips. As his hand slid between her thighs she realized she was already warm and open. Carefully and slowly he explored her, but when she began to move against his hand, he took it away and slid his erect prick against her instead. They were still side by side and it would not go in. "Farther back," she said and reached to help him, when it shrank suddenly limp against her.

"Jesus," he said between clenched teeth. "Useless hanging thing! God damn it."

She lay a moment recovering herself. It was so strange to stop suddenly in lovemaking, right in the middle, to stop cold. It felt like falling on your face. Then she curled close to him again. "When it rises again, as seems inevitable, would you consider this? Could we maybe have oral sex? I think it might be easier. . . . Or would that . . . freak you?"

"To eat you? I'm not sure I'd be efficient. I wouldn't guess it's exactly the same. But with some instruction, why not?"

"Because we're different. Some men might . . . I mean, I feel timid about it myself, and at least I did blow my boyfriend a lot."

"Tell me about him," he ordered and his hands began to move over her again.

Billy or Cliff? "You mean Cliff?" She selected him instinctively. "He didn't talk much. He didn't trust words, he thought they were how people pushed each other around if they were too smart to have to slug you. His father had worked for the railroad—"

"Physically. What did he look like?"

"He was on the short side but built like a boxer. Compact, broad shoulders, slim hips but good thighs. He used to run in the dunes. I'd run with him. At first I did it because I was crazy about him, but then I did it because I came to like running. Even after everything else was crummy and mean, I still liked running with him. It's good for your leg muscles to run in sand, it takes twice as much effort . . ."

His hands on her were no longer light and tentative. "Describe his face."

"Brown eyes, a big sharp nose, thick brows, broad cheekbones. Medium brown hair thick and wild halfway down his back. I mean, it was longer than mine and much thicker. He walked with a rolling gait, a sort of exaggerated swagger. Winter or summer he never wore anything but old jeans and a tee shirt and a leather jacket. Not like yours. Studded and heavier."

"Describe his prick."

She laughed. "I couldn't! Bernie, I can't make that many comparisons. It seemed big to me. Oh, yes, and purplish. I remember thinking once that when he was excited it was the color of a rutabaga, you know?"

He laughed then. "I bet that would have taken the stuffing out of him, to know to you he had nothing in front but a Swedish turnip! Did he fuck you a lot?"

"It seemed like a lot. I wasn't into it that much. It was something I did because we were supposed to and I was hung up on him."

"Did he eat you?"

"No. I only blew him when I had my period."

"Show me," he said coaxingly, putting her hand on his penis. It was hard again. Always going up or coming down, like some demented elevator, like a balloon with a will of its own. How odd men were.

They shifted about in the bed, settling into a side-by-side reversed tangle. Running her fingers the length of his shaft, she felt quite nervous, as if the thing might suddenly go off wetly or shrivel again, but it just stayed there with a little vein ticking near the head. She opened her mouth quite wide, afraid she might bite him, and tried to remember how she had used to do it. All she could remember was getting sand in her hair and her jaw muscles aching with fatigue when Cliff took too long to come. "Hold it at the bottom," he said. "Is this right for you? Is that your clitoris?"

With rueful politeness they gave each other directions. It could not be called easy; it did not feel natural. She imagined it was making love with a dog who spoke English, it felt so odd and lumpy. Yet she did respond. Even with interruptions and corrections and adjustments, her body was ready, and once he actually settled into a rhythm of tongue and fingers she came before he did. When he actually began to come she panicked and held him spurting against her lips rather than inside her mouth, from a quick fear of choking. "Should I have kept you inside?" she asked him when they were settled back afterward.

"It feels better if you do," he said mildly, yawning. "How amazing. We did bring that off."

Loosened and glad, she felt easy. She leaned over, kissing him lightly. George had not come back from Puerto Rico, materializing as they were making love. The idea that he might had been floating like a submerged image in her head, like the buzz of nervous energy in the jewelry store when she had observed Bernie shoplifting, part anxiety, part subliminal excitement. Incapable of wantonly taking a chance herself, she wondered if she did not enjoy being forced into danger. Perhaps I get people I am close to to manipulate me into doing the things I secretly am curious about. She saw herself with Val, who also liked to be naughty, stealing a whole Camembert cheese from one of Lena's parties, to eat for supper the next two days. Had Val ever confessed that to Lena? It had been awkward to make love with Bernie, but she felt closer for it.

Her muscles one by one sighed and floated. She lolled in the tepid dark.

"You did get some pleasure out of that?" he asked doubtfully.

'I'm not that hard to please. It was nice, Bernie, you were right."

"Are we technically lovers?"

"Technically? What nonsense is that? If Val and I were lovers, you and I are lovers. But what does that mean? We're friends. That's what we were half an hour ago, it doesn't go away or turn red or something."

She was standing in a kitchen that was hers and Val's although it seemed to be twice the size of their old kitchen and boiling with light. She was at the stove making coffee; yes, she was making breakfast for Val to bring it to her in bed as a treat. Then Valerie came up behind her—she was simultaneously standing at the stove measuring coffee into the drip pot, and floating up someplace where she could omnisciently watch Valerie steal across the floor toward her and slip her arms around her waist. Valerie hugged her close and she melted with pleasure.

She woke gradually in the dream and then she was puzzled. She was aroused as in the dream, arms around her, lean flat arms covered with curly brass hair hugging her back against bony, angular . . . Bernie. Yes. Oh. They were in George's big kingsized bed (although she should think of it as Sue's also, she did not) with the sun bleeding in through tortoiseshell blinds and light green draperies. It felt late. The bedside clock radio that flashed digits said in inch-high letters that it was nine-thirty: later than she had slept in months.

"Good morning," Bernie murmured at her ear and tickled around the lobe with his tongue. "King-sized bed is wasted on us. We slept curled up like two kittens in the middle. How delectable to wake up with an erection and something to do with it. I adore making love in the morning, it takes the hard edge off the day. In fact sometimes there's no point in getting up at all."

189

"Good morning." She began to turn but he held her fast, one hand making slow circles around her breast, the other edging under her to caress her belly. She yawned again and cuddled closer. Her eyes shut.

"We're prefectly matched, me so gabby and you so silent. We could go on indefinitely. I talk for an hour and you say yes or no. It's deeply satisfying. I won't let you go back to sleep." He brought his hand between her legs and began to excite her, more confidently this time.

"I normally talk as much as you do. Almost. This is the last day of my vacation."

"Let's make it a good one." His mouth burrowed in her nape and along her shoulder. His teeth closed lightly on her skin, worried a fold. "Do you like biting?"

"Not really. It hurts."

"I'd let you bite me too? All right, all right. I won't bite. I'll only squeeze." His hands were hard, rough on her. If she had not awakened already excited, he would have hurt her. She felt confused. She did not like the way he was holding her, her back to him with her hands lying open and useless before her. This was a position which gave him all the initiative and control and there was an edge to that control, a slight stain of sadism in his excitement. Was he making up for what he might conceivably define as failure? She was not at ease. At the same time if he continued touching her just that way she would come in a few minutes. She yawned sleepily, groggily, trying to throw off the sense of sinking in layers and layers of warm cotton. She was not really awake yet. Her mind and body felt ill-coordinated. His hand on her seemed miles away from her puzzling brain.

He eased her over on her stomach and moved onto her. She thought he was going to enter her ass. "I don't want to do that," she began, and then realized he wasn't.

He entered her vagina from the back, thrusting hard, and she winced with pain. Even though she was wet with excitement still from the dream, it hurt at first. It felt strange in her, the alien object pounding. She could not move at all in this position but only lie and be pierced and hammered in. But she adjusted to him, easing and
190

shifting around till the discomfort lessened. He was not heavy but she wasn't used to having anyone lying on her, so the weight on her back made her feel a little claustrophobic, a little squashed. She wriggled around under him but still felt pinned down. If they ever did anything like this ever again, lying on her belly was never going to be her favorite position. She felt too powerless, too contained. Her breasts were flattened by his weight. She could hardly move. Even if the thumping inside had aroused her, the complete passivity would have stolen the excitement away again.

She suspected he had chosen the position not by chance but because it gave him maximum control and because it emphasized the buttocks. The banging against her behind did not excite her and she wished it would end already. Performance, it was all performance. She began to feel hostile. She would have liked to wake up cuddled and loving, with kisses and conversation. He must have wakened some time before her and worked himself up on sexual fantasy until he was ready to stage his scene.

Finally he came with a shuddering groan. The liquid felt hot in her as it began to drip along her thighs.

"Oh my god!" she cried out suddenly. She started up and bucked him off, relaxed as he was.

"What's wrong?" he asked drowsily. He rolled over onto his back and lay smiling, looking pleased with himself. "Wasn't that something? Where are you running off to?"

"The bathroom. But it's hopeless." She made herself pee. Then she began going through Sue's drawers for a douche bag. Sue did not seem to have one. She came to stand beside the bed wrapped in a towel. "We're both idiots. Complete assholes."

He sat up rubbing his eyes. "What's wrong? I thought you came. Didn't you come?"

"No, of course I didn't. How would I come? But you did. That's what I'm talking about. We both forgot that makes babies!"

"Makes what?"

"Babies! We're . . . interfertile!"

"Just from that?" He sat on the bed's edge stretching. He stared at her as blankly and incredulously as if she were telling him there was a lion in the bathroom.

She wanted to beat on him in exasperation. "That's how it's done! We're both prize jackasses. We forgot. We just plain forgot that's how you make babies. I haven't had to use contraception since I was in high school!"

"But don't women take something?"

"Now why in hell would I take the pill? Valerie can't make me pregnant. I haven't taken any of that crap since I was sixteen! Oh, we're idiots!"

"Well, we could have a baby." He yawned again, looking even more pleased with himself. He couldn't see past his newly fledged prick. "How else would we get one? I like babies."

"Look, it's me that would be pregnant! And I am not, am not, not, not willing! We're assholes, that's what we are."

"You know that term is anti-gay," he drawled, hugging himself across his chest. "Like cunt for a woman, you know?"

"We don't deserve a license to walk the streets with adults. We don't deserve to survive. We're too stupid!"

"Speak for yourself, honey." He got up, chin in the air, and stepped into his pants. "I for one am hungry. You can have breakfast with me or you can stay upstairs by yourself and scream at the hamsters. Fertile little bastards. Maybe you can make them miscarry!"

He went down to make breakfast while she rummaged a few minutes longer for a douche bag before she gave up. She felt raw and sore as she moved, and sperm was sticky on the inside of her thighs. She took a shower, scouring herself. Then she dressed, stripped the bed, gathered the towels and came downstiars carrying the laundry. She could smell coffee and bacon, and her stomach shrank into a hard ball. There must be something she could do. She hated to feel so stupid. At fifteen she'd acted with more intelligence. Her body did not feel good. Her waking excitement had been battered into resentment. Because they had had oral sex at night, that had put her in a position where she had felt constrained to go along with him in the morning. It was so complicated, thorny, confusing.

"It's a drag trying to cook in a filthy kitchen. I told you I'd cook if you cleaned up, but you didn't take that bargain seriously," he said, slamming plates down on the table.

"You know why I didn't get to it last night. I'll do the dishes right after breakfast."

"*I know* . . . Don't drop innuendos on me. I didn't rape you this time."

She sat down and he brought out the bacon and eggs. It looked so good, English muffins in the toaster, she said appeasingly, "It looks delicious."

"Hmmmm. For all I know, *you* can get pregnant eating eggs." He was sulking determinedly, in full pout. "You didn't say a word about it. Not this morning, not last night. I certainly don't know a thing about contraceptives. Where would I have learned? Getting fucked doesn't make *me* pregnant. It seems to me a real long shot to imagine that five minutes would do it to you. After all, people spend years trying to have a baby!"

She put down her fork, annoyed again. "Oh? Remember how you were conceived? A bit of bad luck for Mommy."

"Don't throw my mother up to me. I adored her."

"I wasn't throwing her up."

"Besides, you'll probably eat and then throw up. That would be par for the course." He buttered an Englsih muffin, glaring at her. "You're just having a reaction and taking it out on me. A lesbian withdrawal syndrome."

"I fail to see how spending one night with you makes me a withdrawn lesbian."

"Because it felt good, you're taking it out on me. How am I supposed to know if you come or not? You'd rather preserve your purity and not enjoy it. You didn't want to come! That's why you're pissed."

"Oh, so I made you do it and got myself pregnant. That's what men say. She got herself pregnant. With who? The family dog?"

He took the untouched bacon from her plate. "Don't you want any? Are you turning into a vegetarian too? Well, my goodness, two minutes in bed, and you're convinced you're pregnant. I certainly seem to have sullied you." He got up for coffee and came back with the pot, rolling his hips and waving his arm in the air. "First you punch me in the belly and almost kill me—that's how Houdini died, did you know that? You could get a manslaughter conviction for that. Now you carry on as if I'd overpopulated the world single-handed before breakfast. It's dreary, that's what it is. Like stupid pricks who pick me up to ball and then call *me* queer. The morning-after syndrome, that's all. Dreary!"

She had already stopped being angry and she stared at him. He hated her. She stared at him while no words came to her. What he had said about the morning-after syndrome reminded her that there was something called a morning-after pill, which she had certainly described, pro and con, to raped women ten different times. She had just forgotten it, never expecting it to apply to her. She would go and get one.

He hopped up, letting his chair fall over backward. "Well, shit! Cheerio, my deario, you can stuff it in the orifice of your choice. You can stuff it and cook it and eat it by your lonesome." He stormed out and grabbed his jacket. Then he ran back in again to shout some more at her. She felt frozen, staring at him. "I'll hitchhike home and I'll get laid by someone who likes sex, actually *likes* it, can you imagine? No, you can't. So I disappointed you, huh? I know what you did in bed with Valerie—you tortured her. No wonder she ran off with a rich middle-aged dyke. I'd never have looked at you twice if it hadn't been for you hanging around Honor. Waiting for a chance to make her miserable too, I suppose! Well, you won't get it. I'll see you never get your hooks in her!" He was white with anger, burning, rigid. He stood there with his leather jacket on waiting for her to say something, but she could not. Nothing. She could not even quite look at him. Then he left.

She did the laundry and wept, she washed the dishes
194

grimly, she cleaned the house and fed the fish and hamster and watered the hanging houseplants, the spiderplants, the begonias, the African violets, her face stiff and masklike. In the bathroom mirror she glared at herself and clenched her teeth. She must take herself in hand. Before she left, she was satisfied the house was cleaner than it had been. She did not eat lunch, fasting for her excesses, her sins and failures, the mess she had made. A mess with a man. She was deeply embarrassed.

thirteen

Monday morning she went over to Student Heath to get the DES pills. They had told her she had to come at ten, which meant missing Walpole's seminar, a genuinely bad idea. His methodology seminar was the traditional one in authenticating documents, archival work, dating techniques. Walpole viewed her as an emanation of George, brought in unnecessarily from the outside. He had contempt for women students and pretended to be unable to learn their names. They were all Miss . . . Eh . . . to him. One time she had dragged herself out of bed with a hundred-and-one-degree flu fever to attend his class. Now she was sitting on a bench outside gynecology waiting and waiting for her name to be called.

She sat there her entire seminar. A lot of action over the hot weekend, probably. Today it was cool and raining. The air smelled foggy in the waiting room. She felt conspicuously on display for two hours. She had arrived early, hoping to see a doctor and get to Walpole's seminar. She tried to study, but every time someone walked in, through or past she cringed. She had to look up to see if it was anyone she knew. She had a fantasy bordering on conviction that Tasha was going to come by. She had decided to say she was having trouble with her periods. She would not admit to anyone why she was here; but it would go in her record. She was sure every lesbian in all of Detroit would know before noon where she was and why. It was incongruous, it was humiliating. She disliked herself for getting into a smelly situation. DES caused cancer. Wonderful. Maybe she should take a chance on getting pregnant. She had looked up the matter in *Our Bodies, Ourselves*, and they seemed to suggest she might be better off taking her chances (4 in 1000). But an abortion would be worse: Pregnant lesbian seeking abortion wants hand held. It would be too ridiculous and she would have to keep it as secret as a Victorian lady hiding her shame. She did not wish to parade her foolishness in front of strangers, let alone friends. Better to take the cancer chance, sweat on display in the busy waitingroom. Then she could forget.

"Why don't you go on the pill?" the doctor asked, reaching for his prescription pad. "We recommend that over the IUD for most cases."

"This isn't going to happen again. I don't need the pill."

"You didn't think it was going to happen this time, did you? We can put you on Enovid."

"It's not necessary. I don't intend to have it happen again. I haven't needed contraception in . . . two years," she said, unable to be more truthful, with him peering at her in that paternalistic way.

"If you're afraid of the pill, we can fit you for a diaphragm. But we can't have you coming in every week for a morning-after pill. The receptionist will make an appointment for you to come back in two weeks for an IUD or a diaphragm. Have you ever been pregnant?"

"No," she said, seeing the miscarriage. Don't let them put it on your record.

"The doctor who examines you will decide. See the receptionist. Take one of these every morning for four more mornings. If your menses are delayed past two weeks, make an appointment. Every morning for four more mornings."

She did not make the appointment. As she hurried in the rain across a campus crisscrossed by commuters, she felt nauseated, although whether from the shot or depression she could not tell. The rain pelted her hair flat to her skull and tried to creep into the neck of her jacket. She felt extraordinarily sorry for herself.

Chilled, she bent over old real estate records in the anteroom of George's office. Hot coffee alone kept her moving. Around four, George called her in. "Shut the door." He frowned. "You look under the weather. Are you coming down with something?"

"I got soaked. . . . Is everything all right at the house?"

George had returned with sunburn and he was still bright red, lit up. "Good job. Except that you could have given the lawn a soak. Not cool to let it dry out. The rain will help now."

"Sorry. I didn't think of the lawn."

"Keep an eye on it next time. Sometimes you have to touch the ground between the roots to be sure." George stretched, running his hand gingerly over his arm. "Still tender. I hope my tan doesn't peel off and wash away. How was your vacation?"

"Fine."

"You went to Grand Rapids?"

He would not let her off the hook. She nodded. "But that's over now."

"Too bad. . . . Is Cam living with Mark Hennessy?"

"Cam? I don't think so. They're seeing each other."

"She changed her phone number this morning." He pointed to a card in the Rolodex on his desk. Silently they compared the numbers.

She scratched her head. "I know she wanted to leave home. I can find out from her sister Honor. You don't mind, do you?"

"Why should I?" He flexed his arms behind his head, gingerly, and stuck his feet up. "I like to keep on top. Actually, I'm not sure I love having my secretary shacked up with one of my assistants. We'll see. I could imagine situations where it might be sticky." He peered into her face. "You look awful today. Are you coming down with the flu?"

"No. I just didn't get much sleep."

"Are you in some kind of trouble?"

"No. My personal life is not exactly wonderful at the moment, but I'm okay."

"You don't look okay. . . . Mark came to me this morning by the way and told me in all confidence that you are a l-e-s-b-i-a-n. I was a mite annoyed. I said, 'Fine, I imagine some other ambitious grad student will come to me privately next week and tell me you fuck ducks. It will mean as much.' But I was annoyed."

In her slough of misery one more bit of trouble hardly mattered. "I had the feeling he was chewing on that."

"Hope it doesn't spread. I'm behind you, but we have enough campaigns under way."

"I'm not looking for a fight either. Maybe he'll let it drop."

"Why does he have it in for you?"

"I don't know." She tried to rise to an analysis, but she felt bogged in self-pity. "He was interested in me at first, I can't imagine why."

"You're attractive and he's on the slow side."

There goes Mark's assistantship, she thought, and felt a stab of remorse. She disliked him but felt unworthy of judgment today.

"I think he's more likely professionally jealous," George said, stroking his mustache with that look almost of feeling himself up. "I think it's more likely my attention he craves. He's becoming a nuisance. There are at least ten brighter, harder-working students in this department who don't have assistantships. . . . My neighbors, the nosy ones, told me you had a young man with you this weekend. Are you branching out? Or was it just someone awfully butch? They're not too bright either."

The neighbors really do talk; she had not thought of neighbors since childhood. The woman next door calling her over: "I haven't seen your daddy around lately, little girl. What happened to your daddy?" Even at eight she knew enough to lie. "Oh, him." Her mind hardened to frozen slush. She could think of nothing to say.

"Who is he? What were you doing with him?" George was watching her with slightly malicious and slightly possessive curiosity. "Are you lately hetero after all?"

"He's gay! And I can't stand him." To her humiliation her eyes began to burn and two tears trembled in the corners. She sat stark still hoping that if she did not move they would be reabsorbed and she could pretend nothing had happened.

He patted her shoulder. "This is all fascinating. What have you got into?"

"Nothing I haven't got right back out of, believe me. I had a rotten vacation! I want to work like hell and forget it."

"A gay young man. What were you *doing* with him?"

"Just fucking up things, George! Please."

"If it's work your broken heart requires, we've got plenty. That's a new one. Those in the straight world who used to ponder what lesbians do together can put that in the hopper and bounce it around. I don't mean to be facetious, Red, but beyond the novelty, I wouldn't think it a profitable direction."

"I'm just going to work."

"Fine. Let's see what you had time to do with those correlations while I was broiling myself like a piece of prime steak." He put down his feet to signal he was ready for business, but he was still smiling, his eyes crinkled at the corners.

Leslie was sitting crosslegged. Her thighs were stiff from exercising after a whole week off. She had several bruises on her forearms she had not squeezed out. Usually she took the time to deal with bruises so that they were neither painful nor visible, but she had cut short the treatment, impatiently hating her body too much to tend it carefully. It was Tuesday afternoon and she was studying the history of the cotton industry from 1812 to the Civil War, the slight pain of her body a counterbalance to the unceasing pain in her head.

The phone rang. She reached to pick it up without moving from her crosslegged position. "Leslie here."

"Yes. Honor here. 'Here' is a dirty drugstore on your dirty corner. I can't figure out how to get your attention otherwise. You don't seem to have a normal doorbell."

"It's broken. Come back and I'll let you in." Carefully she put away her book and notecards and glanced at the room. It was neat. There was hardly enough in it to create clutter. Had she known Honor was visiting, she would have got some flowers to soften it. She liked flowers against her stark backdrop. A vase of daffodils decorated an entire room for her. One big yellow rose was furniture. But she had not known and she felt ashamed, as if her room was not good enough for Honor.

She ran down two steps at a time, waiting so that Honor would not risk being hassled. She watched the girl swinging languidly along in a trench coat, a shiny black bag over her shoulder and a chiffon scarf wrapped artfully around her hair. Her eager stare in all directions contradicted the studied languor of her gait. She looked in her twenties except for her expression, the open, eager, pink curiosity. But she pulled her face into a mask when she saw Leslie, and Leslie felt rebuked.

"You finally came to visit me," Leslie said as they climbed. "I hope you didn't get too wet?"

"That's what raincoats are for, even though Mama pretends to think I'll die of pneumonia if the dew touches me." Honor stopped so abruptly inside the door Leslie almost ran into her back. "Bernar' certainly wasn't exaggerating. It's a nun's cell. Every time I think dear Bernar' is stretching the truth, he surprises me by his accuracy. . . . Does one stand?"

"You could sit on my bed, if you wouldn't mind."

"I don't see a bed."

"My mattress."

"Hmmm." Honor carefully removed her raincoat, turned several times until Leslie took it from her and hung it in the shower. Then with haughty dignity she lowered herself to the mattress and took up a position sitting with her legs to one side in a neat Z. She was wearing a calf-length dark shirtdress in a small figured print, nylons and built-up shoes that looked clumsy to Leslie.

"I came," Honor said with distinct utterance, spitting out the words, "because I gathered I would not see you otherwise. Yesterday was Monday. I waited, of course, expecting you. You neither came nor called."

Leslie clapped her hand to her mouth. She had simply forgotten. The week of vacation that had felt months long had thrown her schedule completely off. "I wasn't feeling well so I had to go to Health Service in the morning. They kept me waiting till noon. I'm sorry I didn't call. There's no way I could have come yesterday, but I should have called. I missed my morning seminar, and when I got to our office, George was waiting for me with a lot of work."

"I find it interesting. I found it equally interesting on Saturday."

"Honorée, do you have a serious heart condition?" God, it seemed weeks since she had sat in the livingroom staring at Honor's mother.

"No, do you? Bernar' said you told him some fairy tale about my mother warning you off because of my heart. Really! That's a bad Victorian novel. Do I lie on a chaise lounge and cough delicately into a lace hanky?"

"When I arrived to pick you up Saturday, your mother told me you were at the doctor. She warned me against . . . She said you were in danger from too much stimulation because of a heart condition."

"I did have to go to the doctor, but only because of my stupid gym class. I have a note letting me out, but they said the note was too old. The doctor's a friend of Mama's and he doesn't see why I have to prance around shooting baskets to survive adolescence. He says I'm mature for my age and it's not surprising I loathe group games. He hated them himself. . . . I think it's unfair and rather mean of you to blame Mama for your not waiting. She told you where I was. You could easily have waited. Is it so dreadful to sit in my livingroom talking with Mama? She said you seemed terribly jumpy."

"Did you have rheumatic fever?"

"As a child, yes. But it's not a major illness nowadays, Leslie! I was anemic for a little while. Mama makes a fuss, but that's no excuse for you."

"Honorée, she said you were at the doctor's and she implied you'd be there quite a while."

"Why didn't you wait? Why didn't you come back if you were too nervous to sit in the livingroom waiting? Why didn't you call? Really, Leslie, you think I'm a child, don't you? You took my absence as an excuse for going off alone with Bernar'."

"But Honorée, you're the one insisted I pick you up first because you didn't want your mother to know you were going to spend Saturday with him."

"It's the way you went off with him. You were the driver. It was your car—I mean, George's—but you were the driver. What could Bernie do? You arrived and told him that fantastic story about my having a heart attack and then you took him off for the day in the country without me. I think it's mean. Absolutely mean."

"Your mother said you couldn't go. Bernie was anxious. He'd arranged to get the day off from work."

"He would have waited till Sunday, he told me so. He was willing. We would have had to leave early to get him to work by four, but we could have all gone. No, Leslie, it was your choice. And I repeat it, it was traitorous and disloyal." Honor shifted her feet so she was sitting bolt upright on the mattress. "If you believed your own story, why didn't you call me the moment you got back in town? But did you call Saturday night? No. Sunday morning? No. Sunday afternoon? Sunday evening? Monday? Did you appear when you always appear Monday? Well, did you?"

"I've been feeling rotten. Ill," she said, improving on it. "I spent yesterday morning at Student Health Service."

"Ill—like my magical heart condition? Really, Leslie, I'm ashamed of you. And deeply disappointed. Why didn't you simply admit you were romantically interested in Bernar'? It isn't necessary to connive to get me out of the way. After all, I live at home and it's easy enough for you to meet. That is, if Bernar' had proved interested. Oh, Leslie, I am disappointed in you. You go on how you care about women, but you're just like the girls at school, who'll do anything for a boyfriend, really!"

She felt as if she were sinking in mud. She could not rouse herself to indignation, for she felt guilty. She had acted badly. It was hard for her to think how to defend herself, because she felt indefensible. "Is that what Bernie told you?"

"He came to see me Sunday. *He* came over yesterday. I didn't have to confront him in his lair like a wounded animal. Really, Leslie, you must think I'm a complete fool! Did you have any friendship for me at all?"

"You're being foolish now. I feel a lot closer to you than I do to Bernie, believe me." That at least was true and her voice sounded convincing for the first time. "Bernie and I had a fight, did he tell you that?"

"What about?"

"I can't talk about it."

"Why not? Bernie can."

"I'll bet!"

"What is that supposed to imply?"

"That he lies compulsively. Continually. It's a reflex action."

"And you don't lie by commission. Just by omission. You let silence make the implications you won't stoop to make yourself!" Honor tossed her head back, her eyes glittering. Her face seemed to shine with anger, to become clearer and brighter until it burned on the air.

Leslie had a sense of avalanche, of things starting badly and then gathering a strength of their own momentum and plummeting down gathering trouble. She had the feeling if she could only break from her daze of guilt she could stop Honor. If she could speak firmly, she could abort the scene; but she could not summon the strength. Her guilt seeped like gas through the air, and Honor caught it in her nostrils and was infuriated.

"Beyond your facade of strength is just weakness. Self-pity and mushiness. You're a fake, that's what you are. You're just as silly and weak as Cam!"

"Has she moved away from home? In with Mark?"

"Don't try to change the subject. Yes. Isn't that ridiculous? Mama is furious. Now she's practically chaining me to the wall. She's terrified I'll suddenly elope with the mailman." Then Honor remembered she was angry. "You appear strong, but inside you're weak and conniving. You're trying to make trouble between Mama and me, between my best friend and me."

"I don't trust Bernar' any more, you're right, and I fear your mother's possessiveness. I'm concerned for you."

"I don't believe you. Not after Saturday! I'd looked forward to that all week. You'd just gone on a trip, but you were too piggy selfish to wait for me. Then you took Bernar' back to George's house. Keeping it all to yourself! You lie to me and patronize me and impugn Mama and Bernar'. They're the ones who love me. All right, what's your side of it? What happened so you aren't speaking to each other?"

"Nothing that matters." She could not even look at Honor.

Honor sensed her guilt and it maddened her. She looked beautiful and cruel, her teeth avid. Leslie could not break free: the scene was a nightmare coming true. Honor blended with Valerie. Both fused into one beautiful woman she loved who would not love her because she was not worthy; she was guilty, ugly, vulnerable, her guts spilling like garbage on the floor. She had ruined things again; she had let the woman down. She had failed her beloved, and now she was to be punished. Her mother shouting, "Get out of my house!" She felt guilty before the woman, unworthy; and self-pitying guilt welled through her, making her weak.

She could not justify to Honor forgetting her existence for three days almost entirely. In no way could she make that pass away from between them. Between them also lay the corpse of the night with Bernie. There were too many questions she could not bear to answer.

"You won't even lie to me! You don't care that much. You disgust me! Stay in your cell. Lock yourself in your little jail. You'll be ashamed to show feeling, but you can have a good cry anyhow. Really, you're a complete fraud. I don't ever want to see you again. Ever!"

Honor gathered her wet raincoat, slipped it on wincing and banged the door wide to leave. She did not bother to shut it but clattered downstairs. After a while Leslie closed it. She had not the energy to cry. She simply went back and sat down stunned against the wall. She felt as if she had been turned inside out. Then she picked up her book and resumed studying. She did not study well but she studied. She could not imagine trying to do anything else at all.

fourteen

It rained for two weeks, every day. She sat in her room working with her jacket on. She went to class, she went to work, she went to George's, she went to the dojo and she went to the bars. Of the two likely bars, she hated the Queen of Hearts less than the Pig's Whistle. She went after karate, regularly, and on Friday and Saturday nights. The smoke gave her a splitting headache and the bartender glared at her while she nursed her one beer. She did not approve of one night stands, thinking them a male mode of sexuality, yet that was all she went to the bars for. She stayed one hour. At the end of that time she had a partner or left. "Your place or mine?" "Yours," she said. It was easier to get out of a strange apartment than to pry someone from her bed. "I have to go to work," was her exit line.

She spent one night apiece with perhaps eight women. Only one of them kept turning up, Debra, a small wistful ex-acidhead with sad blue eyes and an air of feathery vagueness. Debra decided she was in love with Leslie and fastened on her from the time she walked into the Queen of Hearts. She liked Debra but didn't want to sleep with her again. She recognized she was still too involved with Honor and Bernie to care for anyone else. It had stopped, suddenly as a film breaking and with that same sense of coming abruptly out of an anesthetic in a strange glaring room, with pain too, unfamiliar pain everywhere through her, occupying her entirely.

Finally she called Tasha, who invited her over for Sunday brunch. Because of the rape project and meetings, Tasha's social times tended to be mornings and lunches. Tasha lived in a house with four other women on the east side, a few blocks from the river and the waterworks. They lived in a pleasant neighborhood, racially mixed and working class, with good-sized houses that came cheaply and big bosomy trees, all leafed out now. It was strangely lush, the grass tending to be less clipped than in the suburbs, the fat old trees meeting over the streets and shooting up tall and green behind the houses too in the ample yards. The neighborhood had a staid seedy bucolic air. As Leslie climbed the shallow wooden steps of the big front porch, she felt a pang of regret that she had given up coming regularly to the house, with its mellow easy atmosphere, that she had not spent more time with Tasha, who liked her so much.

Music played upstairs; a woman was singing plaintively. Another woman chatted on the phone in the front hall, sitting on the stairs in a yellow terrycloth robe with her hair in a turban, laughing into the receiver and eating a piece of toast with marmalade, while a white and tan dog lay at her feet with its tail thumping and its eyes on the toast going down.

Tasha took her into the diningroom, a big room with a bay window lined with shelves of plants. A big blond in a kimono nursing a baby nodded at her: Sherry, a straight woman she vaguely remembered. Leslie said, "You had your baby."

"April nineteenth. Look at him, isn't he something?"

"We're not an all-woman house any more." Tasha was smiling, bringing in from the kitchen a pitcher of café au lait and a fruitnut bread, still warm. "You want some cheese too?"

"If you have some."

"I remember you're a cheese lover. This is Rae."

A Black woman with honey brown skin had followed her out of the kitchen. Rae was big, much bigger than

208

Tasha, with square-rimmed reading glasses she tucked now in a pocket of her long dark red and white djellaba. Was Rae the same woman she had seen with Tasha putting up posters in the gay bar that time? Yes, she thought so. A big stately woman with a round smooth face, Rae looked her over slowly and carefully with a not entirely friendly regard. She must be living in the house. "You're living here?"

"No, I live over on John R." That was all she said.

Tasha came back with the cheese and this time Leslie looked at her more carefully. Tasha was wearing a new-looking blue version of a mechanic's jumpsuit that did not conceal her figure. In fact she looked good in it. "Where did that come from? I've never seen you in anything but overalls."

"I stole it off the rack in Hudson's," Rae said before Tasha could phrase an answer, flushing as Rae went on: "But I would have paid for it even, if I had to, worse luck. I don't like going out with a woman who wants to wear a paper bag over herself."

That little fantasy she had carried over of getting involved with Tasha all conveniently now and assuaging her loneliness went pop like the hot air balloon it was. She was in a mood too to feel assaulted by the image of women coupled off. Rae sure was taking care to inform her she was Tasha's lover. She drove it back and forth like a truck. As if she could read Leslie's mind, she flashed a big smile, her first. "Just making things clear. I like to be real clear, you know?"

Tasha beamed. She was so happy that she did not even push Leslie about coming back to work on the rape project. She was tremendously sympathetic that Leslie had finally altogether broken up with Valerie. Leslie felt a trifle dishonest, because most of her pain had nothing to do with Valerie, and she wasn't about to explain what it had to do with. But the comfort and the homey atmosphere were soothing anyhow. Rae relaxed now that she had made her hegemony clear. Rae was a big woman, but she moved powerfully and well; she strolled across the room centering it on herself. When she got up to get more coffee or use the telephone, everyone watched her. It would have taken effort not to. Trust Tasha to take on a Black lover, Leslie thought sourly. Any Third World lesbian could have her for a wink. But she felt jealous. Rae would turn anybody on.

Because of Debra's quiet persecution, she quit going to the Queen of Hearts and tried the Pig's Whistle instead. She disliked it. There were more men, more straight couples slumming, more johns cruising, and heavier old fashioned sex roles, the butches and femmes of yesteryear. Every time she talked to a woman, somebody was ready to slug her. She could not take it. She stopped going to the bars as abruptly as she had started and settled into celibacy again. She caught up on her sleep and worked even harder.

Her sensei, Parker, said she was improving and that she must try for her black belt in a month.

"That soon?"

"You can make yourself ready, if you work the way you've been doing these past couple of weeks. Instead of the sloppy way you were doing in April."

She had a new kata to learn. It was the most beautiful she had studied and she did it for pleasure as well as the coming test. One particular set of kicks and blocks she loved, for it was a stately swift dance.

Late Monday night she was working on the Simpson papers. When she took a break and was practicing her new kata in the women's room, she caught sight of herself in a mirror and her mouth opened in astonishment. How graceful, how strong, how good she looked! In spite of her quick success in the bars, she had been feeling so ugly that her reflection attracted her gaze as a stranger glimpsed dancing in a crowd might. Under fluorescent light her hair was dulled, but her body moved like a big cat in swift dignity. She thought of Rae. She was pleased. She bowed to herself and blushed. At that moment she began to forgive herself. At least her body was trying to live up to her standards; her body was good the way a good bird dog was good (her old dog Satan, a part-Labrador retriever), the way a good race horse was good, good as a nursing baby. She, that querulous conversation within, she must try to be worthy too.

Tuesday when she packed her rucksack with books and papers and got ready to leave, Cam was loitering in her raincoat at the door.

"You left home, you moved out, um?" Leslie said, slowing her stride to Cam's and simultaneously worrying about the time. She had to catch the Woodward bus.

"Oh, Mark's been after me to live with him. . . . His parents send him money and he's got a really nice apartment in a high rise. It's a studio but it's air conditioned. That seems silly now . . ." She put up her umbrella and motioned Leslie to come under it. "But in a month it will be too hot here to live, you know. Oh, I guess you don't. Mark says you come from a little town on Lake Michigan?"

"Mark seems to think he knows a lot about me."

Cam fiddled with her scarf. They walked down the block together. Cam seemed nervous. "Is something wrong?" Leslie asked finally.

"I've been worrying. . . . Honor is such a baby. She doesn't know a thing yet, believe me. It's all talk and pretend. She imagines she's sophisticated because she read *The New Yorker* for a year when she was fifteen. Honest to God, she used to read it cover to cover. She got me to give her a subscription for Christmas. She'd read the listings of what's going on about town—New York, in Detroit yet! As if just reading about all that stuff was magic." Cam brought herself up short and tugged at her scarf.

"She just doesn't like being patronized. She doesn't like older people coming on as if we know everything just because we're older, especially just a couple of years older." Was Cam an intermediary? She felt a stir of hope. Honor had asked Cam to speak to her. That was why Cam was so awkward. She would provide an opening. "I guess I've annoyed her that way myself."

"But she is young! She's just seventeen. I know she

told you she was a year older. I hope you didn't believe her? She really hasn't had any experience at all."

"We've all had experiences," Leslie said slowly. "Even in sense deprivation, you have experiences."

"Don't try to misunderstand me," Cam said shortly.

"I'm not. And I am not understanding." She felt her defenses hinge down. She stood straighter, she took longer strides. "I know Honor is young. I couldn't hardly miss that. She's in high school, after all."

"You know what I'm talking about."

"No, I don't." Leslie's face froze. Her back was hardening concrete.

"Honor is very innocent, and if anything happened to her, it would be just terrible. It wouldn't be fair! She doesn't have any experience even dating boys!"

"Are you worried about Paul?"

"You must think I'm stupid or something. Mark had to tell me you're a homosexual."

"If Mark had to tell you, it can't be very important to your understanding of me, can it? Do you imagine Honor doesn't know?"

"Well, I hoped she didn't!"

"Why? It's good for her to know different kinds of women who've made different choices—work choices, living choices, sexual choices. What's the point of her growing up imagining everybody lives in a daddy-mommy-baby family and votes Republican? If you think loving women makes me less fit to be her friend than loving men or dogs or vibrators, you just have to be crazy!"

"If I told Mama, she'd never let you in the house again."

"How does she feel about your living with Mark?"

"She doesn't understand! She's locked in some weird Victorian notion of how people live and I can't get through to her! Okay, I don't want to tell her. . . . But I don't like your hanging around Honor either."

"You used to see her as hanging around me. Look, I've never gone to bed with a woman who wasn't at least as interested as I was. Honor doesn't attract me that way.

212

I don't like straight women. I don't usually like straight women as friends, and I sure don't need them as lovers."

"If anything happens, Mama will think it's my fault. So will I. Because I could tell her."

"Then you can set your mind—if that's what you call it—at rest!" Leslie pivoted. She saw her bus coming and sprinted for it. The rain felt good pelting her. As soon as she was packed swaying in the late rush hour mass, she began thinking of all she should have said. "You're a woman who hates women. I've heard you putting yourself down. Do you think Honor should trust you over me? You do nothing but criticize her. You're jealous! You don't respect her." She almost missed her stop.

Tasha was trying to include her in social events, inviting her to eat at the house, inviting her to a party there. It was a nice quiet relaxed talky party, mostly women, five or six men, but everyone seemed to come in couples and know each other. She got into an unavoidable argument with the blond with the baby, Sherry, who was spouting nonsense about matriarchal prehistory, the worst kind of undocumented unproven wishful thinking.

"But writing came in around the beginning of patriarchy," Sherry said. She smiled a lot when she argued, as if to make contact across the words. "The first thing they did with it was to cover up the past. To rewrite the old myths. How can you expect we'll ever find a nice box in the desert with a scroll in it saying, This is how things were before the male revolution, folks, with nice cross-dating in a language you happen to be able to read."

"But your history isn't history, it's comic books. You just make it up wholesale to be the way you want it to be," Leslie said coldly.

She felt as if the other women around her were annoyed with her for starting the argument with Sherry. Tasha came over and tried to mediate. "You don't really disagree about the facts we know. I think you just attach different importance to the evidence that remains." Tasha looked momentarily pleased with herself as if she had produced a formula that had to work.

"I don't give women license to do slipshod work," Leslie said, mostly to Tasha. She was annoyed with Sherry, all that smiling and nodding and really an inflexible position behind it. "I have to work twice as hard and be twice as good as the men in my department just to survive."

"Twice as good at what?" Tasha laughed. "Not helping old ladies across the street. Goodness has nothing to do with it."

"As a woman I have to be more scholarly, more precise, better documented, with sounder statistics. Why can't Sherry see that?"

"Cause it's like studying theology. Can't you see that? The winner gets to tell about the fight." Tasha was glowing again. She would never be pretty—her features were crowded into her small triangular face—but she gave off a sense of loving energy that could replace prettiness.

"And to describe the loser," Sherry said, patting Leslie's arm. "We don't *have* a history."

They were trying to charm her, to cajole her into backing down, and she resented it. Tasha was saying, "You still admire that macher George. You think his way is *the* way. What are these damn Simpson papers you talk about? They're just a bunch of rich crooks. Essentially they're paying you off to put their house in order."

"But they had an effect on how things are here. They made choices that shaped Detroit."

"Boy, I don't doubt that," Tasha said, laughing. "If you really did an exposé of them. Or even just so we'd understand how they screwed us. Is that what you're doing?"

"Not exactly." Leslie sighed. Tasha was attacking just where Leslie feared the most. She wanted to leave. "But after all, I'm educating myself. Later I can do what *I* want."

"Leslie, why don't you get involved in the women's school? Use your skill now for us. Rae's teaching a course on the history of Black women. You could do a history course. Local. Women's history. Whatever."

214

"Not old wives' tales, which is all you people care about," Leslie said gruffly. "I don't have the time."

George was always pulling her into the domestic corners of his life. Almost she expected him to summon her to take notes while he was sitting on the toilet. He did not have her sense of privacy. Sometimes that made her feel like a servant, a real domestic. "You're part of the family," Sue was always telling her, but never said which part. Sue had grown up with Black servants and had one still in the cleaning lady who came three times a week. Leslie felt bogged down in their domesticity, always alien to it, the behavior of a different species, the dominant species which threatened the existence of hers, heterosexual man and complaisant woman and their offspring. Yet at times she could feel their house as a refuge. George is my protector, I shall not want.

He was talking in exuberant snatches over his shoulder as he roughhoused with Davey and Louise on the floor of the family room (TV, comfortable furniture, toys scattered so that the unwary foot would crush plastic). She could not watch George with his kids without feeling envy. Yes, she envied Davey and Louise the love they got without having to beg, a father who played with them on the floor, in the yard, who took them to the zoo and sailing and thought that was fun. She envied them the room each had, the fish, the hamster, the clean nice furniture. She envied them the creative day care, the Montessori kindergarten, the gentle exciting grade school they had started, the chance to be precocious gifted children. Who wouldn't be a charming bright-eyed genius with that kind of attention? She would not mind being George's kid instead of his research assistant. Louise's finger paintings were thumbtacked to the walls of his office. Imagine her own father putting up some daub Leslie had smeared, even if he'd had an office. The only time she'd drawn on a wall she'd had her face slapped and had to wash the wall down. Nothing remained from her childhood, nothing cherished by anyone; even her outworn clothes had been used up as rags.

George was especially exuberant because this Thursday evening there was something to celebrate: he had got his Rockefeller grant for the book they wanted to do. They would have the money for the capital investment project. "It's going to be real on a scale that'll make an impact if we do it right, if we carry it off elegantly. Nothing is more satisfying than busting myths," he said, lying on his back while Louise bounced on his chest. "I'm going to take the myth of the robber barons and reduce it to rubble. The development of industry was always intelligent and efficient. Money's always had the smarts here. We'll demonstrate it, and that's going to put us on the map." It meant a good dissertation for her, better than the previous game plan, with money to support her directly on that work. "We'll farm out the boring papers," George said. He didn't mean it—he'd keep control and of course the money and credit. But he'd let the papers absorb more grad students who were protégés of others in the department, and he'd withdraw his best talent into the capital research.

"Get trucking on your topic," he ordered. "I want a proposal from you by next week. Ow! Ow! I give up, Davey. Uncle!"

"Next week! I can't."

"You've been dawdling. You haven't got years and years, Red. How long do you think I'm going to stay here?"

"Do you have another offer?"

"Sure. Not one I'm ready to take. Hey, you watch it, you're ticklish too, lousy-Louise. Grrr. I don't even have to touch you to tickle you. Watch, I'm just going to point my finger at your belly and you're going to be tickled. One, two, three. . . . See, I told you. . . . This book is going to do it, but why sit it out here till the book's done? We'll make the move on the basis of the first papers we present. Full steam ahead."

Cold iron in her stomach. So soon. Would he take her with him? She couldn't switch schools again in mid-Ph.D. She had to finish before he left, or she was done for. She had better be done with everything but her dissertation by halfway through next year. She felt harassed, evicted. Now the dissertation topic would come right out of the work with George, and she would be paid; but she had to rush. Why, how lucky to have lost all her human relationships in the course of a week, because from now on her social life would be confined to saying hello in the elevator.

The food was set out, the wine, the cans of soda and beer, and now students and staff were arriving. Leslie was startled to see Mark and Cam come in with Honor. What was Honor doing here? Why had Cam agreed to bring her, after that wonderful chat? She suppressed the impulse to bolt the room. If Honor came knowing she would be here, perhaps there was a chance to reconcile. She hung back, watching. Honor was more dressed up (the gauzy blue gown) than anyone except Sue, who had on a long maroon dress.

She ran errands, she kept an eye on the supplies, she had earnest fleeting conversations, she sat at George's feet, all the while wishing she were home in her neat stark room alone. A headache made a lump behind her eyes. Everyone seemed to be smoking more than usual and the air felt stuffy and soiled.

Honor danced up to her. "Aren't you going to speak to me?"

"I wanted to. I wasn't sure that was what you wanted."

"How humble. And perceptive. I wasn't sure I did either, but I'm bored. What a lot of dull forlorn people one must encounter in graduate school. Perhaps everyone who likes people at all or is good at doing anything must leave, abandoning the sad cloddy types to plod along."

"Maybe it's more like the Army. A few years under an alien regime, with no time to do anything you want."

"Well, my life is definitely more interesting. . . . Definitely."

"I'm supposed to ask who or what, aren't I?"

"You know *who*. Bernar' and I have been getting closer and closer. It was perceptive of you, Leslie, to think of him in a way I hadn't. How fascinating you should have done that."

"You give me too much credit. I think of him as a snake in the grass."

"Oh, pooh! Just because he rejected you. You must be more broad minded. We can't all be attracted to each other, can we?"

"What happened between him and me isn't what he told you. You'll fingure that out sometime. . . . So you think you're in love with Bernie?"

"How blatantly patronizing! I *think* I'm in love! I *think* you just insulted me. Good night." With a flounce of skirts she stalked away, over to George, who was poking the fire. As Leslie watched, Honor took up a position with one arm against the fireplace wall and began flirting outrageously with him. Soon the other students were drifting away resentfully, because George was no longer listening to the bright remarks they spent ten minutes thinking up. He was not even looking at them when they spoke. Honor was putting on a performance for Leslie's benefit that Leslie thought was at least equal to her Cecily.

I won't give her the satisfaction of standing here suffering, she told herself and marched to the kitchen. There Sue was in an odd petulant mood. She was drinking a lot, not wine but vodka mixed haphazardly with whatever came to hand: orange juice, ginger ale, cola. "He's going to be a big success, isn't he?" Sue took her by the hand, squeezing.

"Sure," Leslie said awkwardly.

"I never expected it. You figure on that? Why, when I took up with him, sending my parents climbing the wall, he was a campus radical. He organized a teach-in, he was a hippie with hair down to his waist who used to hold his jeans up with a piece of rope. I just don't know, and that's the bottom truth, Leslie. Life is full of surprises, ain't that the truth? You know he got kicked out, fired from his job at Champaign-Urbana? In 1970 when I was carrying Davey? He was just an assistant prof. And for a year he couldn't find a job sweeping streets. We had to live off my parents, which was no treat! I swear it would've been less of a hassle to go on welfare! That's because I didn't come into my own money till I was twenty-five. That's how my granddaddy set it up. Honey, the first thing I ever did besides buy a decent king-sized bed and a whole bunch of clothes for Davey and George and some halfway decent maternity clothes for me—I was carrying Louise by then—was to pay my parents back every red cent we'd borrowed from them." She paused, lost. She could not remember what she had started out to say, and turned appealingly to Leslie.

"You had a real hard time starting out," Leslie edged away, hoping to turn Sue off. She was not sure how much of this Sue really wanted the others in the kitchen to hear. "I told George I'd bring him a refill."

"He ought to be drinking real bubbly tonight instead of that sour-piss white plonk."

She took a glass of wine to George, who received it with a quick automatic wink and turned back. He was still talking to Honor, who was baiting him about how boring she found the idea of quantitative history. "Sounds just like painting by number. What happens to Cleopatra's nose and Napoleon's personality?" Honor was touching her own long nose flirtatiously. Then she stopped abruptly, looking startled.

Leslie turned and there was Bernie unzipping his jacket in the foyer. She gasped and tried to compose her face, which felt twisted out of shape. He strode toward them. Then he saw Leslie and came on more slowly. Their gazes crossed like live wires and then immediately withdrew, in shock. They both at once looked away.

A kind of anger propelled her forward. "Good evening."

He choked on an answer. He turned his head as if to look at her, then looked past her.

She found herself able to smile then, a strange sneering sort of cracked smile she could feel hardening on her face, but she was proud of it: not to let him know how shaken she was. "What a surprise," she said coldly.

"I imagine so." He turned indolent and haughty. He tossed his head. Like a girl, she thought. "Thought you had the field to yourself. Tough titty. Here I am bold as brass."

"You always did like to make yourself at home chez George."

"Didn't do you any good, catching Honor without me, did it? I bet you tried too," he crooned.

Honor stepped between them. "Bernar', what are you doing here? I didn't expect you."

"Oh, just thought I'd give you a lift home."

"But Cam would. She brought me, after all." There was an edge of peeve to Honor's voice.

Maybe she did come to see me, Leslie thought, and I blew it. He's jealous of me with her, I can see it. I didn't flatter her enough.

"I wasn't sure, since she's living with Hot Pants. Anyhow, often you get bored at parties, and want to leave early."

"How thoughtful of you," Honor said with a wash of sarcasm. "I'll get my wrap. But you know I can't ask you in. Mama'll have to suppose Cam brought me back, since otherwise she'll get terribly suspicious."

"Come again," George said after her. "We do this every Thursday."

"I may do that," Honor called back. "I just may. We have an argument to finish."

"Is that her boyfriend?" George asked as they left.

"Not exactly. She's seventeen and lives at home. He's more a friend than a boyfriend."

Slowly people left. Midnight was the unofficial deadline. As twelve approached, she helped Sue put leftovers away, throw trash into bags, wash up. They were alone in the kitchen. The very last students were hanging around George and the embers.

"I know what I started to tell you." Sue gripped her by the shoulders. "About George and how he used to be. It was a big rebellion for me, you can't imagine how strict I'd been raised. I don't mean Eastern proper. I always went hunting with my granddaddy. I could ride and shoot from the time I was knee-high to a horse. I mean . . . what you do and what you don't. And you don't marry a pinko Yankee with hair to his waist. It's a wonder how George has buckled down. Of course I believed in him,

220

but I never did believe it would turn out . . . I mean, that he'd make it."

"Are you relieved? Or . . . not?"

"I'd have to be a flaming idiot not to think it's real nice to have my hubby doing well. Folks admiring him. Better pay. All that goes with it. We won't stay here long. The weather's something else. The city's just a ratty slum; nobody lives there. Just people shooting at each other. I'd like to live some decent place where it isn't cold and mean two-thirds of the year. It's nice to live in a place that likes to have you around, where you can ride without freezing to death or getting half-drowned trying to cross the street to get into your car."

"You'd like to be in the South?"

"The schools he has eyes for are in the East. Except California. I'd like that. It's closer to home and the climate's grand. I don't mind heat, I'm used to it. Besides you always have air conditioning. . . . You know, it was his bossiness. Wanting to get there and being impatient. That's what it was. I don't think George was ever properly pink. He was just in a hurry and that's where the action was."

"He's sure . . . er . . . conservative now." Leslie was thinking of the robber barons. "He still likes to stand things on their head, but it isn't political."

"Oh, it is, sugar, but it's horse-trading politics. The kind I understand. . . . He hasn't taken up with anyone here, but he will. It's only a matter of time. Isn't it? Only a matter of time?"

"Maybe he won't. He's busier and busier."

"He'll always find time for that. . . . You're the only one around here I feel at ease with. I know you see how it is. You've never been interested in him that way and that makes me feel real relaxed around you. His men grad students are scared to look at me. If I say a word about him, they put their tails between their legs and leap over the nearest fence and gone. . . . But you listen. Cause your heart is in the right place." Sue squeezed her shoulders, leaning forward.

She had an awful suspicion. She was scared. She stood

221

very still. She did not move. She did not take a breath. Tails between their legs and gone, exactly how she felt. Out the window. Down the drain. Don't move a muscle but say something, anything, quick. She's drunk and amorous and you're in trouble. "I do see. Yes, I see you're a wonderful wife and mother, just a wonderful wife and mother. I think you're really lucky, but no more than you deserve, to have such wonderful gifted children as Davey and Louise. I really admire you being such a wonderful mother to them. Davey's doing well in school too, isn't he? Reading by himself, I noticed."

"He's smart, he takes after his daddy, but he likes to read just like his mommy." Sue looked dazed, as if she had lost what she meant to do or say, but hung on to Leslie's hand.

I'm chicken too. None of us dare touch you. Besides, I don't like to get involved with straight women. It takes a powerful attraction to yank me through that barrier, and I don't feel it. Please let go my hand, pretty please.

"Well, good night, all. See you downtown," George boomed in the foyer and shut the door. Leslie gently withdrew her hand and went back to washing the glasses in the sink.

fifteen

"There's only two seasons here, winter and the Fourth of July," George groused and sent her on errands. The sun was glaring from a hazy sky, while bare arms, bare legs, occasional bare chests danced along the streets. Students were sunning wherever they could find a free patch. Everywhere trees grew, Detroit was so fiercely green it oozed. Residential streets were tunnels of green under the stately old trees.

She was toting her rucksack loaded with books along Woodward, the broad street that ran straight for miles and miles and miles, splitting the city into east and west sides. Woodward was either a slow roiling river of cars gutter to gutter, or it was empty as now at two o'clock in the afternoon. Detroit was a shift city, she thought. People were either commuting or else there was no one on the streets. The sky looked huge overhead, the clouds oversized as they puffed along. Everything felt flat and far apart, as if made on a scale for something other than people: a landscape for beings the size of large combines or earth moving equipment. She was swinging along under her load, feeling good. She was sweating, but to do anything physical on a university day was a gift.

When she fumbled for her key, she saw someone had stuck a sheet of paper in her box. Probably a throwaway: Madame Nosis, Spiritual Advisor; a special on pants at the Kleen World Kleeners. Lined page torn from a notebook. Neat curling handwriting.

May 14, Sunday evening about 9 P.M.

Dear Leslie,
    Mama thinks I am doing my homework, but I had to write you at once.

She looked immediately at the signature, Honorée. Then she started the letter again.

> This isn't an easy letter for me to write. First of all, I want to offer my sincerest apologies for that horrible day in your apartment when I lost my vile temper. After listening to Bernard pick me apart, I can sympathize with your feelings that day. I realize now why you didn't fight back—I couldn't answer Bernard because I was too numb. I had trusted him completely and had no defenses. I know why many of the things I said hurt—it was excruciating for me to know that part of what Bernard was saying was true.
> It wasn't pleasant to be told I retreat behind a wall of dreams and the security of my home and Mama's protection. I do not remember what I said to you on that day in question; that incident is hazy in my mind, which proves I feel dissatisfied with my role.
> I wish I could make up my mind about Bernard. It would be easier without nagging doubts. Can you forgive me? You are the only person who can perhaps understand and help me. I hope for the good fortune of regaining your friendship. I have so much to say to you, if you want to listen,

Your Honorée

Now what had happened? She, she was to forgive? Leslie found herself smiling. She had permitted Bernie to seduce her from considering Honor; she had let a man distract her from her friendship with a woman. Honor had been correct to be angry and jealous, but not to believe Bernie's lies. Now he must have lied himself into a corner. She had to know. She had to forgive Honor, if only because she missed her and her life felt empty of everything but work. She was the only person who could see through Bernie's manipulations, who could unmask him to Honor.

She wanted to run to the telephone; she found herself fluttering around the room. An excited warmth simmered through her. No, no, mustn't. This wasn't a lover. Honor was impossible as a romance, tremendously young and naive. The objections that had obtained still held. No. If she went to Honor, it had to be strictly sisterly. No gain. No blurring of the clear lines of the situation through personal desire. She stood before the mirror over the sink to make sure the smile was gone from her face. She looked serious, responsible. That was how it should be.

"Hello, Honorée. Leslie here. I got your note."

The conversation was brief. She had the feeling someone else was there at the other end. Mama? Bernie? Her scalp bristled. Bernie was there behind Honor, running some tricky selfish number, so that Honor could not speak freely. They arranged to meet in the Art Institute Saturday morning. She noticed that Honor carefully did not use her name.

Honor was waiting for her in the Rivera Court. "I loathe this room." She stood immediately, wearing loose white pants and an embroidered blouse, carrying an oversized straw purse.

"I kind of like it." Leslie looked around. She'd never been in the building, and the murals were impressive. "They're powerful." Monumental benign presences loomed there, all engaged in labor, all producing.

Honor led the way through the medieval rooms, past a rebuilt chapel to a circular staircase down. "This is one of my favorite, favorite places. You have to understand that the museum is mine. Ever since I was a little girl and Mama brought me here so I'd learn to love beautiful things, even before that, when Mama was carrying me and used to look at paintings so I'd be artistic." Honor stopped halfway down the stone stairs and sat abruptly near a slit of window. "If I sit just here, I can imagine that outside that window is some wonderfully romantic landscape like the South of France. I've been coming here for years to get away from Mama and my sisters. Where I could come and gossip with my best girlfriend Barbara back when she was still a human person with interests other than her dogfaced boyfriend."

Leslie leaned against the dark stone wall near the window, which had a yellow bulb behind the lattice, waiting for Honor to stop bubbling irrelevancies.

"Mama never minds if I'm going to the Institute or the library. But if I'm going to a movie she wants to know which one and is it a good movie and why do I want to waste my time on trash and the ads sound suggestive and so on. The museum's a free place where I'm allowed to go and escape."

Leslie shrugged. "I've never been in a real museum before."

Honor got up, dusting her pants. At the bottom of the stairs she craned to see her behind. "Did it leave a smudge? I think just because it's a castle stairway it won't be covered with good old Detroit dirt."

On the ground floor Leslie followed Honor into a cafe. The walls of the courtyard were brick and the architecture Romanesque, but the roof three stories up was a modern glass fantasy and the food came from a cafeteria line. By the time they were seated with orange juice and tea at a table, Leslie was annoyed. "Did you really want to talk to me? Or did you just want to see if I'd come when you called?"

Honor cupped her chin in her palm, her big golden-brown eyes melting with remorse or a good imitation. "I'm dreadfully sorry for how I acted. . . . But you know I felt quite hurt. . . . Now I need your friendship. Did you come only to sit around acting aloof?"

"You seem cheerful enough for both of us."

"I'm chattering. It's a defense. Can't you sense that?"

Leslie sighed. "What's up? I saw Bernie come to get you at George's."

"I swear he did it to check up on me. . . . I scarcely know where to begin. Right after that dreadful week when you and I quarreled, Bernie told me he loved me. I said, of course, and I love you too. Even more than Cam, next to Mama. And of course Dad."

"And he said that wasn't exactly what he had in mind." Leslie's voice rang out shrilly in the closed-in courtyard, louder than she had intended over the murmur of flirting couples and the muted clatter of dishes.

"What he means isn't clear." Honor frowned at her bitten nails. "I must stop that, it's an ugly habit. . . . He confuses me. Sometimes he seems to mean as a friend, a brother. And sometimes—you know—as my lover. It keeps shifting. Every time I think he may possibly, just possibly, mean he's fallen in love with me, I think I'm wrong and I must have a dirty mind or something. . . . Do you think I'm crazy?"

"Not for an instant. I recognize Bernie's touch at work." She sat up straight. "Has anything happened between you?" That weasel, he was making love to Honor. As soon as she was off the scene. As soon as he'd got rid of her. As soon as he'd hopped out of her own bed— But don't think about that. Bury it quick. Raw mistake.

"Oh, dozens of scenes every week. My life is much more thrilling. But how can I tell if I'm imagining half of it? You don't understand. Mama has a tremendous imagination and I know I inherited it. We're terribly alike, Mama and I. In some ways."

Yeah, she imagines wasting diseases. "You'll admit she exaggerates sometimes? About your being sick and things?"

"Oh, you know Mama, she's always worrying. . . . But when I was, oh, nine, ten, she got a notion that Dad was seeing another woman. She's always trying to find out what he's doing, he's so secretive. It's because she doesn't want him throwing away money on wild inventions. But she overheard some conversation with one of his cronies about an Adeline. . . . He was staying out late at night, disappearing weekends—like he does half the time anyhow, you never know where he is. Finally she confessed to me what she thought. . . ."

"Your mother told a nine-year-old?" But of course she'd always known too what was going on between her parents, even when her mother thought she was successfully lying about where her father was for two weeks.

"Mama *always* confided in me. . . . Anyhow, we played detectives. Yes, we honest to God followed Dad. . . . Adeline turned out to be a stupid motorboat one of his friends had on Lake Saint Clair, and they were rebuilding the engine together. . . . I could be just as full of nonsense about Bernie. . . . I think Mama writes novels in her head too."

"Has he . . . made love to you?"

"Not *yet*." Honor smiled as if she was quite proud of herself. "But I think he's *thinking* about it. . . . Mama's getting very suspicious. It's such a drag, I feel like saying, But, Mama, he's homosexual, you know. I'm disgustingly safe."

"But you don't quite believe that."

"Oh, he's been more open with me now that he doesn't have you to confide in. I don't believe he *is* anything, like some fate off an astrology chart. But he told me more of his experiences. . . . Besides, I'm discussing what I feel like saying to Mama. . . . It's part of what confuses me, Leslie, about what's happening!"

"Why don't you ask him what he has in mind?"

"Leslie! What am I supposed to say? Voulez-vous accouchez avec moi? Really! . . . Leslie, what did you quarrel about?"

"Thought you believed what he told you."

"If only you'd tell me your side! Don't you think you owe that to me?"

"I'll think about it." Leslie had no intention of doing so. "It's not something I feel I can talk about just yet."

"Did you quarrel . . . about me?" Honor leaned forward, her lips a little parted.

Leslie was startled. "About you? Why do you ask that?"

228

"Well . . . Bernie said the strangest thing once." Honor looked down into her lap. "When I told him I'd broken with you, after that awful Tuesday, he seemed glad at first. Then he started pacing and he said in a low nasty voice, I'm quoting him, that I'd be sorry and I'd come to love you." A golden eye glinted from under lashes, watching her for a reaction. "Why did he say that?"

"I'm so lovable," Leslie said. "Can't think of any other reason." Honor was flirting with her, she knew it. I must not be rigid, she thought, I must be open to her. Better me than Bernie, after all.

"So you'll come over Monday, the way you used to?"

"This Monday I can't. George and I have a meeting with the foundation people. . . . I'm eating supper with them. I don't know how long it'll run, but I'll come over Monday night whenever I get away."

Sue presented Leslie with a summery outfit, crushed natural cotton pants and a striped natural and brown top, from Greece. Sue said, "Oh, my sister Rosalyn bought it, but it's miles too tight on her," but Leslie could see it had never been worn, and the label was from a boutique in a nearby mall. She imagined George and Sue consulting about how to get her into something more acceptable to meet with the foundation people, and Sue concocting the story about her sister.

In the mirror at the Japanese restaurant on the first floor of a local hotel, Leslie looked herself over. She actually liked the way she looked in the loose light pants and the top with its vague suggestion of faded awning stripes. In fact, she looked forward to getting away from George and the two men and going straight to Honor's in her new outfit. She had an excuse for arriving dressed up, because she was coming from the meeting.

At eight it was not yet dark; the night was mild and felt spacious. Almost, after the rather sumptuous dinner with teriyaki and saki and a plum liqueur afterwards, with her head a bit detached from her shoulders, a balloon on a string, almost she would have liked to hail a cab on the sidewalk outside the restaurant. But she resigned herself to a brisk walk and a couple of buses.

By the time she came down Honor's street she was sober, but the night was soft and gentle enough to keep her mood good. It was a long lingering twilight, a night she could imagine sleeping outside with a lover. The air felt just the same temperature as her skin. It was neither warm nor cool but perfect and sensual. She wished she could be with Honor in some more pastoral setting, on a lake, on the screened-in porch of a lake cottage; there must be a hundred thousand such objects within two hours' ride of here. The lake would look lighter than the shores, reflecting the pale gray of the sky that still retained a faint plum glow. . . . Car in the drive? In fact there was Bernie's Mustang parked across the street, and in the drive was a '71 Chevy she vaguely thought she had seen before, right there in that drive.

Damn Bernie. Damn Honor. What was he doing here when Honor knew she was coming? She felt like turning on her heel and leaving. She was furious. Yes, she would simply turn and walk off and leave Honor to her own devices, the little two-faced conniver. She was surprised by the rush of her own anger, ashamed; she must not yet be as sober as she had thought.

She stood undecided on the front walk and then she heard loud voices inside. "No!" Honor was wailing at the top of her lungs. "You don't understand!"

A fight? She went forward hurriedly and climbed the rickety front steps, hopping over the broken one to bang on the bulging screen door perfunctorily.

". . . think I find it pretty hard to understand! I think it'll take some tall explaining," said Mama Rogers' very loud voice.

"Hello?" Leslie said. "I'm here!"

"Oh, Leslie! Come in!" Honor ran to the door and almost embraced her with relief. "Oh, Leslie. . . . How nice you look. You're so dressed up!"

"Er, yes," Bernie said. He was standing in the livingroom barefoot, wearing Honor's lavender dressing
230

gown, looking awkward with discomfort. "We were actually expecting her some time ago."

"Oh were you?" Mrs. Rogers said. She was holding something to her face, an ice pack, and when she took it away to speak, her right cheek looked swollen. She wore a baby blue pants suit, and she was shining with anger. She stood very straight, her shoulders thrust back, springy with indignation, her face flushed, her eyes glittering. She looked ten years younger. "Do you always lie on my daughter's bed in a dressing gown when you're expecting company?"

"I explained about the bicycle accident. The construction site. I hadn't expected a big puddle there."

"And then you got off your bicycle, got in your car, and drove over here to take a bath. Of course. I understand completely."

"Leslie, how come you're so dressed up?" Honor asked ingenuously. "Where were you?"

She wants me to impress Mama with how respectable I am. Why not? Just so it doesn't rub off on Bernadine in the bathrobe! She addressed herself directly to Mrs. Rogers. "I couldn't tell exactly what time I'd get free. I was having dinner with my faculty adviser, Professor Sanderson, and two men from the Rockefeller Foundation. I'll be working on a project that they're financing, and I was having dinner with all of them near the University."

"How fascinating," Mama said, and turned back to Bernie. "I suggest you put your clothes on and go home." Briskly she turned back to Honor. "Why don't you get Leslie some lemonade?"

Honor backed reluctantly out of the livingroom, throwing a glance of appeal to Leslie. What was she supposed to do? And what had been happening? She glared after Bernie's retreat into the bathroom. "Is something wrong?" she asked Mrs. Rogers. "Your face looks swollen."

Mama Rogers snorted, still standing with the ice pack to her face. "When I was eating in the cafeteria, I felt this awful sensation, and then a piece of my crown broke right off. I almost swallowed it."

"That sounds painful," Leslie said, still standing also. She wouldn't sit until told to. She did not want to leave, but she was not sure she was going to be asked to stay.

Bernie bounded back in with his clothes on. They did not look markedly muddy, although he had obviously tried to do what he could in that line. He opened his mouth to speak, but Mrs. Rogers cut him short. "Good night, Bernard. I'll say good night to Honor for you. I know you have to be hurrying along, immediately."

Bernie opened and shut his mouth and then fled, saying at the door, "I'm terribly sorry, Mrs. Rogers. . . . Really, I think you misunderstood. . . ."

"How stupid of me," Mama said dryly. "Good night."

Honor came dashing back in. "Where did Bernie go?" She had made up a pitcher of frozen lemonade, obediently.

"I sent him home. Sit down. Won't you sit down too, Leslie? I'm sorry you came all this distance to walk into a family altercation. You might as well have a glass of lemonade before you go home too."

"Thank you," Leslie said humbly, glad of any delay. At least she wasn't being kicked out with Bernie. And Bernie was gone. She felt an enormous relief. She had managed not to look at him, not to speak to him. But she felt a loose raw anger in her just pushed down. She looked now at Honor, asking with her eyes what had happened.

"Mama came home early because she hurt her tooth," Honor said. "Does it hurt terribly, Mama dear? Did you take any aspirin?"

"Were you smoking marijuana too?" Mama asked icily, sitting down on the couch with a deep sigh of exasperation.

"Mama, I don't know what you're talking about? I've never smoked anything. I don't care to. He was merely smoking a regular cigarette."

"You're not as good a liar as you imagine," Mama said. "I have a nose. I caught Cam with that three times already, and you know it."

"I didn't know what he was smoking, and I think it was just plain old tobacco without a filter. I certainly wasn't
232

smoking anything." Honor clasped and unclasped her hands and then forced herself to stop. She shook her hair back and tried to adopt a confiding manner. "Mama, really, how could you be so rude to him? He lives in a roominghouse, he's a student putting himself through college. He doesn't have hot water where he lives."

"Do you invite every young man you meet to come and take a bath at our house, alone with you?" Mama took down the ice bag and groaned. "I'm ashamed of you. You show no sense at all. There's something absolutely out of control in a young high school girl entertaining a man older than herself alone in her house at night. Him with no clothes on except her own dressing gown. Her in a provocative dress."

Honor was wearing the apple green dress with the deep V-neck. "But Mama, you made this dress for me. What's wrong with it?"

"It's not suitable for wearing in the house alone with a man. You know that. Why did you put it on?"

"Well, Leslie was coming, and she was going to be dressed up too."

"I presume she had a reason, since she was coming from an important dinner."

"Mama, Bernard's my friend. He's not going to . . . attack me. Really. I'm not ten years old. How could you throw him out of the house without consulting me? While I was in the kitchen making lemonade!"

"I asked him to leave and I don't want him back. If you want to have him over when I'm here, that's one thing. You can invite him to luncheon this weekend. But not otherwise. Do you hear me?"

Honor sobbed into her hands for a moment as if experimentally. Her mother did not even look at her but put the ice pack back against her face. Honor put down her hands and stared at her mother. "How can you be so angry at me? I didn't do anything!"

"Oh?" Mama glared at her over the ice pack. "Perhaps I came home too soon?"

Leslie felt a strange grateful kinship to Mama Rogers, allies in their opposition to the slimy Bernie machinations.

As if Mrs. Rogers sensed their bond, she turned suddenly to Leslie without bothering to remove the ice pack. "What do you think about the situation, Leslie?"

"Oh . . . I wasn't here . . . I don't really know Bernie that well, but I'm sure he's not . . . dangerous."

"I thought you were friends," Mrs. Rogers said with sly curiosity, putting down the ice pack.

"No," Leslie said shortly. "We're not."

"I thought you were," Mrs. Rogers looked as if she would have liked to ask a great many more questions, but politeness restrained her. She glanced at her daughter again, her eyes narrowing. "You're not to have him here again without me. Do you hear me, Honor?"

"Mama! Don't you trust me?"

"Perhaps you trust yourself a bit too much!" Mrs. Rogers spoke quietly now, but her anger had not abated. Her eyes flicked over her daughter warily, with a certain disgust and almost a certain amusement. Leslie felt as if Mrs. Rogers was rapidly constructing a great many scenarios in her head about what might have happened, and liking none of them.

sixteen

The following Monday Leslie came to Honor's in her old late afternoon time slot. They were operating in awkward carefully arranged shifts. Leslie was to leave before supper, Bernie to arrive at six for the early evening shift, and he was to clear off by nine-thirty to be out of harm's way long before Mama got home. Leslie and Honor sat at the kitchen table about five-thirty. The evening was cool again but clear, in the fifties.

"Oh, I admit it looked wicked," Honor said. "In point of fact, I had a ticklish feeling that something was in the air. . . . You know, Mama is really unfair to him. He has no hot water at all in that dreadful depressing insecticide-smelling roominghouse—"

"Oh, you've been there?"

"Only for a moment! But who would have expected her to get so upset? I've never made her that angry. Nothing I've been able to say has got around her yet. I'm sure it was her tooth hurting so much. I always been able to talk her around before. . . . What's that?"

A key turned in the door and Mrs. Rogers walked in.

"Why, Mama, hello." Honor sprang up. "Did your tooth start bothering you again?"

Mrs. Rogers kissed her on the cheek. "I had my hours changed. Isn't that wonderful? Your dad's not going to be tremendously pleased, but that's the way it goes. You can't please everyone, can you? I need to spend more time with my darling daughter." Mrs. Rogers went to hang up her old black cloth coat, trimmed with fur that had long since lost its luster and most of its hair. "I'll be working nine to five. We can eat supper together the way a family should. After all, soon my Honor will be going to college. I have to enjoy your company while I can, don't I, darling? How are you, Leslie? We haven't seen you since last Monday. Have we?"

"I've been working very hard," Leslie said woodenly. "I'm going to have to get my degree work done faster than I expected."

"Then will you go back to— Was it Frankfort? Lake Michigan anyhow. It must be beautiful there."

"I'll go wherever I can get a job." With George. Whither thou goest.

"Mama, how does it happen you didn't tell me you'd changed your hours?" Honor asked carefully. Her face looked pinched. She could not conceal her lack of pleasure.

"I wanted to be sure it was really going through. I didn't want you to be disappointed if they couldn't give me the day shift. . . . I have a surprise for you." Mrs. Rogers clasped her handbag before her meaningfully.

"Oh, what's that?" Honor asked dully.

"I got it on my lunch hour today. Heavens knows, I'm a bit overweight, how can it hurt me to miss lunch once in a while?" From her handbag she took a small box wrapped in white tissue paper.

"What is it? Honor took it, excited now. "Can I open it?"

"Certainly, darling. What else is it for?" Mrs. Rogers moved closer, standing at Honor's elbow. "Do open it."

It was a watch. "Oh, Mama! I can't stand it! It's beautiful. Oh, Leslie, look! How does it go on? What a darling bracelet! It's a real bracelet too, not a cloddy band. Mama, it's heavenly, it really is. It's exactly what I wanted."

"It's a good watch. Don't leave it on while you wash your hands. And don't forget it on the wash basin. It's a lady's watch, Honor, its not meant to take a beating."

236

"I'll be ever so careful, Mama, truly I will! It's exactly what I've dreamed about. Exactly."

Hmmmm, Leslie thought, what a clever bribe. She felt sorry for Bernie and automatically she glanced out the livingroom window. It was about time for her to leave and she was about to say so when she saw his broken-backed Mustang parking across the street. Oh, shit, she thought, and moved right up against the window. He got out of the car and began to cross the street. It hurt to see him, it hurt. She felt a little dizzy, as if something was pressing hard on her forehead. He saw Mrs. Rogers' old Chevy in the drive and slowed his steps, looking hard at the house. Leslie held up her hand in a stop sign.

Bernie waved back. Then he saw it was her and he stopped abruptly, scowling. Thinks I haven't cleared out on time. She tried shaking her head.

"What's wrong, Leslie?" Honor asked. "Isn't it a beautiful watch?"

"It's lovely, lovely." Leslie jumped away from the window. "My goodness, it's close to six. Isn't it?"

"I can give you the exact time on my stunning seventeen-jewel timepiece. It is now six oh five exactly." Honor was imitating an operator. Then she listened to herself and her eyes grew larger. "Oh." Casually she drifted toward the front windows. Bernie stood across the street leaning on his car and watching the house. Honor winced. She tried to make a concealed go-away wave as she turned back to the room. "Why don't we invite Leslie to stay for supper? I'll make supper for a special treat, Mama. Wouldn't you like that?"

"I don't much feel like scrambled eggs tonight, and I'm sure Leslie, if she accepts your invitation, would want something more substantial."

"Mama, I can do more than make scrambled eggs. You go change and relax and I'll make a tunafish casserole. You'll be surprised!"

"I wouldn't mind the surprise at all." Mrs. Rogers chuckled. "I'm weary enough. All right, I'll change. My feet are killing me."

As soon as Mama shut the bedroom door, Honor flew

237

to the window. Bernie was slumped across the street staring at the house. Honor waved wildly, Go away. He waved back briskly. "What's wrong with him?" Honor asked. "Standing there like a prospective burglar casing our house. Like a peeping tom! Leslie, go out and tell him to go away."

"No." Leslie shook her head. "I don't want to speak to him. I won't run errands to him for you."

"Leslie!" Honor pulled the blinds shut. "Let him stare at a blank wall then. What's wrong with him?" She got busy in the kitchen as Mama came back and dropped on the couch with a sigh. She was wearing a flowered housedress and old blue mules. "Maybe I'll watch the evening news," she said, flicking on the television. Then she frowned. "Honor, why did you shut the blinds? It isn't even dark yet."

"Oh, let it be. It's cozier this way." Honor came quickly back to the livingroom carrying a stalk of celery. "Who wants everyone looking in from the street?"

"Really, if you're that nervous, I don't know how you stood it alone in the evenings. It's high time I changed my hours."

Leslie did not want to encounter Bernie, but she had work to do and she did not want to eat what she saw Honor putting together with a self-important frown. It did not look edible to her—cornflakes and tunafish and celery and pimientos and mayonnaise about to be baked in the oven. She decided to take a chance on Bernie. When she walked out, he was sitting in his car. He had the radio turned to a rock station and he was sitting in the driver's seat slumped over the wheel glowering, drumming his fingers on the wheel. She grimaced and walked on, staying on her side of the street.

Then she stopped. It really was absurd. It was still broad daylight at six-thirty and Mama might decide to put the blinds back up at any moment. She could not help seeing Bernie—or hearing him. Honor would be in more trouble.

She turned back and crossed the street, coming up behind him. He did not hear her, with the radio blasting

238

away. She kicked the car door, standing there feeling like an imitation punk with her hands shoved in her jean pockets. "Hey," she said roughly, not looking at him, "her mother came home early. She's had her hours changed. Surprise. You better get out of here." Then she turned on her heel and marched off. Behind her the radio ceased. She walked more quickly. Then she heard him gun the motor. He could not exactly get off to a squealing start in the old Mustang, but he turned it around in a driveway, and then went past her at what speed the wreck could summon, barging up the street leaving a wake of oily smoke to envelop her.

She thought she had avoided looking at him, but nevertheless she had seen him out of the corner of her eye. She kept seeing his face: haggard, furious, chewing on something—some sour rind of anger, of disgust, of frustration. He looked awful. He looked sick. What was wrong with him? Why was he acting so crazy? It did not concern her. It had nothing to do with what had happened with her, because he had run from her to Honor. He had run straight from her to tell Honor he loved her, interchangeable women. Never mind him, never mind him. Forget him. Never think of him again. Forget him as he had forgotten her. If only he was out of her life for good, out and gone. What a relief that would be. Never to hear his name again. She was proud of herself for having summoned the raw nerve, the strength to speak to him, for Honor's sake. That made up secretly a little of the shame she had toward Honor. That was one stroke back from the thing she had done. But she was bothered by flashes of his haggard, desperate face chewing on cold anger as he slumped over the wheel with the radio on raucous and loud. It was not the face of someone in love, she thought. Only someone in raw need.

Tasha was insistently showing her the rooms of the women's school, some freshly painted and inviting, others still begrimed with the dirt of decades. Two of the rooms were ready for use.

"It wouldn't be like the rape hot line," Tasha was saying. "I can understand your getting tired of doing that month after month. It's such an emotional drain."

"Can you understand? You never let on you could."

Tasha shrugged. "To me it's important to continue. . . . But this is different. It's not emergency work. It's not tending the wounded, Leslie."

"Aren't we all wounded?"

"Aw, don't bullshit. We're all wounded some, but you don't have any trouble recognizing somebody who's bleeding. Here you'd be working with women who want to learn what you'd be teaching them. You'd get feedback. You'd feel better, not worse."

"Like the stupid fight I got in at your house."

"Was it so stupid, Leslie? I mean"—Tasha took her arm—"do you really think that quantitative stuff helps anybody? I mistrust it too."

"You mistrust everything academic."

"But I don't mistrust knowledge. I really don't. Tell me what you're doing at school. So I'll understand. What's that foundation paying you to do?"

"It's pretty technical—computers and that stuff." Leslie felt rotten. But she just could not tell Tasha what George had told her, the way he had described it. George liked to make things sound . . . oh, stood on their heads. She had to think up some way to describe it to Tasha so it would sound better. She had to think up some way to describe it to herself. "What are you living on, Tasha? Is the women's school paying you?"

"You have to be kidding! We're still raising money for the building. We need everything—tables, chairs, equipment, everything!"

"So what are you living on?"

"I still got unemployment from the hospital job. Maybe six, seven more weeks," Tasha said.

"Then what?"

"I'll find something. Another hospital job. Why worry now? I want to get the school on its feet first."

"If I quit George, I wouldn't get unemployment. I wouldn't get anything but a job waitressing. I can't even type."

240

"But, Leslie, Rae works full time as a nurse. I'm not asking you to give up but one evening a week. . . . And you won't look at the work you're doing."

No, I won't, Leslie thought, feeling herself clenched tight. I won't. You can't make me. "Tasha, I don't have any free evenings. I really don't."

"Why don't you make one free?"

"It's fine," George said, slapping his palm down on her thesis proposal. "We'll take it to the committee, but we'll carry it. Good job. Now an outline. Let's say by the end of June."

"I can't."

"Red, you have to." He grinned his little square grin, enjoying applying the pressure. "You've got no choice. . . . Okay, dismissed. And send in Hennessy. I have a little bad news for him."

What was the use of good news to her about the proposal when it only made him push her harder on an impossible schedule? She felt as if she were staggering out of his office. Hennessy was down the hall in the room where the teaching fellows and research assistants in the department hung out, where they shared desk space and met students. She came in a little shyly, because she did not spend a lot of social time with the other students, two thirds men, and because she had her own desk outside George's office. This seemed a traditional smoke-filled room, a male enclave. It took her a moment through the haze of smoke and her shyness to pick out Hennessy straddling a chair backwards and boasting, as usual, to the only woman in the room. "So I walked into my bedroom and what was all over the floor but a woman's black lace undies—"

"Hey, Hennessy," she said gruffly, to cover her embarrassment. "George wants you."

"How come?"

"How would I know?"

"I thought you were into all his secrets, hey, Red?" Hennessy very reluctantly rose from the chair, and the

241

woman with evident relief pushed out of the room past Leslie.

"It'd take ten r.a.'s to keep track of George's secrets, don't you know that?" She walked beside him back to the office. He was looking a little worried, his broad forehead wrinkled, his mouth pouting more than usual.

"What did he say, exactly?" Hennessy asked.

"Just to tell you he wanted to see you," she lied nervously.

Cam was on the phone. She blew a kiss at Hennessy. "Hi, darling. Hey, Leslie, it's my sister, but she wants to talk to you." Cam did not look at all happy about that, but handed her the phone and looked down as if going on with her work. But Cam did not resume typing. She pretended to be proofreading.

Leslie had to take the phone call at Cam's desk, sitting on the edge. "Leslie, here. How're you doing, Honorée?"

"I'm furious at Bernie, just furious!"

"What did he do now?"

"I walked into school this morning and there was a note stuck to my locker. Anybody could have read it, it wasn't even sealed. Listen to this: 'My sweet love, Don't let your mother's tyranny'—spelled t-i-r-a-n-y—'keep us apart. We can beat the rap if we stick together. I'll be on tap all day hanging around this dump. Know I'm always with you and never letting go. Love, XXXX, Bernie.' He stuck it right on my locker!"

"How did he get into the school?"

"I don't know! He didn't have a pass and there's a cop. I was working on library staff at the check-in desk when he came barging in as if he owned the building. I didn't know what to do!"

"Why didn't you tell him to go outside and wait?"

"He wouldn't, Leslie! He just wouldn't. . . . I got Phyllis to cover the desk for me, and I went into Conference Room Two with him. That's where we keep pamphlets. Its right off the library, the walls are half glass and everybody could look right in and see us having an argument. Mrs. Schumacher, the librarian, stuck her head in to see what was going on. Heaven knows what she thought. I pretended I was helping him find a pamphlet, but I was supposed to be at the check-in desk and she knew it. . . . He's going to get me in trouble at school. He never finished high school, and I'm afraid he's going to see that I don't."

"You were embarrassed." Honor was so young, Bernie and she kept forgetting. Honor was embarrassed in front of the kids she went to school with. Leslie felt a moment's twinge of sympathy for him but she quieted it. "What on earth does he want? He sounds desperate."

"He's certainly making me desperate."

"Er . . . has your mother actually forbidden you to see him?"

Honor sighed. "In effect."

"So that's why he's desperate."

"Why can't he be patient? After all, I'm lying to her for his sake. I'm sneaking around. He's putting pressure on me to lie and sneak around still more. He doesn't seem to understand that I do live in Mama's house and she works hard to support me, and she and Dad have saved for years so I can go away to college. I know all that. I'm not stupid. I'm not blind. She wants me to have what she couldn't. She wants that as desperately as Bernie wants me to go sneaking around the streets to see him!"

High melodrama, that's what it was. She wondered how much of it Cam could follow, pretending still to proofread the same page of a speech George was delivering. "I'll meet you later and you can tell me what he really wanted in Conference Room Two."

As Leslie went back to her desk, she smiled wryly: Letters, phone calls, assignations, rendezvous, accidental meetings, meetings not accidental, scenes of high passion and great wordiness. Avoiding Bernie as much as she could, Leslie was playing against a hidden antagonist. Bernie and she were fighting for Honor, but she was committed to taking no satisfaction except the moral one from her struggle. She must try to remember that. Since Monday of last week she had managed to avoid the sight of him, although his name was always on her lips. Out of my life, she thought, I want you altogether out. So I never

243

hear your name again. It always hurts. To say your damned name hurts. She imagined him dead, struck down suddenly in the street by a car, and she felt a sense of enormous relief.

Hennessy came bolting suddenly out of George's office. "What's up, baby?" Cam said to him.

"Come on," he said. "Come outside a minute." Then he glared over Cam's head at Leslie. "I bet you're behind this."

"I don't know what you're talking about," Leslie said nervously, half rising. George must have told him his assistantship would not be renewed; he wanted to give it to that guy with all the mathematical background he had fastened on as the star of his methodology seminar. She could not say that, though, since it wasn't arranged yet and George would not let her reveal his plans, so she was stuck with the lame pretense of knowing nothing.

Cam gave her a puzzled glare and followed Hennessy into the hall to hear his news.

She ate nothing. She could not. She was tight and loose at once. She was tight because it mattered, it mattered a lot. She was astonished to find out how much she wanted that rag, how much she wanted that authentication. She did not like looking into herself and discovering such a passion lurking where she had thought of herself as being pure. But she was loose because she was convinced that she was ready. Her body had never felt so good.

From the moment they bowed in, from the first ceremony, she felt right. Somewhere in her a superstition curled that she was acting correctly in her life and that therefore she was going to perform well. The day was long and most of it was spent waiting and watching. Everyone must perform, from the black belts to the white belts, even the children. There were special exhibitions by her instructor and the instructor of the school they were holding the ceremony with. There was a visiting expert who gave a demonstration also. When she performed her kata, she knew she was good. Her dance was beautiful and swift and strong. It was how it should be. The kata

244

danced her. She felt less sure in combat because she was overmatched. The Black woman she was fighting had twenty pounds and three inches on her, and no matter what anyone said, that counted. She was good, she was very good. Leslie wished briefly she was watching her from the sidelines instead of out there in the still center facing her. Her heart failed her and she lost a point right away. Then she decided she must flow with it and do the best she could.

She lost the match but won her belt. At the ceremony she kept waiting for the pleasure, the triumph to hit. She felt weak and almost depressed. She went out for a Chinese meal with the other students from her class, and for once their sensei went with them. She ate, she tried to chat, she accepted congratulations, but she kept feeling strange. It was hard to remain at the table throughout the long talkative meal.

"I've been cruel to him," Honor was peering into Leslie's bathroom mirror. She had no hesitation about coming to Leslie's now and in fact dropped in more freely than Leslie really liked, when she was trying to clear up her end-of-term work. "Look at the gorgeous earrings he gave me yesterday. Aren't they wonderfully gypsyish?"

"I wonder where he stole them."

"Leslie! Do you suppose he did?" Honor sighed, making them swing and tinkle. "It's so sad. I can't wear them anyplace where Mama might see them. But at least I can wear them in school."

"You really shouldn't just appear without calling. Most of the time I'm not home."

"Oh, I don't mind dropping by George's office to look for you. It's a treat to get out of the house, and I can always say I'm coming to see Cam."

"I got my black belt, Honor. I won it." She watched Honor's face carefully, hoping to taste some victory or satisfaction in her reaction.

"That's wonderful. But I like coming by here. . . . It's really to much . . . stuffier somehow with Mama home all the time. I'm not used to it! I'm used to more freedom."

She needed intimacy: someone paying attention to her, a woman giving her attention, so she could feel what was happening in herself, so she could sort out what was wrong. Somehow a phase was over. "I've lost all sense of purpose in my karate. I've got the black belt, and I don't know why any more."

"Well, I never did understand it. I suppose it's like getting a badge in girl scouts or an A in English comp." Honor stole another glance at the earrings, setting them tinkling.

"I just can't remember why I've been doing it, I can't remember why I've been pushing myself harder and harder. I can't remember."

"Leslie, we've been too hard on Bernie. It's not his fault Mama is mistrustful of him—and he took me out for an Italian ice. I had such a marvelous time with him. We've been misjudging him."

"But he hasn't misjudged anything," Leslie said sourly, putting away her problem like a game Honor refused to play. "Mama gave you a watch, so he'll give you earrings."

"Leslie, he can't be that calculating. Really!" Honor touched the earrings. "Do you know what he said about you? He said you fall in love with people who are different from you because they're different, but then you try to turn them all into yourself. You try to turn everybody into you."

"Nonsense!" Leslie said angrily. She was in this game to win nothing, she must remember that. Slowly with each day of struggle she was beginning to relinquish Honor. "How would he know? How would he know anything about who and how I love?"

"I guess we all think we observe each other accurately," Honor said. "That's how you think you know he's calculating, isn't it?"

Leslie paced across the room angrily from the window on the fire escape to the window overlooking the busy street. Something caught her gaze. She swung back and looked again. Damn him! "I see we have a stake-out across the street," she said lightly.

"A steak house?"

"Bernie on guard. Watching this very window." She stared at him through the window and balefully he stared back at her. He had made no attempt to conceal himself but stood in the middle of the sidewalk.

Honor ran over to the window, nudging her aside. She laughed and waved. "What a surprise! Shall I ask him up?" she said wickedly.

"He looks so happy in the street. Perhaps he'll serenade you," Leslie stalked away from the window.

"Are you jealous? Bernie says you're jealous."

"I say Bernie's jealous, and there's the proof." Leslie pointed at the window. "Your faithful dog."

"It is a little heavy . . . but oh well. I'll go down and see what he wants. Maybe he'll give me a ride home."

seventeen

"He's driving me crazy! Look what he stuck on my locker! Everybody's teasing me. And my counselor called me in to tell me all visitors have to check in to the office! Thank God it's too late to affect my recommendations for college. . . . Look at it!"

Bernie had written on a page torn from a notebook. She had a brief pang of conscience, that she should not read his letter to Honor. But after all, how could she give advice? And she was curious, she would admit silently to herself.

> Dearest Honoreé.
>
> After a blinding flash of pride, I need time before I can see what I did wrong. And you jumped on me so hard, all for what other people say. Who cares? But this is more than an apology, an apology only says I'm sorry, this says I love you.
>
> Baby, I'm sorry more than I can say for my "pushing you." But you have to believe me. I'm sincere not only in what I say now but in everything I ever said to you.
>
> Others around you accuse me of many things including lying, as if I could ever lie to you. Perhaps my greatest thanks to you is due for the few moments when I learned what it feels like to know a

home and a family. I want to prove to you how much you mean to me. I miss you, I know you are missing me. You have to see me and let me explain and show you. I have a lot to say to you about yourself too.

Love,
Bernie

"Now read my reply and tell me what you think." Sitting on the faded couch, Honor handed Leslie two pages written in dark chocolate marking pen on a moss green notepaper she had just bought. "Doesn't it look good enough to eat?"

Leslie sighed, carrying the letter to the chair by the window where Honor's father usually sat. A light dusting of ashes littered the floor around it. She began to read: " 'My dear Mr. Guizot.' That's overdone. Call him Bernie. You never had a relationship where he was mister."

"Poor letter. I see you'll have to be recopied."

"Should I write in the margin things that need changing?"

"Like my English teacher? Don't look gloomy, Leslie, it's a privilege that I trust you to the point of showing you such personal correspondence."

"Oh, Bernie's love letters. Wow, what a treat."

"Is it a love letter?" Honor sat up, smoothing out her denim skirt. She had not changed from school. "Do you really think so? Rather than a letter of brotherly affection? He's told me I remind him of his lost sister."

"Oh, has he? Ann-Marie, you mean?"

"He says she resembled me physically. She was beautiful and rebellious and couldn't tolerate hypocrisy. . . . But is it a love letter?"

"Is that what you want me to tell you? The hell with that. With one hand you wave goodbye. With the other you want a romance."

"But if he really loves me. . . . Oh, never mind. Read my letter."

Leslie picked up the moss green pages again.

I am writing to you a day after receiving your note because I feel obliged to give some sort of answer. I hope this will terminate all correspondence between us (that includes phone calls and standing staring at the house under streetlights too!).

I regret more than I can say those foolish phone calls and the afternoon I said I loved you. Mama martyred you before me. In resentment I persuaded myself I loved you. So you see, I have no feeling you at all. I dislike even to hear your name mentioned. Please do not try to see me or communicate (this includes following me to school!).

I cannot forgive the unkind things you said about Mama. She is not "crazy" or "repressed" and if she is "possessive" what do you call yourself? As for what you said about Leslie, she has never done anything such as you insinuated to or with me. I shall have the generosity to believe some of what you said is true.

What I said once in anger, I repeat in calm—you are cold and calculating. You made me think you needed me and used my blind faith against me. I never want to hear of you again!

Sincerely,
Honor Rogers

"You stopped calling yourself Honorée?"

"My French period is fini. I'll recopy the first page right now. Then we can walk to the mailbox."

Leslie picked up Bernie's letter again. Others around you have accused me: Mama and her, yoked in unlikely harmony as his enemies. What had Honor said about him thinking of her as his dead sister? The line she too had fallen for. Was there a different model Ann-Marie for each target? Did he have a whole wardrobe of dead sisters? Did he have dead brothers for his male lovers? She felt cheated and robbed. *Had.*

The sound of tearing paper caught her attention. Scraps were floating in the breeze from the opened windows to litter the old rug. Honor had buried her hands in

250

her hair and was moaning, "Oh, I can't do it! How can I hurt him this way?"

"What did you do that for?" Leslie cried out in irritation. "Do you mean what you say or not?"

"What should I do? He says he loves me. If he really loves me, I should forgive him. I should go to him."

Leslie looked at her coldly. The sun shimmered on Honor's loose hair. Her body inscribed a poignant arc of sorrow. Leslie had a barely controllable desire to kick her. Instead she got to her feet and wandered past the couch, her hands thrust in the pockets of her jeans. On or off, on or off, let's get done with this charade. Off with him finally. Enough! She sat down beside Honor, not too close, and tapped her shoulder. Honor's amber eyes welled a couple of tears. "So, kid," Leslie said, with grating heartiness, "what do you want? His head on a platter? You want him for a secret boyfriend while your mother chews nails? You want to end up going to City? Fine with me. I'll see you, at least till I clear out of here."

"But he's sorry for how he acted. And he loves me!"

"So do I. So what?" Leslie said, who did not feel loving at all. "His letter is designed to get you back. Okay, while we're working, let's write three or four letters. It'll speed up events if we have the letters of reconciliation and rejection on hand as events demand them, instead of having to sit down each time and grind out a new one. I'll write the go-away letters and you write the ones that say come back."

"Leslie! You make it gross." But Honor was faintly smiling. "It is awfully dramatic, isn't it?"

"And you're enjoying it. You gave him the only home he ever had! For five minutes he knew the joy of groping his dead sister."

"Leslie, how can you say that—that I'm enjoying it? It is laid on a bit thick." Honor stooped and began to gather the scraps. "I guess we could stick these together and copy it. Tell me. Should I really?"

Mama came home from work before they had taped the letter back together. I swear Honor never intended to send it, Leslie thought glumly as she left. She'd be happy to keep both of us dangling for a year. As she says all the time, what else is nearly as interesting?

She had tried to talk to Honor about the women's school, but Honor yawned at the idea. "Ugh. I'm sure it's like the girl scouts all over again. I hated every moment of it." But the women's school troubled Leslie, it made her fidget and squirm in her life. She had stopped altogether going to karate; she had quit cold turkey, and Honor's melodrama had filled up all the chinks in her life. But it didn't quite work.

This time Leslie invited Tasha out to breakfast, and she was amused to noticed that Rae came too. The day was perfect and blue. Rae wore leather shorts, well studded; she was a woman who dressed herself fashionably. She had got Tasha into a French sailor shirt. In front of such dyke splendor, Leslie felt seedy. She did not know if it would be worse if Tasha knew all about George and the capital development project, or all about her tug-of-war with Bernie over Honor. Over the waffles she hemmed and hawed. Finally she said, "I have been thinking about the women's school."

"You'll teach a history class!" Tasha got excited at once, knocking over the syrup that Rae automatically caught.

"No. Not really. I think not. . . . What I was thinking about is—"

"The women's school. Sure." Rae grinned cynically at her.

"I could teach karate. Self-defense, if you prefer. I have my black belt now."

"Honestly? That's marvelous. . . . What's a black belt?" Tasha asked.

"It's a rank," Rae said. "A high one. Black's beautiful in karate."

"Anyhow, I think women would be interested. I'll bring it up at the collective tomorrow. Want to come to the meeting?" When Leslie made apologies, Tasha went on: "I'm sure they'll be excited. . . . But why don't you do a history course anyhow?"

252

Thursday afternoon Honor appeared at Leslie's apartment disheveled and close to tears. "Look! He broke my watch!"

She took it. "It's still running. Only the catch is broken."

"But Mama just gave it to me. She'll say I'm not mature enough for a watch of my own. That I'm too careless to have nice things! How can I tell her that *he* broke it? I'm not supposed to be seeing him. Now I'm in real trouble." Honor flung herself on the mattress.

"I hope you didn't tell your mother you were with me. I'm tired of being a cover for that weasel." She stood arms akimbo.

"Bernie showed up at the bus stop. He cut classes today and he talked me into cutting. I haven't done it since Barbara and I went to see a Robert Redford movie. Of course I was ever so much younger then, that's when I used to like him. Anyhow, Bernie said he could forge a note in Mama's writing saying I was ill."

"So off you went."

"I hardly ever get to see him, I'd been seeing him briefly after school, but one of the neighbors told Mama. I swear it's too tacky—the neighbors spying on me!"

"Can't you stand up to her? I think Bernie is effort down a rathole, but do you want her to dictate who your friends are?" Bernie got rid of today, me tomorrow.

"But she's still trying to decide whether they're going to let me go away. I'm accepted into the U of M at Ann Arbor, Ohio at Athens, and here. She won't let me go farther. I want to go East, but she won't hear of it. I got accepted into Barnard, but no scholarship so I can't go." Honor sat up, sticking the pillow behind her, and sulked. "I want to go away, so right now is a rotten time to persuade her she can't trust me. Of course she can't." Honor smiled. "Have you any delicious wine?"

"I'm not going to send you home smelling of alcohol, as well as with a broken watch. . . . I don't think I can fix this, but I might be able to stick it together. How about herb tea?"

"Mint? Please do fix the catch. I'll be so grateful!"

Leslie put the watch on a plate and squatted over it tinkering. "What happened today that he broke your watch?"

"Nothing!" Honor turned away. "I don't want to talk about it."

"Something he did?"

"The whole thing. Why go over it? It's too painful."

"What happened?"

Honor gave her a long look of reproach. "You won't even tell me what happened last month."

She looked up from the watch to stare at Honor. "Did you sleep with him?"

"Leslie! But I did let him . . . kiss me, embrace me. Oh, why? I'm feeling almost a . . . physical revulsion." Suddenly Honor began to sob into her hands.

"A physical revulsion?" Leslie was interested. "Was he rough?"

"Only when he tore the watch from my arm. He said it was a bribe from Mama to stop seeing him. Isn't that unfair? I've been begging for a watch for a year, it has nothing to do with him. As if I could be bought off!" Honor dabbed at her eyes.

"He wants you to be lovers now?"

"So he said." Honor lay back, pouting again. "I don't believe him. I don't believe he wants me. In a way it's insulting. I think I have a beautiful body. I imagine giving it to a man as one of the . . . well nicest presents."

"How can you talk as if you were a box of chocolates?"

Honor giggled. "I think I'd be more fun than a box of chocolates. . . . But, Leslie, of course I'd be *giving* myself. I don't know the first thing to do. They don't excite me, those books that explain sex as if they were teaching you how to repair your own car. Cam tries to get me to read them. Someone will initiate me and then I'll feel differently."

"You can initiate yourself. You can masturbate, you can experience orgasm. You don't have to go blindly and stupidly into sex."

"It was pretty blind and stupid this afternoon! Oh, I'm

254

furious. It was ugly! It's not fair. . . . And he said vicious things about Mama. I'll never forgive him, never! That my own mother acts like a lover to me. Did you ever hear of anything so perverse? Mama never even kisses me. Nobody in our family ever hugs except Cam. I hate him!"

"Then give it up. Quit it."

"Will I have to?" Honor sighed. "Yes, it's too messy. . . . I want things to be mysterious and romantic. That's a choice too, and I'm making it. I understand, don't you see? Romance fascinates me. School is boring. I don't know what I want to be. I expect sometime in college I'll take a course and figure it out. That I want to be an anthropologist or a neurosurgeon or a professor of something." Honor made her eyes enormous, pulling her hair forward across her high cheekbones. "I'll relinquish him! It's over."

It was a faint feeling she tried to suppress, faint but not suppressible. Honor lay on the mattress with her hair spread artfully and looked at her through her lashes, a glint of amber eyes. Am I to seduce her? But she keeps saying, A man, he. She leaves me no space in which to imagine myself with her. Yet she lies there seductively. She can't be unaware; she never is. She was ready to go to bed with Bernie this afternoon, and then she didn't; and it's still on her mind.

Slowly, hesitantly, Leslie came to sit on the edge of the mattress. Very lightly she took Honor's hand. Honor let her hand be squeezed and returned the pressure. Leslie knew she had to keep talking, but her mind was stuck. Say something. "I think Bernie's desperate. Yes. He wants to make love to you to hold on to you. You deserve better than that."

"But he doesn't really want to! That's what's so nasty. It's all a big put-on. I'm in a lot of trouble at home, and it's not even real!"

She could not put her arms around Honor. She was afraid to. She had little experience in making passes. Always she had been approached or it had been clearly mutual, as with Valerie, as in the bars. Women understood each other with little soft inviting gestures or open flirtations. It seemed frightening to reach out suddenly and with clear sexual intent take hold of a woman who might not like that. It seemed almost hostile. She needed a sign from Honor, unmistakable. She talked randomly. "Have to get ready for George's soon. It's another Thursday and I help Sue set up."

"Oh, maybe I'll go. But I can't tonight. . . . But it was interesting."

They babbled on, neither listening to the other. Finally Honor looked at the clock. "Oh, it's four-thirty! I'll be in trouble even deeper. I have to leave at once. Did you fix my watch?"

"I stuck it together with a bent pin, but it has to be fixed by a jeweler."

"Oh dear. Thanks for the help. Maybe I can sneak it past her. But how will I ever take it to a jeweler's? It's so complicated!" In a swirl of skirts Honor was gone.

Why didn't I do something? She wanted me to, Leslie thought. Or did she want to reject me the way she felt rejected by Bernie? Leslie leaned her head against the door. I'll never know, will I? The truth is, I didn't want to. I feel cold and calculating, the way I describe Bernie. I feel distant and manipulative. How can I reach out to her? I don't even know if I like her any more. All I know is I want him out of our lives. I don't want to win her; I only want to defeat him.

eighteen

"He's writing me letters, leaving notes. I never know when he'll show up, the last of the Mohicans with his hand on his heart at the bus stop. It's absurd, Leslie. I'm beginning to loathe him! No, we must see him. We must have this out and bring it to an end. He says if I'll see him, he'll call off his campaign." Honor nudged toward her the plate of carrot sticks, radishes and celery. Honor had suddenly gone on a diet, and there was no more fudge in the Rogers kitchen.

Leslie took a radish. "Okay, *you* have to see him. How does that translate into *we* have to see him?"

"You don't want me to see him alone, do you? Besides, you're in this all the way." Honor grimaced as she bit into a carrot. "You've been influencing me, you can't deny it. It's time to stand up to him in person. I need your counsel. I may even need your protection!" Honor tossed her hair, looking not at all worried.

"You just think it'll be more dramatic with all three of us there."

Honor put her hands together as if praying. "Don't you long to confront him? You've said such dreadful things about him."

"Dreadful? Have I?"

"That he's a compulsive liar. Manipulative. Cold and calculating. A desperate psychotic personality."

"Oh, but that's true. I mean," Leslie said hesitantly, "he is like that. Isn't he?"

"And you don't think those are awful things to say? You're silly, Leslie, honestly." Honor pushed the plate resolutely away. "Enough of that cellulose! We'll meet at your house. That strikes me as safe. The scene can't go on forever, because everybody will be too uncomfortable."

Honor was so decisive, Leslie couldn't believe it. She kept waiting for the inevitable tears, the comments about how they had once again misjudged poor Bernard. "But why wait till Saturday? I could take off work a little early Tuesday and we can get it over with."

"I'm very busy this week, Leslie. It's close to graduation. We'll do it Saturday."

"You're not just putting it off? You'll change your mind about him before then."

"Really, Leslie, you talk as if I'm changeable. I see what has to be done now. It's over, and we just have to get him to realize that and clear off." Honor went into the living room to phone. "Hello, may I speak with Bernard Guizot, please."

Leslie could not stand listening. She did not know why, but she could not listen. Honor sounded mocking and superior. Leslie hurried into the bathroom, shut the door and ran the water to drown out Honor's voice. Honor's and Mama's panties hung drying over the curtain rod, large and larger nylon pastels. Maybe she was a fool to hide in the bathroom; Bernie would talk Honor around. Honor had been in a cold fury with him ever since the scene with her watch. Maybe graduation was making her so preoccupied and brisk. She could not even remember her own high school graduation in the fog of misery that had hung over her senior year, but she supposed it was a more invigorating occasion for Honor.

When she ventured back into the livingroom, Honor was lying in the middle of the room tentatively struggling through a few sit-ups. "Under control, Leslie. At least the arrangements, and that's half the battle, isn't it? This is a lot of work." She stopped to catch her breath and sat up with her arms tucked around her legs. "We meet at your apartment at two Saturday afternoon. I have to return some books to the main library from a paper I was writing. I'll go there first in a great hurry and then come."

"Come early. I want you there when he arrives. You get to my place by one-forty-five. No, one-thirty."

"Don't be silly, Leslie. He won't bite you. Just because he pulled the watch off my arm is no reason for you to be afraid of him." Honor gave up on the exercising and stood rubbing her back.

"I'm not afraid! But we ought to get it over with. I have tons of work to do. Finals are next week."

"Good! You can work right up until two. I'll be on time, don't worry. I'm depressingly punctual now that I have my watch. I like to look at it on my arm, and every time I look, of necessity I see the time. Not an unmixed blessing." Honor brushed at her skirt. "It feels like summer already."

"It could be a nice summer," Leslie offered in mild hope. "We could go swimming. . . . If you ever do that?"

"Why not?" Honor said bravely. "I have to get out of the house more. Mama is driving me crazy! I am not used to being . . . patrolled!"

Afernoons in the country. . . . Bernie and the rowboat . . . forget. It could be nice, simple, a real friendship with healthy outdoorsy things to do. She must be having a good effect on Honor. Honor was becoming visibly less fey, less withdrawn and sheltered. Less weird, really. "Are you fighting a lot with her?"

"More just bumping on each other. She wants me to stay home tonight and watch a Bette Davis film on UHF. . . . We've seen it before, it's about a governess in nineteenth-century France who loves this nobleman, but purely. I'm tired of all that. . . . I think I'll call up Cam and get her to take me to rehearsal. They're opening *Rhinoceros* in a week."

"Paul? I mean, you'd like to see him?"

"*Paul?* Don't be absurd, Leslie. He's crude. He's just a Motor City Joseph Papp who didn't make it in the big

259

time. Besides, I bet he's like Bernie underneath. I just want to get out."

If I wasn't so frantically busy with finals, Leslie thought, there are lots of things we could begin to do together.

Whenever she thought of Saturday, she felt distressed and agitated, almost excited. Finals were comimg and she had a lot of preparation. She spent as little time on the project as she could get away with. Fortunately, George was cutting corners too. He said he wanted to get home early and play outside with the kids, for he had just bought bicycles for everyone, including a reluctant Sue. One of his current subjects was how the bicycle was the most efficient machine for transportation ever invented. It was elegant in terms of energy use. Secretly she hoped he would pull a muscle and shut up. She still dreamed of a motorcycle.

When he left early again on Tuesday, she had to call the house to ask about some computer runoff. He was not at home. She immediately tried to cover. Normally, she would not have let Sue know he had left the office. What Sue knew and what Sue really knew were two different matters. But Leslie had not even noticed him faintly interested in anyone; now she had given Sue an early warning.

Friday he kept glancing at his watch. About one-forty he was off, saying he had errands to run. He combed his hair carefully, he smoothed his mustache and sucked in his little pot. Then he whistled as he ran down the steps instead of taking the old cranky elevator. Yes, George definitely had something going.

At four he came whistling back. He did not look rumpled as he tried to cram three hours' work into one. His mood was expansive. He even let Cam take off early to go to the special rehearsal for the Ionesco play they were opening, whereas earlier in the week he had said quite coldy he needed her until five. Cam and Mark were still sharing the studio apartment his parents paid for. Cam was no longer friendly to her. When Leslie entered the women's room, Cam fled.

When she stopped by Friday at Tasha's house to find out what the school collective had decided, she was directed to the women's school, where Tasha and Rae were sanding floors. They were both close to the same color with sawdust stuck to their faces, arms and hair with sweat. They seemed in a good mood, though Rae complained her back was breaking.

Tasha sat on the front steps, fanning herself with a newspaper. "We definitely want your course. In fact people are already signing up."

"Really? Do you think there'll be enough?"

"Too many," Tasha said firmly. "It's hard to find a woman qualified to teach martial arts. Mostly, you know, you get a woman who's just a step ahead of the class, and people can get hurt that way."

"I have a lot of ideas how to teach women. I don't know if they'll work . . . but I'm willing to try if the others are."

Rae sat down, squeezing between them, but she gave Leslie a broad smile. She was acting friendlier, as if she was classifying Leslie as interested in the women's school rather than in Tasha. "How come you changed your mind? About teaching here I mean."

Leslie scratched her head. "I'm lonely, I guess."

"Well, you teach karate, you know half the class are sure to fall in love with you." Rae gave her a curious head-tilted-to-one-side look. "You like that?"

"Leslie, that can't be your real reason," Tasha said. "It's important for women to defend ourselves!"

"It has to do with feeling weird after I finally made black belt." Leslie paused, groping for words. "Like it maybe really is crazy to do all that effort for nobody except me." She could feel both of them listening carefully, intently. She felt a sense of at-homeness with them, an ease of discourse, of communication, that she did not really want to feel. "That if I don't share it, something's wrong. . . . Most women never get a chance to follow through on anything the way I've pushed myself with karate." Bernie would understand her reluctance to enjoy the coziness of the ghetto: that only here could she talk

261

openly and be listened to with full attention and sympathy.

"Mmmmm." Rae rubbed her nose. "It's owing back to where you come from, maybe. I can dig on that. When you achieve you either hate the people where you come from—like you made it and they didn't and they're shit. Or you want to go back and take along what you learned, to share it out. People come out both ways, I guess."

"But professional training is the same, right?" Tasha said. "All that grad school. Don't you want to share that too?" She never gave up. "Lots of women would sign up for a history course."

Was it because Tasha needled her politically, questioned her about her work, shook her confidence in her own righteousness that she had not been attracted to Tasha for so long? Or was it just because Tasha was not as pretty as Honor? Leslie was not comfortable with the question, no matter how she answered it to herself. In no way could she doubt that Tasha was a better person, and far more affectionate. Rae looked at her still with eyes of delight, and seemed always restraining herself from a hug.

Saturday morning she did her washing at the laundromat and her shopping for the week at the Starlite Supermarket. Passing a bakery, she was struck by an impulse like a bright ball rolling across her path, and she popped inside. "How much is that chocolate cake?" She bought it, a chocolate cake with chocolate frosting for them. She had to be crazy. But they both had such sweet tooths. Hardly anyone ever came to her house; not since she had lived with Valerie had she "entertained," but she kept the notion from her mother's fussing when relatives visited that company got at least a cake. Maybe Honor would hang around.

Another thing she did was steal irises from a bed outside a boarded-up house. She clipped them with her pocketknife, carrying off an armload of purple, of white, of brown and gold irises that filled her head with their nonsweet fragrance. She imagined a lover Iris who smelled like that. The chamber of the iris was a vagina. Women

262

were taught to be ashamed of their organs, but flowers held theirs in the air brightly colored and flagrant. The scent made her giddy as she climbed to her room.

At one-thirty she jerked smooth the bright blanket on her bed. She rearranged the irises in their bottle. The day before she had swiped ground coffee and a filter from the office; now she improvised a drip pot from the teapot and made coffee for them. At a quarter to two she suddenly pulled off her jeans and put on the crushed cotton pants and the striped top Sue had given her. At five to two she went downstairs and propped the outer door open with a brick.

At ten after the hour someone knocked. Please, Honor, she thought. Perhaps Bernie would not come at all. What had he to gain? Why did he seek the meeting? It had to be Honor. It wasn't. She blinked, her gaze sliding from his face. "Come in," she said in a high squeaky voice and immediately began taking surreptitious deep breaths. She backed out of his way and after a quick imploring glance down the stairs, hoping to see Honor, shut the door. They stood about in her room looking at stove and refrigerator respectively.

"I thought she'd be here," Bernie said plaintively. "Do you suppose she's not coming?"

She had to look at him. He was wearing a black tee shirt and jeans. His skin was golden tan and his eyes darted like minnows, silver and fast away from her. He was as nervous as she was and that heartened her. "She said she had to go to the library first to return some books."

"Why couldn't she go afterward?"

She realized she had never thought to ask Honor that. "I'm sure she'll be here soon. Unless her mother?"

"She just wants to make a late entrance." He leaned on the refrigerator. "Is that coffee?"

She nodded, unable to understand why it hurt to look at him. But it did. It hurt her. They both went on standing six feet apart not knowing what to do with themselves until she had the idea of pouring coffee for him. Then she brought him the cup. The handing over of the cup was as

263

formal as if some document of state were being exchanged, some prisoner sent over a hostile border. She did not come as close to him as she normally would have, and he reached out his hand farther. They both carefully calculated so that no part of their fingers touched. The calculation and the nervousness were so visible that a quick spasm of amusement tightened his face around his mouth.

Leslie offered, "Perhaps her mother kept her from coming."

"That woman's a vampire," he snarled. "Do you realize that if Honor is not pried out of that house by force, by guile, by some damn means, she could end up like that?"

"If we don't scare Mama, Honor will go away to school in the fall. There's no chance of her hanging around there. Don't you see that? Even Cam flew. Do you want some cake? I bought a chocolate cake."

"You did what?" He stared at her. It was the first time he had really looked at her and then he got stuck as she had. Nervousness sputtered between them. "No, thanks. . . . When do your finals start?"

"Monday. And you?"

"The same. I'm not done till Thursday."

Neither of them could think of another word to say and they were both looking everywhere rather than at each other. Finally Bernie seized a piece of cake. Leslie went over to the window and looked out on her fire escape, the expanse of tarred roof. "Maybe Honor dreads this too. So she puts it off by being late."

"Not bad." He meant the cake. He was licking his fingers. "Did you dread it, Les? Did you?"

"Are you kidding? Why would I want to go through this?"

"Distasteful, isn't it? It's amazing what you put up with, out of a sense of duty."

"What does that mean? Honor's my friend."

"Once you were my friend. Remember?"

"Once you were mine, Bernie. But you couldn't wait to become my enemy. With Honor."

"But you outgeneraled me. You make a bad enemy.

264

You hang in there and fight, fight, fight. . . . Did you ever stop just once to think what that whole business between us, even giving it your own distorted interpretation, might have done to me?"

"No. I was too busy finding out what it did to me." Now why did she say that? She wanted to retract. She felt she had made herself vulnerable, but he was too angry, too excited to notice.

"Well, I'm not asking you to think now. If you'd cared for me at all, at all, you'd have had patience with me. You'd have tried to understand."

"Cared! You cared so much you couldn't hardly wait to run home and start writing love letters to Honor."

Bernie looked startled. He poured himself another cup of coffee. "Come now, they weren't exactly love letters. Did she think they were?"

"You rather gave that impression," Leslie said dryly. She felt better. As long as they talked about Honor she felt on hard ground.

"You wouldn't say that if you'd read them. You didn't, of course?" He paused. Leslie said nothing, embarrassed. He took silence for assent. "They were just pleas she not forget our friendship. Knuckle under to Mama. Follow you over the side."

"That's not the impression you gave Honor. And you know it. You've been hounding her like a despairing lover."

"I've been frantic. I couldn't let go. You can't imagine how important she is to me. But the harder I've tried to hold on, the worse I've done. I've tried to tie her down. . . . But I won't lose her. You and her damn mother have given me a hard time, but you'll end by helping me. Because you martyr me in her eyes. You'll see today. It's one thing for her to act cold to me over the phone. When we're face to face she won't hold out. I'll win, Leslie."

"What will you win? What will you win this time?" She poured herself a cup of coffee with the sense of its being a strong drink. She hardly ever had coffee; she considered it a poison. "I wouldn't be surprised if she crumbles this afternoon. If you walk out of here arm in arm, what then? You want to hold on. You want her so close she can't form a judgment against you. That drives you into trying to make love to her. You're asking more than she can give. And assuming you can give what you can't."

"What did she tell you?" He frowned, rubbing his knuckles.

"What did she tell me about what? She told me what's happening."

"I wonder." He grinned. He paced from the refrigerator to the window. "Oh, I have no doubts at all you believe you acted for the best throughout."

"Not throughout."

"Except for minor slips. But I'm sure through these last weeks you've been reasonable. Calm and dispassionate, like a doctor cutting a small malignant tumor in plenty of time to save the patient. Even I, the tumor, admire you."

Leslie put her cup on top of the refrigerator. The coffee seemed to hurt her throat. "You don't see that what you want you can't have in this situation. It isn't me in your way."

"You asked nothing for yourself except that there should not be too many melodramatics. I think you've even lost your feeling for Honor." He stopped dead in front of her. "Do you love her still? You don't, do you?"

"I had to control it. Or like you I'd have tried to get what I couldn't."

"So you won nothing. Your conscience is clear."

"Who won anything? What is winning, you damn fool!"

He took hold of her arm and then looked startled that he had done so. They both jumped and then stood there bristling. "Why didn't you tell her? I kept waiting for you to tell her. You feel hurt, but you go out into the world to protect your sisterhood. Didn't you realize, you idiot, that you could have told her nothing, nothing at all that would have finished her with me more quickly?"

She nodded. Her throat was closed. She nodded again as if afraid he might try to shake words from her.

"It would have hurt her pride to know we'd slept together. You can't imagine how. And lied to her. Kept it from her. Why did you?"

"I wasn't protecting her."

"Were you ashamed? Was that it?"

"I was ashamed."

"Of me? Why? Was it that bad? Was it really so bad we both had to run off?"

It was all still there untouched. The pain, the outrage, the anger, the connection, it was all still there molten and raw and tangled. It was between them like an aborted baby. Maybe they hated each other. She did not know what to call the pain. "Why did you run out of the house? It was you who ran!" She heard herself speak as if it were someone else's high angry voice.

"I hurt! You pushed me away. How could you? And why didn't you tell her? I have to know. I kept waiting for you to tell her. It would have done so much damage. Why didn't you do that to me? Why didn't you, damn you? Why?"

She was braced so hard that his shaking simply did not move her. His face looked hot as the sun. "It belonged to me."

"How you turn the knife!"

A knock at the door. It took them a moment to hear it. They both moved forward, paused, looked at each other—startled by how they were standing, bodies almost touching. Like conspirators, she thought. God, it's so strange. They were both getting control of themselves, as if they were twins, as if they were of some secret family, looking at each other almost with pity, almost embracing. The disengagement from the wrestling of anger was painful too. They were so passionately caught. Then Leslie went and opened the door.

"I could hear you shouting but I couldn't make out what you were saying. I hope I didn't miss anything exciting. Sorry I'm late, but I had to pick up a few books. I decided I should read up on history, Leslie, so I can understand what you're doing."

"Oh, that's wonderful, but you should have let me make up a reading list—"

"I've asked Leslie to be present because you've made me feel I can't trust you," Honor said, putting down her book bag. She was wearing her drawstring pants and a low-cut ruffly summer blouse. "And because I think she's really a party to what's been happening. Don't you think so, Leslie?"

She produced a throaty noise and looked at the stove.

"No doubt," Bernie said. "How much a party you might be surprised yourself."

"First of all, I told Leslie pretty much everything. I showed her your letters and mine."

"No!" His face jumped. "They must have amused you. Did you roll on the floor giggling?"

"Don't look up, Bernie. The light in the ceiling's too high for you to reach in here." Honor turned to Leslie to add, "Breaking light bulbs with his bare hands is one of his ways of showing mental anguish. Why not just bang your head on the floor? It gives as much proof of sincerity as breaking a bulb, and it's less of a nuisance with the glass underfoot."

"It's lucky your mother kept you locked up at home these past two weeks, because I might have wrung your neck."

Honor touched her throat with a shudder. For a moment she looked frightened. Bernie shook his head roughly, clawing his hair back. "I'm sorry. You know I don't mean that."

Honor smiled, her lips pulling down. "I know. You're much too docile. I'm looking for a man who'll do what you only talk about." She gave him a sly look and continued at once. "I mean a man who'll slap my face."

"Nonsense," Leslie said. "If someone really slapped your face, you'd be furious."

"You judge by your own standards, Leslie, because you need to feel in control. I'm strong in a different way. I'm only interested in a man until I find out whether he's pushable. Pushable—that's a good word."

Honor was torturing Bernie in some way Leslie could not grasp. She could only feel the sense of torture. Bernie said angrily, "You picked that up from Paul. 'Push-
268

able—that's a good word.' You have his tone down pat. Did you practice it?"

"How can you compare me to that old flop even *you* weren't attracted to! Really, when I met him I was too easily dazzled—by him and by you."

Bernie recovered himself. He lit a joint, he strolled to the window and back with exaggerated ease. "You know, Les, old trooper, you didn't use half the ammo you had. Bet you didn't tell Honor I tried to rape you?"

Honor gasped. "What is this? You never said a word."

"Bernie apologized afterward," Leslie said limply.

Bernie started to giggle. He laughed too hard, sputtering smoke.

"Would you have forgiven him if he had succeeded?" Honor folded her arms.

Bernie stopped laughing. "No, she wouldn't have. Besides, she punched me in the belly. *She's* not pushable, Honor."

"Oh, me and Ann-Marie?" Leslie said sideways, only to him. "*My* model Ann-Marie?"

"How could you keep that back, Leslie? When did it happen? You must have thought it was very funny when I confessed I had let Bernie . . . kiss me."

"I wasn't amused, actually."

"I seem to have been the subject of many busy hours retelling juicy scenes. What fun." Bernie cut himself a big piece of cake.

"More fun than that dull session in your room with you screeching at me and hounding me out of my mind." Honor screwed up her nose in disgust. "You practically ripped my clothes off. And then nothing! After all that build-up. All that carrying on about how you love me and you just have to. That seduction was a big nothing!"

"Wasn't it?" Bernie was eating cake. "For both of us, I mean. You lying there like an overstuffed pillow expecting to have wonders performed on you."

They glared at each other. Leslie felt horrible, she felt mangled. They had tried to make love. She did not want it to happen, she did not want it to have happened. It was not jealousy, it was pure pain. They had mangled some-

269

thing between them and she was at fault, somehow she was at fault.

"We're embarrassing Leslie," Bernie lilted. "She doesn't want to know."

"What is there to know? Nothing happened." Honor looked for a moment as if she would cry. "Nothing at all. Just nothing! After all that carrying on, you wouldn't do it. You couldn't! As if I'm not pretty enough, not good enough. Something's wrong with you, that's what's wrong!"

I mustn't let him tell her, I mustn't, she thought. Fast into the breach. What's a breach? She felt as if her head were flying apart from the inside. "We were friends," she said suddenly. "Isn't there something left?"

"Wash your mouth out." Bernie gripped her arm hard. Then he let go as if he had been burned. The painful grip of his fingers remained.

"After what we've said, do you think he and I could sit down and drink tea?"

"Why not? It's only words!" Leslie said desperately. "Words don't change anything."

"Don't they?" Bernie laughed bitterly. "There's no difference between saying I love you and saying I hate you?"

"I have only one thing left to say to you, Bernie." Honor picked up her purse and went to the mirror over the bathroom sink to comb her hair. With her back to the room she said, "Goodbye. I know you'll make sure we never meet again." Her eyes were expressionless in the mirror, her teeth slightly clenched as she drew the comb slowly through the long lustrous hair.

"Sure. I got nothing left to gamble with, so I'll pick up my bod and go home—wherever that is. Bye-bye." Looking straight ahead, he walked out, still carrying a piece of the cake. Leslie heard his steps cascading down. It was over so quickly her eyes remained on the space he had occupied in front of the refrigerator and she stood with the awkward bridled feeling of having been about to speak and having lost the occasion.

Honor snapped her purse shut. "Oh me, oh my, that was awful, wasn't it? Now cut me a little piece of that cake. I just couldn't eat with him here." But Honor nibbled only half. "I don't know what's wrong with me, I don't feel like enjoying it."

"He left so quickly."

"He knew it was blown. Do you think he'll leave me alone now?"

"I think he will."

"Leslie, look outside. Make sure he isn't hanging around in the street."

She looked out obediently. "I don't see him. What would he be waiting for?"

"If you'd gone through these past weeks, you wouldn't ask. Is it really over? I'd better run." Honor stood up, rather slowly, and looked around as if she had forgotten something. "Oh, my books."

"Yeah. . . . What did you get?"

"Never mind. I'm late."

"Oh, where are you going?" She had thought Honor might stay. But she didn't really care. She felt listless, exhausted.

Honor paused in the doorway. "I'm almost scared to go down. I just want it over and done with! I'll see you Leslie, soon." Then she screamed. "Oh, look what he did!"

He had smeared the chocolate cake all over the wall. Leslie got a rag and sponged it off as well as she could, but the stain remained. Then she sat down on her mattress, her knees folding stiffly. She felt obsessed by a sense of cheated anticipation. All had gone off as it must that afternoon, and the struggle was over. But something she could not define had not happened.

nineteen

Finals were over, the streets sizzling all day. Night was a lid clamped on a boiling pot. Leslie kept hearing gunshots. She kept trying to persuade herself she was hearing firecrackers, but she had grown up in hunting country. Half the city must be at war. Yet the police had never looked more sinister to her, cruising by armored, as if from a different entirely mechanical planet. She was sweating in her tee shirt and working on interminable computer runoff, trying to catch up on the project work she owed George. When she discovered she was missing a whole file she needed to proceed, she felt a mixture of dread and pleasure. Her room was so hot that to walk outside would be a relief; yet walking on the streets at night was popularly supposed suicidal. Not even the men she knew used these streets where a predominantly white army of occupation fought it out with a predominantly Black population in a rotting network everyone with money had fled decades before.

She had to walk to George's office to pick up the file, or give up for the evening. She was behind, she owed him two weeks' work, and it was too hot to do anything pleasant. It was her own stupidity she must blame. It wasn't that the hour was late: nine Friday night. She had to go and that was that.

When she arrived a light was on in George's office, the inner office. She was startled and afraid. Burglars? But who would steal what from George? She felt like slipping away leaving the mystery to solve itself, but she forced herself to knock. It could be a cleaning lady. There was a longish silence and then George asked in a loud hostile voice. "Who is it?"

"Leslie. Just picking up a file I forgot."

Conversation inside, a light female voice consulting. Oh, shit, she'd walked into it. But why on earth was he meeting his girlfriends in his office? She'd never known him to do that.

"I'm leaving now," she called and started out. The inner door opened.

"Hold on," George called. "Just a moment. Come on in."

Reluctantly she crossed the outer office to the inner. He had installed a couch recently on which Honor was sitting, brushing her silky hair. "Hi, Leslie. I'm supposed to be watching a play Cam's in. Fortunately I went to rehearsals."

"Foresight, that's what I like. Smart cookie. Listen, Leslie, could you walk Honor over to the play? Then I can take off. I'm running a little late. She can slip into her seat and Cam will take her home afterward and everything will be fine and cool and nice."

"Sure," Leslie said. Her face was numb with novocaine. She could not smile back at them. Her face would not work. It felt as if pain and anger were braided with spikes into her gut. She wanted to say, I'm a woman too. Why am I supposed to walk her around? And if you think lesbians don't get raped, you're crazy. But she could not help being aware *that* had nothing to do with her anger. Honor with George. No! She was very angry, and she had no right to be. She wanted to say to Honor that now she knew why she had been willing to get rid of Bernie suddenly, to let him go, to send him away. Yes, he had got in the way at last. Damn them both. Damn them.

George had his briefcase packed. He seemed not to want to walk out with them but to send them ahead. Leslie tucked the file she had come for under her arm and walked with Honor to the elevator. As soon as the doors wobbled shut, Honor burst into an aria of self-congratulation. "Aren't you going to ask me millions of questions? Aren't you surprised? I was going to tell you soon as I got the chance."

"How long has it been going on?"

"The 'it' would need definition." Honor tossed her hair back, smoothing her muslin dress. "I'd say in some measure from the first time we met in front of the fireplace in that gloomy house. I always knew a real attraction would be just like that: immediate, overwhelming, unmistakable. Like a thunderclap."

"George is into the thunderclap business," Leslie mumbled. They crossed the lobby, where a security guard sat reading a newspaper, looking up to eye Honor's behind long and carefully.

"Oh, he's certainly experienced. I was right about that too. You see, Leslie, I did know what I was looking for in a man. . . . Things really got going the week Bernie broke my watch. I was trying to find you. You weren't home, so I went to the University. Neither you or Cam was around, but there was George. . . . I could tell he was waiting for me, looking for me, just the way I'd been looking for him. It was so immediate, Leslie. From the time our gazes crossed that day I knew something was happening at last! He called me into his office and he shut the door, he wasn't hesitant at all, he had that wicked grin on his face."

"He's always looking, you're right about that."

"Leslie! You're jealous. How disappointing. I know he's dreadfully attractive and it must be hell to work with him. I'm sure I couldn't. Besides we have such different relationships with him."

"Damn right. You're in the relationship of being exploited."

Honor swished her hair in annoyance. "Leslie, you're being absurd. I know what I'm doing. Just what I always said I would. And he's crazy about me. He's told me he loves me. I'm not a fool. I'm still going to college in the fall. I'll go to Ann Arbor and it'll be even easier to see him than it is living at home. Ann Arbor's only half an

274

hour from his house. I'm patient. I only regret I didn't have the courage of my instincts all along. I'm ashamed I ever let Bernie touch me, I'm really ashamed. He isn't a man. It's not as if I expect George to leave his wife tomorrow, after all—"

"You asshole!" Leslie grabbed Honor by the arm and then she slapped her. Immediately she was horrified. She did not slap hard. She pulled the punch as she swung so that as the hand landed she was only tapping the cheek; but the will, the wish, the anger were there, ominous to her.

"Oh!" Honor stopped short. Her hand went to her face. She stared at Leslie and then she began to weep.

"I'm sorry. Forgive me, I'm terribly sorry. Look, I'm worried about you. I know George."

"No you don't! How could you? You're only his employee."

"Ah, poor lamb, I do know him. And so will you. I'm sorry I hit you, Honor, I had no right. You're correct saying I'm jealous, but not of George. That academic fucker with a mustache and a rich wife."

"She bought him, didn't she? Ten years ago he was a handsome dashing young radical, just the sort of thing a rich girl needs to make her life complete. I see more than you think I do. I see he's trapped in a life that frustrates him, with a rich redneck of a wife like a millstone around his neck. I see that you hate me!"

"Honor!" Gently she touched the girl's face. Honor turned away. "I'm sorry I hit you. Say you forgive me."

"I could say it, but it wouldn't mean I did." Honor felt her cheek again. "You're right, I mean you were right when you said the time we had that awful scene with Bernie that I wouldn't really like having my face slapped. It isn't anything like my fantasy."

"Well, one more fantasy down the drain." She felt as if moment by moment, slow step by step, she was staving off a sleetstorm of images. Maybe she only wanted to believe George was using Honor for a quick affair. This time he could be in love. He seemed to be breaking his own rules: Never in the office, not on weekends, reserved for family. Maybe he was madly in love. After all, she loved Honor; why shouldn't he? Who wouldn't prefer Honor to Sue, when you came down to it? He'd have to be crazy not to. "There's the theater. . . . Does Cam know about George?"

"Are you serious? I can't trust her. She'd get excited and flap around terrified about Mama. She wouldn't see how much in control I am. I said I wanted to sit at the back to watch the audience. What reason would she ever have to suspect I met George in the lobby ten minutes after the play started?" Honor laughed, and Leslie knew she was forgiven. On shaky ground. Honor needed a confidant. She needed someone to listen to her talk about her romance. "Really, Leslie, I feel like a heroine in a spy movie, clever and mature and wonderfully cool. It's fun. I always knew life could be like this, if I had half a chance!" Honor slipped into the theater and Leslie set off at a brisk march for her apartment, the file still clutched under her arm. If I ever got drunk, it would be tonight, she thought, their bodies crushed together in her mind. She felt ill. Obscene, that couch in his office! She would never sit on it as long as she lived. Why not get drunk? Always as she entered or left her room, she passed that chocolate stain, suggestive as old blood on the wall of the stairwell.

She bought a bottle of red wine, random red she thought, and set out to drink it lying on the mattress. She waited for it to blot her mind but nothing happened. She did not feel drunk. After she had consumed half the bottle, she trotted into the bathroom and suddenly threw it up and felt better. Then she lay on the mattress trying not to think. She kept seeing them together, George on Honor. She felt battered.

Finally she must have dozed, because she woke from a dream with no sense whether she had been asleep a minute or an hour. Bernie was lying naked in the cultivated earth of a flower bed, a bed of day lilies. Their long grassy leaves bent over him and the orange trumpets nodded above him. She was leaning toward him. Was he asleep or dead? He was beautiful lying there on the brown loamy earth with the orange bells tolling over him and pollen smeared on his chest. She bent closer to him, filled with tenderness that rent her, and when she touched him she woke.

She got up slowly, kneading the muscles of her abdomen which protested having vomited. She stood at the window looking out on the fire escape and the flat asphalt roof and the skyshine beyond, the neon sign blinking on and off in magenta and green. She had to do it. She had to. Pain and love braided irrational and spiky through her. She had to. She dialed his number. She hung up, terrified at what she was doing. But pain freed her, jealousy freed her, everything was tearing loose as if in a storm and floating free. She dialed his number a second time and this time she did not hang up.

"Who?"

"Bernie Guizot."

"Oh, Bernie. He gone."

"Gone? Oh, he's out. I'll call back later." It must be late now. "Tomorrow. I'll call tomorrow."

"He move out. Gone to California hitchhiking with his thumb stuck out. You a friend of his?"

Leslie had trouble answering. Finally she said, "Yes."

"Well, he left a lot of books and school stuff here. He says he don't need it where he going. He done with school, I guess, but it seems like a real waste to me. I could give it to the Goodwill, but if you a friend of his, if you want any of it, you can come on over and get it. He paid up to the end of the month, so I didn't clear out his room yet, if you want any of that stuff for school. You a student too?"

She put down the phone, resonating in all her nerves, ringing to her finger ends. Gone. Lost. She had the same scrambled sense of being bottled up, of unfinished business, of connections hanging loose she had had ten days before when Bernie had turned and left the room, the building, their lives. He was crazy, he was a liar, he was devious and desperate and emotionally violent, but they were connected and now the tie was roughly cut. She was bleeding into the air. He had given up on respectability, on academia, on getting ahead, on clambering into the college-educated working class—the degree-bearing home-loving regularly paid medically insured so-called middle class. He was gone, back on the road, on the streets. He had been straight for almost two years and what had it got him? There was plenty of room at the bottom.

It was George's last Thursday night, for he took a summer vacation from them. Although she wasn't feeling social and dreaded standing around and making conversation, she looked forward to getting out of the city, to sprinklers turning on lush lawns in Farmington Hills, where George lived. Green velvet in the twilight. The night hummed electrically. She had done well in her classes, top notch, and in celebration and in recompense for what she would not think about, for what she was blocking from her mind daily to function, to go on working with George, she had given in to herself and she had done it; she had bought a small red bike, a Honda, from a departing student. A little beauty.

Going to George's was a pleasure. She felt happier than she had in months, since that day on the water she held herself rigidly straight not to remember. She did not want to arrive at George's, ever. She could keep going. Past George's. The mythical male open road past the filling station and the pile of wrecks in the junkyard, into the oil slick sunset. Even if all her human relations had combusted, that was bullshit. No, her life was here. In fact she arrived early to help Sue in the kitchen.

She walked into a fight. The children had been given supper already and were stashed upstairs in the family room in front of the television set with the puppy. Suddenly in the last week Sue had changed her mind and given in to Davey and Louise's perennial clamor for a dog. A clumsy Great Dane puppy, rawboned and bigeyed, was peeing on the family room rug upstairs. On the phone Sue told her, "He'll be a protection. You know how unsafe it is."

The children and the guard puppy were upstairs, but
278

Sue and George were having it out in the kitchen. They had a habit of fighting in the kitchen ever since she had known them, arguing in tense unnaturally soft voices so the children would not hear. The children were watching reruns of *The FBI* and wouldn't have heard them if they had shot each other. She wanted to go upstairs with the kids and Hoover's blood-wet dreams until peace had come, but both Sue and George with different excuses drew her in.

"We have to get ready. All those students will be coming any minute." Sue made as if to begin cutting cheese.

"But you like students so much. Suddenly." George sounded sour. He was whining. "I think Sue needs help, Leslie. I think she needs help badly, but she won't do anything about it."

"You mean in addition to the cleaning lady?"

"Psychiatric help," George snarled. "She needs a doctor."

She was having trouble looking at George. She did not want to see him. It would pass, it would go away. She kept her eyes on Sue instead.

"He thinks I'm crazy," Sue said airly, chopping the cheese into big crooked yellow hunks. "What's sauce for the gander is sauce for the goose, sugar."

"When you put on that fake drawl, it drives me ape."

"I come from Texas, sugar. Did you forget that? I wouldn't if I were you. We have an open marriage. Wide open. That wasn't my idea. Ever. It sure as . . . heck wasn't my idea. Here I am bringing up two children, keeping house for you and entertaining—"

"Leslie does most of that and you know it."

"I do not! I just follow directions on Thursday nights." Leslie was getting very nervous. She edged toward the door. Upstairs the puppy was barking.

"I thought you'd straightened out since we moved here. It's a step in the right direction, a better position, and you got all that old grant money you were crying for. I think you'd be too busy, the way other women's husbands are. But no, I thought you'd straightened yourself out and quit that funny business. I mean, how old do you have to be? Sixty-five? You have two children. I'd think you'd leave tom-catting around."

"How can you stand there and say that to me after what you've done? You're the one disregarding the children. The mother has a responsibility!"

"I got a sitter." Sue smirked.

"You're home with them, you have to take care. I do a lot for them. I spend more time with my kids than ninety-nine percent of men do."

"Sugar, if your thing doesn't bother the children, I don't see why my thing does. So there! Sauce for the goose!"

"If you don't quit using that inane expression—"

"You'll what? Are you going to threaten me? Leslie, I'm sure this is a real riot for you to listen to, because I'm sure you know as well as I do he's carrying on again, this time with a . . . a nymphet. Did you ever read *Lolita?* She's a high school student, a child. Do you believe it?"

Nervously in narrowing circles Leslie arranged sesame crackers on a plate. "You've lived this way a long time. Why are you disagreeing now?" He was in love with Honor, that must be it. He was really in love this time. He would leave Sue.

George whined, "She's taken up with one of my students. My *student,* do you believe it? Really, even if you weren't my wife I'd be embarrassed. Embarrassed for you."

"I think Mark's quite attractive. And I surely do think it's unbecoming to you to be so jealous of me." Sue laughed flirtatiously.

Leslie realized that Sue was enjoying herself covertly. For the first time in one of their fights Sue felt herself to be in a winning position.

"Jealous!" George sputtered. "I'm humiliated!"

"The difference in our ages, of which you are making such a silly fuss," Sue went on languidly, "is much less than the difference between you and your new young high school sweetheart."

"She's mature for her age," George snarled. "She was the one who pursued it. She's old enough to chase men.

She comes on like the marines. They start running around very early nowadays."

"Up here in the North, maybe. I'm really amazed, George, absolutely stunned how upset you are, I really truly am. I'll bet Leslie is too. I never in my life imagined you'd carry on so about it. I really never thought you cared that much what I did in that line. And especially considering the way you've been handling yourself of late, George. For instance, Friday night. Now I know there's no departmental meeting late Friday night. That's a bad joke to play on your ever-loving wife."

Georre was chewing his mustache. She had never seen him do that. She could not help enjoying the sight just a little bit. The doorbell rang. "Oh, god!" he groaned. "They're here. Fuck them all."

"Sugar, you've tried. We'll carry on, don't worry about us. You just go and talk at them the way you always do." Sue turned her back.

When they were alone in the kitchen running around, Sue took the time to murmur at her ear, "I know that kid isn't in love with me. He's got a pretty young girlfriend who's nuts about him. Why should he need me? He lives with George's secretary. But he has gall, he has guts. You have to give him that. Let's say it right out—he has balls! My, isn't George livid? I was so amazed when the kid propositioned me. I was a little drunk, if you know what I mean. I sobered up like judgment day and all I could do was stare. I thought he'd lost his mind. He doesn't like George, you know that? But he told me he'd been eying me for months and trying to work up the courage! Imagine. I was touched, frankly. But I'd never have done it if George wasn't acting like a ninny about that child. He's going to get into trouble, and I can't tolerate that. It has to be nipped in the bud."

"You're very worried about it? That he's serious?"

"Serious? Don't be silly. Some high school floozy bold as brass? You know she even called him at home the other day?"

"She isn't a floozy. . . . I think she was a . . . virgin, you know."

"Oh, Leslie, you're naive. So what? So was I. And I didn't chase after him, you better believe it. And I didn't try to take him from his lawful wedded wife. Cherries are still ten for the dollar around campuses, you know that. George could care less. . . . Leslie, he couldn't get up in the morning without me! He wouldn't know what clothes to put on. He wouldn't know where to find his socks!"

Mark did not show up that evening, although every time the door opened George glared at it. He was edgy, irritable. When people were finally leaving and she was picking up, he slapped her somewhat too heavily on the shoulder. "I'll get that punk." George was still chewing on his mustache. "I'll have his ass barbecued on a pole! I'll kill him academically. He better start learning how to pump gas, because that's all he's going to be doing from now on. Just because I had his assistantship dropped. His punk revenge—can you imagine the nerve? On a pole, I'm telling you, over a slow fire."

She taught her first class. It went far more slowly than she had imagined. They covered less than a third of what she had anticipated, and she realized she was going to have to rethink her plan. They were working in the basement of the house, covered with what mats they had been able to find and some old carpeting. She had to get more mats. The class was full, twenty women, all she had been willing to take, and there were women waiting in case anyone dropped out. She felt good about that.

She had meant to start teaching them to fall, but instead the first class was all exercises. It moved her, watching the women begin trying to use their bodies in a different way. She looked at them—skinny from dieting, thick around the middle, soft bodied, bulgy, floppy, all the marvelous round shapes of women—and watched them trying to stretch, trying to touch their toes, trying to do sit-ups. She could pick out the ones who had done at least something physical before. It moved her, watching them strain themselves. She had to keep a sharp eye out for those who would not be able to get out of bed in the morning. Grunting, moaning, sweating, they gallumphed
282

around, awkward, earnest. Sometimes she almost felt like crying. They had put themselves in her hands to learn something new about how to be in the world, a new relationship to their bodies, to possibilities. She was to teach them a slim measure of safety and strength.

"We won't stay with the karate ritual that men have developed," she said suddenly. "At the beginning of the class instead of bowing we'll hold hands in a circle. Would you like that?" She wanted the class to feel warm. She began to remember hating her own body, she began to remember feeling afraid, unable. She wanted each of them, she wanted the weakest, flabbiest, most out of shape woman in the class to be at ease. If she could not love anyone else, maybe she could love her students.

She stood in Bernie's old room. It was up under the eaves and faced the next house. He had done his best to make it warm and livable, the ten by twelve feet of it with a bed under the slope of the roof and a desk in the dormer looking out on what light there was. He had tacked up reproductions; from somewhere he had got travel posters and a woven hanging. The bedspread was the inevitable Indian cotton. Half his clothes were still in the closet.

"He just take what he can stuff in that duffel, put it on his shoulders and go off bumming," his landlady said from the doorway. "If you a friend, you may as well take the books or whatever you want. They just going to haul it away."

She could find nothing to indicate where he had gone—no note, no map, nothing. No letters summoning him. The room was surprisingly free of personal clutter, things with names on. Some roses withered in a vase with a little stagnant water at the bottom, far below their dead stems. She could not think what to take, yet she felt the need for something. A French dictionary? Not French-English, but French to French. But what would she do with it, except remember him and never use it? She ended by taking a cashmere scarf she remembered him wearing back in the winter. He had not bothered with it, although it was handsome. Burt had given it to him, she remembered. That was her souvenir: her assertion of dumb connection. The landlady was watching her with a pitying expression. Was she so obvious? She thanked her profusely, took the scarf and left quickly. Her bike was chained to a tree outside, and she was glad to roar off down the street.

"I don't understand it! I don't understand! It doesn't make sense. How could he change!" Honor raised her head to speak. Then she let it fall again into Leslie's lap. "Overnight. It can't be real. No! I don't believe it!"

They were in Cam's livingroom. Cam pacing, smoking a filter cigarette, pacing. Leslie sat on the daybed which Cam had hastily closed. A tag end of sheet stuck out from under the cushions. Honor lay half across her crying. She had been crying for perhaps an hour straight. Honor's face was swollen, her lids red and enormous, her nose sore, her hair plastered to her cheeks. It was as if she had been broken and her lifeblood oozed from her eyes in water. Even the daybed was damp by now. Mark had been sent to the library, into exile from female troubles.

"He's so attractive to women," Cam said. "I never believed those stories he told me at first. I thought he was just trying to impress me. But it's true! They fall all over him."

Honor clung to Leslie desperately. "Why did he say that? I can't believe it! I can't. He'll change his mind, he has to. He loves me, I know it! He said he loved me, he said it twenty times, I swear it." Honor wept and wept. Leslie stroked her back. There was nothing sexual in it. She felt only pity and a little boredom, because an hour was a long time to sit on a brown and orange tweed daybed, lumpy and prickly under her, and to listen to the hum of the air conditioner, Cam's worrying and Honor's sobbing.

"I'll tell you how it happened," Cam said. "She came right up to him, that cow, and she put her hand right on his prick as he was sitting there. Do you believe it?"

No, Leslie thought, I remember that story. But he did

284

go to bed with Sue, somehow. He really did. Nobody else would for seven years, and then he did. Maybe he was as surprised as she was.

"He's dropping out of school, he's lost his assistantship. At least he'll never see her again. He doesn't love her or anything. It was just sex. I could have killed them both, but never mind. I don't know what we'll live on. I have to get a good job."

"Oh, George won't fire you, don't worry," Leslie said. "He said you're a good secretary."

"Won't fire me? Leslie, I quit!" Cam chain-lit another cigarette. "I quit this morning."

"You quit?" Leslie sat up, automatically adjusting Honor.

"You don't think I'd go on typing that creep's letters after what he did to my sister? Making him coffee. Saying, Yes, sure, of course, all day. I wouldn't give him the satisfaction."

"Wow," Leslie said. "I know you need the job."

"Oh, I don't expect you to quit," Cam said hastily, trying to make her feel good. "I'm just a secretary. I'll get another job." She paused by the daybed. "You want me to hold her for a while? Your arm must get tired."

"No, it's fine," Leslie said, feeling rotten.

"It's easier for you to comfort her. We've never been physically affectionate. Something in our house keeps us from it. . . . Poor kid. . . . At least Mark *says* he's not interested in Sue, if I can believe him. I always thought he was making up those stories!"

"Maybe he was," Leslie said, who was sure of it.

"How do I know she won't come after him?"

Honor was slowing down. Perhaps she could not cry any more. She blew her nose repeatedly, she filled paper handkerchiefs and gasped for breath. Leslie hoped Honor was almost done crying. She was late for work: for George of course. She imagined slitting his throat with a thin sharp knife. She imagined pushing him out one of the windows of his office, watching him float down in the air, turning over and over. She had a large sharp ax on her shoulder and she was cutting him up like firewood, hacking and

285

hacking. She would never be free of anger or of dependence. How could she have hit Honor? She would never be able to hit George. Even after she got the infernal degree, she would still need him. She would need him for ten years. She couldn't even speak her mind to him.

What could she say to Cam, who had stood up for her sister and quit George? What could she say, that she was too important to do that? What could she say, that her career was too important? That security meant too much to her? That she needed money and respect and prestige and a toehold in the middle class more than Cam did? Some reckoning was coming due. She had to face what she had not been facing.

Honor sat up, blowing her nose. "I love him, Leslie! I do. It can't be over. He can't mean it. She has some hold on him. He doesn't love her, he can't. I know he loves me."

Me. Who do I love? Nobody. I'm afraid to. I've protected myself too well. Nobody. I wouldn't take a big enough risk to love her, poor heavyhead like a huge baby on my shoulder. I came closest to Bernie, but not that close.

At the window Cam chain-lit another cigarette and fingered the stiff ends of her hair. "I better bleach my hair and take a hard look at my clothes and start reading the want ads. We're going to be short on the green stuff. Honey, Honor I mean, if you want to stay here, I'll call Mama and tell her I'm taking you to something, we'll make up a good story. You can sleep with me and we'll send Mark to a friend's. No! I don't trust him out of my sight, that two-timer. You can use my plaid sleeping bag."

Honor felt her cheeks as if they were strange to her. Then she stared at her hands. "I don't have anything. Not even a letter. He never wrote me a letter." Slowly she put out her tongue and licked the salt from her mouth. "I know he loves me!"

"I don't think it has anything to do with love," Leslie said, working her arm free. Her biceps felt cramped. Funny, you could study self-defense but not self-opening.

286

"I think love's a rarer phenomenon than we're led to expect."

"Leslie, you're my only friend. Oh, I wish I could talk to Bernie now. Maybe we could call him up. I got so mad at him, but at least he was always my friend."

"He's left town."

"What will happen to me? I feel such pain I think I'll die!" Honor pushed her hair back, groped for her purse where it had fallen. "If you don't call it love, what do you call it?"

"Pain. I call it pain." Leslie got Honor's purse for her. She watched while Honor wiped her face, combed her hair, dabbed at her rumpled dress. "Do you want to stay here with Cam?"

Honor shook her head no.

"Do you want me to give you a ride home on my bike?"

"No!" Honor snorted. "Can you hear what Mama would say? I'll go home on the bus. I'll sit way at the back so if I cry nobody will see."

"Are you sure you don't want to stay, honey?" Cam asked, sitting down with the newspaper and a marking pen.

"I have to go home," Honor found a small square of mirror in her purse and squinted into it. She stared at herself with a blank resignation, as if looking through her face to something else. "Tomorrow I'm supposed to start work as a receptionist for my doctor—the one who gives me the notes letting me out of gym."

"Nine to five?" Leslie asked her, to make her keep talking.

"Yes, Monday, Tuesday, Thursday, Friday, and then Saturday morning. He's given me the job for the summer. . . . I have to make money for school, if I want to go away. . . . It won't be bad, he has a crush on me."

"Okay, then. I'll leave you. I'm late for work." And George, always George, the lord who'd given her a job, her powerful protector and friend. Her owner. What did he offer her besides security, a well-paying job eventually, work she wanted to do? That's what it came down to. She

287

was not ready to give him up. She wanted what he had too badly. She had to stop wanting that, and she could not stop. Not yet. She wanted to live in Tasha's world only in her spare time. She got on her lovable small secondhand Honda, that ate up her extra pennies and made her feel good, and headed for George.